PRAISE FOR JAMES A MOORE

"Where *Seven Forges* teased a reader with the Sa'ba Taalor and their strange land, *The Blasted Lands* goes a long way toward fulfilling their promise, revealing much more about their culture and history as well as hinting at the origin of the waste lands themselves. And while the Sa'ba Taalor are still the stars of this show, Mr Moore has also deftly turned the Fellein characters into more than cardboard scenery for his master race, as Drash Krohan, General Dulver and Andover Lashk shine in their own special ways. All in all, this novel was a great read, and this series is definitely one to watch for any true fantasy aficionado."
Bookwraiths

"From living mountains to the secret behind the veils of a nation, Moore pushes and pulls the story through questions and answers, keeping the reader on their toes. For me, *The Blasted Lands* is more immersive and thrilling than some of the fantasy masterpieces. Moore shapes a story which appeals to fans of all types, showing how fantasy can be a grand equalizer. The Blasted Lands does this and more, making it not just a sophomore book in a series but a genuinely good story."
Literary Escapism

"I thoroughly enjoyed *Seven Forges* although I was left speechless by the ending and left wondering for days whether there was to be another book in the series. There were so many threads of stories left open that I need to know what happens next."
The Bookish Outsider

"*Seven Forges* is a well-written fantasy adventure with a very interestin
*Celticfro

"The end of the book had me on the edge of my seat, wanting more. I will definitely be reading the next book in the *Seven Forges* series as soon as it comes out."

Avid Fantasy Reviews

"The race of the Sa'aba Taalor are the newest and freshest I've read in decades. Where many writers will have gods who are nebulous and unreachable, many of Moore's gods respond immediately. I think I like his creatures the best – the Pra Moresh. Here Moore's horror roots allow him to really shine. His descriptive prose and keen eye for the horrific proves that he's a master architect of the gruesome and prognosticator of fear. I raced through the first two books and can not wait for the third. If you have yet to try these, then do so on my word. You'll thank me for it."

Living Dangerously

"*Seven Forges* is an excellent, enjoyable, and thoroughly entertaining fantasy debut into a new world of swords and sorcery, complete with romance, intrigue, and danger."

Attack of the Books

"James A Moore dedicates *Seven Forges* in part 'to the memory of Fritz Leiber and Robert E Howard for the inspiration.' That dedication sets the bar high, and caused me a bit of readerly apprehension, because so many writers have imitated badly those two greats of the sword and sorcery tradition. Moore is far more than an imitator, though. He does some fresh, counterintuitive things with the genre conventions. More than once, he startled me into saying out loud, 'I didn't see that coming.'"

Black Gate

"Moore does a fantastic job of building worlds and characters in *Seven Forges* as we hop on board the train that is about to meet its doom."

Troubled Scribe

"Wow, that twist. In some ways I think I should have seen it coming, and I kind of did, but *Seven Forges* just lulled me into security and BAM! Craziness!"

On Starships & Dragonwings

"The story is just as epic as the cover art. I am not going to go into specifics because I don't want to give any aspects of the storyline away, but let's just say this is fantasy on the scale of Terry Brooks or Brandon Sanderson. It is that good... The book starts off with a bang, pretty much from page one, and continues on through the climax."

Shattered Ravings

"*Seven Forges* is a perfect story of political intrigue, brutal fighting, beguiling magic and assassinations. I think you can safely say that I 'quite' (read absolutely, fully, thoroughly) liked the book. The build up of Seven Forges was done in an excellent way with first a heavy emphasis on the characters and the obscure Sa'ba Taalor and later neatly shifting the focus onto another developing storyline, but still keeping the exploration of the world at the front. *Seven Forges* has the WOW factor."

The Book Plank

JAMES A MOORE

The Silent Army

SEVEN FORGES, BOOK IV

**ANGRY
ROBOT**

ANGRY ROBOT
An imprint of Watkins Media Ltd

Lace Market House,
54-56 High Pavement,
Nottingham,
NG1 1HW
UK

angryrobotbooks.com
twitter.com/angryrobotbooks
The final showdown

An Angry Robot paperback original 2016
1

A catalogue record for this book is available
from the British Library.

ISBN 978 0 85766 507 2
EBook ISBN 978 0 85766 509 6

Set in Meridien by Epub Services.
Printed and bound in the UK by 4edge Limited.

This novel is gratefully dedicated to Phil Jourdan and Paul Simpson for keeping me in line, and working miracles on the edits. It is also dedicated to Marc Gascoigne and Mike Underwood, because I enjoyed the hell out of our conversations at World Fantasy.

Special thanks to every reader who has followed along with me through this tale. I hope you've enjoyed the journey. Special thanks also to Penny Reeve, for all that you do that so very few people get to see.

ONE

The kings gathered together, those of them who were near the place where Canhoon had once rested in the ground, and stared at the vast landmass rising above them.

It was an impressive sight. Canhoon, surely the oldest of the cities in the Fellein Empire, a vast city with millions of inhabitants, had risen into the air, soaring higher and higher until it seemed only a little larger than a fast ship.

Tuskandru stared at the retreating stone cloud and felt his jaw clench. He had been patient. He was ready for a proper war.

Next to him, Tarag Paedori crossed his massive arms, which was an impressive sight in full plate armor. Tusk would not have thought it possible, though he'd never worn such heavy armor himself.

"I do not like sorcery," the King in Iron stated. "When I meet this wizard you've spoken of, I plan to kill him first."

"He is not so easy to kill, I expect." Tusk looked away from the dwindling city and back at where Canhoon had been. Most of the city had risen, but everything between the Mid Wall and the Outer Wall was still there, broken and scattered by the tremors caused when the city rose. Only Old Canhoon had taken flight. Tusk could see people there, looking out from their homes or simply wandering around, shocked by what had just happened. It was not a common occurrence to see a city rise into the air and fly away. Where once the city had been, a deep wound now lay, so vast that it was hard to contemplate. Waters from the river were already raging into that gash in the earth and in a day or so it would likely be a lake.

"What now?" he asked

"Kill the people left behind. And then..." Tarag Paedori removed his massive iron helmet shaped to look like the face of his god, Truska-Pren. "Then we chase the city."

"How?"

"It is a very large target, Tusk. And it does not move so quickly that we cannot follow. Sooner or later we will have a chance to find our way to the heart of that city. The Daxar Taalor would not call us to war if it was not time for the Great Tide. This is merely an effort to escape from the gods. It will fail."

Tusk nodded his head and then gestured for Stastha to call for war.

She raised her horn and gave the signal. Immediately the Sa'ba Taalor who followed Tusk stopped gawping at the dwindling city and prepared themselves, calling out their praise for Durhallem.

"To war!" Tuskandru's voice rang out in perfect unison with that of Tarag Paedori. "To war and kill your enemies!"

More horns sounded, but Tusk barely noticed. It was time to honor his god with offerings of blood and bone. Tusk lived to serve.

The three figures walked across the silence of the Blasted Lands, moving at a steady pace. They struck an image that was not easily forgotten in the vast desolation. A heavy layer of dust covered them like a mantle, spilling from their hair and drizzling down their clothes. There were two men and one woman. The first of the men was a massive brute, a towering member of the Sa'ba Taalor, with gray skin, long dark hair and eyes that glowed in the growing darkness. Next was a young woman who seemed almost childlike in comparison. Her hair, though currently hidden by dust, was thick and blonde and curly and her heart-shaped face bore a blank expression that made her look younger still. Behind them, the other man moved on, his head lowered toward the ground. If he saw anything at all it was only the blanket of fine dust and ash that covered the world around them so completely.

The first of the trio was called Drask Silver Hand. His name came from the fully functioning metallic hand at the end of his right arm. In the past someone looking at his silver limb would have been able to clearly see where the flesh and the metal had been placed together; there had been a deep seam of scar tissue and open spaces where the fusion of skin and silver had not fully connected. That scar was gone now, replaced by thin tendrils of silver that pulled the flesh close to the metallic hand.

Drask looked at his hand several times as he walked, watching the silver threads pulling and tightening. It was a fascinating process for him. He flexed his metallic hand, watched the tendons, real and artificial alike, pull and turn.

To his side, sometimes lagging behind, came Tega. The girl was still in her teens, and her skin was soft and flawless where Drask was hard and his flesh marked by hundreds of scars, some fine and some substantial. Her eyes were blue and did not glow with the same inner luminescence that marked all of the gray-skinned Sa'ba Taalor.

Trailing behind the both of them and never looking up

from his feet, Nolan March plodded steadily along. He had the swarthy complexion of a northerner. His hair fell around his shoulders and draped down in front of his face like a veil. Anyone who could have seen his face would have been surprised by how calm he looked, as that was not usually the case. Nolan was not known for his patience, though he was now disturbingly placid.

They did not speak. Though they walked at a solid pace they appeared to be in no urgent need of reaching a destination.

They did not stop to eat or drink. They simply walked across the desolate wasteland. Two of them looked to where the City of Wonders now rode among the clouds. Nolan March did not look up. He was no longer capable of lifting his head. He had lost that ability when Drask broke his neck. By rights he should have been dead, but that was true of all of them.

They walked on in silence, fully aware of the gods and all that surrounded them. Drask's face did not carry his usual expression. His brow was knotted with concentration as he considered the implications of what was happening to him, and what had happened when he fell into the liquid fires that fed the Mounds. Those vast structures, long forbidden his people by their gods, were no more. They had shattered when the energies far beneath them bathed three mortals in what should have never been seen by any but the gods themselves.

To the unwary observer, it might have seemed that they were struck dumb by the things they had seen. That was not the case, at least not for Drask. He simply chose not to speak as he considered the information moving through his skull, ricocheting through his mind like a burst of lightning captured inside him. Power coursed through his body, but he was not yet certain what it was meant to do. He supposed what was happening to him happened also to the others, but he did not contemplate that fact much as yet. He was still adjusting. The silver hand was the very least of the changes going on inside his body. It was simply the most noticeable.

The lack of a raging storm on the vast plain should have worried him. For his entire life, for over a thousand years, the Blasted Lands had raged around the Seven Forges. The mountains were still there, visible from even this vast distance, but the storms were gone, the cold had abated, and the dust and grit that had scoured flesh and stone alike for a millennium was now a fine powder that buried his feet to the ankles if he stood still for too long.

He had long since accepted the voices of the Daxar Taalor as they spoke to him. The gods of his people whispered in his mind, spoke through the Great Scars they had gifted him with over the years, and were his constant companions in many ways. They might not always be speaking but they were always present. They were still there, still in his mind, but now they did not speak. Like him, they were contemplating what he had become.

Or maybe they were fearful of what he would decide to do with the power that was now inside him.

He looked to Tega and she in turn looked back. He could sense the changes taking place in her. Could sense the metamorphosis taking place within the chrysalis of Nolan March's flesh, as well.

The gods had not prepared him for this, for any of this. The power inside him roared and flashed and bloomed throughout every fiber of his being, though to see him from outside, a person would not have guessed.

He did not know what they were becoming.

Still, it would be interesting to find out.

• • •

"So, are we walking back to Fellein?" Andover looked out across the Taalor Valley, which was already changing, losing the vitality that had made it stand out so much from the Blasted Lands beyond the edge of the mountain.

They stood once more upon Durhallem, the great obsidian mountain. Above them the volcanic heat still melted the ice, but there was something different now, something lacking that Andover Lashk could not quite place.

Delil stood next to him and stared out at the foliage in the valley below.

"No." She touched his shoulder with her hand and then pointed out into the valley a good ways off, closer to Wrommish than Durhallem. Where she indicated, there was motion. Whatever was down there was large enough to shake the trees and rattle the ground.

"Mound Crawler?"

Delil shook her head. "It's not violent enough for a Crawler."

Andover looked at the sway of the distant trees and nodded. He had still never seen one of the gigantic beasts and he was perfectly fine with that, though there was a part of him that was deeply curious.

Tusk had killed a Crawler by himself. The thought was staggering.

"This feels wrong. All of it."

"The world is changing, Andover. The Daxar Taalor have willed it and now we must follow through with their desires." She sighed and pointed to the Blasted Lands. They had been standing together when the world shook and the light filled all of the raging, frozen hell beyond the mountains. The very clouds coming from the Seven Forges had flared silver and white for several seconds and then the winds that had roared against the sides of the mountains since the gods had lifted them from the ground had suddenly ceased. He had not been aware of how much the distant roar of those winds could always be heard until they were suddenly silenced.

"We need to hunt for what is down there before we head for Canhoon?" Andover asked.

"What is Canhoon?"

"Where the Empire is now if Tyrne was ruined."

"Yes, we do."

"It's a long walk."

"It is as long a walk as the gods decree, Andover." He flexed his hands and looked at the disturbance far below.

"What is down there, Delil?"

"There are many tests before any of the Sa'ba Taalor. If you would have a mount, you must tame one. What you are seeing below are new mounts. They are angry and they are hungry and they will try very hard to kill us."

Andover felt his stomach flutter at the very idea. He had grown so used to fighting that he sometimes forgot to be afraid. The mounts, however, were a good reminder. Delil had explained that nothing in the Taalor Valley was accidental and that nothing went to waste. He was not quite afraid. He knew fear very well, had been intimate with the sensation many times, but they no longer spoke as often as they had in the past.

The Broken, the Pra-Moresh, these were creatures made by the gods. They were obstacles for the Sa'ba Taalor to overcome.

Below, in the valley, the leaves of trees that had always been green and vibrant were changing, shifting into shades of brown and gold, and fiery orange and red hues. Delil had already expressed her shock at the notion and had only calmed down when Andover explained that the leaves always changed where he was from.

When she asked him why, he could only shrug. Perhaps, he had mused, because the gods were leaving the Taalor Valley and offering their followers the whole wide world in exchange.

"We are to get mounts?"

"No, Andover. We are to choose them and they are to choose us."

"Where do the mounts come from, Delil?"

"They are gifts of the Daxar Taalor, provided we can prove worthy of the offering." That was her only answer. He already knew, however. Whether they were punished, rewarded or redeemed, the mounts were also Sa'ba Taalor, or at least they had been.

The great predatory beasts were larger than horses, thicker in the body and muscular. Though he had yet to see one of their faces beneath the armor their riders provided for them, he had seen them eat meat and rend flesh with ease. He had seen the great mounts cover vast distances in single leaps. They were not status symbols, but they were also hard to earn.

"How do we capture mounts?"

"How do the Sa'ba Taalor do anything, Andover Iron Hands?" Delil smiled at him, her face wrinkling with pleasure. "We fight and we demand their submission."

Andover nodded his head. In his very soul he had known that, but there had been a hope for a different answer.

Not all prayers are answered in the method we prefer.

"So now we go to them? We choose the ones we want to ride?"

Delil laughed, her voice filled with amusement. "They are already looking for us, Andover."

"They are?"

"Oh, yes. Mounts need to find riders. There are very few left in this place." She slowly unwrapped a thick metal chain from around her waist, examining the links as she slipped them through her hard, callused fingers.

"Is the chain the best method for taming a mount?" He watched her hands, the surety with which she moved, the casual stance she took as she coiled the length around her wrist, holding the majority of the chain in her hands on either side.

"I do not know, Andover. I know that we will have a chance to tame the damned beasts. And they will have a chance to hurt us." She dangled a heavy weight from the end of the chain. The sphere of metal looked to weigh close to four pounds. A blow from that lump of iron would leave a skull caved in.

"So you will beat them to death before you tame them?" He couldn't keep the humor from his tone.

In the distance he heard a roar coming from the valley below.

"Use what you will, Andover, but be prepared to strike hard and fast. When they come for us they will be hungry as newborns."

Andover considered his choices. He had his axe. He had his bow and arrows. There were a few ranged weapons.

And there were his iron hands. Solid iron, flexible, capable of tearing flesh if need be.

"Should we go looking for them or should we wait?" He looked toward Delil, his eyes taking in the details of her body and her muscular arms. He stared at her simply because he needed to think of something pleasant before the enemy came and the fighting started.

The Pra-Moresh had the decency to advertise their arrival. The Sa'ba Taalor called them "Cacklers" because of the fearsome beasts' insane laughter and weeping combined. Long before they came for you, you knew they were on their way. It was both terrifying and a chance to prepare yourself.

The mounts were different. They were large, sleek, predatory nightmares. They were often silent and they stalked whatever they intended to kill.

Andover wanted desperately to reach for his axe, but did not dare. The idea was to capture a mount, not cleave it in half and there was nothing about the obsidian blade and handle that Durhallem had gifted him with that was meant to be a weapon of submission.

Besides. If he could not handle the threat with his iron hands, he was not worthy of the challenge. Delil herself, along with Drask and Bromt, had taught him to use his body as a weapon. He had learned well enough to survive several encounters.

His confidence dwindled a bit as Delil let out a deep, stressed breath and muttered a prayer to her gods.

Andover thanked the Daxar Taalor for their blessings and then stretched his arms, rolled his shoulders and looked away from the woman at his side. He had changed since he met her. Not only was he now taller than her, he was also not afraid of what was coming. Wary, yes, but not fearful.

The trees lower down in the valley shuddered and shivered closer to them now. Close enough that he knew the mounts were coming.

"Where do they come from, Delil? The mounts? What have they done to be reshaped as beasts instead of as men?"

"Do you think they are being punished, Iron Hands?" There was a faint note of teasing in her voice.

Andover tilted his head. The idea that it wasn't a punishment had never really crossed his mind. "Are they not?"

"No, Andover. It is a second chance."

"You said that about the Broken and the Cacklers."

"No, those are punishments. They carry a chance of redemption. The mounts are a second chance for those who have done the impossible and grown too old to fight any longer."

Despite himself Andover laughed. "That can happen with your people?" It seemed nearly impossible. The Sa'ba Taalor worshipped combat and war. The very notion of anyone living long enough to grow too old to fight seemed absurd.

She shook her head and crossed her arms. "How many of my people have you seen?"

"Thousands and thousands."

"How many mounts have you seen?"

"All told? Maybe a hundred."

"Now you know how often a Sa'ba Taalor grows too old to fight."

There was logic to that. He nodded and once again looked around.

They stood in an area that was mostly stone and little shelter, but the closest shrubs and trees that could hide one of the great mounts were not far distant.

He had seen the beasts leap. He knew they could come quickly if they chose.

The first of the massive things came from the side and he looked directly at it. Like the Sa'ba Taalor, their mouths were slashes across their face that sometimes bisected or intersected the larger maw. Great Scars, marks that showed the favor of the gods. The first one had three such scars. The eyes were large and glowing, the face bestial, designed to bite through meat and bone with ease.

The monster ignored him completely and charged for Delil. Part of him longed to protect her, but that notion was cast easily aside. The woman was more than capable of defending herself.

And if he even tried, she'd cave his skull in for his troubles.

That was the last thought he managed to complete before the time came for instinct over consciousness. The mount that ran at him was fast. Its fur was dark black and its eyes shone like silver coins as it burst from the closest trees and bounded across the remaining distance between them.

That great gash of a mouth was open and showed teeth the size of his hands.

The impact lifted Andover completely from the ground and hurled him effortlessly. The weight of the mount was more than he'd expected, more than he was prepared for, and he hit the ground on his back and did his best to roll with the blow instead of breaking under the force. He was moderately successful. All that saved his arms from being skinned was the leather hide that tore away as he spun and tumbled.

Not far away something growled. He could not honestly say if the sound came from one of the beasts or from Delil.

Or maybe it was from him. Andover rose into a crouch, his feet wide apart, his body low to the ground. His arms were spread and his fingers hooked into claws as the thing facing him rumbled and locked eyes.

He chose not to wait, but instead ran for his enemy. The mount raised one massive paw to swat him down. Andover dodged hard to his right and rolled under the advancing beast. With a single swipe of a blade he could have gutted the thing, but instead he let the monster move past and rose as quickly as he could.

The idea was not to kill it, but to show it exactly who was going to be in charge of their relationship.

The great back of the thing was to him for the moment but it was already turning, planning to come for him again, no doubt. Andover jumped, his arms stretched wide, and as his chest crashed into the broad back of the mount his arms swept inward until his hands found each other on the opposite side of the mount's neck. The mount roared and threw itself in a half circle, and Andover clenched metallic fingers together, locking his grip across the corded muscles of the wide neck.

He hunched his body forward until his legs were around the broad abdomen of the mount and gulped in air. Fear surged through him again as he tried to hold on. One thing to face the damned thing in combat and another to try to ride it. He'd never even been on a horse's back in his life and the mount was bigger, and far deadlier. It twisted its body much as he had seen cats do and tried to reach him. Andover's knees slipped and he scrambled with his legs, but his grip was sure enough for the moment.

The great mouth opened in a screech of anger and Andover pulled his arms in closer, drew himself up the great body until his legs were in a better place. The pulse of the thing's heart pounded against his arms, and he squeezed harder still, feeling the pumping blood through the thick neck muscles of the mount. It grunted under him, and still he held on. It tried to turn its head enough to bite him, but could not.

The monster rolled over onto its back and he felt its crushing weight grinding down on him. His breath was caught in the mane of the brute, his face buried in the thick coat. His hands trembled but held and his legs stayed tight to the sides, boot heels digging into the ribcage of the monster as it rolled and scraped and tried to peel him away.

The leather of his pants tore at the knees and the seam along his left thigh split and ripped away, taking flesh, drawing blood.

Andover roared himself, pain lashing at his senses.

Enough. This would end now.

He squeezed harder still and the great beast gulped for air. The weight lifted off him and he gasped, but did not dare let go his grip. The brute had him in size, strength, ferocity and weapons if you counted the claws and teeth. Letting go would be enough to get him killed in seconds and he knew it.

A sound erupted in his head. It did not bother with his ears, but instead filled his mind. He tried to shake the mental noise away but it would not go. Gods had spoken to him but this was different. When the Daxar Taalor spoke there was a feeling that came with it unlike anything he had ever experienced in his life, a sort of euphoric awe. This was insignificant in comparison but enough to distract him

The mount tried to roll again, slamming him into the ground, and Andover drove his heels into the sides of the great beast to hold himself in place and then choked harder still. The noise in his head grew brighter.

The thing made a noise that was part snarl and part stuttering, slurred words. The noise in his head clearly said, "I yield."

The sound in his head and the rumbled noises. They were linked.

Andover did not let go his grip, but he eased it.

"Then roll off me!" He wheezed the words more than spoke them. The weight of the beast pinning him in the dirt was substantial.

The pressure shifted and then eased and the world came back into view, replacing his close and intimate view of the hairy skull of the mount.

It did not lie. He knew that. The mount spoke the truth when it said it yielded. Sometimes he wondered if the Sa'ba Taalor even understood the concept of lies, but he knew better. Of course they did. King Glo'Hosht and the followers of Paedle most certainly understood the power of deceit, even if the rest did not.

He let go his grip on the mount's heavy neck and staggered back four steps before landing on his backside in the dirt. Dark spots ran before his eyes and he breathed in deep gulps of air, already doing his best to get back to his feet. Delil was nearby and the other mounts as well. They might be allies if things went well but right now they were monsters.

Andover adjusted and adapted, as he'd been trained to do, and pulled his axe free, holding the obsidian in a hard grip. He looked at his mount, which was now settling down and waiting. He looked toward Delil and saw her, where she was pinned under the mass of her assailant.

Every muscle tensed, ready to move toward her.

Delil grunted, struggled, her arms trembling; the chain in her hands rattled with the strain.

The beast over her was a heavy gray form that dwarfed her. The chain was wrapped around its muzzle, and around its neck. Where Andover had held onto his attacker from behind, Delil was clutching the front of the thing in a death grip, her body literally pressed between its wide-set forelegs. She had managed to wrap the length of chain around both the front paws in an elaborate web of links that had the mount struggling to move without falling face first into the dirt.

The fall would have worked to the creature's advantage, except for the blade pushed against its stomach. A dagger was resting against the soft part of the belly, braced against Delil's knee. She had a sheath there. He had no idea how she'd managed it but the blade was now where it would do the most harm.

Her face was buried in the thick mane of the mount. Behind

her, several of the other creatures were already moving away. They had no choices here. They would not locate another here to choose them and so they left.

Delil released the chain from the thick neck and gently pulled it away from the torn, bloodied mouth of her mount. She fell back, panting, as the brute stepped back and carefully extracted itself from the length wrapped around its paws.

Delil looked toward him for a moment and sighed. She closed her eyes and gulped in breaths as the mount slipped back and settled down.

"What is your name?" The words were muttered and spoken directly into his head again.

"I am Andover Lashk of the Iron Hands." He looked toward the black mount. It came closer and nudged him gently with its muzzle. The teeth in that mouth could have taken the head off a horse with one bite. He knew that. He also knew that he now had nothing to fear from the mount. "And what do I call you, my friend?"

"I am Gorwich."

Andover carefully ran his hand through the thick black mane, fully aware that his fingers could pull hair without trying very hard. Best not to anger his newest friend.

Delil sat up and winced. Her side was bloodied.

Without another word he moved to her. The fight was done, her challenge completed. Now he could help her without fear of interfering with the ritual of companionship. That was what it was. He knew that now. How else to choose a worthy rider for a mount? How else to see if a mount was a proper fit?

Deep claw marks ran down her side and scored her ribs.

He reached into a sack at his side and pulled out clean cloths. "Do you need bandages?"

She shot him a look that told him it was a stupid question;

he nodded and urged her back so he could clean the cuts as best he could.

Behind her the very beast that had torn into her now paced nervously, a worried expression on the broad, feral face.

IT IS TIME, ANDOVER IRON HANDS. The words filled his head. The voice was that of Ydramil. The god spoke and Andover listened. There was no choice in the matter. Gods could not be ignored.

Andover nodded and pulled back his cloth. He was not surprised to see that the wounds had stopped bleeding. The Sa'ba Taalor were a strong race. She would heal.

He could not have said which gods spoke to Delil but he could see the subtle shift in her expression as she listened.

A moment later they were moving. The mounts went with them, and the four of them walked together toward Durhallem's Pass.

It was a long way to Fellein and they had to be where the gods demanded in time to serve properly.

TWO

Desh Krohan looked at Merros Dulver and shrugged. "I've considered what you asked for earlier. Well done. I never would have dreamed up this possibility." He referred to the general's request to have communications passed from one sorcerer to another in an effort to save time. Considering that no horse known to man would be able to reach the city for some time, that was a request he was glad he'd approved.

Dulver was currently looking over the outer edge of the only barrier that stopped any of them from falling to their deaths. The great stone Mid Wall had been designed to stop invaders from entering Canhoon. Built by sorcerous means it had held any potential invaders at bay since it was created. Now it held the city of Canhoon together, or at least stopped the foolhardy from spilling over the edges.

Merros looked his way with wide, glassy eyes. He was shocked. A great percentage of the population felt the same way. Those few that saw Desh Krohan walking from the palace very nearly competed to look away and cower. He was the foremost sorcerer in the entire Fellein Empire. They had no doubt that he was responsible for all of this. They were right, of course, but only in an indirect way.

"Are you well, Merros?"

Usually the general was fast with a return quip. Just now, however, he was shaking a bit. "I had no idea."

"That cites could fly? To be fair, it doesn't happen that often." He wanted to be sympathetic. He was trying, but he'd been here before. He'd been one of the sorcerers who made Canhoon rise in the past and sail above clouds. He'd been part of the reason for the Silent Army rising from the ground and stopping the invaders of the past. His was the sorcery that rebuilt Canhoon when an earthquake shattered the greatest city built since Korwa. It unsettled him a good deal that he couldn't remember the details of those events as clearly as he wanted, but a lot of centuries had passed, and he didn't know how clearly he recalled the events from his youth.

All of which, aside from foggy memories, would have made him feel absolutely spectacular about his abilities, if he had any control over the Silent Army rising from the ashes and then lifting the City of Wonders into the air to avoid the invading Sa'ba Taalor.

That was all beyond him. The Silent Army had brought themselves back to life – and, from what he was hearing, had either sacrificed or caused others to sacrifice themselves in the process. Over a thousand. One for each of the unmoving stone soldiers that now stood as silent sentinels over the entire city. Canhoon rode the winds – or at least seemed to as it moved far above the ground. How far? He could not say. He would have others looking into the matter soon enough. For now he knew that the city moved toward the east and that it was not responding to any attempts by him or the other sorcerers to tell it where to go. Not that they'd had much time to try anything.

Which was why he was here now, looking for Merros.

Merros Dulver was a good and a strong man, but he really didn't much like sorcery, and he'd seen enough in the last few days to change his perspective about how the world was supposed to work. Little things: people appearing and disappearing in places where they shouldn't have easily been able to go, that was annoying. Desh knew that. He'd seen the general's response to the Sisters' comings and goings. Only a few days earlier Desh had been asked for assistance by the Empress herself. He had avoided saying yes for as long as he could, but there comes a time when actions are required.

With one stroke Desh Krohan, First Advisor to the Fellein Empire, went from possible charlatan to man to be feared. Even now, had he bothered to look in the opposite direction, he would have been able to see the scorch marks left on the terrain by his actions. Not seeing them would have been the challenge, as the land was burned for miles.

Now this. The city was moving itself and what should have been statues at best were now surrounding the city and had come to defend the citizenry.

Merros Dulver was a little shocked? Only because the implications had not completely settled in yet. He would likely be truly worried later, after he'd given the situation some thought.

"There's nothing under us, Desh. I can see the river. I can see trees down there, but they are so tiny…"

"They are the same size they always were, Merros. They are simply farther away than you might expect."

"All the gods, Desh. How do you handle this?" Merros shivered. It wasn't the surprise or the fear that caused his body to shake. It was the cold. Thinner air and colder weather were only a few of the challenges that came from their new, higher, altitude.

Desh looked out over the landscape far below, where the Jeurgis River glittered in the fading sunlight. He could see the chaos in the towns beneath them. If being on a floating city was disorienting, how must it be for the people who realized that it wasn't a storm cloud above them, but a landmass? How deeply afraid might they be that the approaching mountain-sized structure meant their death?

"What is the other choice, Merros? Neither you nor I were ever meant to merely watch the world as it changes. We are not the sort. We prepare and we fight."

The general nodded and shook his head. "Have you discovered where the city is going?"

Desh shook his head. "We're... investigating. It will take a while."

"Let's hope whatever is keeping Canhoon this high in the air does not decide to drop us somewhere along the way."

Desh did a few quick calculations in his head and then scowled. "Try not to put notions like that in my skull, Merros. It's enough to wreck my cheerful disposition."

"This is your territory, not mine, First Advisor. Might I suggest you seek a solution?"

"As I said, we're investigating. These things take time."

The general looked away from the view below and stared at him for several seconds. "Yes, well, sooner is better I suspect."

"What are you so worried about, Merros? I mean beyond the obvious."

"We are currently heading, near as I can tell, directly east."

"Yes. I gathered as much myself."

"I was looking at the maps yesterday. I've been looking at them a lot. What is the one distinct landmark that is east of us?"

"Oh. Damn."

The mountains. Fellein was a vast continent and most of it was easily traversable but there are always exceptions. In this case the Arkannen Mountains rose from the fertile lands like the spine of a god and separated the west from the east.

"Wait. There's always–"

"Yes. The Lishter Gap." Merros gestured with his left hand. "It's a lovely notion. It is also few hundred miles to the north of us."

The Lishter Gap was the only actual break in the mountains. The granite and marble range was as tall as it was long, and the only spot aside from where the river cut through was the Lishter Gap where the Imperial Highway ran. The choice for travelers was always simple. Take the river, or take the gap.

The problem that they faced was that the cut between the mountains where the river flowed was not nearly as wide as the city. There was a very real chance that Canhoon would smash into one of the peaks, and while Desh was a man who believed in the impossible, there was nothing in his arsenal of spells that would make moving mountains easy. If there were, he'd have long since done something about the volcanoes burning to the west.

Desh had not yet discovered if there was a way to actually *steer* the city. He was working on it, granted, but there was very little time left for trial and error. Relatively speaking at least. Surely there was still time left.

Hopefully.

"Enough of this," said Desh. "I came to find you because we have several different problems facing us, not the least of which is what to do with all of the extra people in town."

Merros nodded. For a moment he looked decades older than his age. Then he inhaled, squared his shoulders, and with a few changes in posture and a hardening of his features he went from a worried man to a general.

He did not look at the edge of the wall again as he started walking toward the palace of the Empress. "So let us be on with it. The day is not growing any younger and I'd like sleep at some point."

Summoning the heads of the military and the City Guard was not challenging. The Fellein Army was nothing if not efficient, at least that was what Merros kept telling himself. The men that stood before him were as stressed as he was, and they were looking to him for answers. He would give them their answers, too. Whether or not they liked them was another matter entirely.

Taurn Durst, his personal aide and one of the largest men in the entire army, bellowed everyone to attention. They quietened quickly. They'd learned what happened to those who did not respond properly.

Durst stood at attention next to Merros and waited, his eyes scanning the crowd as if he might be looking for assassins, or possibly fresh prey.

Merros stood ramrod straight and looked out at his commanders.

"Yes, we all know that the city is in the air." A few of them chuckled. Most did not. "We are very aware of that fact. The bright point here is that the Sa'ba Taalor did not take our city. The darker news is that we are now completely isolated and facing new troubles."

Several of the men tried to speak up and Durst shouted them down, demanding silence.

Merros took his time, looking from face to face, making sure they knew that he was talking to them, and not just talking to hear his own voice. "We have food. We have fresh water. Thank the sorcerers for that. I don't know where they store it, but I've been assured by Desh Krohan himself that we have supplies enough to last us for several months. That is a blessing. There are other troubles, however. The weather, as you can feel, is much colder at this height. Any of you who have ever had to cross over the mountains know what I mean. We are going to have troubles keeping everyone warm. We need to find places for everyone to stay. That was an issue before this happened. It's only going to be worse now."

One of the men called out, "Not to be inconsiderate, but why is that a problem for the army or the City Guard?"

"Because we are all here together. Because if we do not have warm clothes and shelter for people, they will feel obliged to find it on their own, even if they have to break into someone else's home, or steal their cloaks. Reprol, is it?" The man nodded. "Do you have family here?" He nodded again. "You have to work. If you are not home, who will make sure it isn't your home that is broken into, and your family that remains safe?"

Reprol had the decency to blush and look down as he considered those words.

"Hear me out. We are all in this together because there is nowhere for any of us to go. We need to find shelter and warmth for everyone before this entire affair becomes a riot or worse. There are a lot of soldiers here. There are a lot more people who are not soldiers, who have lost everything, and who will, if they must, turn on us and fight for whatever they can reclaim. We will not let that happen. That is the end of this discussion. We will help because we must if we wish to stay alive.

"Now, I've put the problem on the slate for you. Let's hear some suggestions."

They were slow to speak, but speak they did. They had families to consider, after all.

Tataya and Pella sat in Desh's chambers and waited for him. He was busy and they knew that, but he would want to see them, and so they waited.

They had already moved under the city and seen what there was to see. The foundation was solid. A few open gutters spilled dribbles of water from within the bowels of the city. No spare debris fell away any longer. There had been some, but it was negligible in comparison to the sheer size of the base of their airborne city. They did not speak of what they had seen. They did not speak of the questions they had asked.

They did not speak of the answers they were given by their sister, Goriah, as she tore apart her funeral shroud and howled her agonies into the air of the cold, dark chambers where she rested even now.

Fair to say that there was little that scared the Sisters, but after the recent grisly work they'd employed him for, they were suitably afraid of Inquisitor Darsken Murdro. He had a commanding presence. He had a reputation for finding the darkest secrets and unearthing them. He was of the Louron, which in and of itself was enough to make some nervous, but now? Now he had shown them that he could wake the dead and make them tell their discoveries to the living.

There were secrets kept by every living being. Those weren't the secrets that bothered the Sisters.

It was the secrets of the dead that worried them. More importantly, how Desh Krohan would respond to those secrets.

The Sisters waited in silence, uncertain they wanted to know the answer to that particular query.

• • •

Darsken Murdro walked along the edge of the Mid Wall and observed those around him. From time to time his staff tapped the ground in a measured thump, but otherwise he was silent.

There was a pathway around the Mid Wall that he was certain was not deliberate. People were avoiding touching the barrier, as if it might be paper and would slip away from them should they try to use it as a support. Refugees with nothing were still avoiding actually using the wall as shelter. Instead they took whatever supplies they had and placed them on the ground a dozen feet from the edge.

The people around him were scared. He could understand why. Their world, or at least a portion of it, had been torn from the ground and raised into the sky. That was the sort of thing that tended to make people edgy.

On the wall itself stood an army of silent statues. They were made of stone. It was impossible to miss that. Just the same, from time to time they moved, looking in one direction or another, shifting their weight to favor this leg instead of that. Far more unsettling, occasionally they would melt into the very stone of the Mid Wall and step out in a different spot, as if they were dropping through water.

He could understand the wariness of the homeless masses forced to stay near the wall. It was late, the sun long since set, and cold enough to leave most breathing puffs of steam as they huddled together or jealously guarded what they had left in the world.

Darsken moved among them but was not one of them. He walked because he needed to clear his mind from his earlier work.

He needed to prepare himself for when Desh Krohan came for him as he would inevitably do. It would not be long now. The Sisters would have spoken with the First Advisor, and he would want more answers than they could provide.

Darsken leaned against the cold stone wall and closed his eyes for a moment. Not far away someone made a gasping sound, surely thinking he must be mad for daring to touch the Mid Wall. Madness was always an option, of course. Sometimes it seemed a delightful distraction from the world around him.

"Why did I say yes?" he mused to himself. The sorcerer had asked his assistance, nearly begged him to speak to dead Goriah, and he had agreed. His logic was sound enough. Better that he take the risk of speaking with the dead than the sorcerer himself do it.

Inquisitors were trained in necromancy. They had to be in order to gain certain knowledge that would otherwise be lost. Once set on a trail, the Inquisitors almost never let go until they found the answers to their questions by any means necessary. That was the true reason they were feared. There were always rumors that they tortured their targets, and from time to time they earned the secrets they needed that way, but mostly the Inquisitors knew that torture was almost never a reliable method of gaining information. People would lie to escape the pain of a hot brand or metal pinchers. Empathy, observation and patience. Those were the best methods.

Still, when necessary, any tool in the box would suffice to find the answers required.

Desh Krohan could have performed the necromancy himself. Would have, very likely, despite the laws against it, because it was one of his.

Emotions ran hot when a loved one was murdered. Had the sorcerer been the one to work the magics he might well have handled everything perfectly, but he might also have let his emotions best him. It was an easy thing to do. Darsken knew all of the Sisters, had spoken with Goriah on many occasions and had liked her well enough. He had worked with her on a few cases that had been of importance to the sorcerer and his Sisters alike.

His feelings for her would have never been a problem. If she called for vengeance he would not have responded. If she begged for another day, another year, he would not have been swayed by her desperate pleas. That was why he said yes when the sorcerer asked his assistance, because he would not be weakened by the bonds of familial love.

Not far away from him he heard people making more noises. He did not need to raise his eyelids to know that the sorcerer had found him.

When he opened his eyes Desh Krohan was before him. The sorcerer wore his robes of office and there was no face to be seen within the shadows of the dark cowl.

Darsken Murdro was not a man who was afraid of much. Inquisitors were trained to ignore fear in its many incarnations. Fear was a tool of the trade and nothing more. Still, seeing the sorcerer before him, looming out of the darkness, he felt a shiver in his guts.

When the First Advisor to the Empire spoke his voice was a whisper, soft and cold, delivered from only a foot way. "You claim you can bring Goriah back to me?"

"I can." He resisted the urge to lick his lips. If a hundred men held blades to his throat he would have shown no more fear than if the only threat was a pleasant breeze. The sorcerer made no more impact.

"How? Without sacrificing another life, how is that possible?"

All magic had a price. It was possible to raise the dead. It had always been possible. Necromancers merely spoke with them and there was a cost. But to resurrect a dead form and give

it life again was far different. The very best you could hope
for was a life for a life and usually the cost was far higher. A
hundred lives. A thousand. Even then there was no guarantee
that the person brought back would be complete.

"I have ways. You know this. You know what Inquisitors do
and why it is allowed."

There were a hundred thousand ways to learn the truth.
Some of them cost the person being questioned more than
discomfort. Some lost years to the Inquisitor. It was far easier
to take a bit of life force to get the truth than it was to get
answers by pulling toenails or cutting away fingers. The ethics
of the situation never got considered. There were truths to be
found. Some truths could make a difference between whether
or not kingdoms went to war.

That life was stolen away and not often returned. Instead it
was held for other purposes, if an Inquisitor were wise.

Darsken liked to think he knew a thing or two about wisdom.

Desh Krohan nodded his head. Not in agreement to a pact,
but in consideration. A moment later he was gone.

Darsken did not pursue him. He would decide for himself if
he wanted his Sister returned to life.

The Inquisitor waited for several minutes, listening to the
wind and the sounds of people moving, adjusting and trying
to get comfortable in the cold and darkness.

After a time he moved for his home, and occasionally
the sound of his staff tapping marked his way along
the cobblestones.

Deep in the ground, beneath the palace of the Empress, there
were rooms and chambers and hallways that remained hidden
from most. A select group was trusted to know the truths that
rested underground. Most were students of the sorcerers who

knew that their ability not to speak of what they learned was one of the first lessons they must take to heart.

Failure to keep a secret would be discovered. It always had been. The secrets under the castle were kept well indeed.

It was in one of those rooms, a comfortable enough affair for all the secrecy, that Cullen sat on a pallet for sleeping, wrapped in a thick fur, rocking slowly back and forth. Deltrea was with her, as she always was. Hours before she had been in one of the towers of the palace, but as soon as the armies of the Sa'ba Taalor attacked, she was taken here for her own protection.

The sorcerer wanted her undamaged.

"Are you still in pain?" Deltrea's voice was grating on her nerves. She had been more tolerant of her friend when she was alive. These days, the voice of the woman was inevitable.

"Yes. I am in pain. Why are you still here, Deltrea? Why do you keep talking to me?"

"We have already discussed this." Deltrea leaned against the wall of the nicely decorated cell, her shoulder and arm pushing against a tapestry that did not ripple or notice her at all. "Either I am a ghost or you are mad. Only you can decide."

"When Desh Krohan comes again. I will ask him if you are real."

"If you do that and he says I am not, how will you respond?"

Cullen shrugged. "Either way, at least I will know."

Deltrea sighed and then squatted down until they were at eye level again. "Does it hurt? That great thing inside you?"

"It's not a thing and you know it. It's the Mother-Vine, whatever is left of her."

"What makes you say that?" Deltrea leaned closer. "You did not make that claim before."

"What else could it be?"

"Does it hurt? Carrying the Mother-Vine?"

"It would hurt less if she would stay still."

Deltrea eyed Cullen's stomach. "Well, you don't look pregnant."

Cullen laughed softly. "I am not pregnant. I don't rut like you do. I choose my mates more carefully."

"More like you don't choose at all."

"That is still more carefully than you. How many men did you fuck before you died?"

Deltrea did not answer, but instead crossed her arms and stared at the ground in sullen silence. It seemed there was a way to shut her up after all.

The sound of the door opening was loud, and Cullen looked toward it as the sorcerer entered.

The first time she'd seen him, his hood was up and he terrified her. This time his cowl was pulled away and down and she could see his face. It was a good face. Lean, but not narrow, kind without being weak. She liked him instantly.

The thing that was twisting around her guts seethed and pulsed deep inside her, and she stifled a moan.

"You mentioned a name when you came here, child," the sorcerer began. "Do you remember?"

Cullen nodded. "Moale Deneshi," she said softly. "She is the one who sent me here."

"She has been dead for rather a long time, Cullen." He walked through where Deltrea was squatting and came closer until, finally, he too lowered himself to her current height.

"Rude," muttered Deltrea.

"I don't step aside for specters. Sets a bad precedent."

Cullen gasped at his words. "You see her?"

Desh shrugged his shoulders. "I sense her. I could see her if I wanted, but I have no need. She is not here for me. She is here for you."

"What does she do? Why does she follow me?"

"Likely she feels you need protecting or she is simply confused."

"I'm right here, you know. I can hear the both of you." Deltrea crossed her arms and sighed.

The sorcerer completely ignored her. "Moale Deneshi is dead," he said to Cullen. "Why do you claim to speak for her?"

"She's not dead. She is inside me."

The sorcerer looked into her eyes for a moment and then placed a hand upon her head. The hand drifted slowly down to rest on her abdomen and, much as part of her was offended by the familiar contact, she knew he wasn't trying to molest her.

"How is that possible, child?"

Cullen opened her mouth to answer but instead felt her lips move of their own volition, speaking words that made no sense at all. They were a language she did not understand.

Desh Krohan nodded his head as if he understood. A moment later he rose and smiled wearily down.

"Get your rest, Cullen. We will talk soon."

He left a moment later and closed the door with a gesture. She did not hear a lock engage.

Part of her wanted to test whether or not the door was truly sealed, but she decided against it. She was safe. She had food, water and shelter. That was more than she could have said before wandering into the city. Trecharch, her home, was dead. Destroyed by the Sa'ba Taalor. She saw no reason to go elsewhere.

Deltrea apparently agreed. Her friend had slipped down the closest wall and leaned against it, looking at the space between her sprawled legs as if the floor there held the most astonishing secrets.

"Why so quiet, Deltrea?"

"I'm dead."

"Well, yes, but you knew that."

"Yes, but there was the chance that I was just your imagination and now we know better."

"And that makes you sad?"

"No. Confused. If I'm dead I have no idea why I am still here when everyone else has moved on."

"I know why."

"You do?"

"Of course. I've never needed a friend more in my life."

"I thought I annoyed you."

"You do. Doesn't mean we're not friends."

Deltrea nodded. "I feel a bit better then."

"Yeah?"

"Yeah. It's good to be needed."

For a while they sat in silence.

Captain Callan looked at the towering waves behind his ship and wished that he had not. It wasn't the waves. They were bad, but he knew well enough how to ride through a storm and could safely take his chances. He also knew that Vondum was even better than he was and as Vondum was at the helm he should have felt plenty confident.

No. It was the massive vessel behind them that was the problem. His ship – really, if he were being completely honest it was more of a large boat – could survive the waves only by riding up whatever wave came at them and slipping over the top before it crested. They were far enough away from the shore that most did not crash down upon themselves.

The black ship of the Sa'ba Taalor cut the latest wave in half, like an axe blow through soft, pampered flesh. Water flew away from the prow of the vast, black vessel, and even from the distance that still separated them – a dwindling distance, thanks very much – he could see the shapes of the sailors riding those waves, waiting for the chance to destroy him.

Two days ago he'd had a chance to take the river east. It seemed a great deal like he'd made the wrong choice.

Canhoon had lifted from the ground and into the air and he and his shipmates had stared on, stunned.

They had talked of trying to follow it and decided against the notion. What if it fell? That suggestion by Vondum had put an end to the discussions.

The sea with all of its current troubles had to be a better idea.

Surely the ship was not as large as the city. He knew that, but it was perspective, really. In comparison to his boat the damned black beast tearing through the waves may as well have been as large. The whales of Cormadun were not as large as that ship and the whales were gigantic, terrifying beasts best thought of only when on the land.

"Hold yourselves to the rails, lads!" He could barely hear Vondum over the wind and the thunderous backdrop of the burning seas. The only way to get where they needed to be was to pass by the land growing where the Guntha used to have their islands. The storms there were always rough but not so dangerous that a good sailor couldn't manage.

Now this, the ship, that was a different tale entirely. He grabbed hard at the closest rail and felt the boat beneath him shift and buck as his first mate tried to compensate for the waves and the vast nightmare heading for them. He dared another glance and saw the ship of the Sa'ba Taalor slam into the next wave, shrugging off the sea's attempt to thwart it from its hunt.

One of his men reeled across the deck and grabbed at the railing, barely catching himself before he'd have been tossed over the side. Thimms was a good man, but Callan would not go after him if he went swimming. There was the rest of the crew to consider, and his own hide besides.

"There's another from the east, Captain!"

"What?" Surely he'd misheard.

"Another of the damn ships comes from the east!" The clouds impaired easy viewing of anything, but he looked where Thimms pointed and cursed. There was, indeed another ship. It matched the scope of the one already chasing them.

A moment later there was a sign of hope, a faint light of potential safety.

The ship to the east was not alone. Several smaller vessels were running around it, moving like cats surrounding a massive bear, but they were there just the same.

The Brellar had arrived.

"Might have a chance at that." He whispered the words like a secret prayer and watched as the smaller ships moved around their prey.

The Brellar were terrors. They owned the Corinta Ocean and the seas beyond as well, near as he could tell, and they owned them because they were the fiercest warriors on water.

They had also been paid very handsomely to be here and to fight the Sa'ba Taalor. Because they were honorable enough in their way, they had even shown themselves as the enemy approached.

The ship to the east shifted itself. The great black hulking shape took a turn that should have been precarious and in the doing crashed its prow into the closest of the Brellar vessels with an impact that could be heard even over the wind and the storm.

The Brellar was not fast enough and in seconds the greater ship shattered the lesser on impact. Wood and bodies flew away from the crashing ships; both looked exclusively to be Brellar.

Whatever was in the way of the turning ship was ruined or dragged under the keel. Callan looked away, not in horror but out of necessity. The other black ship was gaining on them.

The waves surged, the ship under him shuddered but it rode another crowning wall of water to the crest and dropped down on the other side. Callan held onto the rail and felt the muscles in his hands screaming at him as his body rose and fell at the whims of the water.

The black ship was closer still and he saw one of the forms on that ship holding what might be the longest bow he had ever seen.

A moment later an arm was drawn back and a missile released. He did his best to watch the shaft move through the air. He missed most of the journey but saw it land in the back of Vondum's skull.

Vondum dropped to the deck. He didn't need to guess. He knew the man, his friend, was dead.

He also knew they were all dead if he didn't get to the wheel soon enough to stop the ship from foundering. Wind and rain and waves were his enemy right then, and Callan crouched low and ran along the deck as quickly as he could.

He did not run far before the arrow punched into the meat of his calf. Did he scream? Gods, yes. Did he fall? No. It wasn't choice. He hopped on one leg and made it to the helm, grabbing at the wheel and missing the first time.

Vondum's body was in the way. Thimms was there an instant later rolling the corpse to the side. He stayed, too, holding an arm around Callan's waist and bracing his captain as best he could. Thimms was a smart one. He was carrying a shield.

This was a simple affair. They lived or died together.

The black ship came closer, and Callan turned away from it, intent on riding through the storm and outracing the bastards coming up behind them.

THREE

The veils became a necessity. The winds were gone but the dust and grit of the Blasted Lands remained, and wherever the waters had receded, the dust lifted with each step they took and grew in clouds that surrounded them.

They had no food and very little water, but for the mounts that seemed not to matter.

Andover stared at the Edge as it grew closer. When he had entered the Blasted Lands, an eternity or so earlier, the storms had kept him from seeing anything at all. He had no real scope for how vast the barrier was. It was not as towering as the mountains, but it seemed to go on forever in both directions.

"Do we know where to climb this great thing?" He spoke in his usual slightly puzzled tones.

"The Temmis Pass is that way." Delil pointed south. "Another three days at this speed. If we let them run we will be there tonight."

He nodded and looked along the great stone wall. There were spots where they could climb. "We can go up here if you like." Again that ghost of his former self railed at the notion. There were large stretches where the climb was easy, especially now that the winds were gone, but other places where they would struggle.

Delil looked to him. "Don't ask me. I love climbing. Are you up to the challenge?"

He grinned. There was no more to say. Within minutes they were scaling the sheer stone surface. The way was much harder than he'd expected initially. The endless winds had scoured large areas nearly smooth.

Iron hands dug into stone where necessary. The mounts took the walls in leaps and bounds, their thick claws allowing purchase, their powerful bodies perfectly designed for pushing themselves in areas where human forms could not compete.

There were no Broken here. The Pra-Moresh did not attack. The winds did not slow them. The way was hard but without the challenge and risk of possible attack, Andover found himself oddly disappointed.

Life is pain. Life is struggle. A life of ease was no longer what he wanted from the world.

When they finished the arduous climb he looked down into the vast, motionless valley of the Blasted Lands and frowned. Far, far away he could make out the Seven Forges.

When he turned and scanned the desolate horizon in front of him he frowned again. Far to the south a column of smoke painted the air. Far to the north a caul of lighter colored smoke hazed the skyline into a soft blur.

He pointed to the finger of black smoke in the south. "That was Tyrne, I think."

Delil nodded. "Yes. It is so. Durhallem now rests there."

"How can a mountain be in two places at once?"

"Not the mountain. There are two mountains, yes, but Durhallem, the Wounder, the god, now rests where Tyrne once stood."

Completely unaware of the action, Andover tilted his head in the way of the Sa'ba Taalor, asking a silent question.

"We move to the desires of the Daxar Taalor, Andover. They do not abandon us, they move with us. They are claiming Fellein as theirs. They are making themselves comfortable in their new lands."

Andover nodded. "So the first of the gods to move? Which was that?"

"You do not know the shapes of the Forges as well as most. You have also not seen it, but the first to move was Wheklam. Donaie Swarl took her black ships out into the waters and found the spot that Wheklam wanted. I saw it in a dream. It was impressive to see."

"Are you a follower of Wheklam now?"

"I follow all of the gods, but Wheklam has asked that I learn his ways."

"And will you?"

"Why would I ever deny a god, Andover?"

He nodded his head, expecting no other answer from her. Gorwich moved close and nudged Andover's arm with his muzzle. He scratched idly at the broad face.

The Forges were still alive, still active, even if the gods were moving from one place to another. Both he and Delil had asked for and received the "Blood of the Mountain," literally the white-hot metal they pulled from Durhallem.

Andover had metal hands. Delil did not. Neither of them were burned by the metal as they pulled it out and shaped it like so much clay. Both of them should have been ruined by the contact, but that was the blessing of the Daxar Taalor. They were given wondrous gifts in exchange for their loyalty.

Gorwich likewise had been rewarded. The armored mask over the head of his mount was crafted in short order.

Gorwich's mask closely resembled the shape of his face, but Andover had lined the edges with barbs, the better to dissuade fools from trying to cut at the mount's muzzle or head. Was it necessary? No, but Gorwich seemed to like it.

"Delil?"

"Yes, Andover?" She was currently climbing onto her mount, and preparing to ride again.

"If the Forges are moving so far apart from each other, does that mean the Sa'ba Taalor will have to choose only one god each? Fellein is vast. A thousand or more times the size of the Taalor Valley."

Delil shook her head. "The distance we rode to the Seven Forges. How long was it?"

"I could not say. The storms of the Blasted Lands hid so much from us."

"They hid nothing the gods did not want hidden. Sometimes a trip to the Taalor Valley is a trip that takes months. Other times a day or only a few hours."

Andover frowned, considering that.

Delil continued. "The time it takes to reach any place we are required to go is changed by the gods themselves, Andover. If they wanted us at Canhoon now, if they needed us there, we would be within sight of the city. That is their way."

Andover rubbed his iron palm on Gorwich's neck and then climbed onto the mount's back. If his weight bothered the great beast, it gave no sign.

"So let us see how quickly they want us there," he said. "But let us be careful. We are now in a land where the Daxar Taalor are not the only gods, and there are enemies here who would see us dead."

Delil smiled and patted the hilt of her long, thin sword. "Finally," she sighed. "A war."

• • •

Drask Silver Hand raised his eyes from the ground before him and frowned.

"I tire of this." Neither of his companions spoke. He was not completely sure that either could any more.

"Brackka! To me!" Drask roared the words and the air around them shimmered as the dust at their feet rippled, impacted by the sound waves.

His voice echoed far further than should have been possible. In the far distant remains of the Mounds, half hidden by the settled ash and soot, a shadow was burned into the very stone where Brackka had stood when Drask and the others fell into the glowing essences that powered the endless caverns of the forbidden underground realm. The resulting contact between living flesh and reservoirs of power locked away in the Mounds had been... explosive.

Drask was not even now completely certain what the energies had been. He only knew that they were still changing him, altering his mind and his body alike. One look at his silver hand was enough to make that point clearly. Striations of silver ran all the way up to his bicep now, slithering slowly up from his wrist like arteries of liquid silver.

He knew something else as well. He knew that Brackka was dead, and how he had died, burnt into naught but a shadow.

One last thing he knew. He knew that when he called for Brackka, his mount would come to him.

In the distance, in the Mounds, left far behind, the shadow of Brackka rose, and pulled itself away from the stone. It moved quickly and took on flesh as it ran toward Drask's voice. Flesh, and familiar armor, leather and straps and supplies and a dozen weapons long since forged by Drask.

By rights it should have been days or at the very least a long night before Brackka could reach Drask.

It took only minutes.

Drask did not wish to wait for his mount, and so he did not have to. For some beings, time works differently.

There was a moment of joy when Brackka got there. He patted his friend's thick neck and ran his flesh fingers through the thick mane and murmured nonsense to his longtime companion.

And all the while he contemplated what it meant that he was able to so easily bring his friend back from complete destruction.

What, he wondered, makes a god a god?

Merros walked the Mid Wall, looking into the stone faces of each of the Silent Army. They were easy to tell apart. Some were male, others female. All wore the same armor, archaic breastplates and helmets that did not cover their faces. Each looked slightly rough, reflecting the fact that they appeared carved from the very stone of the wall. But each had a different face.

Each still had the features of the person who had died for them, that they might live again.

Now if he could only remember the face of the Pilgrim, a man he had all but ignored, Merros might be able to get somewhere with the notion of speaking to the literal army of stone men surrounding the city.

The top of the wall was clear of refugees. It seemed the notion of staying near the moving statues unsettled them. Merros could understand that. Sorcery of any sort made him uncomfortable.

"I called for you." Nachia's voice, coming from behind him, was more amused than annoyed.

"I have not received a message, Majesty." He turned and bowed formally. Nachia stood with two soldiers: Darfel, her bodyguard – chosen by Merros himself – and Lauro Larn, the grandson of General Dataro Larn, who before his death had been one of the men who held the seat Merros himself now claimed. Both men nodded and stayed properly at the Empress's side.

"Likely the messengers are looking in and around your offices." Nachia raised one eyebrow and crossed her arms. "Where one would expect to find a commander of the armies in a crisis situation."

He felt his skin blush a bit. "I've been trying to remember exactly what the Pilgrim looked like." He gestured to the closest of the Silent Army, a female. "Before he turned into one of these."

Nachia did not bother answering him, but instead stood face to face with the feminine statue, looking up to stare it in the eyes. Male and female alike, all of them were taller than the Empress.

"I am the Empress Nachia Krous of the Fellein," she said formally. "I would speak to the one who called himself the Pilgrim and I would do it as soon as possible. Please convey that message to him."

Merros stared at her, not quite sure when she had lost her faculties.

Nachia looked back at him and frowned. "It can't hurt to ask."

"They're *statues*, Nachia." He shook his head, immediately regretting the tone. A wise man did not scold his Empress, especially in a public setting, and doubly so if her name was Nachia Krous.

Nachia shot him a withering stare. "I know they're statues,

Merros. I wasn't the one trying to find one out of a thousand or more. Also, they're statues that move."

"Well, yes, there is that. It's why I was hoping it might be possible to talk to the one called the Pilgrim."

Nachia stepped back and so did her guards. It only took a moment for Merros to understand why. To his right and slightly behind him a stone man was rising from the ground. The shape was definitely one of the Silent Army.

He was tall and he stood straight, one hand resting on the hilt of a sword made from the same substance as everything else. His face was familiar, but if Merros were honest with himself, he would never have located the one from the thousand others. There simply weren't enough remarkable features.

The expression, however, he would have remembered. The face twisted into a cold scowl.

"You have called me, Empress. I have come." The Pilgrim's voice was oddly hollow, as if coming from a vast distance. There was a faint echo as well, making Merros think that the source of the voice came not from the mouth but from deep within the chest. Merros repressed a shudder. Sorcery.

Nachia stared up into the Pilgrim's visage and then pointed a finger toward Merros. "He wanted to speak with you."

The Pilgrim regarded him coldly. "You are General Merros Dulver."

"Yes."

"I remember you. What do you ask?"

"I was, well, I was hoping you could explain to me why you have come here and where you are taking Canhoon."

"The gods have summoned us to come and protect their city."

"But where are we going?"

"Where the gods command." The Pilgrim stared to the east.

"Can you tell us what the gods want?"

"What they have always wanted. The safety and fealty of their children."

Without waiting another moment, the Pilgrim started to melt back into the stone.

"Wait! We have more questions!"

The stone face turned to look at him again, and that scowl deepened. "We are here to protect the Empress of Fellein. For that reason I answered your query, but we do not serve you, nor do we serve the Empress. We serve only the gods. This body is not designed for speech. We are called the Silent Army for a reason. No more questions will be answered."

With that, the form of the Pilgrim melted once more into the Mid Wall.

Merros stared at the spot where the stone man had been and made an obscene gesture. When one considered his position in the city it certainly seemed there were a lot of rude people around him.

The Empress spoke. "Well, I'd wanted to know if you'd had any luck figuring out where we are going. I guess I have my answer."

Merros shook his head. "Near as I can guess we are going straight east. If that does not change, the only thing we are going to meet is the mountains. After that the only thing we are going to see for quite some time is the river below and then Lake Gerhaim and Goltha."

"How do we get out of this, Merros?" Nachia's voice was soft and worried.

"We work on solutions. If that doesn't work I might suggest that the Sisters teach us how they fly."

"The Sisters fly?"

Merros nodded. "Oh, yes. Apparently it's contagious.

They've lifted the entire damned city."

Nachia swatted his arm and laughed. "For that humor alone I'd keep you in my court, Merros."

He had no response for her.

Instead of speaking he merely broke protocol and put a companionable arm around her shoulders. She did not protest, but instead leaned into him. It was only for a moment that they acted human, and then only because they could trust the witnesses.

The columns of the Sa'ba Taalor moved along at a steady clip: the riders with mounts to the front, the rest behind them, trudging over terrain that was sometimes rough and rocky and often pleasantly flat near the edge of the river.

From a distance they could see the City of Wonders as it moved steadily through the sky.

Tusk moved along beside Tarag Paedori, who rode his mount contemplating the vast stone cloud on the horizon as if it might be an apple he wanted to take a bite from.

Their scouts had prepared them. Up ahead was a small town. Beyond that was a great stone structure, the likes of which none of them had ever seen before. All they knew was that both were occupied. The scouts had been warned not to engage the enemy.

The King in Iron shrugged his shoulders and rattled in his armor. Tusk smiled. He knew he was not the only one who was restless.

"Durhallem says the city ahead is for me. The tower is for you." He spoke conversationally, knowing full well that Paedori's god had spoken to him as well.

"So it shall be, Tusk."

"I think we should send the scouts ahead a day or more,

to see if there are opportunities to reach the city in the sky."

"You are thinking of the mountains ahead." Tarag Paedori nodded his head as he spoke. "This is wise. Send Stastha with them if you like. She is a good strategist and can assess better than most, I think."

Tusk made a small gesture and Stastha immediately rode forward. "My kings." She lowered her head for only a moment. The horns on her helmet rose from near her neck and thrust upward like the tusks of a great boar. She looked toward Tusk and studied his face.

"We will send you ahead, Stastha. Go to the mountains. Seek weaknesses and ways that we might reach that city. They will not escape us for long."

Stastha looked toward the horizon. The mountains were several days away at a guess, but the city only moved at one speed and the mounts were capable of covering the distance at a much greater pace.

She nodded and Tuskandru continued. "Be aware. They must know we are here, and arrows from that height would cut through any possible armor."

"I will only approach the city in darkness, my king." Tusk felt himself stir. Stastha was a woman he admired for her strength and her tactical skills. Her scars fairly glowed in the sunlight and he found himself in a mood to examine them closely.

Now was not the time.

"Make Durhallem proud, as you make me proud, Stastha."

She smiled at that and nodded her head. A moment later she was moving forward, calling names. Several other riders obeyed her summons and joined her.

"It is a small town?" Tusk asked.

Tarag nodded.

Tusk sighed. "I want that city, but this should whet the

palate, yes?"

"I am curious about the tower. Why is it all alone? What is there and who protects it?"

"It is my experience that something all alone is more deadly than a gathering of like minds."

Tarag nodded and frowned. "Unless you are talking of the Pra-Moresh. They are much worse in packs."

Tusk chuckled deep in his chest and then spurred Brodem forward. The beast let out a rumble and charged forward at great speed. Behind him others began to ride faster, a few pulling out their horns for when the time came to announce themselves.

Tarag Paedori looked to Kallir Lundt, the Fellein who now sported a face of iron and served him loyally. "It is time, Kallir. Find four others to come with us, the rest will continue on the path and seek whatever they can find by way of combat."

Kallir nodded his metal face and then looked over his shoulder, seeking the ones he felt best qualified and deserving. He had watched all of the Sa'ba Taalor close to Tarag. "Ehnole, Tenna, Mardus, Kopora!" he called and the followers of the King in Iron responded, sitting straighter on their mounts and looking toward him.

It was Tarag who finished what he started. "We ride!" There was nothing more to say. The six of them moved forward and the rest of the long columns moved on. The followers of Tarag Paedori were, easily, the most disciplined of all the Sa'ba Taalor, that is to say, the best at following orders they did not like. None would dare disobey a king. To do so was to disobey a god. Still, Paedori's army waited with more patience than most, fully prepared to take down the vast, floating city above them.

• • •

Andover Lashk looked at the lake where Canhoon should have been. It was an impressive lake, to be sure, but it was not what he'd been expecting to see. A few buildings remained around the edge of the water. Most had been destroyed by whatever catastrophe had removed the city itself.

The lake's waters were clear enough, but along the vast shoreline the remains of hundreds, possibly thousands of people had been stacked in heaps and then burned. Ashes coated stacks of bones and partially ruined meat. Andover did not have to guess what had happened to the dead. The Sa'ba Taalor sacrificed the dead to the gods, preferably by tossing them into the heart of one of the forges. When that was not possible they were burned. On occasions when necessity demanded, he knew that the dead were eaten. The Daxar Taalor did not believe in waste.

Amid the rubble great storm crows hopped and lurked, mostly silent save for occasional caws, eyeing everything with cold contempt. He had never seen so many gathered in one spot before. It was a sight to behold.

Delil looked at the birds, too. They did not exist in Taalor. They were large and gray and gave off a certain air of menace.

"Where is Canhoon?" Andover spoke out loud, simply because he was surprised. There had been a vast wall around the city, at least according to the paintings he had seen. He had never once left Tyrne before he came to the Blasted Lands, and could only trust his memories of a life he had almost forgotten. There was evidence of the wall, broken stones and shattered gates, but mostly there was debris.

Ydramil's voice filled his head. THE GODS OF FELLEIN HAVE MADE THEIR FIRST MOVE. THEY WOULD FIGHT US AND THWART US. THE CITY OF CANHOON RIDES THROUGH THE SKIES, MOVING TO ESCAPE THE SA'BA TAALOR.

Movement from the right made him look that way. Several people were gathered together near one of the portions of the wall that had not collapsed. They were ragged and scared. Their clothes did not match and if he had to guess, they were as confused by the lack of a city as he was.

He slid from Gorwich's broad back and landed with ease. "Why are you here?" he called out in his native tongue and the group flinched.

They understood him. He had been like them once upon a time. Now he felt like he was staring at a different species entirely. They were so pale, so pink. It was not long ago that he was the same. It was an eternity ago.

"There is nowhere else to go." It was a woman who spoke from beside him. She shivered as she looked up at him. Her hair was fair, her skin sunburned from seeing more of the daylight than she usually did, and her clothes were the sort of finery he remembered from Tyrne, only now they were badly weathered. There was a time she would have held his eye and he'd have thought her lovely. Now she was dirty, unkempt, and shivered with fright at the sight of him. She was weak, and that weakness made her ugly in his eyes.

"You come from Tyrne?"

"From where it was." Dark blue eyes looked up at him with dread. She did not see a person from her home. She did not see a Fellein. She saw a Sa'ba Taalor, one of the people who had come into her world and started shattering it. Her eyelashes fluttered rapidly as she attempted to blink back tears. "Everything I had is gone. And now Canhoon has gone as well."

"You have your life and your health. If I followed Durhallem, you would no longer have those." He tried to keep the contempt from his voice. She was one of the wealthy, one who had likely never worked a day and could not understand a world that did not adore her for her looks.

"You... You won't kill us?" There was something about her tone that set his nerves on edge and he moved his right hand, stretched the fingers as if to relax tension, and then did it three more times, quickly.

That was all the warning that Delil needed. She drew her sword and moved into a crouch.

Andover grabbed the woman by her arm and brought her in front of him, striding hard toward the small gathering of people and the wall where they waited. Iron hands crushed soft flesh with bruising force.

She wailed out her fears as he pushed her along in front of him, holding most of her weight with ease. Her feet scuffed and dragged and tried to hold the ground but he did not afford her that level of control.

"I will kill her! I will gut her and let her bleed in the dirt. Show yourselves!"

The three men who came from behind the wall were fighters. They were hurt and they were desperate, but they were armed and carried themselves like experienced soldiers.

Swords. Three swords. For a moment he'd been worried about arrows. That was still a possibility, but not as likely now.

"Don't! Don't do that!" The man who yelled at him was heavier than his fellow refugees. Likely he was well trained, but he was also in bad shape. Somewhere along the way he'd earned a deep cut along his left thigh and the wound was festering. His eyes were too shiny and he licked his chapped lips constantly. He was suffering from the Plague Winds.

"Drop your weapons or I'll kill all of you." Andover's tone was conversational.

He looked them over. There were ten people all told, three

armed, and only two of them seemed likely to last more than a few seconds in a fight. The man with plague shook his head and muttered to himself.

"I do not care if you live or die, but I also don't trust you at my back," Andover continued. "Leave here. Go west. Or I'll kill you all."

The plague man charged, moving surprisingly well on his festering leg.

Andover's axe removed most of his head in the first swing. The return arc brought the obsidian axe into a guard position even as he tossed the girl away and prepared for a proper fight.

In an instant Delil was next to him, standing at his side and watching the gathered people.

The mounts looked on, aware, standing close, but not joining the fight yet. They had not been invited.

"Leave. Now." Andover's voice was not loud. It did not need to be.

"We have nowhere to go!" the woman screamed from where he'd thrown her. She did not attempt to rise. Instead she sobbed, her body shaking with her misery, and lowered her face toward the ground.

Andover felt no pity, only disgust.

Delil looked his way for only a moment. "Let the mounts feast. They are hungry."

He nodded and Delil called to them to have their meals.

The two armed ones tried to defend themselves against the great beasts and failed. While they were dying Andover stared at the woman on the ground. She reminded him a little of Tega, but without the strength he had always sensed in his first love. Love? No. Infatuation. But it had felt like love, once upon a time.

"You are alive. That is my last mercy." He spoke to the

remaining seven who had not been slaughtered. He looked at the woman on the ground as he spoke. "Leave. They are still hungry. They'll eat all of you if we let them."

That did the trick. Even those who'd been staring on in horrified fascination as the mounts started their grisly feasts got the hint at that point and started moving. Supplies no longer mattered.

"Where will we go?" the woman tried one last time as she rose to her feet.

"I don't care."

Delil reached past him and slapped the woman hard enough to knock her back to the dirt. "Leave before I forget Andover's mercy!"

She took two steps after the woman, who scrambled to her feet and staggered toward the west as quickly as she could, wiping the blood from her mouth as she ran.

As she started her third step, the arrow took her precisely at the base of her skull. Delil fell forward and landed hard on her face.

There was no thought in the action; that had been trained out of him. Andover spun, even as his hand grabbed at a short spear from the quiver at his hip and he spotted the archer and threw his weapon.

The archer tried to turn away and dodge. The spear's tip punched deep into the muscle of the young man's shoulder, until it broke skin on the other side. The man might have thought of running, but the pain was too large for him to ignore and he staggered, then screamed, eyes locked on the weapon in his bloodied joint.

Andover called out, "Kill them all!" and charged the young archer.

Young and desperate and hungry to survive, the archer

swept his bow around despite the wound in his shoulder, and tried to draw a fresh arrow. The notch did not match up with the bow's line before Andover cut him down.

Another step and he was reaching for the closest of the natives and grabbing at her hair with his iron fingers. She slipped past and screamed and he cut her down just the same.

It was not a battle. It was a massacre. The mounts did their work and Andover did his and none of it changed the fact that Delil was down and dead. He had tried for mercy and been rewarded with the death of his closest friend.

Had there been any doubt in the desire to follow the Daxar Taalor, it was removed in that moment.

FOUR

Nachia seemed remarkably calm on her seat. She was not on the throne. Unlike her cousin and generations before him, she seemed perfectly content to hold off sitting in her seat of power until she absolutely had to.

Also, she knew about the enchantments layered into the very wood and stone of the vast structure. It offered protection and made sure that the person sitting there was never too comfortable. She would never say so to the old man but she agreed with Desh Krohan's agenda when it came to the throne: no one should ever sit there long enough to be comfortable.

As she looked over the maps of the area around and below, she tapped a finger on the thick paper and shook her head. There was simply no way around it: the mountains were fast approaching and they would be a problem.

Merros Dulver entered her throne room and stopped long enough to bow formally. She had told him not to stand on ceremony when there was no one around, but he seemed incapable of obeying that simple request. He'd already told her once that she had bodyguards around at all times. He considered them people. She had flushed with embarrassment and he'd chuckled at her discomfort.

Sometimes, she wanted to gut punch him just for the look on his face. Sometimes, she wanted to aim lower. Her self-control was one of the things no one understood about her. They'd have given her a second empire if they did. She chuckled at the notion, as that would be a fitting punishment for any who truly believed themselves free of all sin. She knew better and her self-control, while impressive, had not stopped her throwing a few things and screaming more times than she cared to think about.

That was before the coronation. Now she waited until she was truly alone before she had her tantrums. One must keep up appearances.

Merros eyed her cautiously. "You're studying the maps again?"

"Well, I suppose I could dress up in my finery and stalk the Mid Wall, but it seems someone else has already taken that task, and besides, I should hate to have people thinking I wanted to start a trend."

"Better stalking walls than Pathra's hideous curled hair." Desh's voice came from behind her and she resisted the urge to jump out of her seat and scream. She supposed she had that coming, as she liked using the same hidden passages.

"Honestly, Desh. That hair should have been a lesson."

"That hair should have seen his hairdresser executed for starting one of the worst trends in the history of your family."

"There's always the chance she died with Tyrne." She kept her voice low, as the sorcerer had before her. Only Merros heard both of them and he was properly appalled.

"If you're both quite done mocking the dead–"

"Only their hair, dear boy."

"–we should discuss the latest intelligence." As Merros

spoke he moved the ring she had been using to mark Canhoon on the map and replaced it with a crest of the Empire that was a bit larger and had more weight.

"So, tell us what has happened, General Dulver." Nachia crossed her hands over her chest and stared archly at him. He did not wither. Had he been the sort to wither under that sort of expression he would have never been a successful general.

"The scryers have done their best and it's quite astonishing what they can learn. The armies of the Tuskandru and Tarag Paedori are still behind us, but they've sent a few small bands to get ahead of us and to find out what lies ahead and on the ground below."

"Really? Have we actually seen any of these scouts?" Nachia leaned back in her seat, the better to look at Merros's face.

"We have. There are a few of them almost directly under us, moving in the shadow of our city."

"And can we do anything about them?"

Merros smiled. "Possibly. We are working on ways to surprise them from above."

Desh stared at the map and nodded his head. "I might be able to help with that. It's something we can discuss."

He leaned over the map, studied it carefully and then pushed the crest three inches further along the river's line. "We continue to follow the river. I've checked and there are slight variations in our course to compensate. Also, we're moving a little faster than we thought initially. I have made adjustments."

"Still no luck in finding out what to do about the Silent Army?"

"There's nothing we have found so far. They did not work this way before." Desh crossed his arms. "We summoned them and they only did certain things, like defend the city.

This is new. They could not speak before and they did not act on their own."

Nachia sighed. "We might yet have to go to the churches and ask the leaders."

Merros shook his head. "I already did. They seem as baffled as we are. I have witnessed several groups from different churches placing laurels and treasures at the feet of the statues. Tributes, I think, but I've seen no response."

"No more from this Pilgrim of yours?"

Merros shook his head. "He's not mine, I assure you."

Desh nodded. "Yes, well, if he were, there'd be no real problems, now would there?"

Nachia barely moved, but her eyes flicked from one man to the other. "What of the other kings of the Sa'ba Taalor?"

"Sorry?" Merros seemed surprised by the question.

"There are seven kings. What of the other five? Where are they and their armies?"

"Well, quite honestly, Majesty, we're not completely sure. One of them we believe is on the ocean. The black ships have moved to the south and have been engaging the Brellar."

"How have our associates been doing?"

"It seems they've been having a few successes and a great number of losses."

"How many losses?" Nachia asked and prepared to hide the wince that she knew would come when she heard the numbers.

"Well, the Brellar really do have a great number of ships. Somewhere over a thousand. Which, truly, is a staggering number, but they are spread all along the edge of Fellein. They've lost over fifty ships."

"That's not so horrid, really. I mean fifty out of a thousand?"

Merros nodded. "True enough, but they are not happy with

our previous arrangement and would like to renegotiate."

"How did you receive that information? I thought only a few of the Brellar spoke our tongue."

"A good number understand the tongue well enough but few speak it, true." Merros nodded again. "They have sent back a couple of messages on the bodies of their dead. It seems they really don't have time to be more personal than that as they are retreating from the Sa'ba Taalor as quickly as they can."

"So. No navy then?"

"Not as such."

Nachia stared long and hard at Desh Krohan. Hard enough that he fidgeted. That was effectively a gigantic victory.

"Is there nothing that you or the sorcerers can do, Desh?"

"I'll look into the matter, Majesty." The chill from his voice nearly matched the weather outside. As the walls were beginning to get a layer of ice, that said a great deal.

"Desh, you know I would not ask..."

"Yes. I am aware of the dire situation, Nachia. You have seen one demonstration. I cannot promise that any actions taken wouldn't destroy the sea life for a hundred miles in all directions."

Nachia thought back to the vast swathe of lightning blasts Desh Krohan had cast from one hand in her presence. She recalled very clearly the devastation he'd wreaked at her request.

"Please give careful consideration, Old Man. I need the help." Desh did not look old. He was. He had been around since the first rise of the Silent Army over six hundred years earlier. He looked to be roughly forty and was handsome enough to distract her sometimes.

She pushed that thought aside. While she could use a

distraction, she'd not try seducing him again. That hadn't gone well the first time and wouldn't go well now, she'd have wagered.

Nachia looked at the map though it offered no new information. "Are we safe from the Sa'ba Taalor if they should try to reach us from below?"

Merros gave her an arch look. "You mean if they should grow wings?"

The first Advisor said, "The entire city has been destroyed and rebuilt. I for one am not moving under the city to discover anything, but the Sisters have traveled around the underside of Canhoon and spoke of many openings in the belly of this floating nightmare."

"Openings?"

Desh shrugged. "As I said, the city has been rebuilt many times. They could lead almost anywhere or nowhere."

For twenty more minutes they discussed the minutiae of the war on as many fronts as they could be certain of. There were seven kings. They could account for five. The other two either were not involved or were better hidden than they wanted to think about. Likely it was the latter of the two.

In the far east, the armies of the Sa'ba Taalor were already making their mark. Elda was gone, destroyed and buried under a growing mountain of fire. From Elda the Sa'ba Taalor marched north, heading along the coastline and striking wherever they found people. The news was grim whenever they found a city or town. They did not leave survivors. Danaher was a vast city, but it was currently engaged by the Sa'ba Taalor and not doing well.

Morwhen was to the north and had already sent forces to stop the Sa'ba Taalor if possible. Theorio Krous himself was leading the charge. Having seen the man, there was the possibility that he could match the savagery of the Sa'ba Taalor.

Nachia thanked her general for the news and smiled warmly. He really was a wonder. Despite everything he maintained a level head and that helped her do the same.

When Merros headed away, back to his office to find out the latest details, Nachia asked Desh Krohan to stay behind.

As soon as he agreed, she dismissed the guards to the outside of the room. There were few times she actively told them to stay out of range and this was one of them. They were trained well enough not to react openly. Desh was not. He looked genuinely puzzled.

Before he could make any comments at all, she spoke.

"I can't forbid you to do anything, Desh. I mean, I could, but you and I both know it would be a waste of my words. So I'm just going to say this and have it out in plain view between us for you to consider."

She took a breath and considered her words.

Desh watched her, unblinking, his face calm but cautious.

"You should let Goriah stay where she is."

The sorcerer paused for a moment then said flatly, "I'll consider that."

"You are the one who wanted necromancy outlawed. I looked into it. You were the one who said it was too dangerous."

"I'm well aware of what I said, Nachia." His voice was colder still and his expression was impossible for her to read. She had nearly grown up on the man's knee and she could not guess what he was thinking. That was a first for her.

"There's always a price. That's a phrase I've heard from you all of my life, Desh." She fought against the tears that wanted to sting her eyes. She did not want to have this argument with him. She did not want to give him any reason to grieve. "There's always a price. Always. Your words."

If she could have, she would have looked away. She would have pretended that she did not know what was in his heart. She knew how much the Sisters meant to Desh. They were his chosen disciples. They were very nearly his children.

"I did not break the rules for your cousin. I will not challenge the laws for my Sister." His voice shook with rage and guilt. He was still thinking hard of lifting Goriah from the dead.

"You know I won't punish you if you do this thing, Desh. It's not in me to punish you, even if I could make the punishment stand."

She stood up and stepped toward him where he stood in his robes with his arms locked behind his back, lest he make a gesture that was too harsh to forgive. Or perhaps lest he cast a spell and shatter her body.

"Do not do this thing, Desh. I don't know if you could forgive yourself."

"There is always a price, Nachia. I am aware of that."

He turned and walked away and she let him. She could have commanded that he stay and he would have, but she had already done all she could to convince him. If he listened she would be grateful. If he did not, she could cause him no harm. The trouble with sorcerers is that they were sorcerers and oh, so very powerful. Even when they tried to hide that fact.

They gathered in silence. Deep beneath the main hall of Dretta March's home, in the area where foodstuffs were meant to be stored.

Swech settled in a familiar corner, swaddled in a heavy cloak to fight off the cold. Next to her was Jost, who was often her shadow. Jost was dressed in leathers and had a fur cloak as well. She sat cross-legged and had her hands propped on her knees.

Jost was the one who stood out. Her flesh was gray and her Great Scars made clear that she was a different beast altogether. The rest were cloaked in Fellein skins, hidden behind guises chosen by the gods. The only other exception was Glo'Hosht. The King in Mercury revealed nothing, including gender. The king's skin was gray, of course, but no one could have said anything more.

When Glo'Hosht spoke, the others listened.

"It is time. The waters must be tainted. The grains made to rot. It will not kill them. They will not be in the air long enough to starve, but it will anger them and make the Fellein desperate."

The King in Mercury looked to a plain woman with blonde hair shot with silver. Swech did not know her. She was a stranger, but if Glo'Hosht accepted her as one of the chosen of Paedle, then it was exactly so. "I have given you the means. Go to the wells beneath the castle and let them know that nothing is beyond our reach."

The woman nodded and rose. She was pale, but Swech could see that this one had been training her body, just as Swech had been training the body of Dretta March. There were fresh calluses, a few fresh scars… inevitable marks of transformation.

The man who sat closest to Glo'Hosht was little more than a boy. He was familiar to Swech, having helped her poison the feed in all of the stables. Even now the city had a problem with dead horsemeat. The citizens could not eat the stuff for fear it would poison them. That was wisdom: it would indeed have killed them all.

"Find the larders. Ruin them." Those were all the words Glo'Hosht spoke to the boy. In response the lad rose and walked away. He was not a boy. He was one of the Sa'ba Taalor and he was a trained killer. He showed no signs of recent change in his body. He did not train himself to be stronger, knowing full well that he could not change his size. Instead he used that size to his advantage. He was a child, an urchin, not seen as a threat by anyone. That was a mistake as well. Swech had killed her first enemy when she was six.

Glo'Hosht spoke without looking away from the retreating figure. "As for the rest of you, it is time to spread fear..."

Half an hour later, Swech moved through the Inner Wall Commons. The area was lush with shops and people, and as always was crowded. These days a good portion of that crowd were refugees seeking a place to stay, food or new ways to make enough money to arrange for food and shelter. It was an endless cycle that affected increasingly more of the city's dwellers. The wealthiest of them came here to shop. Now they had to move their way through the crowds of beggars, prostitutes and cutpurses.

Swech moved in the shadows. She dressed in black and hid her face away. She did not wear a cloak. It would have encumbered her too much, but she wore leathers under thinner clothes and she sported enough blades to scare anyone who knew what she was capable of.

Small, skillful hands reached out to test her awareness. Pickpockets abounded. Her fingers caught the hand of a young one testing her mettle and she broke the fingers quickly. There was a gasp. The pain was a potent, living thing, but the penalty for being caught stealing in that district was far harsher than a broken finger and rather than cry out, the child slipped away, unseen.

The people around her were desperate. She knew that. She was one of the reasons it was so. Her people had caused this because her gods demanded it. Swech had no pity for them. They were the enemies of her gods and that was all that mattered.

A man noticed her and opened his mouth. She shut it for him. One step closer to his side and then the blade kissed the inside of his thigh even as the man smiled, expecting a different sort of touch. He was drunk and he wanted to pay for a woman. She was sober and killed him for his trouble. As he fell back against the wall, she gripped his arms and lowered him gently. The look of surprise was still on his face as the light in his eyes left him. The blade would have killed him in any event, but the toxins guaranteed his silence as he died.

A member of the City Guard stood nearby, his eyes already bored with dealing with so many people. The air was cooler, but the sheer volume of bodies ensured that everyone stayed warm.

The man tapped the hilt of his sword as he looked around. He glowered at a thin man who got too close to him and sent him along with a boot to his side. So many like this: a little power and they could not possibly let a person stand their ground. This was preferred. This, the need to express their contempt.

Swech felt nothing for the man or the guard. Still, she let the thin man live and broke the guard's neck with a vicious blow to the side of his throat. When he fell, she caught him. He was still alive, but only for a moment.

Seven deaths in, someone finally noticed her.

She had been careful, because that was her duty. She was to spread as much panic as she could. Seven bodies lay behind her and even in a crowd as vast as this, that was a lot of death to go unnoticed.

As a merchant who'd bumped into her slumped and then fell over, bleeding, a woman who'd approached the collection of fine scarves and cloaks the man had to offer saw her pull back the blade and screamed as loudly as anyone Swech had ever met.

The small blade in her left hand sailed and buried itself in the woman's cheek, ensuring more screams, more chaos. Most of the poison had long since worn off the blade and it would take at least another minute for the screamer to die. In that time Swech intended to kill as many people as possible.

The people around her were scattering. They moved away from the screaming woman and away from the table of woven fineries.

And Swech moved with them, slipping among them and cutting, striking, breaking as she went. A man gurgled out his last as his throat vomited a crimson stain. Next to him a woman let out a scream as Swech broke three of her ribs and shoved her aside.

People continued to flow like water away from a scalding hot stone, but they were not fast enough. Swech moved with them, her face covered, her body shielded. A man with a dagger tried to stop her and she blocked his strike, broke his wrist and shoved the blade he proffered into his own stomach as he went past. He grunted and fell, the pain a sudden and overwhelming thing that stole his breath. He might well live, but he would suffer greatly.

Her foot kicked at a kneecap and the leg it belonged to folded the wrong way. As the screaming victim of her kick started to fall, she stepped in close and flipped him to the ground. He collided with three others in the process of collapsing and took them with him.

Three sharp jabs and the City Guard coming to investigate stepped back and fell to his knees. His throat was punctured, as were his ear and his eye. His sword fell from his hand.

Swech leaned down and caught it.

The sword was well made and properly sharpened. She slashed several people with it and then left it buried in a screaming man's guts as she moved past.

The effort was starting to weary her. Her muscles were beginning to protest. The crowd was now panicking, running into each other, shoving others aside rather than moving past them. They were no longer people. They were a mob.

Swech moved along their edges, not foolish enough to risk being inside the mass of crushing bodies. Where she moved, she struck, cutting, wounding and occasionally killing as she headed for her point of exit.

Her work was done for the moment. The Inner Wall did not stop access for the people of Canhoon. Not unless the horns were sounded and all the access points were sealed. Swech made her way to the top of the wall with ease, only pausing once to stop a terrified man from pushing her back down the stairs as he climbed. She just made the wall before the City Guard came down in force. By the time she reached it, her face was uncovered, her hair was loose and displayed, rendering the appearance of merely being a patron of the shops complete. She even managed a look of panic, which was easier than she'd expected.

Below her the crowds pushed and fought and screamed as they tried to escape their possible demise.

Elsewhere, Swech knew, others were causing the same sort of chaos. She could hear the voices of the Daxar Taalor and knew that they were pleased.

That news pleased her as well, but she did not show her satisfaction until she wound her way through the narrow alleys and streets of the homes that were closest to the palace.

There were preparations to make. Her man was coming over and she had a meal to prepare for him.

Theorio Krous was a man of his word: four legions of his finest soldiers left Morwhen and headed west, toward the City of Wonders. Even with the city soaring toward the east – an accomplishment he knew of but did not begin to understand – it would be weeks before they met up.

In the meantime, there were members of the Sa'ba Taalor heading in the direction of Morwhen and he had no intention of waiting for them to show themselves. With that in mind he took six legions with him to meet the enemy in combat.

Theorio Krous was a member of the same bloodline as the Empress Nachia. Thirty years her senior, he had spent his entire life dedicated to the goal of winning any and all encounters of a military nature. Morwhen trained some of the finest soldiers in the world.

He planned for battle. He trained for it. He thrived as a result of it. He and his would take care of the matters on the eastern side of the Empire because they had to be taken care of. They would fight and they would either win or they would die trying.

If death occurred, it was a natural part of life. If victory occurred it was because of his might, and when the time came he would claim his rightful prize.

Nachia Krous would either be his grateful bride, or she would be his unhappy wife. He would be satisfied with either result. Sometimes a woman who struggled added to the pleasure. Not always, but he could accept that sometimes a woman needed to be taught her place in the bedroom if not in other areas.

She had not yet been made aware of his plans, of course.

Most of his communications had been with Danieca Krous, the girl's aunt. Negotiations continued apace, but things would work out his way, especially after he beat back the savages from the Blasted Lands.

His men traveled as lightly as they could; still, it took time to get where he was going. The first few weeks they saw nothing but the Imperial Highway and the dark clouds gathering to the south.

Everything was made perfect. The men were armed with bows, two spears apiece, short swords and small shields. The crest of Morwhen and the crest of Fellein were both present on the shields, and via random inspections Theorio made absolutely certain that swords were kept sharp and armor properly tended to.

When they rode down the highway to meet their enemy, the sounds of men walking and horses charging was a glorious thunder.

None would ever doubt Theroio's bravery. He led the charge as a king should, traveling down the road surrounded by his closest and bravest. A contingent of lancers was followed by archers, themselves followed by bannermen who announced their approach.

Should the need arise there would be trumpets and horns to make clear their intent.

Though the Imperial Highway was a vast thing – and called the Emperor's Highway in some places – it was well maintained. He took full advantage of that.

When they stopped for any reason they made sure to keep to the road and as theirs was a mission of great importance, any who crossed their path were wise to step to the side and let them pass.

As they approached the Rehkail River their forward motion

slowed to a gradual halt. The hills around the river had always made the bridge difficult to see from a distance, but Theorio knew the path well enough. When they reached the bridge, the great stone supports looked wrong. They had been altered.

He and his two oldest sons, Roon and Horden, stared long and hard.

"They've added something to them." Horden squinted across the distance, trying to make out the details. As they continued to stare, four figures came forward and crossed over the bridge, heading for them. They did not carry banners. They did not bring a retinue. It was only four men on the strangest looking horses Theorio had ever seen.

Theorio's first view of the Sa'ba Taalor was enough to make him understand the dread lesser men felt. They were, indeed, striking figures. Each carried several weapons. The largest of them had a vast disfigurement that he covered with a faceplate. His eye and the area around it were sealed within a stained bronze sculpture that closely resembled the rest of his face, but only if it had been forged from–

"By the gods. That thing across his face moves...." Horden's words rang softly out, but in the silence it was enough to nearly sound like a scream.

His son was right. The metal moved. The sculpted eye within that metallic socket shifted and adjusted as the men came closer.

"Do we go to meet them, father?" Roon's voice was quieter still and he bristled. Roon had spent years waiting for a proper conflict. He was a strong lad, and a gifted fighter.

"They send four and we send four. Come with me, Roon. Horden, hold here." He pointed to two guards he knew were skilled swordsmen, trained by him personally, and then he rode forward.

Once they had covered about half the ground between his army and the bridge, Theorio came to a halt, the other three taking position behind him.

Ensuring his voice carried the proper tone of command, Theorio called, "Who are you?" He was a king, and not easily to be denied.

The four strangers came closer and Theorio could now see that they did not ride horses. Near as he could figure they were riding bears. He had heard of the creatures, of course, but had never seen one in his travels. He had never heard of a man riding a bear before, but what was before his eyes proved the possibility.

"I am Lored, chosen of the Forge of Ordna and King in Bronze," came the reply. "Who are you?" The voice did not sound overly impressed. More amused, really, and that was not at all the reaction he wanted or expected.

"I am Theorio Krous. King of Morwhen."

"Then you are who I was told to wait for."

Lored smiled. His mouth split in the most hideous way, showing more teeth than should have been possible and great wounds that looked like they sported more teeth and tongues to boot. Theorio stared with sick fascination.

Theorio was wearing proper armor and a black uniform under it. The man he faced wore furs and leathers and had armor over his vitals as well as a large buckler on his left arm. He did not carry a sword, but instead sported a very large and brutal looking mace.

"Why were you told to wait for me?"

"Because according to great Ordna, you are the king of all that is north of here."

"Who is 'great Ordna'?"

"Ordna is my god. He chose me to serve as his king and to

be his voice among my people and yours alike." Lored smiled. "Ordna is the God of Bronze, of long-ranged weapons and siege warfare. He has chosen me as the best among his people to represent his methods of combat."

"What is a siege engine?"

"Do you see the towers of the bridge?"

"Yes, of course."

"I have chosen them as the anchors for my siege engines. These are powerful weapons designed to attack many people at once, or to destroy the walls of the very greatest of fortresses. I have already used them several times in my combat to the south of here. They are very effective weapons."

"I don't have any walls here to knock down."

It was meant as a joke. Lored allowed a small smile. "You have many troops. I could kill several hundred with a wave of my hand."

"Are you a sorcerer?"

"No. I have siege engines."

"What do they do?"

"In this case they hurl great stones and burning collections of oil and smaller stones that will scatter when they hit the ground and burn everything they touch."

Theorio considered that notion. "How many of these weapons do you have?"

"Currently there are eight of them built and waiting to destroy whatever I aim them at."

"And where are they aimed?"

Lored's smile came back, wide and enthusiastic and utterly terrifying in the number of teeth it bared. "They are aimed at your soldiers, of course. The better to kill them if you do not surrender to me."

"I do not believe in surrender."

"I am offering you a kindness. Should Tuskandru be the one to attack, you would all be dead within a day. My way, you survive and consider attacking again when I am not prepared."

"When you are not prepared?" Theorio stared at the gigantic man in front of him and tried to look past the scars that covered all bared flesh. He was trying to imagine what sort of hellish things might have scarred him that much in the first place.

"If I am being honest, I am always prepared, but without hope we have nothing, yes?"

"I cannot surrender to you. I think you are lying."

Lored raised his left arm and made a fist. He then brought the fist down hard.

One of the odd collections of lumber atop the closest bridge tower shuddered and rumbled, and then something sailed through the air, trailing a thick streamer of smoke.

"What have you...?"

Theorio turned and watched that vast something rip through the skies with the speed of an angry storm crow past him.

"A demonstration to tell you the truth of my words, King Theorio." By the time Lored had stopped speaking the missile hit the first column of Theorio's soldiers. Whatever held the smoking mass together broke, and true to the King in Bronze's words, flaming stones exploded across the ground and all over his troops as the mass rolled and tumbled to a stop.

Horses shrieked and bucked and threw themselves and their riders hard. They were burning and so were the men riding them. The soldiers screamed as well and beat at the fires that licked at their tunics and their bared flesh.

Theorio stared on, horrified. This was not warfare. This was a massacre.

"How did you do this thing?"

"My god, Ordna, told me the secrets. I listened to him."

Theorio drew his sword and prepared to fight. An instant later an arrow drove through his wrist and forced him to drop the weapon.

He screamed a lot. The damned arrow hurt.

Throughout, Lored looked at him with a small smile.

When he was done screaming, Lored looked at him and asked, "Will you fight or will you surrender?"

"We fight!" Theorio roared the words and drew his dagger from its sheath. He'd pry that maddening metallic mask away and cut out whatever was under it.

Lored roared and reached forward, a brutal smile on his face. "On this we agree, King Theorio!"

His great mace swept around and slammed into Theorio's forearm, shattering bone and pulping meat. The dagger fell to the ground and Lored hauled the King of Morwhen from his saddle. Theorio Krouse was a strong man and he fought hard despite his injuries.

While he struggled Roon charged forward, low over his horse as he'd been taught, one of his spears held at the ready.

The world tilted and Theorio groaned as the thing under Lored moved, lashing out with thick paws and slapping Roon's spear aside. His son was prepared, he was braced, and so he sailed from his saddle and fell to the ground as the strength of the creature simply overwhelmed him.

Lored's powerful arms were not injured and did not bleed. The man hauled Theorio to him as the King of Morwhen's horse ran from the great beast beneath the King in Bronze.

Theorio watched while his son was mauled, his face ripped into shreds by the claws of the monster. As he struggled, more of the giant stones soared past him to crash into his troops.

They were prepared for warfare, but not for this.

Lored pulled him higher still until they looked eye to eye and Theorio thrashed, trying to break the grip. His arms would not work, his legs were at the wrong angle to help him.

"I was told to take you alive, King Theorio! Fight me and the rest of your people die!"

Theorio did not surrender. He fought with all that he had. He bit, he screamed, he spat and he even drove the point of the arrow piercing his wrist into Lored's face.

He did not die that day.

Nor did he win.

When they reached the Edge, Drask called for Brackka to stop and his friend did. To make the ascent possible, he tied Nolan March to Brackka's back and then they all climbed. It would have been easier to find the Hallis Pass, but he wanted Tega to learn how to climb, as she never had done so before.

By the time they had finished the ascent, Tega's hands were bloodied and torn. She stared at them for a few moments before healing them.

They stood on the ground of the Wellish Steppes, and not a hundred yards distant was a large outcropping of shale and stone. It could not quite be called a hill, but it was certainly more than a boulder. Drask looked at the stone and nodded his head. Beneath that stone, the Wellish Overlords lay trapped, locked in a semi-slumber. They could think, but they could not move. They could starve, but they could not die. It was a proper punishment.

"The Wellish Overlords: they were the last great enemy of the Fellein, is that correct?" Drask was not certain where the information came from, but it was in his head. Best that he doublecheck its veracity.

Tega nodded slowly as she sat down and watched him make a fire. She still had a dazed, nearly sleepy look on her face, but she seemed more coherent now. That was a good thing. Drask grew tired of only his own thoughts for true companionship and it seemed neither Nolan nor Tega had been capable of much actual thought since the lot of them had bathed in the energies of the Mounds and then absorbed them.

"That was a long time ago," Tega said. It was the first time Drask had heard her voice in many days, bar the occasional grunt of exertion as they climbed. "Several hundred years, I think. They came for the people of Fellein and tried to take Canhoon by force." She paused and looked up at the sky. There were clouds here, and a breeze, which was more than could be said for the deathly still Blasted Lands.

"Desh told me how they were stopped, but it has been a long time and I don't recall clearly." She frowned. "I am having trouble thinking."

"It is getting better though, yes?"

She nodded softly and smiled. She had a lovely smile, even if it was completely unmarred. Drask could appreciate the aesthetic of smooth skin, even if he preferred the stories that scars told on well-healed flesh.

He looked at Tega's freshly healed hands. There were several new scars there from her climb.

Drask asked her, "Why did you wait before you healed your hands?"

"I wasn't sure I could do that."

He looked back at the stillness of the Blasted Lands and nodded.

Finally, bored with watching Nolan stare at the ground, he moved over to the boy and moved his head into the proper position. Muscles were not a problem, but several fragments of broken vertebrae had to be moved before they could be mended. When he was done Nolan looked around and frowned with an idiot expression. Drask could not decide if his mind was broken too, but for the present time left him alone.

"Your people. Do they truly worship gods?" Drask asked Tega, who was holding her hands before the fire.

She was a long time answering, "Some of them do. Most, I think, consider the idea for a while and then pretend."

"That is the problem with distant gods. Faith is not always easy in silence."

In the back of his head there were seven gods doing their very best to get his attention. He had not yet decided if he felt like listening to them any longer. The world sometimes changed when you were transformed, and while they seemed to want to talk to him, Drask was not certain that he wanted to hear what they had to say.

The gods had lied. They told him that the Mounds were forbidden and he believed them. They said that the world was changed by the Fellein when they destroyed Korwa, and for his entire life that truth had been accepted, but now, he was no longer completely certain. If gods lied, what did they tell the truth about? How could anything he had believed be considered the truth without examination?

"Your Desh Krohan, can he do what we can do now?"

"No." Tega frowned. "At least I do not think so."

Drask looked toward the still silence of the Blasted Lands. With very little effort he could see the footprints where they had walked across the vast, motionless expanse.

"I do not like it."

"You do not like what?" Tega moved closer and put her arms around his bicep. Her hands were tiny. She was tiny.

Ignored by them both, Nolan let out a low moan. He

blinked slowly but his eyes remained unfocussed even if they were no longer staring at the ground as they had these past days. Slowly, he moved to join them by the fire.

"All my life the Blasted Lands have raged and thundered and now they are too quiet. I do not like it."

Drask concentrated and willed a change. The air far below stirred, and a moment later the winds roared, spiraling outward from where he stared, taking the dust and grit with them. He made the air as cold as ice and waited as the storm he created grew and spread across the still wastelands.

Drask nodded. "That is better."

Far below him and under the great stones that held them pinned in place, the Wellish Overlords let out a noise that none but Drask and his two companions could hear. Not even Brackka could hear the sound. Still, he looked to Drask and smiled in the way of mounts.

Drask smiled back, glad he'd resurrected his trusted friend.

"Where do we go now? I can feel that Canhoon has moved and Tyrne is gone."

Drask looked down at her. She looked back up with wide, guileless eyes.

"Canhoon moves. So do we. We will find it."

They sat at the fire and waited for a while. They were not tired and they did not need to eat, but some habits are hard to break after a lifetime. Eventually they rose and all three climbed atop Brackka's broad back. Tega rode in front of Drask, and because it was easier than teaching him, Drask tied Nolan to the saddle.

When the mount started moving, Drask patted his neck and said, "Go very fast, Brackka. As fast as you can."

The miles tore past.

• • •

The town was larger than he would have imagined and that pleased Tusk. The ride along the river was easy enough and the town was open on all sides. It was not a place that dealt with war. It was a village that dealt with boats and fish.

Currently there were several boats along the docks. Some were small. A few were impressively large. They could have potential.

There were also many people along the shoreline, most looking toward Tusk and his people. Perhaps a hundred of them appeared armed. The rest stood in their crowds and looked on, faces painted with dread. It was not an expression Tusk was used to, but he understood the meaning. They thought they were going to die and that there was nothing they could do about it.

There was no thrill in that sort of enemy, only a mild contempt.

When he got closer, a small contingency broke away and approached. "You wish to take the city?" one asked. His language might be different but the meaning was plain enough.

Tusk contemplated answering the man in one of his own tongues, but decided he was not in the mood to toy with them. He said in the tongue of the Fellein, "I am here for your city and all that is inside it. I do not care if you wish to fight or if you wish to surrender."

"We are just fishermen and merchants." The man who spoke to him had leathery skin and hair that had been bleached blonde by the sun. His eyes were blue and he stared at Tusk with a wince on his face, as if he already knew that whatever arguments they might make, Tusk and his people would answer with steel. "We do not wish to die."

"My god does not believe in mercy."

The man looked him up and down for a long moment.

"Who is your god?"

"Durhallem. The Wounder. The Unforgiving. He is a god of war, and he is the god of obsidian and his way is the way of combat."

"Durhallem does not accept surrender as an option?"

"No."

"Will you wait here for a few moments? I would discuss with my people." It was a different sort of request. Normally people tended to beg or to fight. Either way, they were met with the same answer. Durhallem did not take prisoners.

"You may discuss the situation among yourselves. If you attempt to attack, we will kill you."

The tanned man looked at him. "You are four times my size. I am carrying a skinning knife that I do not think would even part the fur on your... on whatever beast you ride. There will be no treachery."

Tusk nodded and leaned back in his seat, wishing that Stastha were here to see this. She would have had a few sharp comments and would have made him laugh.

After nearly ten minutes the man came back. "We wish to join you and follow Durhallem."

Tusk leaned back a bit more. "Repeat that."

"We wish to join you and follow Durhallem."

Behind him a few of the other Sa'ba Taalor talked among themselves. They did not speak the Fellein tongue and could not understand what caused Tusk's expression. They merely knew that he was surprised.

"In all my years none have ever made this offer."

"In all my years I have never had the followers of a war god come to my doorstep."

"True enough."

Tusk spoke to Durhallem and his god spoke back.

"Durhallem would require a test. A proof of your loyalty to him."

"What would he require?"

What indeed?

Tusk asked and Durhallem answered.

The king nodded. His god was wise.

"Do you have a forge here? A metal worker's forge?"

The tanned man nodded. "Yes. Of course."

Tusk nodded in turn. "There will be a test of loyalty. Also, you will need weapons."

"Weapons?"

"A god of war does not ask that you follow with kindness in your heart. The Wounder will make great demands of you and you will have to prove yourselves in combat. Do you understand this?"

"What do we get from Durhallem in return?"

"Prove your loyalty and the Wounder will tell you himself."

"The god would speak to me personally?"

Tusk nodded. "The god would speak to all of you. All of the followers of Durhallem have heard from the Wounder and follow him by choice. We are born to this. This, what you ask, it is a new thing and requires… improvisation. You must show your loyalty. Then you can speak to Durhallem. Then you will have the chance to join his brethren under my command."

"And what is your name?"

"I am Tuskandru, King in Obsidian and Chosen of the Forge of Durhallem."

"You are a king?" He sounded surprised.

"What else would I be?"

"I thought perhaps a general."

"I am a king. In the army of Durhallem I am also the general."

"Ah. I see."

Tusk, who knew what Durhallem had in mind, nodded. "You will. Soon enough you will."

As they moved along, the hundred or so with weapons very carefully set them aside. It was one thing to attack and defend if you had to, but the word had already spread, and the invaders were so very large in comparison. And so very many.

Tuskandru's army numbered in the thousands, and even the children who walked with them were armed and looked ready to kill.

Tusk gestured to a small girl who was lean and hard and looked like she might have been from Fellein, save for the scars on her body and the slightly feral way she stared at everyone. The tanned man looked at her with a worried expression.

"Mendt." The girl moved closer. "Gather coins. One for each of the people in this town." He looked at the crowd that was now moving cautiously along the edges of the Sa'ba Taalor.

For their part the followers of Durhallem noticed the people and remained prepared. Sooner or late everyone encountered the followers of Wrommish and learned that even a small person without a weapon could be deadly.

"What is your name?" Tusk spoke to the tanned man.

"Bram Littner."

"Bram Littner, tell your people to each offer one coin to Mendt and the others with her. It does not matter what size coin. The value is of no concern."

Bram nodded. He held up his hands and called out loudly in his tongue and Tusk listened. A moment later he sent Mendt on her way and told her to gather the coins and to choose others to help her. Being a wise young warrior, she chose several skilled fighters to back her. It was not that she could not handle herself, it was rather that the coins would be heavy and she wanted to share the burden with others who could carry it.

It was almost an hour later when the column stopped at the small forge and settled down. The people of the city were surrounded by Tuskandru's Sa'ba Taalor. Mendt had collected an impressive number of coins.

"Bram Littner, are you a leader of your people?"

Bram nodded his head and worried at his lower lip.

"Then you will lead in what comes next. You will feel pain. Life is pain. Try not to scream."

Bram looked at him and nodded again. He was very scared. He had right to be.

"This thing you do, it has never been done before. You understand this? Those whom the Wounder chooses to fight die. This is... This is as close to mercy as I have ever seen from my god. This is a rare blessing."

Tusk plucked the first coin from the collection. It was a large coin and golden.

"You would follow Durhallem in the ways of war? You would become a disciple of the Wounder?"

"Aye. Yes, I would."

Tusk nodded his head and placed the coin firmly against Bram's head. "Do not move. This is your test. This is how you prove yourself to your new god." Even as he spoke, he placed one hand against the back of Bram's skull. With the other, he pushed the gold coin against Bram's forehead.

For Bram and his people it must have been a momentous thing, but for the followers of Durhallem, miracles were not uncommon. The metal glowed hot against Tusk's hand but he was not burned. Instead all of the heat seared into Bram's forehead and the metal fused with the flesh. Skin burned and metal ran and Bram screamed. He did not stand still but tried to fight, as was to be expected. Two of Tusk's followers grabbed the man's arms and held him as still as they could while he bucked and howled and roared in agony.

Tusk stepped back and nodded, pleased with his work. The men who held Bram let him go, setting him on the ground instead of letting him fall.

All around them the people of the town murmured and tried to retreat, but it was too late for that. They were completely surrounded by the Sa'ba Taalor.

Tusk spoke loudly, roaring to be heard over the noises of the crowd. "This is the price you must pay! If you would follow a god you must make sacrifices!"

Bram stood. The gold of the coin was fused with his flesh. The metal was flush with his forehead and ran in swirls. Though his skin was burned, it was clear that the redness and even the bleeding was fading away.

The gold of the coin was not perfectly round, but had melted and smeared as it was held in place. There was a pattern there. A thick line ran through the melted lump.

Bram spoke up. "I have felt pain, but it's gone now. I am not injured." He sounded surprised. Several of the city dwellers came closer and looked at his face, frowning.

He said softly, "This is how we survive the day. This is how we learn to know a god. We must do this. As we discussed."

The next to come forward was a portly woman. Her hands held on to the hands of two children.

"Must we all do this thing?" She did not ask Bram. She asked Tuskandru.

"Pain, or death. All must choose."

Tears glistened at her eyes, but she did not move away. "We will be healed? Like Bram?"

"Yes. Durhallem demands a sacrifice, but he does not demand a life of misery. You must be tested. This is the test."

She looked to her children and spoke solemnly. "I will go first, but if we are to be together you must do this thing. It will hurt, but I will be here for you."

They were young. The oldest perhaps five years.

They watched and screamed as their mother was marked.

She watched and held them as each of her children endured the same.

Each person in the town was marked by Tusk, save a few that foolishly tried to escape.

They were struck down quickly and their bodies were laid out beside the forge for all to see.

As he made his mark upon the town, the fire in the forge glowed brighter and brighter.

The processing of every member of the town took most of the day and the following night.

Through it all Tusk spoke to the new disciples of Durhallem. He remained a calm, strong voice in a nearly endless series of screams.

After they were touched by Durhallem's gift the people of the town were allowed to rest. Most gathered together in the area around the forge. Some wandered back to their homes, as once they had been tested they were free to do.

When the next morning finally came around, the people who had been marked by Durhallem were gathered together again.

They had been tested. Afterward, they were given the blessing of Durhallem and allowed to speak to a god.

None of them were unchanged by the meeting. Each of them was made to reach into the blazing coals of the forge to receive Durhallem's blessing.

FIVE

Captain Callan woke up in the small cell and groaned. Every part of him hurt, but especially the wound where they'd pulled the arrow from his leg.

There had been a brief moment when he thought he and his crew would escape the gray-skins. That moment was crushed when the great black ship cut his little vessel in half. Each of the black ships, in addition to being nearly impossibly large, also had sharpened metal along the keel. That metal destroyed wood with ease and his little ship was no exception.

Wounded as he was, he thought he was a certain candidate for death, but the Sa'ba Taalor came down and grabbed him.

The woman who came for him was lean and hard and heavily scarred. She pulled the arrow from his leg and lifted him like he was a child. When he tried to struggle she put him down and beat him until he thought his seams would split.

When he came to, he was in the cell, three sides wood and one iron bars.

"You are alive and awake. This is good." The voice was heavily accented.

It was not the same woman who'd bested him so easily.

This one was scarier. She wore cloth pants and a leather vest over a white shirt. The fabric was made to breathe and hung loosely except where she had pulled the fabric tight with leather straps to hold the sheaths for her knives. She sported several knives along her arms. Her mouth was scarred in several spots, and her skin was dark gray and seemed almost corpselike. Her eyes glowed in the semi-darkness of the ship's hold. On the top of her head a deep blue scarf ran around her hair, binding it, and then dropped along her back. The scarf was tied to her waistline loosely allowing her to move her head easily.

It seemed an elaborate effort, but he decided not to focus on that. Instead he looked carefully at the sword she was sporting.

"You are Callan?"

Callan nodded, suddenly very aware that he had to piss and that he was also extremely thirsty.

"I am Donaie Swarl; I am the King in Lead, Chosen of Wheklam." The words meant nothing. She was obviously not a king. Kings had finery and were, as a rule, men. But she had a sword and that was enough for him to let her keep her delusions.

"Majesty." He nodded his head. "I'm sorry, but who is Wheklam?"

"Wheklam is the god of the sea, and seafaring warriors."

"I like him already."

She nodded her head and crouched down until they were eye to eye. "He likes you, too. He favors you. Your crew is dead. They served me no purpose. Your ship is gone, as you tried to flee."

He nodded his head. "Sorry about that. I thought you were trying to kill us."

"We were." Donaie, King of the Mad, nodded. "We would

have killed you, too, but Wheklam said you had a purpose."

"What purpose is that?"

"You can talk to the scarred people, yes?"

"Scarred like you?" He shook his head.

"No. The others. They... write on themselves. They carve words in their flesh."

"Oh, yes. The Brellar. I speak their language."

"Excellent!"

Without preamble she opened the door. Apparently it wasn't locked. He hadn't bothered to check, really, as the light shone through several portholes and trying to sneak off the ship would have required darkness. Still, in hindsight, he could have at least looked into the matter.

Hard, callused hands grabbed Callan and pulled him to his feet. He did his best not to scream at the pain in his calf. It was bandaged and he could see that it had been cleaned, but still.

Despite being a dead shade of gray, she was attractive enough. Still, he blinked when the scars around her mouth moved as she smiled her approval. As a rule, he found all women a worthwhile pursuit. He decided he could make an exception in this case.

"You can stand. Good. Come with me."

Donaie Swarl moved and he followed. Her back was to him. He had no weapons, but if he were fast enough he could surely take her.

Callan shook his head. No. The way she moved, he had no doubt it would be a mistake. And anyway, there was nowhere to flee. They wanted him alive. There would be chances to escape later once darkness fell.

Callan could see other cells down the hallway they walked. They were, universally, uninhabited. They were slavers' cells. He recognized them easily enough to understand that he was not on one of the black ships. This was a Brellar ship. Above him the deck would be vast, with enough space for three hundred men to stand comfortably apart from each other.

As they walked up the narrow stairwell to the top level – several flights that made his calf scream with each stair climbed – Callan's eyes adjusted to the changing light. He saw more and more of the scars that crossed the woman's body. The Brellar inflicted scars on themselves, but these were different. He could see that they overlapped in many cases and some were faint with age, others newer. This was a lifetime of fighting and injuries. He had heard of the Sa'ba Taalor from Tataya, but he had never seen them up close until now.

They were scary people. They were, judging by this one, survivors at any cost.

The sky outside was overcast, and a quick look around told him they were near the shores of Roathes. The villages that should have been there were little more than ashes among more ashes. The hot air here was acrid, but calmer than the last time he had been through. Far behind him, he knew, there was an island growing in the sea. A fiery mountain at the center of that island continued to bellow fire and smoke and cast lightning into the waters. But it did so with less violence than before.

The waters around the ship were littered with flotsam, jetsam and corpses. The sharks would come soon, he knew, even through the ashes that poisoned the waters, for they could not possibly resist a feast of this scale. Close enough to see but not to get caught in any currents, two of the great black ships waited, their decks covered with more of the gray-skins.

The deck Callan stood on was covered with the prone forms of the Brellar. They were not dead, but they had been beaten and subdued.

Standing among them were dozens of the Sa'ba Taalor. He looked first to the Brellar, who mostly lay still, their eyes searching their environs or closed to avoid the glare of the day. The Sa'ba Taalor did not wear much by way of armor and several of them had cuts freely bleeding, or newly crusted. They also had weapons. Sorts he had never seen before. There were swords, to be true, but there were other things that looked designed to break bones and heads with ease.

Judging by the ruined flesh on a few of the Brellar, they did their jobs quite well.

"You will speak for me." Donaie Swarl looked his way. "And you will speak for them. Do not lie to me. I will know. My god will tell me."

"Othea is my god. Also a god of the sea."

Donaie looked at him for a moment. "What does your god tell you right now, Callan?"

"Nothing." He frowned.

"Then listen to my god and listen well. Ask the questions. Answer them truthfully, and you will walk away from this intact." She tilted her head for a moment and nodded. "Wheklam says you may even have this ship if you do this thing. You like to barter, yes?"

"Yes. I do. Indeed."

"Then that is the offer that Wheklam makes. Safety and this ship in exchange for truths."

"What of the people already on the ship?"

"You will be captain. That will be your decision to make."

He nodded his head. As they'd spoken, several of the Brellar had looked around to see his face. He recognized Tomms, one of the chieftains of the Brellar.

"Tomms. You are alive."

Tomms looked his way. "Yes, and thanks to you, they now know my name."

Callan shook his head. "They want to speak to you. I am to translate."

Tomms sat up. No one stopped him. His face was swollen on one side, bruised and bashed. His lip on that side was smashed and bloodied and would heal poorly. The scars on his body glistened in the sunlight.

Donaie walked Callan closer, holding his arm.

"I want to know about his scars. Why does he scar himself? Do his gods demand it?"

Callan asked the questions, moderately curious as to how Tomms would answer.

"My gods demand nothing. We write our victories on our flesh. We tell stories of what we have achieved in our lifetimes."

Callan looked to Donaie Swarl and answered truthfully.

Her face took on a different look. Rage made her terrifying as she bared her teeth and her scars split baring even more.

"What do his gods say to this?"

Callan translated.

Tomms answered, "We have no need of gods. We find our own way. We are our own gods."

Callan hesitated for a moment. He did not know that the Sa'ba Taalor would not like the answer, but he could guess.

"These are his words, yes? Not mine."

Donaie Swarl nodded agreement and he repeated Tomms's answer.

The woman of the Sa'ba Taalor strode over to where Tomms lay and grabbed him by his hair. She ripped hard and he followed, screaming in pain even as he stood.

Tomms brought his arm around and struck her in her side, his fist dealing a brutal blow. None of the Brellar were bound, they were merely subdued. At the sound of combat several of them started to rise.

Donaie Swarl barely flinched. She brought her free arm around and slammed Tomms in the face with the palm of her hand, sending him staggering back as she let go of his hair.

"Tell them to stop or they die faster!"

Callan repeated the message and the Brellars who were rising either froze where they were or stood the rest of the way with their hands above their heads, clearly showing that they had no weapons.

Donaie spoke again. "Tell them. Let them know that they have marked themselves and bragged for the last time. The gods decide who survives scarring, no one else."

He repeated the words, and Tomms looked directly at the King in Lead and spat blood and a tooth onto the deck. Through his ruined lips he said, "Fuck your gods."

And Callan sighed and repeated the words exactly.

The reaction was immediate. The Sa'ba Taalor brought all their fury upon the Brellar. Not a single one of them touched Callan, but as he looked on, the Brellar were cut, beaten and broken. Some used their hands. Others used swords. Some brought up their metallic clubs with heads the size of Pabba fruit and smashed them down on the skulls of their enemy.

Through it all, Callan watched. The Sa'ba Taalor acted with rage. They did not forgive and they took no quarter.

It took a few minutes to finish the massacre. Callan stood still throughout it, not daring to move, lest he catch the attention of the gray-skins.

When it was done, Donaie Swarl gestured to one of her followers, who took up a horn from a satchel at her hip and blew a sharp note. Moments later one of the black ships started moving in their direction.

"The ship is yours." She dismissed Callan with those words.

"Why did you kill them all?"

"His words offended our gods. His scars offend our gods. His people offend our gods, and so we will kill all of them."

"What of the corpses?" When Callan spoke that time it was more to himself.

Still, the king answered, "It is your ship. Do with them what you will."

He did not speak to her again as she climbed the rope cast down from the black ship. A score of ropes fell and the Sa'ba Taalor scaled them.

Callan was left alone with the dead.

He waited until the black ships were far in the distance before he started screaming.

The keep ahead of them was not large, but the gods wanted it taken. That was enough for Tarag Paedori.

He looked back at Kallir Lundt, and asked, "Do you know this place, Kallir?"

The Fellein looked at the tower and the surrounding walls with metallic eyes. His face was metal, a gift from Truska-Pren.

"I do not. The town we passed, Inbrough, that I know. I have seen it on trips down the river in the past, but this?" He shook his head in the way of his people. "This has been built in the last few years."

Tarag looked the structure over. It was large enough to host as many as twenty, he guessed. Had they built it into the side of a mountain the size would be impossible to guess, but the short tower and the surrounding wall were freestanding. The wall surrounding it was only fifteen feet in height. That barely qualified as anything but decoration in the Taalor valley.

Without any preamble Tarag urged his mount forward. The

great beast let out an amiable rumble and obeyed. The path leading to the strange standalone tower was hardpacked dirt and little else.

The others followed as he knew they would.

The gate in the wall was open. The King in Iron rode toward it with one hand on his sword's hilt and looked around carefully.

He slowed only when he realized that the aperture in the wall didn't have an open gate. It had no gate at all.

That was enough to give him pause. True, there were no other structures around, but that didn't mean there were never visitors. The paved pathway was a sign of that.

"What sort of town builds a wall and forgets to build a gate as well?"

Kallir shook his head. "None that I have seen of any size. Most of the towns I've seen that had a gate needed it to keep out marauders. The land is mostly calm, but there are always exceptions."

Tarag shook his head and moved forward again, riding through the opening, his eyes sliding over the landscape inside.

There was only the one structure and none other.

No people were moving about the courtyard.

The tower was large enough. Close to fifty feet in height, and built of good stone, if he could judge by appearances.

Its door was too small for his mount to join him, so Paedori slid off the great beast's back and passed through, drawing his sword.

There was only one person standing on the other side of the door. He was a broadshouldered man, balding and bearded, wearing casual clothes.

"You are Tarag Paedori, the King in Iron." It wasn't a question.

"Yes I am."

"Good. Excellent." The man nodded and moved away from a table where he'd been looking at several thick volumes. "My name is Jeron. I am a sorcerer. We are going to have a discussion."

"What do we have to discuss?" The man was a fool. But he was also a sorcerer, or at least made that claim and, having seen what one of the sorcerers could do, it was best to at least hear him out.

"Why you are going to leave Fellein and never come back."

"Truska-Pren demands that I be here. He will have his revenge for what the people of Fellein did to the people of Korwa." He would have laughed under many circumstances. But the man was an unknown quantity. It was best to respect the unknown.

"The people of Fellein did not destroy Korwa." The man looked at him with cold eyes. "The Wellish Overlords did that."

"So you say. My god says otherwise."

"Your god is wrong."

He kept his place, but it was not easy. To insult the gods was beyond mere folly.

Jeron smiled. "I have proof. I have testimonies from hundreds of witnesses."

Tarag looked on, not moving. "Where are these people?"

"Well, they're dead." He shrugged and gestured back to the books. "They have been dead for almost as long as Korwa, but they were there to see the final days. They survived the experience. They wrote their tales down and I have spent hundreds of years collecting them. The truth has always been my passion."

"You would have me believe books over my god?"

"I would have you consider all possibilities, the better to decide if this war should happen." As the man spoke there was a change in the pressure in the room. Tarag Paedori looked around and noticed that the door through which he had entered was gone.

"Truska-Pren has given me life. He has offered me a kingdom and the chance to lead the greatest armies that the whole of the world has ever known. Do you know what he asks in exchange for this?"

"No. I do not." The sorcerer had crossed his arms over his chest.

"That I obey him."

"Well, isn't that what every god asks?"

"I do not know every god. I only know Truska-Pren." A small lie. He had spent time in the presence of all the gods, as virtually every member of the Sa'ba Taalor did.

"We have so much we could share, Tarag Paedori. We have a different world filled with its own wonders. You could teach us of your gods and we could teach you the history of the world beyond the Seven Forges."

The King in Iron stepped closer. "I know your world. I have listened to a thousand tales about it from one of your own. A soldier who has seen much of your Empire. If I need to know more, I can ask him. Or I can ask Truska-Pren. Either way, I would learn what I need to know."

Jeron opened his mouth to counter, but before he could, Tarag continued. "Do you know of my people? Of my gods?"

"No. I don't."

"Yet you would have me choose your words over those of my gods?" He simply stared as he spoke. This man, Jeron, was mad.

"Well."

"We will teach you of our gods when you are given the choice to follow them or to die."

"That's not the best solution."

"It is the only solution. It is what the Daxar Taalor demand and they are the gods of my people."

Tarag did not alter his position. He did not have to. He merely continued to stare at the sorcerer, letting the learned man make his first move.

"I cannot let you attack Canhoon."

"Are you the one who lifted the city into the skies?"

"No. But I have enough power to level you and your army."

"You are not a god. Do not presume to stop the armies of a god."

Two strides had him moving past the startled mage and grabbing one of the ancient books.

"You trust in words written in the past. I trust in words spoken to me by a god."

"Your gods are not–"

"A wise man," Tarag interrupted, "does not insult a god in the face of the faithful."

Jeron closed his mouth and nodded. After a moment, he asked, "What do your gods say to do?"

"I have been tasked with conquering Fellein in the name of my gods. If I must kill every person in Fellein to do so, I will."

Jeron sighed, nodded and then threw both hands in Tarag's direction.

The energies hit him in the side. He could not have dodged even if he'd been given warning. As Tarag turned, he felt the book in his hand crisp and ignite. The volumes on the table, the table itself, did likewise.

The clothing on his body was all that stood between his metal armor and the waves of heat that hit him. Tarag Paedori turned to face the man trying to kill him and let the burning ruins of the book fall to the ground. The sword in his hand was starting to glow red.

"You would seek to kill me with fire?" Tarag grinned.

He walked a pace toward Jeron the sorcerer, who looked at him with a shocked expression.

"I am the chosen of Truska-Pren, the God of Iron. When I talk to my god, I walk into his heart, the very center of a mountain filled with molten iron." He took another step forward as his armor grew hotter still.

"My god protects me from that heat as he does now." He shrugged and the armor screamed, metal tortured by heat moved and moaned.

He reached out with one gauntlet and grabbed Jeron before the man could move away. The reaction was immediate. Jeron screamed as his flesh began to burn. His left arm caught on fire, the cloth blazing and burning the skin underneath. Tarag's other hand reached for the sorcerer's face and caught his bald ear and half of his scalp.

Jeron tried to pull away, but Tarag Paedori hauled him closer, letting the man thrash against the burning metal that covered his chest and body.

A moment later he let the man drop to the ground, blistered, burning, breathing.

Jeron was still alive, much as he might have wished otherwise.

"You are not a warrior. You are not a fighter. You are not important. Your Empire will fall because the gods demand it. People like you, like your Empress, you only delay the inevitable. We have spent a hundred lifetimes preparing for this. What have you done?"

When he looked again, the entryway to the room was there once more.

Tarag Paedori thanked his god and then called in others to search the keep.

There was nothing useful to find or to have: books, and one ruined old man.

They left the area, heading east again.

A short time later Tusk and his newly acquired boats came alongside them. Tusk rode along the shoreline. The boats were handled by the Sa'ba Taalor who also followed Wheklam. Most of the recently converted walked along the shoreline behind Tusk and in front of his troops. They were, he explained to Tarag, earning the respect of their fellows.

To Tarag's eyes, they looked like they were suffering and miserable. Life is pain.

"Durhallem wanted to convert them instead of killing them?" Tarag frowned at the notion. The Wounder was not normally so generous.

"He says we should try new things." Tusk shook his head. "Who am I to argue with a god?"

"No one."

"Exactly."

"What happened to your armor?"

Tarag looked down and saw the heavy scorch marks where flesh had burned and where, frankly, metal had glowed hot enough to soften and lose a bit of its previous form.

"A sorcerer tested his power against a god and failed."

Tusk laughed at the very notion.

"We ride. Let us reach Stastha and hear what she has to say."

Tusk smiled at that notion. "Indeed!"

A moment later they moved on, and both signaled for the horns. It was time. War was upon them. Glorious, wondrous war.

They passed odd outcroppings of ruined stone wall and occasional buildings that rose toward the skies above, and Tega explained to Drask that this had been the edge of Canhoon. The lake that replaced the city was calm enough, despite the easterly winds.

Across the ruins, Drask saw the Sa'ba Taalor before they saw him. They were too distant to recognize and so he rode closer, his companions on the back of Brackka easily compensating for the change of pace. Though Nolan still did not speak, at least he no longer fell from the mount at every change of direction or speed.

Two mounts rode ahead of them. One carried a male warrior; the other carried a corpse.

He would not have recognized Andover Lashk if it had not been for the iron hands.

"You have changed a great deal, Andover Lashk of the Iron Hands." He smiled as he spoke.

The boy was gone, replaced by a man. He sported hard scars on his flesh and, like Drask himself, he had seven Great Scars running down his face, angry slashes that fell in a symmetry meant only for the followers of Ydramil. He had met with all of the gods and survived. More importantly, he had been found worthy.

Andover the man looked at him for a long moment without recognition and then he smiled broadly. "Drask! Gods, you are a sight!"

Both slipped from their mounts and hugged each other warmly. It was not a common gesture among the Sa'ba Taalor, but it was a sign of complete trust.

When they broke away from each other, Andover looked to the other two and nodded his head.

Tega stared at him for a long while, her mind processing before, "Andover?"

"It is good to see you, Tega."

She climbed down from Brackka's back without the grace of Drask, but she managed. When she moved closer, Andover realized that he now looked down on her. He had grown a great deal.

His stomach iced over as she stared at him, and froze completely when she touched his heavy arms and looked into his face. How was it that a woman he barely let himself think about could so easily cripple his mind?

Drask could see the questions on the young man's face.

"Tega and Nolan and I met in the Blasted Lands. We did not plan to meet, but the gods saw to it."

"You have changed so much, Andover." Her eyes were wide as she stared up at him. "You look more like Drask than like yourself." That was true enough. Both were gray skinned and longhaired. Their Great Scars were nearly identical. The rest of them was as different as ever, of course. The scars on their bodies told different tales. Drask had one metallic hand and Andover had two.

"You are as beautiful as ever, Tega." The words would have never been spoken in the past. Andover Lashk would have trembled at the very notion. Andover Iron Hands was not quite the same man, though he shared all of his younger self's memories. The world changes, and the wise change with it.

"Why are you here, Andover?" Drask asked.

"I'm seeking Old Canhoon."

"The gods send you to Old Canhoon?"

"Yes. They have not said why."

Drask nodded. "And what is this?" he pointed to Delil, where she lay across the back of her mount.

"Delil. She… She is dead."

"The gods decree that she should be burned. You know this."

Andover looked away from him. The boy's face was a

man's and the sorrow it showed seemed not to fit his features properly any longer.

"The Daxar Taalor do not agree with your heart. What is it that you want from them, Andover?"

Tega stepped back, looking from one man to the other.

"I..."

Drask continued to stare, his gaze unflinching, as the younger man, so changed from what he had been and still changing, look at Delil's corpse and then at the ground. Finally he looked at Drask again and said, "I want her back."

"And have you asked the gods for this?"

"No." His eyes fell back to the ground.

"Why not?" Drask stepped closer until Andover felt obligated to look at him again.

"Because they might say no."

"Very likely they will. She has served her time in this world and nothing goes to waste. But you will not have an answer until you ask." He held up his silver hand. "I had no answer until I asked Ydramil for this. It was not merely given. I had to make sacrifices."

"Who should I ask then?" Andover's eyes blinked back tears that wanted to fall. Another sign he was more Sa'ba Taalor than Fellein these days. When they had met previously the boy would have wept.

"Ask the Daxar Taalor and see if they respond. You have been with all seven of the gods." He gestured to show the Great Scars on Andover's lips. "Ask all of them and see if they answer you."

"Where shall I go to ask?"

"You can ask here. You can ask anywhere. The Daxar Taalor are spreading across this land. They will hear you."

Andover nodded and walked slowly over to where a portion

of the wall that had once surrounded the city still stood.

Tega moved closer to Drask and asked, "Your gods can raise the dead?"

"Yes. I suppose all gods can."

"But you... I felt it... you raised Brackka back from the dead."

Drask nodded. So many tales of the gods and all they had done, of raising the wounded few who survived the cataclysm and helping those last survivors become the Sa'ba Taalor. That simple tale was one of the foundations of his entire life. The gods could raise the dead. He had done so himself now. Had he considered how he had done it for too long he would have been no closer than he was currently to understanding why it had worked beyond accepting that he and Tega and Nolan had bathed in the energies of the Mounds and come away changed.

Did that make them gods?

He looked past Andover and toward the distant City of Wonders. "Yes. I did. I'm still reflecting on that."

Behind him still on Brackka's back, Nolan let out a laugh. It was the only sound he'd made in days.

Andover looked into the waters of the lake that should not have been there and tried to calm himself. The gods had already granted him so much. He needed look no further than his hands.

"Delil is dead."

He spoke the words to his reflection. The wind smeared his doppelganger's features.

His reflection answered him in Ydramil's voice. WHY DID SHE DIE?

Andover shook his head.

When Ydramil spoke again it was with the full force of his power. ANSWER ME. WHY DID SHE DIE?

"Because she was careless."

YOU HAVE BEEN GIVEN GREAT GIFTS. WHAT WOULD YOU DO TO HAVE HER BACK?

Andover looked at his reflection and knew that it looked back.

"What would you have me do?"

Soon enough the gods answered.

SIX

At last, the man came to see her again.

Desh Krohan. He was handsome enough in his way, but haunted.

That was a feeling Cullen understood very well.

"I'm sorry for making you wait. I have been rather busy."

"You have a war on your hands." She shrugged. Not far off Deltrea was doing her best to ignore the sorcerer. He returned the favor.

"Moale Deneshi was my life partner once upon a time. She left me when she said that she had been summoned to a greater duty." Desh Krohan spoke softly and looked at her from the corner of his eye. "I was younger. I never went after her. I had my pride, after all."

"Pride is poor armor, but better than none."

The sorcerer nodded his head. "Indeed. I haven't heard that one in many years."

He sighed and looked at her abdomen.

"In any event, what is left of her is now inside of you. I don't know that either of you planned it, but that is what has occurred."

"How do I get her out?"

"According to her, she needs to stay with you for now. She will only let go of her grip on you when she is ready."

Behind him Deltrea made an obscene gesture, but did not speak.

"Am I to stay locked in here until then?"

"Not at all." He smiled. "That's why I'm here. I'm going to personally escort you to your new chambers."

Cullen nodded. "These chambers. Will I be allowed to leave them?"

Desh nodded his head. "Of course. But because there are some who might seek you out, you will have guards with you at all times."

"What do you mean 'seek me out'?"

The sorcerer shrugged. "There are assassins in this city, Cullen, and they are causing endless grief. If they find out what you carry inside of you, it's very possible that they will cut you open to get to it. They tried to kill the Mother-Vine and all that is left of her is inside you. If they find out they can, they will, cut her out of you to make their point."

"And you are telling me this why? So that I can have more nightmares?" Her eyes narrowed as she stared at the sorcerer. He stared back, studying every detail of her with all of the intensity of a suitor. She was unsettled by the notion. He was not unattractive, but she was also not in the least bit interested.

"I'm telling you this because I want you to remain safe. I want you to be smart and avoid getting killed by the Sa'ba Taalor, who I believe have already managed to infiltrate the city. Not a lot of them, but the ones who are here are killers."

"And you think they would be after me?"

"No. They would be after her. The Mother-Vine." He gestured toward her abdomen. "You. Me. We are not significant. She is. She has a power they would take if they could. That is why you are here. Knowing the name of my old mate and having a few words for me from her, that is not enough. That only gets my attention."

Cullen nodded and rose from her seat. "Perhaps you should show me to this new chamber then."

The walk was long, but not arduous, and they talked as they traversed hidden corridors and stairwells that were built into walls of solid stone.

"What have these assassins of yours been doing?"

"For the last four days, someone or several people have been sneaking among the many refugees we have here and killing them. Not all at once, only a few at a time, but always where there are a lot of people gathered together. We have people watching, but it means nothing. They are very careful and they leave the bodies where they fall, the better for them to be discovered quickly and the better for the bodies to cause a panic.

"It's a brilliant tactic. I'd have never considered it, but the end result is that the people who are trying to survive without proper housing are very anxious and we've had to break up several attempts by mobs to take over buildings."

Cullen shot a look his way.

"Oh, please. No. We cannot take them into the palace. Believe it or not, there aren't enough rooms. Most of them are already being used to store food and supplies. The palace is very large, but it is not a city in itself. The barracks of soldiers have been given to the refugees and that means weapons and soldiers alike are kept here. We were not anticipating having a city lift into the air, nor were we considering how cold it would be up here or that half the city would be left behind. Believe me, there are many things we never once considered."

Desh Krohan paused for a moment as he fumbled a key from his pocket. A moment later the door was opened to her new chambers. They were a vast improvement, with a large bed, a window and a roaring fire. There was a door. It was currently barred from the inside.

"All of this?" Cullen could barely believe it.

Deltrea spat. "How is this even a little fair? I'm dead before I can see a sight like this, and you're still going strong." It was Cullen's turn to make a gesture.

"Through that door, to the right, you will find a small dining room. There is fresh fruit. There is bread. If you wish to join us for dinner you are welcome."

"Thank you. For all of this." It was all she could think to say.

"Stay safe. You carry a great burden. Please honor that responsibility."

A moment later he was gone.

Deltrea shook her head and strolled around the chamber, which, to be fair, was larger than the entirety of both their homes back in Trecharch.

"This royalty thing pays well enough." Deltrea walked over to look out the window and Cullen blinked hard, unsettled because she could see through the form of her friend. The light was too bright through the window and Deltrea cast no shadow. In the woods, in a cell, it was easier to ignore that fact.

Cullen joined her at the window and immediately understood the need for the fire. The ground outside was covered in a thick rime of frost. The trees were coated; the lawn below was white. The buildings were iced over. Small wonder so many fought for decent shelter. Certainly it wasn't a gathering of assassins causing the grief. Just desperate people.

The wall around the palace kept out many more people. No one was foolish enough to try storming the structure, but they were near it as if seeking shelter from the cold.

In the far distance she could see the Mid Wall. Beyond that were only blue skies and, far away but, she had no doubt, coming closer, the mountains.

There were so many people, more than she had ever seen in one place before and the sight of them hurt her head. Cullen crawled into the depths of the bed, warm and secure and despite Deltrea's comforting presence, still scared of what lay ahead.

Three short thrusts into the screaming man's belly as she ducked past, and Jost knew he was already dead, though he screamed on.

That was the thing about the people of the city. They screamed about everything. This one roared that he had fresh meat and people came to him looking at what he offered and hoping it would truly be fresh. It was not. Still they came.

So Jost did them a favor and killed him. Truly that was coincidence. She merely did not like his voice.

When he stopped screaming about fresh meat he screamed for a different reason. So did the people around him as he fell to his knees and took his table down in the process.

The markets were the easiest place to cause panic. They were also the easiest place to kill a lot of people with little effort.

The onlookers backed away from the bleeding man and Jost moved on. Her eyes scanned the area for the next target. The ones that made the most noise or who reacted with violence were the best for stirring the crowd.

It was easier to hide now. The air was so cold that everyone was wearing coats or dressing in shawls or cloaks. Skin reddened in the chill and most everyone huddled down on themselves for warmth.

They did not look up or around as she moved among them.

Her blade cut a woman across the back of her leg, severing tendons. The woman screamed in pain and fell backward as she lost the use of her leg, and Jost danced back, away from the blood spray. Dark clothes alone could not hide the steam that rose from a fresh stream of blood.

The hand that came for her was impossible. Still, it came and she dodged.

Jost looked at the stone wall and watched with fascination as a man walked out of it. He was the same color as the stone, as were his clothes.

She had heard of the Silent Army, but she had not seen one in motion before. They had always been standing still when she passed. A few had changed positions when her eyes were turned but this was different. This was actual motion.

The stone man reached for her once more and Jost stepped back. Her hand tried to block him, but with no real result. He was made of stone. She could not force his arm to move.

"Wrommish!" she called to her god as the thing continued reaching for her.

If the statue moving shocked her, it did far worse to the people in the crowd. They had not fled the dead as quickly as they did the moving stone soldier.

Jost blocked a hand that grabbed at her again, this time with her dagger. There was a scraping noise and the hand was pushed aside, enough for her to avoid it, but there was no blood drawn.

Lifeless eyes turned to look at her. The face of the stone man shifted and the mouth curled into a sneer.

Jost backed away again, fully aware of the people around her and how they were retreating.

The fourth attempt to grab at her met with success. The

hand that caught Jost's elbow was as hard as rock, and despite her best efforts to twist away, there was no give. There was no heat. The moving stone was as cold as the wall it came from.

The hand held her tight and the powerful arm pulled her forward. Jost was a fighter. She had been trained in combat since she could walk, but she was not made of stone. Her fists did no good against this opponent. She moved her body in an effort to lock his joint, but it was useless. On any human being she had ever met the move would have broken the offender's elbow and likely driven bone into meat, but here the end result was the same as if she was hanging from a rock outcropping on Wrommish's heights. She effectively swung herself around on that arm and then found herself pinned to the wall. The soldier needed do no more.

Jost kicked, she struggled, she attempted to cut one finger at a time from the stone hand, but it was useless.

The Silent Soldier slammed her into the wall three times as she fought back. The third time she was knocked senseless. By the time she recovered enough to consider struggling, she had been bound by heavy leather straps and metal chains.

The City Guard were taking no chances.

The soldier held her until they were done.

And for the first time in all the battles, the Fellein had a prisoner of war.

The meal was wonderful. The food was always satisfactory, but this was an extravagance. Dretta had cooked chicken she had likely paid far too much for, and the meat was perfectly seasoned.

Before they ate, they made love. That was even better than the meal. By the time they'd eaten most of the bird, feasted on the fresh bread and cheese and fruit, Merros wanted nothing more than to make love a second time and then sleep in the arms of the most amazing woman he'd ever met.

Naturally, the world interrupted.

Though Merros did not advertise where he went, it was hardly a secret. By the time they'd finished their meal and the conversation that went along with it – and how was it that any person could be so endlessly fascinating? There was nothing she said that he did not want to hear – one of the messengers from the palace had come to interfere.

The business of war waited for no one, and most assuredly not the man in charge of the Empire's forces.

Dretta looked at him with her dark, deep eyes and waited patiently. He looked back and was torn. There was excitement, but there was also guilt when he looked at her. She was an amazing lover. She was the widow of his best friend. There were so many levels of wrong in what they did that Merros could never hope to untangle them all. And he wasn't sure that he wanted to.

"What is it you are thinking about, Merros?" She reached for the bread and wiped some juices from her platter. Gods, she could even make eating fascinating and erotic.

He shook that thought away. It was just food and he was as lusty as a teenager around her.

"We have had good fortune it seems." He smiled.

"Have the Sa'ba Taalor suddenly surrendered?"

"I said good fortune, not an act of the gods." He still smiled. "We have captured one of the Sa'ba Taalor."

"Have you then? Was it the one who killed Wollis?"

"I don't know yet. I haven't seen who, but I must go now, Dretta. We have to find out what we can." He did his best to sound apologetic, but inside surges of adrenaline were kicking around. The thought that they might be able to actually learn something from one of the gray-skins was nearly intoxicating.

Dretta stood and nodded. She even offered a tiny smile. "Go. Take care of what you must, but be careful. I have heard too many tales from you of how dangerous they are."

"I will be very careful indeed, milady. I will also let you know if I learn anything of Wollis's killer."

She moved close and hugged him for a moment that was not long enough by far. And then she stepped back and spread her arms. "The gates here are always open to you."

He smiled at that. The very notion warmed him. She warmed him, despite the cold weather and the frost.

It was a short ride to the palace and the guards at the gates let him in. He smiled at them and headed immediately for the Empress's throne room, where, as he expected, several people already waited.

Desh Krohan looked his way and smiled tightly. "I do not believe it is Swech, but I recognize her. She was among the first of them that we met. One of your ten, I believe."

"That doesn't surprise me. It also explains how she has evaded being captured until now. They were very skilled."

"I don't think we'd have captured her, but the Silent Army interfered."

"Truly?"

Nachia responded, "Had her pinned to the stone wall and wouldn't let her go until the City Guard secured her. Then the soldier moved back into the wall and slipped up to the top again."

"How many dead this time?" It had become a problem, and a serious one. The attacks tended to leave a dozen or more dead every day and the resulting chaos had rendered more and more people too injured to care for themselves.

"Only three by the assassin's blade." The man who spoke

was one he'd met before and one he still didn't much like. Darsken Murdro was one of the Inquisitors. They were unsettling people with methods that Merros was never going to be comfortable with. True, the tales might only be tales, but he didn't like the notion that whoever was going to be questioned would be left to the likes of the man across the room from him.

Murdro continued, "When the statue moved and attacked, the panic that resulted left two more dead. They were trampled."

Desh spoke up, "We'd discussed the possibilities of a curfew."

Murae Pellinger, the man who currently led the City Guard, cleared his throat and looked toward Merros before speaking. Technically the man had the same rank as Merros, but the reality was that Pellinger was only in charge for as long as Merros tolerated him. Nachia had appointed the general head of all military forces and that included the City Guard. Pellinger understood that and was doing an excellent job in his position.

Pellinger said, "We can enact a curfew, but there is nowhere for these people to go. They've made shelters for themselves in tents or on bedrolls. They're curling up in piles to stay warm at night."

"I know we wanted families to have homes to themselves in this situation, but is it possible to add more people to some of the places that have been offered?"

Pellinger nodded. "Some will allow it. Most will do it if they are told to, but while there are several people who have been generous with their properties, there are many more who have offered no concessions and are charging monies that few can afford."

"Who is the new Minister of Lands?" Nachia spoke and

they all looked her way.

"Arlo Lancey, Majesty."

Nachia nodded and leaned back. She was in her throne and leaning to one side. With a wince she rose and walked away from the seat. She shot a withering look at Desh Krohan and said, "Fix that."

"Couldn't if I wanted to." For one moment only, he smiled at her.

She glared and he stared back frostily, with a small smirk. Merros had no idea what they were talking about and tried to bring the conversation back around. "We were discussing the land minister?"

"Arlo Lancey. Old blood. Old money. We should bring him in to discuss how badly his world will fall apart if he doesn't find shelter for more people."

"Majesty?" Pellinger looked her way, frowning.

"Come now, Murae, you know better than that. Arlo is new in his position. Bring him here. Try to make it happen soon."

"What happened to the previous minister?"

Darsken Murdro answered, his voice low and reserved. He had a thin smile on his face, and while he was pleasant, Merros couldn't bring himself to like the man. "He was found a few weeks ago with his throat cut, not far from the docks. Someone killed him and four of his bodyguards."

Nachia asked, "No one was ever captured?"

Murdro looked to the Empress and lowered his head. "The people I spoke to could only tell me that it was a woman who did the killings and that she was dressed in black and kept her face hidden."

"So, Sa'ba Taalor." That was Desh. Nachia and Merros nodded at the same time.

"Likely, yes. When we talk to the one you have locked

away we might find out more."

"I would like to be there when you speak to her, Inquisitor Murdro." Merros spoke calmly and looked at the other man.

Murdro's smile did not change at all, but his eyes looked over Merros carefully. "As you wish, General. As I believe you are fluent in their language that would be extremely beneficial."

Merros nodded and wondered exactly how the man knew he spoke the language of the Sa'ba Taalor. Well, one of them at any rate. There were several apparently and he only understood the one. "Do you have her properly secured?"

Desh answered him. "She is currently unconscious and very well restrained. Tataya is with her and making certain of that."

Nachia sighed. "Kindly go find out what you can. I want to know everything that she knows as quickly as possible."

The Empress strode around her throne room. Merros and the rest followed her with their eyes. "We are still heading for the mountains?"

"Yes, Majesty." Desh didn't seem at all happy to report that fact.

"I thought you said you had several sorcerers working on that problem."

"Yes, Majesty, but they've had limited progress."

She spun on Desh and the First Advisor stood his ground. Few would have.

"Either find a way to move the damn city or find a way to burn down one of the mountains if you have to. It would be a preposterous way for all of us to die."

"All respect, Majesty, but it might not come to that. It's possible that we will clear the mountains completely."

"Desh, make certain of it. I don't care how." He lowered his head and she continued, "I want Arlo Lancey here as soon as possible. Do not tell him why he is summoned, simply make certain that he gets here before the day ends."

Pellinger nodded and left the room. The Empress seldom stood on decorum when it came to the meetings and it was best to do what she wanted.

"If we cannot manage walls for the refugees, then I want tents. I don't care where they come from. The soldiers have their rooms. If they have to give up their tents for this, then so be it."

Merros nodded, but did not try to clarify that the soldiers didn't have personal tents. There had been a time for that, but not in his lifetime.

Nachia looked around the room for a moment and then speared each of them with a hard glare. "Why are you still here? Go! Get me answers, get me results!"

Merros took the hint. He and the Inquisitor walked together to the cell where their first Sa'ba Taalor prisoner waited.

Trying to ignore the presence of Merros Dulver at his side, Darsken Murdro headed for the cell where his next assignment waited. There would have been a time when he wondered why he had been chosen over the other Inquisitors, but he already knew the answer. He was chosen because he was good at his job and because he was currently in favor with the sorcerer and the Sisters.

All that meant was that he had to do his job well. There were a lot of people who thought he was ambitious, and perhaps he was. But they didn't understand the Inquisitors and how they worked.

He would rise to a new rank if it became necessary, but he was in no hurry to get there. The higher in position one rose, the more one became a target. He was respected, he was occasionally feared, and he enjoyed his duties.

People like Merros Dulver could think what they wanted. It changed nothing.

The guards opened the door for them and Darsken stopped at the door and smiled to Tataya, who smiled back and rose from her seat. As always, her beauty struck him. As always he nodded politely and then got to business.

Merros also nodded at Tataya, as Darsken got his first true look at a Sa'ba Taalor. She was lean, all hard muscle, and dressed in the clothes of a street person. Perfectly camouflaged. No one would have reason to suspect her of anything, until they saw her face.

As the girl was unconscious he stepped closer and looked at her carefully. His hand moved across her gray face, feeling the raised flesh of a dozen or more scars under several spots where her flesh was freshly bruised.

At first he thought that an overzealous guard had punched the girl in the mouth until it split several times but upon a second, careful glance he understood better.

"So that is the reason for the veils." He opened each of her mouths, studying the fully developed teeth, the musculature, the tongues. They were properly damp and his hand felt the breath that came from each. If they were born that way it was a wonder they ever knew how to speak.

Merros looked over at the girl and stared at her mouths, horrified. "By the gods."

Tataya spoke softly. "Drask was different. His mouths had more... symmetry."

Merros looked at Tataya for a moment and then looked back at the girl. He took one of the layers of her shawl and drew it over the lower half of her face. "Jost. This is Jost."

"Are you certain?" Darsken did not ask to be rude, but

rather to assess the facts.

Merros was wise enough to understand that, despite his active dislike of the Inquisitor. "Yes. We traveled together for months."

"Do you know if she is fully grown? Her body is that of a young woman, but I had heard the Sa'ba Taalor were giants."

"Not giants. Some of them are very large, yes, but only a few stand taller than me."

Tataya nodded. "They are not giants. They are merely very, very fit."

Darsken ran his hand over the girl's arm and then her leg, nodding. He could feel hard muscle and still more scar tissue under the clothing. He also felt several concealed knives, which he carefully extracted from folds in her attire. He took his time, running his hands in places that might have been deemed inappropriate had this been any other female, but he was not going to leave the young woman in question with any surprise weapons. He had been cut more than once in his line of business.

When he was done there were eight blades, an even dozen small darts and three lengths of wire he didn't quite trust should be left on her person, all set to the side.

"Can you wake her please?"

A word, a gesture from Tataya and in seconds the girl was awake. She bucked and thrashed and tried to get free from the shackles on her legs and wrists.

She failed.

Darsken waited patiently while she tried several times.

Finally he said. "You will find the best way of gaining even a little freedom is to comply."

The girl continued struggling. Merros Dulver spoke and the girl cocked her head and answered.

"I have no answers for your questions." Merros's voice, but he knew the words belonged to the girl called Jost. He did not look away from her, but merely waited for the translations from the General's mouth.

Darsken nodded. "Then you will stay here."

"If that is what my gods demand."

He shook his head. "It is what my Empress demands. Your gods do not matter in this place."

"My gods are all that matter. You will learn in time."

"How many of your people are in Canhoon?"

"Enough to kill you all."

"You will not leave this cell alive if you do not tell me what I need to know."

"Then I will have honored my gods."

Darsken looked to Merros and then to Tataya. "This will take time."

He looked back to Jost. She was staring at him with her oddly glowing eyes. "A lot of time."

Arlo Lancey did not have any bodyguards. Many of his fellow ministers did, but he felt no need to waste his finances. First, he was only the Minister of Lands. He did not mint new coins; he could not change the taxes. He only did what he was told to do. In exchange he made enough coin to live comfortably and he ruled over a small gathering of people who listened to him and obeyed not because he was a harsh man, but because he was pleasant enough to work for.

He did not consider himself a bad man. His predecessor, Lirrin Merath, on the other hand, had been a fat, bloated lump of a man with too many connections, too much money and too little empathy. Arlo had worked with him on many occasions and both of them had understood that land was ultimately power. But where Lirrin had willingly changed the rules as he pleased to gain more power – there was never enough, you see. Power is a feast for fools. The more you have, the hungrier you become – Arlo did not follow suit. He wanted to. Let's not misunderstand that. He would have gladly gained as much power as he could and appreciated the starvation as so many others did. Arlo would have considered being greedier, and he most certainly would have hired bodyguards, but he had been told not to.

One did not argue with the woman who held your fate.

He did not know a name. Not for the woman. He could tell you the name of her god. If he ever failed to remember the name Wrommish, it would be the death of him. That he believed with unyielding conviction. The woman, a little tall, but nothing remarkable, had killed five men in front of him to make her point. The first four were trained mercenaries, capable killers, and she'd broken them in a matter of seconds.

The last one had been his predecessor, Lirrin.

The nameless woman was the enemy of the state. She was a murderer. She was a cutthroat. She had probably had a hand in all of the mindless murders running through the city.

Arlo had no doubt that if he hired bodyguards, she would kill them and then him. She had already said that he would do his job the best he could and follow her orders, or he would die.

He looked at the thin scar on the back of his right hand. All that had happened was a scratch from the woman's nail. She'd scraped him and promised that before that wound healed they'd talk again.

She'd kept her word. The very day he was appointed as the new Minister of Lands, after he'd celebrated with friends, consumed far too much wine and whored his way home, she was waiting for him in his apartments.

She was not there to sleep with him.

"Do you remember the name?" Her words were a soft, silky whisper in his ear as he was drifting to sleep.

He sat up quickly in his bed, heart thundering, breathless and looked around the room.

She had watched him undress, watched him fall on the bed and roll across the sheets before his head found the pillow, and had watched him patiently as he fell into a drunken stupor.

He had never guessed her presence.

"The name." She was just out of arm's reach. Her dark eyes looked at him without even seeming to blink.

"The name?"

"The name of your new god. The name that can save you."

Oh, how he'd scrambled then. His body did not move. It dared not, but he thought hard and sorted through his memories of the night Lirrin died in a pool of his own blood, rainsoaked and lifeless while the shadow-shape of his killer stood and watched Arlo. She had spoken a name. It was important. Had he not been drunk he would have remembered instantly. He looked down at his hand and saw the scratch and then finally remembered, "Wrommish?"

She'd nodded and he'd thanked the new god with all of his heart.

And then she'd explained all that he was to do.

It came down to paperwork, ultimately. The laws of the Empire were clear. The right scrap of paper with the right seal meant that you owned a parcel of land. Arlo was paid dearly to make sure that there was no confusion in the matter. Ever.

He was not performing his tasks to the best of his ability. To do so would have been his death.

The Empire wanted all available lands that were not being

used to hold the people now living on the streets. Several prominent citizens had already offered properties for that very purpose. The people staying there did not own the properties. They were merely tolerated, but it was a step. Others were allowing the refugees to stay for a price. Most were fair about it. Some were not.

There were hundreds of places that could have been offered. They were not, and despite the fact that he had been tasked with finding the owners of those properties, Arlo had deliberately failed.

Sooner or later they would come for him.

He was prepared. If he could just explain to someone the nature of his dilemma, perhaps they could offer him safety within the Palace. He had all the paperwork he needed. It was sorted and ready for them, but he dared not offer it up without some sort of protection.

"Wrommish knows what is in your heart, foolish man. You have prayed to him."

He knew the voice instantly. Arlo turned fast toward it and reached for his sword. It was a foolish thing, ornate and more for decoration than function, but he knew how to use it and he was desperate.

His eye exploded with pain and Arlo dropped the sword, screaming and reaching to cover his wound. His eye could still see but the lid was trying to close over something that was in the way and every motion of any type caused more pain.

"You are a weak man and you would betray me. For that reason you are already dead."

His good eye saw her as she moved away. Anger surged. She had hurt him and she wanted to kill him and while he was not a fighter, there were limits. Arlo surged toward her and promptly fell to the ground.

"Do you know that you can buy a dozen spices here that will kill a careless person? You just have to cook them the right way."

"Why? I didn't do anything wrong."

"They are coming for you and you would have. As I said, Wrommish knows what is in your heart. You prayed to him. He knows all he needs to know of you."

Without another word she knocked his oil lamp to the ground, where it spilled its fiery contents across a woven rug and began to smoke and burn. The rug was a gift from an admirer. It was lovely. It was also flammable.

Arlo tried to reach for it. With effort he could put it out and only get minor burns.

His arms did not move. His body was sluggish. He should have been screaming but nothing happened.

The woman walked away, but as she left she made certain to scatter his paperwork across the blaze. Deeds burn brightly when they burn.

Swech slipped from the window of the apartment easily enough. The rope was still tied where she'd left it and climbing was not a challenge.

She'd hoped Arlo might be a worthwhile investment and he had been, but his service was no longer required.

As she reached the roof of the building black smoke started spilling from the window she had just vacated. The sun was still up, but the day was overcast. They were high enough up that the clouds did not block the sun so much as they swallowed the city entirely.

People moved as if they were traveling through a heavy fog. It seemed to calm them.

Glo'Hosht's voice called out to her, softly warning her that he was present. While it was unlikely that any strike she made toward her king would hit, he was wise enough to warn her just the same.

"My king."

Even through the cloud cover she could now see the smoke rising from Arlo's apartment. Soon others would sound an alarm.

"Swech, Jost is captured."

She nodded. "How?"

"The wall that surrounds the city. She touched it while she was serving the gods. The stone guardians captured her and held her until the Fellein guards took her."

"Do we go to help Jost?"

"No. She must take care of her own. As all of us must if we are caught." Swech felt her hands try to tighten into fists and made them relax. The gods had plans. Jost was not currently on them.

Swech nodded her head in compliance, much as it hurt her. There were no promises. The Daxar Taalor made demands and they were obeyed. They had saved members of the Sa'ba Taalor before, when it suited them. But not this occasion. Jost's fate was her own to decide. If she could not, the gods would handle the matter. The thought that they might not save the girl was painful, but life was pain.

Swech nodded a second time and took a deep breath.

"What is next, my king?"

"These stone men change everything. They only seem to stand at the outer wall."

Glo'Hosht moved and spoke at the same time, gliding over the ground and heading to the next building. Swech followed and looked back at the black column of smoke that had spread in size.

"We could continue what we have been doing, my king. It has certainly unsettled a few of the people and made others desperate. But there are other things we could accomplish."

"What did you have in mind?"

Swech looked back again as flames began to dance across the roof of the building she'd been inside. Smoke pirouetted across the roof and beneath it tongues of light tasted the air and seemed to like the flavor.

The building was going to burn down. There would be no saving it. Most of Canhoon was stone, but there were exceptions.

"Perhaps we consider more of that."

Glo'Hosht looked on and nodded. "Perhaps."

"What I'm thinking of involves at least three of us entering the palace."

"For you that is an easy thing. You have the face of a Fellein."

"There are others. I know that we have been kept apart to avoid issues, but if we wish to strike hard this is something we should consider."

"What are you thinking?"

"Most of the food supplies, much of the clean water, is stored in the palace." Swech stared at her king. "They might find more food, but water is rare here. They depended on their rivers."

There was a very long silence and finally Glo'Hosht answered, "The gods agree. I will be joining you."

"You, my king? Did you not say that would be a challenge?"

"A challenge for many. A challenge for me, but not so great a risk that Paedle does not decree it."

There was no more to say. When gods make demands, they must be obeyed.

Behind them the roof of the apartment building collapsed

and flames roared higher into the air.

Bells sounded. Horns sounded.

"They will come to put out the fires, my king."

Glo'Hosht nodded. "Let's kill as many as we can when they do, but do not be careless."

Swech took no offense at the words. They were often uttered by the King in Mercury, who liked to remind the followers of Paedle that not being seen was their greatest gift.

Besides, Jost had already reminded them of the consequences of growing careless.

SEVEN

How quickly things could go wrong.

Nachia sat on her throne and ignored the pain it caused her to do so. Perhaps Desh was right. The discomfort was a good way to make certain she did not grow arrogant. Or maybe she just enjoyed being reminded of her responsibilities.

Darsken Murdro looked at her and frowned. "She does not speak, Majesty. Her gods have forbidden it."

"Have you tried torture?" She hated the words as she said them.

"No, Majesty. She is not the sort to respond to that method of inquisition. She and her people celebrate the scars they earn as a mark of honor and proof of all they would willingly suffer for their gods."

Merros, who was next to him, nodded. "You were not there when Drask Silver Hand let Andover Lashk bite into his arm until he bled. He never even flinched and I assure you I would have been screaming my idiot head off."

"Then what do you suggest, Inquisitor?"

He lowered his head. "I can discover much, Majesty. I can walk through her mind and learn, but I am not aware of what will happen if she tries to speak to her gods."

"I don't understand."

"Both Desh Krohan and the general have told me that the Sa'ba Taalor actually communicate with their gods. That either the gods actually speak into their minds, or that they believe they can. If I am in her mind when this happens, I do not know if the god will see me."

"And if a god sees you, what is supposed to happen?" She resisted the urge to shake her head. It would not do to insult her closest companions.

"I do not know, Majesty. What are the limits of a god? We have seen that their gods allow them to survive great heat. We have seen that their gods gift them with limbs of living metal. If their gods could walk into my mind as I would walk into hers, then what secrets might a god learn? I hold many secrets for the Empire, Majesty."

She chewed at her lower lip and then forced herself to stop. One must always look calm.

"A notable point, Darsken. What would you suggest?"

"The Sisters, Tataya and Pella, they are capable of seeing into my mind if I let them. They could, perhaps, kill me before the god could glean much information."

Merros was standing to the side of the Inquisitor when he spoke and she could see the general reassessing his opinion of the man. She knew him well enough to read his face: he didn't like the Inquisitor or any of his kind. Not many did.

"Have Pella come to me. I would speak with her about this."

Darsken bowed formally and nodded before he left the room. She had told them they did not need to bow in the circumstances they faced, but most did it anyway.

She waited a full minute in silence and then looked at Merros. "You don't like him."

"No, Majesty."

"Why is that?"

"He and his use fear as a weapon. That I find acceptable. That they use it as their primary weapon is irksome to me."

"Irksome?" She teased with her voice and he grinned.

"I deem the Inquisitors a necessary evil. I do not like them. They have a level of power that makes them dangerous."

"Said the man in charge of the Imperial forces?"

"I have more people looking over my actions."

"What do you mean?"

"If I leave here, you and a few others know where I sleep." She raised an eyebrow at that.

"Are you going to deny it?"

"No. It's important that you are kept safe."

"If an Inquisitor tells you that something is true, what do you do about it?"

"I act on it."

"And how do you know that he tells the truth?"

"I have the assurances of the Inquisitors."

"And are they investigated by you?"

"No."

"None of them?"

"No."

Merros's face worked as he considered that answer. "Why not?"

"Because the vows of the Inquisitors are very complex and backed by sorcery. Should they attempt to lie in their investigations, there would be consequences."

"What sort of consequences?"

"Horrible disfigurement at the very least."

"Beg pardon?"

"Desh Krohan is the one who set up their vows. He attends

all of them. Each and every member of the Inquisition is marked by Desh. They cannot lie in their duties without being disfigured or worse."

"And how do you know this sorcery works?"

"Have you ever been to the offices of the Inquisition?"

"No, Majesty."

"Should you ever have the need to go to those offices, you will find that the people who work as clerks in the offices are all rather heavily disfigured. In the event that they survive the process of lying, they are given a second chance to work for the Inquisition. I say given, but what I mean is they are forced to pay penance. Five years of their lives marked and in pain. If they survive those years they may either leave or once more work as an Inquisitor, with the knowledge that they will suffer the same fate a second time should they stray."

Merros's face was stricken with dread at the notion.

"The Inquisitors agree to this. They know that they must always be trusted. They know that failure to be worthy of that trust brings pain, disfigurement and, if they cause an innocent's death, their own death in exchange."

"Wasn't the Minister of Lands supposed to be brought before me?" Nachia forced her jaw to relax. It wanted very much to grind her teeth to nubs.

"He is proving hard to find, Majesty. Also, it seems his home burned down."

"Are we to assume that was a coincidence?"

"No, Majesty. The City Guard are investigating."

"Make them investigate faster, please, Merros."

Before Merros could say more, Darsken returned with Pella. Five minutes of conversation was all it took to make the arrangements.

The girl, Jost, would talk one way or another.

The fact offered Nachia no comfort.

Another messenger entered the throne room. The girl was slight and winded, and looked around with wide eyes. She bore the scars of surviving the Plague Winds, and as they were slight Nachia found herself hoping they would heal completely. She entered the chamber timidly. Likely she had never seen a room as large in her entire life.

She whispered to the guard, who pointed to Merros.

A moment later she was handing off her package and trying not to stare at Nachia. Nachia smiled at the girl and the girl smiled back. It was a smile that lit her entire face.

Barely looking up, Merros thanked the girl and dismissed her. The stress showed on his face.

"What is it?"

"Something is wrong. People are falling ill."

"Where?"

"Everywhere, it seems."

It was dark out, and the kings gathered. To the west the skies were black, hidden by clouds. To the east they were clear and the only patch of darkness hiding the stars was the distant city of Canhoon and, in the far distance, the frozen waves that made up the Arkannen Mountains.

The bonfire was large and only one of a hundred or more. The Sa'ba Taalor owned the area around the river and they did not hide their presence.

Ganem sat and stared into the fire, her eyes nearly glowing. "How long until their floating city reaches the mountains?"

Tarag Paedori answered, "Two days. We will have troops in position before then. And archers. As many as we can gather."

Ganem nodded. "I have many archers. They are yours, of course." She paused and considered. "Lored is still to the east?"

Tusk nodded, "Mmm. He is making progress. They do not seem to have as many cities there. More villages."

"And Donaie Swarl? She is still at sea?"

"There are people out there." Tusk shook his head. "They have no gods and mark their bodies with scars to tell tales of their greatness." He tore a piece of hard bread and sopped it in the stew before him as he spoke. "The Fellein hired them to fight their water battles. Donaie decided they must die for mocking the gods. She is doing all she can to kill them all."

"The gods agree with this?"

"She would not do it without their wishes. You know this." Ganem nodded her head and looked to Tarag Paedori. "Glo'Hosht is in the city that floats. They are breaking the city into pieces. Well, the people."

The King in Iron nodded. "The fights among the masses are many. They have no place to rest and the skies are colder, as the tops of mountains are colder. The walls are frozen. The ground is hard with ice." Tarag smiled. "And down here, Tuskandru has converted people to his faith."

Tusk chuckled. "I did not convert them. They asked to join us."

"They have been converted? They have heard the voice of Durhallem?" Ganem looked his way. Mercy was not the way of the Obsidian God.

"Durhallem has marked them. Durhallem can speak to them. More importantly, Durhallem can watch through their eyes and know what they think. A few sought to attack us from within their ranks." Tusk paused for a moment, his eyes alight with the memories. "The unfaithful were killed for their insolence. As they reached into the forge, they reached into the very heart of Durhallem. If their loyalties were false, they burned at the touch of Durhallem's wrath."

Ganem nodded. That made sense.

N'Heelis stretched his lean body, scars glistening in the light of the fire. "My people await your orders, Tarag Paedori. Will you have us entering the floating city?"

Paedori nodded. "Mostly your people. Tusk will ride ahead. We have scouts who say they believe they know where the city will come to rest. It is a large area. His army and mine will go there."

N'Heelis nodded and prepared to leave. He paused once to say, "To the north. Wrommish has chosen."

Tarag Paedori nodded his head and watched the King in Gold leave. He looked to Ganem.

"Your archers will work to take the city. Meet with the rest of your people. Head east. As has been said, there are many villages. I want you to take as many as you can."

"Capture or kill?"

"If they surrender, give them Tusk's choice. Should Ydramil wish to take on new followers, make it so. If they fight, break them."

"You do not want them dead?"

"Your god is the Mirror God. Let your enemies reflect on their sins while they die on the ground."

Ganem nodded. There was a certain wisdom in those words.

Tarag Paedori's hands worked on his armor, oiling metal and leather alike. "The city will not escape us. They have eluded us, yes, but there will be no escape."

He looked at the visage of his god, hammered into the faceplate of his armor. "We will win this war for the Daxar Taalor. They have given us so much and all they ask in return is justice for the past."

All of the kings agreed. It was a good thing.

Ganem left that night, riding her mount, Sidian. Unlike most of the mounts, Sidian carried only a few weapons. For Ganem they were enough.

Not but a day's journey to the west, Andover Lashk sat with his companions and ate.

"You have changed, Drask."

"I have changed?" Drask looked his way and shook his head. "You are a foot taller. You have scars over your body that tell tales of endless battles. You walk differently. You speak differently, but you say it is I who have changed."

Andover nodded. "You are the same in your mind, I think. But there is a difference to you. To Tega as well." He looked toward Tega, who was staring into the fire.

Drask nodded.

"Tell me what happened to you."

Drask sat silently for a while and then nodded again. "When I was sent away from you, it was because the gods needed me to break the very rules on which I was raised. They wanted me to visit the Mounds."

Andover pursed his lips in agreement, recalling the horrifying sounds that sometimes came from the frozen ruins.

Drask inclined his head toward Tega and then Nolan. "They were sent with others to see if the secret to defeating the Sa'ba Taalor might wait in the Mounds. I was sent to follow them and stop them."

He looked at the fire for a moment and grew silent as he considered the past. Andover wondered for a moment if he would say more, but Drask was simply marshaling his thoughts.

"We found ways into the Mounds and found something. I do not know what even now, but I have suspicions."

Drask picked at his food for a moment, then took a bite and chewed and swallowed before he spoke further. The look of concentration told Andover that the man was trying to find the right words.

"When I was much younger, and curious, and angry, I killed a man who offended me. He claimed I was weak because I spared another man his life. I did not care of his opinions until he provoked me. Then I killed him to make sure he understood I was not always merciful.

"Because I was curious, I cut him open and cleaned out his innards then studied his insides."

A year earlier Andover would have been terrified by the image Drask produced. Tega turned her head and look at Drask with interest, suddenly curious about his words.

"Have you ever looked inside a human body?" Drask asked.

"Not on purpose."

Drask laughed at that, a deep, hard laugh, and slapped Andover on the shoulder in a companionable way. In the past that slap would have sent him sprawling.

"There are... tubes in the body. Blood flows through them. They are everywhere, and if you have ever cut off a hand or seen one cut off–" and here he showed his silver hand, which had also changed a great deal "–you can see the blood that flows from them."

Tega said, "Arteries and veins. That is what we call them. Blood moves everywhere through them. Even in your eyes and toes."

"Yes. What Tega says. Arteries. We found them in the ground beneath the Mounds. They were filled with light that flowed like blood. And far below the ground we found a great pool of that blood that moved through all of the Mounds."

Drask stared into the fire again. "Nolan attacked me. I had

killed some of theirs. The Daxar Taalor had told me what I must do. I did it." Andover nodded. One did not debate with gods.

"And then the ground we stood on, above the great pool, broke and we fell into it."

There was silence then as Drask looked at his silver hand and the way the metal seemed to have grown into him and continued to move up his arm.

"What was it?"

Drask shrugged his powerful shoulders. "I do not know. The life of the gods? The blood of the gods? Whatever it is, it is now inside the three of us. It filled us as water fills a jug. As blood fills a body. It became a part of us."

Tega leaned forward. "It is power. We have bathed in it and absorbed it. We should have died, but we did not. We should have drowned or burned or both, but instead it fills us."

Drask nodded. "Yes. That is a good way to say it."

"What kind of power?" Andover asked.

"I brought the Blasted Lands back to life. I brought Brackka back from ashes."

"Could you bring Delil back to life?"

"Yes. I think I could."

"But you didn't."

Drask looked at him again studying his face, examining his eyes as if they held other secrets that even Andover did not see. "You did not ask me. You did not ask Tega or Nolan. You asked your gods. They have given you a chance."

"They are your gods, too."

Drask stared for a long time into the flames. "I am not sure that is true any longer. There is much I have to consider."

"Drask, how can you turn away from the gods?"

Drask did not answer.

• • •

How could he turn away from the gods?

Drask considered that question carefully. He examined it as if it were a gem with thousands of facets, looking for the possible flaws on every plane he could study.

He had not turned away, of course. He was looking for answers that, so far, the Daxar Taalor had not provided.

They had but to speak up, of course. He had not answered their queries but he heard the gods. He had always heard the gods, for as long as he could remember, and they had always known his heart. They had not chosen to answer the questions within him; even when he'd spoken them aloud he had received no answers.

His entire world was filled with their lessons, their advice and their truths. Great Korwa, the greatest city ever, had been destroyed by the very Empire he now entered. The people burned.

The gods painted the Sa'ba Taalor in colors of ash to remind them that their heritage was ashes and ruin. Dead and gone and ruined, destroyed by the Fellein because they wanted to take Korwa as their own and in their jealousy they destroyed what they could not have.

They sought the land. They sought the Empress. They sought to subjugate all that was, all that could be.

That was the story he'd been raised with.

Drask could have told Merros Dulver all of that, but it was not his place. The gods had other ideas.

For a thousand years the Sa'ba Taalor had fought among themselves, honing their skills until even the weakest of them was a match for the strongest of the enemies they might someday face.

He looked at Andover Lashk and contemplated that fact. The Fellein boy was gone, replaced by a Sa'ba Taalor man. The scars were real. The gods had found him people to fight and if he had failed in those combats he would be gone. There were no special favors among the gods. He knew that in his heart.

And yet, Andover Lashk wondered how he could turn his back on the gods.

There were no easy answers. Drask Silver Hand found himself capable of miracles, which had always been the purview of the Daxar Taalor. Of the gods.

What need of gods when you could answer your own prayers?

Had anyone asked Callan how he managed to steer his new ship all the way to Louron, he would have been unable to say.

The Brellar ship drove into the shallows around the swampy area and he looked at the ground for a long time, barely believing he could be that lucky. The air was hot and sticky, but compared to the air along the ocean, it smelled sweet.

For whatever reason, the worst of the smoke did not come here. The volcanic ash did not taint the waters as completely. There were fish in the waters here. He had not seen fish in the region since the Guntha Islands were buried under fire and stone.

Louron had an endless supply of rumors around it. Callan did not care. He dropped anchor and scurried his way down to the beach, grinning like a fool for the first time in days.

When he looked around, several of the Louron were around him. They did not seem afraid or welcoming, merely curious. Still, they smiled in the way of their people.

Callan smiled back and spoke slowly. "Hello." Their language was a complex one and he spoke it with all the skill of a three year-old.

A young girl, perhaps all of four, waved and smiled at him,

returning the welcome. Her father, or perhaps her grandfather, was there with her and he nodded.

The man said, "You do not look like a Brellar, but you have their ship."

"Well, mine was sunk, you see."

He nodded and moved closer to the little girl. "You do not look well fed."

"The grays, they took the food and water with them." His tears started and he was barely aware. "They killed all the Brellar and left me with their bodies, you see. Out there."

The man nodded again. "They are not good people."

Callan nodded.

"Come. We can at least give you food and fresh water."

Nicer words had never been spoken. Callan managed to drink and eat more than he should have and felt sick for it. His hosts gave him a place to rest and he fell into a deep sleep.

It was daylight when he woke again.

Three Inquisitors stood over his bed to greet him.

They had many, many questions for the captain.

Nachia greeted the arrival of her brother and his love interest with a certain amount of amusement. Princess Lanaie... Technically Queen Lanaie, but she had not been formally crowned as yet; Nachia made a mental note to fix that situation soon. It would help morale. But first, there was a war to consider. She was a striking young woman and Brolley was enchanted, but she had doubts that it was anything beyond infatuation.

Lanaie had all the charms a man could want, to be sure, but she was as quiet as a mouse and that had never much appealed to Brolley. He liked to argue. He was profoundly good at it. The skill had almost gotten him killed when he ran across the

Sa'ba Taalor, and had nearly started the war between their peoples a good month early. Drask Silver Hand was the man he had challenged. A behemoth of a man who, fortunately, knew enough of diplomacy to let her brother survive.

Brolley had changed for the better since then. He still liked a good debate, but he trained every day, the better to back up his words with steel if the need arose. He was hardly an adept – Nachia could still take him in most situations – but he was getting better. In short, he was growing up.

Lanaie was a different story. She was still surprisingly quiet, but she had been courted by several men and was still being courted. Her uncle, Laister, now deceased, had been actively pursuing the woman who was decades younger than him in an effort to claim her title as his own. He'd failed.

The catch was simple: Lanaie had the title, but she had nothing else. The country she now ruled was burned and buried under ash. It might come back from that, but not for years. All she could claim was a wasteland.

Still, she was pursued, and at the present time Brolley was most earnestly courting her.

Nachia wasn't quite certain how she felt about the situation. On the other hand Lanaie was nice enough.

It wasn't her concern. There were other matters to look into.

"I know you're busy, Nachia, but I haven't seen you in days and I wanted to make certain all was well with you."

Nachia smiled and stepped closer, opening her arms to hug her younger brother. They had often been at odds, but had always been good friends. That was the way with family. Well, some family. The rest of her blood relations were rather debatable.

"It's busy. We're at war. Still, I'm always delighted to see you."

Lanaie bowed formally and Nachia returned the gesture. They were not nearly as close and wouldn't be until she was absolutely certain what the woman's intentions were.

Before she could do more, another messenger arrived with a sealed document. She smiled her thanks to the boy and broke the seal.

The words were direct and she studied them for a long moment, frowning.

"What's wrong?" Brolley stepped closer and she moved back. The message wasn't for him. She trusted her brother, but she didn't want him fretting. There was enough going on that he already knew and she wanted no more of it in his life.

"Not for you, Brolley." She shook her head. "Not this one. This is for me alone."

For a moment the old anger was there. The nearly physical need to show how he could do whatever she could do. He pushed it aside and nodded his head, smiling instead.

"Is this something you need to attend to now?"

"I'm afraid so." She sighed. "Join me for dinner tonight?"

Brolley smiled. "Yes, of course."

A moment later he and Lanaie were gone from the chambers and she was alone with her two mountainous bodyguards. Merros liked to pick men who looked as if they were bred to pull wagons, but they were, as she had already seen, very skilled at their duties.

That didn't bother her. She understood the necessity; though she preferred to handle as much as she could herself, she could not be left alone, not when assassins had already proven they could enter the castle.

No. The problem was with the Temple of Etrilla, where several hundred people were now locked inside and the remaining priests were turning people away from the locked doors.

Those who had entered were beyond sick now. They were dying or dead.

The Temple of Etrilla was one of the larger structures in Old Canhoon. It was nowhere near as grandiose as the palace, of course, but it was built of heavy marble walls and gilded besides. The structure was nearly as old as the palace, and housed as many as a thousand people at a time. In the olden days it might have held more, but there had been a collapse some hundred years back and somehow along the way the land had been used to build other structures. Just as well. Under most circumstances you could not find a thousand individuals entering the structure at one time, but now was a time of need and that changed the way people looked at churches. As Vendahl, the god of wealth and prosperity, was quoted to have said to his followers when he still walked the lands, "When people no longer trust their mortal leaders, they look to the gods. When there is war or disaster, expect the coffers to fill faster than in times of peace and plenty."

Wendtle Hearin was the head of the temple. He was newly appointed, as his predecessor had succumbed to old age and passed in the chaos of the city rising into the air. Still, he was comfortable enough with his decisions. The coffers were full enough for now, and he'd stocked up water and food for the faithful and was offering it out when it was needed. Those who served with him were faithful and diligent. The one exception had been properly punished. Following the rituals of Etrilla as told by Humble Ohlmer, the seventh prophet, the man was stripped of his position and cast from the temple after being marked with a brand to the forehead. Was it distasteful? Yes. Did it hurt him to burn a man's face? Yes. Was it necessary in a city the size of Canhoon to punish a sinner? Yes.

Now, this.

Was it the Plague Winds? It mirrored the symptoms, but that hardly seemed likely. The faithful came to the temple and sat in the pews and waited for their chance to seek solace and blessings from Etrilla. At first Wendtle thought it was merely another day, with a few seeking a chance to seek aid from the gods. But this? This was madness. The sick came in as a nearly constant stream, a trickle at first and then a river and now a flood. He had no choice but to close the doors and lock them. There was simply nowhere else to put the people who sought refuge.

The inside of the temple was filled to overflowing. People sat in the aisles, rested against the walls, even occupied the seats of the great table, simply because it was necessary. At first prayers were offered, and the passing out of food and water added to the tasks assigned the priests. The food would not stay down. The water could not be swallowed by throats that burned with sickness.

The followers were pale and shook with fever, and their skin began to scale as if they had, indeed, endured the Plague Winds of old. But the winds did not strike with discrimination. They burned and struck rich and poor alike, regardless of faith. These were the faithful, familiar faces even after only a few days in some cases. There were the Followers of Etrilla and they were being crushed by the horrid sickness.

Now, despite the cold, the sick continued to come, seeking solace, and all he could offer them were the patches of the temple's lawn that had not already been taken by the dispossessed.

Wendtle barred the doors of the temple and stood before them and did all he could think to do. He prayed to the God of Cities and Towns, and was joined by others. It was all that was left them.

Sometimes prayers are enough. Sometimes faith is enough. It was the only weapon left in his arsenal.

By the time dinner came around, Nachia was hardly in a mood for company, even her closest friends and family. Still, one did what one had to do.

Because there was no other time for it, she had a dinner with her inner council and with her brother and Lanaie besides.

Merros ate. He was a soldier and that was something she quickly learned: when soldiers are told to eat very little stops them from fulfilling that duty.

Desh was too busy discussing everything with her to eat. "I've examined several of the people at the Etrilla temple. It looks like Plague Wind. But it is not that particular affliction. It's poison."

"Well, how are they being poisoned?"

"I've no idea, Nachia. I'm a well-learned man but poisons are not my specialty."

"Is there anyone in your gathering of sorcerers who might know?"

"Corin. I have him investigating the situation now. But the damage is done, Majesty. This is a poisoning. Somehow, someone has poisoned an entire congregation."

"I know a lot of the churches keep emergency supplies." Merros looked up from his food and wiped at his mouth with one wrist. "We had that incident with the horses before everything went from bad to deadly. Someone poisoned their feed. You might have Corin investigate that."

Desh nodded his head. "I will. He was the one who found the poisoned feed, but best to doublecheck."

"Best that we add extra guards to the stores here, too."

Merros looked at his meal and sighed. "I'd be worried about this, but honestly, I'm rather hungry and I've already been eating."

He pulled a sliver of meat from his plate and wrapped it in bread before chewing on it.

Nachia found her appetite waning.

"We are now a little over a day away from the mountains. Have you found a way to make certain we are clear of any obstacles, Desh?"

Desh shook his head. "I believe we will be safe. I've consulted with the Sooth and others have as well. We should be safe. Beyond that, if it comes to that, the only other option at this time is to try to level the mountain."

Nachia took in several deep breaths and finally nodded her head. Desh did not want to use sorceries of that level. As he had already said, there were always prices to be paid. But he would if he had to and that was enough.

"Or," Desh said, looking at Merros the entire time, "I suppose I could grow us all wings and we could fly away to the Great Star."

She looked at Merros and had to stifle a laugh. He was thinking about the level of power it would take to move a mountain, and his attitude toward his food reflected as much. The bread and meat sat on his plate while he tried to manage to finish the bite he had in his mouth without being sick.

Brolley looked at her and spoke his mind, as he was wont to do. "I was looking over the wall. They're close to us, close behind us. We should do something to hurt them."

"Like what?"

"Well, perhaps spears or arrows..." Brolley's face flushed red.

Merros spoke up. "I'm more worried about the ones we

obviously have here with us. We have to stop them. We have to find a way to detect them and capture them."

Desh scowled. "It's not for lack of trying, General Dulver."

Merros raised his hands. Every time the sorcerer called him by his proper title it was an immediate sign that he was irritated. "I'm not accusing anyone of not doing their best, Desh. I'm just speaking aloud. As much as I like the notion of dropping something on our pursuers, our more immediate threat is the group that has caused riots and possibly poisoned our supplies. Again."

"I'm certainly open to suggestions." Desh drank the last of the wine in his goblet and shook his head. "I know you said they were skilled, Merros, but the damned enemy has dead gray skin. How is it that we haven't actually had anyone report seeing any of them?"

"I know many people thought I was exaggerating, but I meant what I said about their skills. Ten of them killed over a thousand of the Guntha because they move like ghosts. They make no noise, they are not seen unless they want to be seen."

Brolley nodded his head. "The one we have – Jost, I think? – she was the one who waited for Desh in Roathes. Well, the ruins. The ashes. There was nothing there but dust and ash and a few burned-out huts but she waited and not a one of us saw her until she wanted to be seen."

Nachia thought about that and suppressed a shiver. Her brother was many things, but he could never keep the truth from his face. The Sa'ba Taalor scared him. That was good. She wanted him scared. Scared people were cautious.

Desh nodded. "We can continue trying to find them. In the meanwhile, the Sisters have come up with a plan for slowing the ones behind us. If it works, it works. If not, we have wasted only a bit of effort."

"What do you have planned?"

Desh smiled at Nachia. "It's a surprise."

That was all he would say.

EIGHT

Andover climbed from the river's waters and suppressed a shiver. The air was cold, but not unpleasant. It was the breeze that sent the chills through him. Despite his training he was not used to the smells of death. The Blasted Lands were to his back and two of the Seven Forges now breathed ash and toxic gasses into the air to the south. Durhallem and Wheklam raged, reshaping the world.

They had swallowed the Guntha. They had swallowed Tyrne, the only world Andover ever knew before going to the Taalor Valley.

For the briefest moment a flash of anger struck him at that thought. One look at his hands was enough to quell that fury.

Tega sat near his bundle of clothes. She looked at him as he approached, but he felt no embarrassment. Flesh was only flesh. He had changed a great deal and though she showed little emotion, he suspected the way she stared was more to do with how much he had been changed in a short time than it was about lust or any interest.

"You are so different, Andover." She offered him his breeches and he took them, sliding them over the scars that covered his thick legs then nodding his thanks as he took the shirt from her and finally his vest. The cloak stayed where it was for the moment, wrapped around his stockpile of weapons.

"I am me." He looked at her, studied her. His heart still felt a flutter when he cast his attention her way, but she was no longer the whole of his universe. There had been a time when he would have killed for her, would have starved for her. When he would have done anything at all, just to have her attention. All she had ever cost him was his hands, and all she had ever done for him was find a way for him to have his hands again.

He looked at his hands for a moment.

"You have changed as well, Tega. You are like Drask. I can feel the differences inside you from here."

"I haven't changed, Andover. I just hold onto some energies. I'm the apprentice to Desh Krohan. The power is there; I could use it if I wanted, but it hasn't changed me."

"What is it then?"

"Just power. Lightning is power. Power is everywhere. In the flames of a fire, in the breeze, in the heartbeat of a person. This is just extra."

"I don't understand." He stood near her and carefully put his weapons where they belonged. There had been no attacks, but only a fool would expect the world to remain unchallenged. There was a war going on.

Tega held out one hand. "I know how to access power. I was taught by Desh. I am... not as skilled as I would like. I have actually destroyed things I only meant to hurt or stop, without trying very hard. But when I finished casting my spells there was always a price. I was as hungry as if I had gone days without eating, or I was so tired that I had to rest. That is why Desh always says that magic has a price. You can do amazing things, but there is always a cost."

She sighed, and then reached up to take his hands in hers. Tega looked into his eyes and spoke earnestly. "Your hands were made of iron, Andover. I could not have accomplished such a feat. I could not have healed your hands, though I stopped them from being completely destroyed." She shook her head. "I could do very little, because the damage was so great and in order to heal the wounds on you I would have had to ruin someone else. I thought about doing that to Purb and Menock, but it was not for me to decide."

She paused a moment then shook her head again. "Fellein has laws to stop me from performing that sort of sorcery, because the cost is too high. There was a time when sorcerers would heal someone who was rich enough by taking the power from the poor or even from people who gave up years of their life for a few coins. People who were desperate. Desh pushed to have the laws put in place that stopped that."

"Why?"

She looked long and hard at him before answering. "Because the weak sometimes need to be protected."

He nodded his head. "I used to believe that. I understand."

"When Purb and his friends broke your hands, they were wrong. You were given a chance to prove that, but before the laws were put there, it was just accepted that the strong should survive. Without those laws, you would not be here now."

"Without the Daxar Taalor, I would not be who I am. They gave me hands and they taught me lessons. The Sa'ba Taalor spend their entire lives learning those lessons. Tega. Had I been raised by them I might never have needed to fear Purb and Menock."

She nodded and stood up.

"Before you were hurt you worked for a blacksmith. You

were learning a trade. You were also punished a few times for theft."

"I stole to live." He nodded. "Mostly fruit or bread after my parents made me leave. If Burk had not taken me in, I would have likely been killed at some point. Even before that, I had a few scars from the lash of the City Guard."

"Burk took you in. He saw you and accepted you. You were not strong, Andover. You were not a fighter. But you learned, yes?"

"Of course."

"I understand that Tyrne is gone. Destroyed. That's what the first people we found when we left the Blasted Lands told us."

Andover nodded and pressed his lips together. "Yes. Durhallem chose to raise his mountain there to teach the people of Fellein a lesson."

"What lesson?"

"That they should have agreed to a peaceful accord instead of insisting on a war."

"And did Burk escape Tyrne before that happened?"

Andover shook his head. "I do not know."

Tega looked away from him. "And I do not know if my mother and father are alive. Or my aunt. Or my little brother. Or my dog." He watched as she blinked furiously to hold back tears. "All I know is that one of the gods you now follow might have killed them all to teach a lesson."

"I am sorry if you have lost loved ones."

Tega nodded. "I am sorry if I did too. And if Burk is dead. And Libari Welliso, who helped me carry you to the palace and a meeting with Desh Krohan." She looked up at him again. "Do you know what all of them have in common?"

"They helped me."

"They did not prey on the weak."

Andover looked down at Tega for several moments. Her face was the same, as beautiful as he had ever seen. The boy he had been still nearly worshipped her. The man he had become could even understand why.

"Why did you help me, Tega?"

"Because Purb hurt you because of me. And because you were always nice to me. You smiled and I liked your smile."

Her fingers moved up and gently caressed the line of Great Scars that covered his mouth. "I'm not even sure if I could see your smile now, Andover. That is a sad thing to me. You had a beautiful smile."

She rose and started to walk away.

"Tega, if I asked, could you bring Delil back to life? Are you capable of that sort of thing?"

"Yes, Andover. I think I could, just as I now have the power to mend your old hands." She gestured toward Tyrne. "But as much as I like you, as much as I used to wonder what it would be like to be closer to you, there is a city full of corpses I would likely want to tend to first."

There was nothing he could say to that. Instead he sat where she had been sitting and thought about Tyrne and all the people he had known.

The mountains were higher than Stastha had thought, but that was a good thing.

The air was thin near the top of the mountains, and from where she stood she could see the great spine of the entire run in both directions. It was an impressive sight.

A large number of small villages ran along the river's edge. Some were still intact. Others they'd taken as they moved, but only when they absolutely had to. There was an army behind them that would want to sharpen blades on the bodies of their victims. Stastha had a different task. She and her small gathering of soldiers were to find the best way to take advantage of the mountains.

The long run of the river was deceptive. Closer to the Blasted Lands the banks of the river were close to the ground, but the closer one got to the mountains, the deeper the cut of the land. The river had hacked a wound into the land itself and cliffs rose high enough to make the water impossible to reach without climbing down several hundred feet. The foothills were deceptive and the land was magnificent to look over. In a few places villages had built bridges between the two sides of the river. Most were in good repair. Stastha left them that way. A person could never tell when being on the other side of a river might be beneficial.

Canhoon was getting closer. Within a day the vast city in the air would be moving along the river to the west and heading for the very spot where she was now standing.

She prayed the gods gave them the best possible weather. Clouds, yes, but no rain or snow. Whatever the case they would be ready, of course, but best if the weather worked with them instead of hindering the cause.

The work was sturdy, but it was also ungainly in appearance. It would do.

Satisfied at last with her work, Stastha took out her horn and blew four sharp notes that echoed between the mountains and along the river below.

The sound came to them as the skies to the east began to lighten.

Tuskandru rose and stretched and walked over to Brodem, who was still pretending to sleep though the sound had awakened him.

"Up, you lazy brute," Tusk said with affection. Brodem let out a good-natured rumble and rolled over, giving Tusk access to the satchel he wanted.

A moment later his horn was out and he was blowing four sharp notes that perfectly mirrored the ones Stastha had just called out.

There were no complaints from most, but the newest among them looked around, shocked by the powerful notes.

Bram Littner, the spokesman for the villages who now followed Durhallem, looked to Tusk. "My king? What do you need?"

"Get up! It's time for war!" Tusk bellowed the words even as his followers rose from their rest and grabbed their belongings. The newer followers had little. Most could carry only a cloak and a few supplies. That was just as well. They would learn today as they had every day since joining the followers of Durhallem.

The boats raised their anchors and untied from hastily crafted stays along the shoreline.

Tarag Paedori bellowed to his people and they responded.

Within ten minutes the Sa'ba Taalor were on the move. Those with mounts took to the lead. Those on the boats were close behind. The stragglers – mostly from the village – did their best, hastened by the younger members of the Sa'ba Taalor, who made sure they moved as quickly as they could.

Life is a series of tests. No one was permitted to fail. Young Mendt and her cohorts kept the stragglers in line. Those who could not follow the orders of their god were not left alive.

Durhallem is called the Wounder for a reason.

They travelled east with every haste. The time had come to show the foolish among the Fellein that no place was safe from the Sa'ba Taalor.

The winds picked up pace and the boats soon took the lead, moving even faster than the mounts. From all points among the gathering horns called out, not to communicate but to call to the gods, to let them know that their children were on the move and eager to serve.

Far to the east Lored ran into a surprise as he moved along the river's edge.

His army was moving, but slowly. The war engines had to be pulled from location to location. It might have been easy enough to build more in their stead, but there were no forests here, only occasional trees and more flatlands.

Bromt suggested taking the river, seizing boats as needed and moving quickly to the west. There was a war going on and there were few threats to them that they had not easily crushed. A few hundred of the Sa'ba Taalor had been badly injured and half that number had been killed.

They wanted war, and they wanted it sooner rather than later. There were also several cities with great walls along the river, at least according to their captives. Best to find them and crush them if they could, and so they rode along the river. It was easy enough. They took boats by force as they went, and killed their enemies in the process.

When the arrows came, few of them were prepared.

Oh, to be sure, there were guards, but whereas usually they stayed alert because they were on foot, the waters made them complacent. They looked for boats and little else. They were foolish.

Lored saw the arrows and called an alarm, but his call was cut short by the arrow that slammed into his own throat and stopped against his vertebrae. He reached for the obstruction, uncertain as to why, exactly, he was having trouble breathing, and then fell back, drowning in his own blood.

The followers of Wheklam onboard the boats steered and turned the vessels, moving them to better defensive positions, but it did them little good. Their assailants had waited patiently and brought their full wrath down from a very advantageous position.

The Imperial archers knew their duty and they did it. Arrows rose and fell and many of them were covered with burning pitch.

The Sa'ba Taalor did their very best, but the boats under them were burning and sinking and they had no choice but to swim for the shores. The problem was that the shorelines were not clear and easy to access. They were rocky outcroppings that led to areas where a person could climb seventy or so feet up a cliff side to reach land.

The dead Sa'ba Taalor burned with the boats, then sank into the fast moving waters.

The rest climbed. The simple fact of the matter is that the people of the Forges were raised climbing mountains. It was among the very first tasks they were given. Many of them, even encumbered with wet clothes, scrambled quickly up the sides of the cliff. The volleys of arrows slammed into the walls around them, stuck to their backs or pierced their limbs. However, the majority of the gray-skinned people carried backpacks with supplies, occasionally their shields, or even weapons, all of which stopped the arrows from penetrating. Those hit occasionally fell back into the river, but not as many as might have been expected. They were trained their entire lives to deal with pain. Unless a tendon was cut or a bone broken, there was little they would not endure.

The arrows continued to come, however, and those who were not quick enough died before they reached the top of the cliffs.

They did not have their siege weapons any longer. They did not care. The Sa'ba Taalor lived for war. Their gods shaped them that way.

The archers on the shores retreated a reasonable distance, but they did not flee. Some of them used short bows and used them well, several arrows held in their hands and fired in quick succession as the Sa'ba Taalor approached. Others used longer bows and fired from a distance. These weapons had greater power and slammed into the enemy with substantial force, often enough to penetrate bone.

As the Sa'ba Taalor charged, their enemies retreated then dropped down to the ground to give the crossbow archers their chance.

Several of the Sa'ba Taalor had bows as well and used them, but most never had the chance. The Fellein archers were better prepared, and their weapons had not just been soaked in the river.

Had the Sa'ba Taalor been alone it is very possible that they would have been killed off in that initial assault.

No one sounded an alarm. No one blew a horn. So the mounts were unaware of a battle until well after the worst of the damage had been done to the boats.

But when they realized the mounting carnage, they did not take well to someone murdering their humans.

The Fellein in the area had never seen a mount before. They had been warned to beware the creatures, but they had no real point of reference. Yes, they had seen bears, and occasionally a mountain lion. Bears did not move the same way, and the mountain lions did not wear heavy armor.

If the armor should have slowed down the mounts, it was not up to the task. Flaming arrows and regular arrows alike did their job and cut into the beasts, but a few still made it to the archers before the fighting was done and even the crossbow bolts that hit the beasts seemed to slow them only when they'd been struck a hundred blows.

Not all the Sa'ba Taalor died that day. Not all the mounts, either. Instead they did what few Sa'ba Taalor ever did: they retreated.

Once they were safely far enough away, the surviving Sa'ba Taalor looked to Ordna for direction after the death of their king.

Ordna was silent for a long time before responding.

If one were to observe the southern shoreline of Fellein, the first sights from the west would be the ruins of Roathes. The bodies of a few could be seen here and there, rotting away, though far less than one might expect considering the catastrophes that had befallen the small nation. Beyond that, the Louron still held sway in an area that was surprisingly untainted by the volcanic activity that destroyed the neighboring Roathes.

An odd sight that one might note would be the activity around a lone ship that was being loaded with supplies by an unusual crew.

For a long span after Louron there were rugged shorelines that belonged to no one. The area had been disputed for generations, claimed again and again by both Fellein and the Brellar. The land itself was inhospitable, the ground unstable and given to collapse. For that reason, the area was finally abandoned by both sides. The Brellar still claimed it was theirs. The Fellein still claimed it belonged to the Empire. But no one fought over it any longer. The neighboring people of Louron said it was best left alone, for angry spirits inhabited the area.

It should be noted that most people in Fellein didn't believe in ghosts. They preferred to believe that any unusual actions were acts of either sorcerers or the gods. Louron was the exception. Most of the people there believed in ghosts and other spirits. It should also be pointed out that Louron was the area that, for the time at least, the Sa'ba Taalor had decided to leave alone.

Almost at the center of the continental landmass, there was a break at the southern end. That break was the mouth of the Parmahar River, which ran from the Corinta Ocean all the way to Lake Gerhaim. In most places the river was over a mile wide and there were no existing bridges crossing it. The waters were deep and fickle and it was best to travel by ferry, which could be found with great regularity and used to cross for a small fee. No one would charge a heavy fee, as the next ferry was never really that far away.

Along the way there were many villages and port towns, most of them small in population and happy to be that way. Larger towns, the local wisdom said, get noticed in times of war. Though Fellein had not been at war for several generations, the local wisdoms still stood and made perfect sense to the people who lived along the Parmahar.

The wisdom of the locals did not mean much to the black ships of the Sa'ba Taalor. They rode up the river from the sea and took their time about it. But first, they let off the remaining armies they carried.

The armies of Ganem spread on both the eastern shore and the western. Those on the western shore saw Ganem first. Days of hard riding found her on the other side of the Arkannen Mountains. She rode her mount and carried her spear in one hand, bucklers on both of her arms.

They cheered when they saw her. The King in Silver was well loved for a reason. In a perfect world, as far as Ganem was concerned, Drask Silver Hand would have been on the western shore to lead the troops.

Instead it was Tenna, who was just as solid a leader, but tended to waver on the path of balance more than her former lover. Tenna would do. She was a warrior first and a philosopher second and this was, after all, wartime.

Ganem sounded her horn as the sun rose and the black ships sailed on, heading upriver with all haste. Tenna sounded her horn in response. Moments later Ydramil's army was on the move.

The small villages had always believed that their size made them useless as targets. They had no strategic value and their people were merely fishers and boaters.

That notion was cemented for them when the great black ships moved up the river, dark sails set and oars cutting the water. None of the villagers were foolish enough to cheer as they went past, but most of them thanked their gods – mostly Othea the River God and Luhnsh the Beggar King – as they were spared assault.

When Ganem's forces attacked, few of them were praying any longer.

As with Tuskandru before, and with the direct wishes of both the King in Iron and Ydramil, each villager was offered the chance to pray to a new god. When each had made their decisions they were converted or killed. As with Tusk, a coin was needed to prove faith and to mark the newcomers among the blessed of Ydramil. Some lived. Some died. All were changed by the experience. While it is true that many converted and were introduced to Ydramil, a great number chose death. The river ran red as the soldiers of Ydramil made their way to the north, following after the great black ships.

• • •

First came the sickness, then came the riots.

The illness that started with the Temple of Etrilla spread. The symptoms were identical to the Plague Winds, meaning that people first grew feverish and then had to deal with the horrible scarring of their flesh, with nausea and chills and vomiting and in many cases the loss of hair and teeth, before death came along to end their suffering.

Once past the walls of the temple, the illness became a flame that drew the attention of the people. When the dead and dying were hidden away people did their best to ignore it, but as soon as the refugees started dying on the streets, panic set in. In a day's time the rumors had become truth in the eyes of many and that was enough to start the desperate attempts to escape their fates.

Those who suffered the pains soon found death to be a mercy. Those who watched their loved ones suffer did not take it well. Prayers were not enough, it seemed, no matter how much the faithful asked for assistance.

Those who did not have loved ones suffering from the Plague Winds did not see the efforts that went into stopping the spread of the illness. All they saw were the infected, who might well pass the sickness by breathing on them. "Spreading the wind," they called it.

The priests did their best. Everyone acknowledged that.

Still, a few felt that the gods were not doing their part and therefore help was needed.

How they got past the locked doors was anyone's guess. But they did. It was easy enough to find the supplies of oil among the dead and dying.

Fire purifies.

The oil was spilled and then set ablaze before the doors were sealed again in the darkness of a cold, wintry night. Snow was falling even as the temple and the faithful began to burn. The snow was silent. The faithful were not.

The temple was made mostly of stone, great slabs of marble. It survived the fire. The faithful did not.

No doubt a few thought that they had saved the city and acted heroically. It was grim work, to be sure, but better for everyone in the end, yes?

The next day a few people were found suffering from the same symptoms. Most were left alone. Two were burned alive, while witnesses watched. The descriptions given were nothing spectacular. The men who did the burning were captured within an hour, but by that point the damage had been done. Parties started spreading, looking to take care of the Plague Winds before anyone else died. Most of them carried lanterns with enough oil to handle the matter.

A surprising number of them were stopped by the City Guard, who took it upon themselves to do their duties without waiting for anyone to tell them to do so. Still, a few slipped past as was inevitable.

Seventeen people suffering from the illness were taken to the top of the Mid Wall by a mob that had had enough. No one would see them or theirs ruined by the disease.

They were right. The Silent Army ruined them instead. Each and every member of the mob was captured by the stone soldiers who rose from the wall and separated the rioters from their victims.

A man named Wilkham tried to protest the way he was being treated. The stone soldier dealing with him grabbed the protesting survivor from Tyrne by his neck and his crotch and effortlessly flung him over the wall and past the small amount of land beyond it. Wilkham screamed very loudly as he rose into the air and then sank, dropping toward the river far below.

The mob that had planned the exact same fate for the afflicted people they'd dragged to the top of the wall tried to escape, but to the last they followed the fate of Wilkham.

By the time the City Guard arrived the situation had ended. There were plenty of witnesses, however, who were glad to tell them what had happened.

The rioting continued, but it did so well away from the Mid Wall.

The following day, as the sun rose, the Silent Army moved. Half of their force stayed along the wall. The other half moved out through the whole of the city, from all points toward the palace. They did not merely stand as statues. They moved. They patrolled.

That was the day the worst of the riots ceased.

While the riots continued there was, understandably, a bit of chaos and occasional bloodshed.

Merros Dulver moved along the streets, on an urgent mission. He had not seen Dretta March in two days, despite his best efforts. The business of running an army was a massive affair.

Word had come in of the successful assault on the army of the King in Bronze, and he had celebrated with a glass of wine with the Empress and Desh Krohan, but that had been all the time there was for celebration. Despite the very best efforts of Darsken Murdro and Pella, he could not gain access to the mind of Jost. She would not talk, she would not break, and all agreed that actual torture would do absolutely no good. The closest they came to actual physical torture was withholding food and water. The problem was, Merros had seen the Sa'ba Taalor move through the Blasted Lands and eat far less than any of his troops. It was possible that they could have ruined the girl by keeping the water away from her, but they all agreed, ultimately, that she would simply die rather than talk. They did not want her dead. She had secrets that they wanted.

Pella and Tataya were discussing the best ways to pull the information from her without risking anyone's mind.

Desh understood the necessity, but refused to be any part of it. No one, not even Nachia, could sway him.

"Torture," he reminded them, "is seldom a useful technique. People will tell you what they think you want to hear. They'll make up all new stories for you if they think you'll listen to them and just stop administering pain."

The way he said it, Merros knew he was speaking from experience. He didn't ask about the exact situations and Desh did not volunteer any particulars.

The girl under Desh's care came with him almost everywhere, but she seldom spoke. Merros was the one who'd found her back when she was seeking the wizard. Still, though she was civil, she had little to say to him. She held her stomach like she was going to be ill, but she never was. Instead she simply followed Desh Krohan around, occasionally spoke to what had to be an imaginary friend and from time to time cried a silent tear or two. That was understandable. The hells she must have endured getting away from Trecharch and marching the hundreds of miles to reach Canhoon must have left her broken. Merros doubted very seriously that he would have been in any better shape than Cullen by the end of the situation.

Having won a victory against the Sa'ba Taalor, Merros and his soldiers were now busier than before. The riders he'd employed were not from Canhoon, obviously, but they were skilled and they were aggressive when it came to defending what was theirs. The plains they ran along were populated mostly by nomads and the occasional town. Had it not been for working out details with Desh Krohan about having the sorcerers pass along information, the attack would never have worked.

Now that it had, he wanted to employ it to better advantage. The Sooth was useful in finding the Sa'ba Taalor, but it had taken troops and, frankly, a little bit of chicanery to manage their one major victory to date. They'd known where the Sa'ba Taalor were. They'd been informed of boats that had been stolen. They'd set a trap and it had worked.

Captain Leno Nethalte had run the charge brilliantly. He was also, fortunately, one of the people who escaped the great mounts that came after the remaining Sa'ba Taalor.

The mage working with Nethalte – he could not remember the girl's name to save his life. It had to be ten syllables long at least – had helped identify Lored, the King in Bronze. They had managed to kill one of the kings. That had to be a morale blow to the Sa'ba Taalor, but he had no idea how good a strike it had been.

He made a note to have Darsken Murdro mention the death to Jost. Maybe that would make her chatty.

Such were the thoughts that were going through Merros's mind as he walked through the market on the way to Dretta's home. He planned to surprise her with fresh fruit. The stuff was getting harder to come by every day, but one of the vendors, who got his fruit directly from the palace, had promised to set aside grapes, apples and Pabba for the general. Sometimes rank had its privileges.

As he approached the trader's table the rioting began again. Merros could not have said what started it, but there was a scream and then a second and as he looked in that direction he saw the fight breaking out in earnest. Three or four men were doing their very best to take down a smaller figure, but it wasn't going the way they wanted it to.

The first of the attackers stumbled back with a deep gash across his throat that bled like a waterfall until he fell backward and hit the cobblestones. That made more people scream, as one would expect, and the chaos began in earnest. The smaller figure brought an elbow around and drove it into the face of her assailant. *Her* assailant. That piqued Merros's already high curiosity and he moved toward the fight. The man who'd been elbowed staggered back with shattered teeth falling from his mouth.

The woman used the broken-faced man's torso as a springboard, planting both of her feet on his ribcage – cracking his sternum in the process – and then used her momentum to knee another man in the back of his head and neck. Something broke and he dropped to the ground.

The movement was enough to let Merros see past the hood that fell down, to let him see Dretta's face as she killed her third assailant. He stared, dumbstruck, and watched the effortless way she drove her fingertips into the throat of her fourth assailant and left him choking on his blood. A move Merros had only ever seen once before.

When Swech killed one of the men who tried to rape her, the first time she entered a city in Fellein.

A man tried to run from her. He held a satchel in his hand, and he was moving at high speed. Dretta pulled a knife from the-gods-alone knew where, and drove it into the back of his neck and he, too, fell to the ground. She pulled the knife from the man's head even as she grabbed her collected groceries and shoved them back into her satchel.

As with so many of the Sa'ba Taalor, she seemed to look

everywhere at once. Still, it took her a second to recognize
him. The blade was still in her hand. It was not the sort of
thing one found in Canhoon. It was a flat leaf of metal that had
been painstakingly sharpened and was designed to be thrown.

It was the sort of blade Swech had used to cut his face, to
kill Wollis March. But that was impossible, of course. Swech
had gray skin and scars everywhere on her body. He knew
that from firsthand experience.

He meant to say "Dretta". He did. But when he opened his
mouth, "Swech?"

Her eyes looked so broken just then. Her face was a mask
of sorrow, even as the blade left her hand and sailed for him.

She was far enough away for instinct to have time to take
over. His arm came up to ward off the blow even as he dropped
down. The blade took him in his hand and drove through his
palm, the tip emerging on the other side.

The Sa'ba Taalor seemed capable of ignoring pain. They
managed to fight when they should have long since collapsed.

Merros envied them that. He felt his gorge rise and fought
not to puke on himself as the wave of pain screamed through
his arm.

The street was cold and hard and he fell on it, holding his
damaged hand in the air.

He looked up just as Dretta, his Dretta, came at him, a thin
blade that was absolutely foreign to him clutched in her grip.
The grip of the weapon was held in her closed fingers, but
instead of the blade coming from one end or the other of her
hand, it ran from the outside of her grip in both directions. A
metal blade sharpened and ready pushed along her arm, past
her elbow in one direction and a solid six inches in front of
her as well.

"Curse you for being so damned smart, Merros." The words

were not spoken in the common tongue of Fellein. They were Sa'ba Taalor.

Merros looked at her and his heart shattered. "Swech. Damn it, no." He could barely breathe.

Her fist struck his face and drew away in a flash, and the double blade along her other hand pistoned back and came for him.

Dretta March's body was grabbed and hurled backward with astonishing force. She tried to catch herself, tried to twist her body, but the attack was too fast and too brutal. She hit the wall closest to them and fell, grunting. She came back up just as quickly and drove the blade of her weapon into the face of her attacker.

The blade was sharp and strong and scraped along the stone face of the Silent Soldier causing exactly no damage. She brought the longer end around to attack him on the backstroke of her swing and had the same effect.

And while she did that, the stone short sword of the stone man facing her cut through her stomach and deep into her chest, cleaving Swech's heart in half.

Dretta March fell to the ground. She was dead before she landed.

Desh Krohan tended to the wound in Merros's hand. "Stand still. You'll only make this worse."

Nachia paced around the room, doing her best to stay calm. Her best was not very good.

"What were you doing out on the streets alone?"

"I'm the general of all the Empire's forces. How would I ever get the respect of the troops if I couldn't walk home alone? Ow! Gods, Desh!"

The first Advisor tsked like a grandmother. "I told you not

to move. You're very lucky the blade didn't sever a bone. It nicked one, which is probably the only reason it didn't go through your hand and into your head."

Desh looked at the wound and winced. He was being kind; the nick he spoke of was a cut though bone. Dretta March or Swech, whoever she'd been, had a deadly aim and threw knives with force enough to kill. His hand was the only reason he was alive. According to Merros the woman had aimed for his eyes.

"Where is her body?"

"Where you don't need to look at it. She's currently being examined by the Inquisitors."

Merros nodded, his lips pressed into a thin line.

"You're either going to get guards or you stay at your offices here in the palace." Nachia was not making a suggestion.

Merros nodded. "I'll stay here. There's no reason for me to leave."

Snow was falling in a fury. By the time the City Guard had brought the March woman's body to the palace she'd been frozen half solid and covered in a blanket of snow.

She'd been taken immediately to Darsken Murdro.

Merros had been brought to the private quarters hidden to the side of the throne room, and that was where he was still sitting, scowling and wincing and occasionally making faces like he would cry if he could get five minutes alone.

"You've torn the bloody bandages again. Oh, to dust with this." Desh moved his hand and muttered a word and Merros let out a squeal of surprise. Nachia saw the small burst of light that moved from sorcerer to soldier. She saw the wound close itself completely.

She stared, and had to force her jaw shut.

"I don't do that often. Don't expect it." Desh actually

sounded different. His words were a little slurred. Not many would have noticed, but after a lifetime with the man teaching her, she knew the First Advisor well enough. "Move your fingers, make a fist, do it often for the next few hours or the scar tissue will steal mobility from you."

"What did you do, Desh?" Merros looked at his hand as if it might be an alien life form and one that was possibly trying to kill him.

"I mended your wound. Don't expect it a second time. It's exhausting."

"I had no idea you could manage such a feat."

"Like I said. I don't do it often."

Merros muttered to himself, "I don't know if I should thank you or strike you."

Desh had a smirk on his lean face when he responded. "Go with the thanks. Striking a sorcerer is never wise. We have defenses."

"Yes, well, then I suppose thank you is in order." Merros was staring at his hand, moving his fingers, making fists, and frowning.

"As I said, keep working your hand or risk stiff fingers and a wrist that won't turn easily. Not the best issues for a swordsman."

Nachia nodded. She'd known that Desh could do that. She'd studied with him for a while; even if she seldom practiced even the simplest spells, she understood the concept.

"What made you suspect, Merros?"

"I've been a fighter my entire life, Nachia. I've trained and worked and even when I left the army I did some work as a mercenary. The only people I've ever seen fight that way were Sa'ba Taalor. They don't swing their fists. They don't... move the same way. She moved her feet along a man's chest and broke him. It barely looked like she was touching him, but his ribs may as well have been crushed by a Pra-Moresh."

He looked down at his hand again. "And the moves she made? Not every Sa'ba Taalor can do them. Swech told me she followed a god who believes in unarmed combat. I can't say for sure if she was Swech. But when I said that name, she tried to kill me."

"If there's a way to know for certain, we'll find it."

"I'm going to have to examine her place. I need to know whether or not she had secrets in there. Gods! How could I be so damned stupid."

Nachia shook her head. "None of that. She looked nothing like Swech. She had letters from Wollis March. She gave no sign that she was anyone else."

Merros nodded, but his face didn't say that he agreed. He was already wondering how best to approach her home and examine it.

"We can send the Inquisitors if you prefer. They are very, very good at finding secrets."

The look that crossed his face was almost pain. "Yes. That would be for the best, I suppose."

Nachia moved closer to her general. "I am so very sorry, Merros." She could hardly be accused of being touchy, but she reached out and wrapped her arms around his neck from behind and rested her chin on the top of his head. Merros closed his eyes and took the comfort offered.

Desh waited a few moments before speaking again. "Should we discuss why it is that the Silent Army is now policing the Mid Wall for us?"

Nachia nodded against Merros's hair and sighed. It was likely to be a long conversation.

• • •

There was nothing.

Pella stood by him throughout the process of him meticulously searching the body of the dead Dretta March. First Darsken examined her clothes and removed each item, carefully setting aside each of her numerous weapons. He scrutinized them, too, and noted that several of the items had poisoned reservoirs. There were also three metal vials that contained powders or fluids. Those were set aside as well, the better to let one of the sorcerers who dealt with potions examine them.

The body was female. There were no indications that she wore anything to hide who she was. If she were, in fact, a member of the Sa'ba Taalor, they had changed her appearance completely. Just to make absolutely certain, he peeled the flesh from one of her arms, examining the layers of skin carefully.

Pella tried examining the body with her sorcerous skills and came to the same conclusion. This was a human body. Nothing more. Nothing less. The cause of death was violent trauma and a sword through her chest.

There was one peculiarity.

While necromancy was forbidden in Fellein, Inquisitors were allowed to make exceptions and Darsken chose to use that loophole. The flesh was marked, the blood was employed and the air in the dead woman's lungs was taken into his own in an effort to draw in any last remnants of her spirit that might linger.

There was nothing.

Darsken frowned and tried stronger magics, the sort that he used only when seeking to draw the spirit back to the body. It was a sorcery he did not like to use, but he had to know.

There was still nothing. Whatever had been inside the woman had been destroyed beyond his ability to find even a trace of her essence.

"Have you ever run across a situation like that before, Darsken?" Pella, who had been watching everything and writing notes for him could not quite grasp how that was possible. She was not alone.

"Never in my life. Not once." He frowned and ran his fingers over the designs on his staff. "I have examined bones that were hundreds of years old and there was still something. The flesh you gave me from the dead soldiers who attacked, even that had some essence. It was how I identified the bodies. If I had not been told the name of this woman, there would be no way for me to know it."

The body remained a mystery. It did not move; it did not reveal any secrets at all. On a few occasions a body might try to leave after necromancy had been employed and for that reason Darsken always placed a few markings on the corpses to be safe. He did so again, before he and Pella sought out the Empress. He needn't have bothered. The body did not rise nor did it attempt to.

The body of Dretta March – born in flames when Swech needed a new form – remained unchanged save for the start of atrophy.

The Arkannen Mountain Range was close enough to see, but more than that, it was close enough to feel. The air moved between the mountains and swept across Canhoon. Anything left unanchored in the streets was taken by the breeze and carried over the side of the floating city and discarded down below.

The Sa'ba Taalor watched the objects falling from above with a wary eye. It wasn't that long ago that a dozen or more screaming people plummeted from above and crashed into the ground with violent force. Even those that hit the river failed to survive the fall. It was simply too high.

The weather was going bad, at least for the people of Canhoon. The clouds were coming hard and hiding away even the hint of the mountains. No one was quite certain how far they were from the risk of collision. No one was happy about that fact, either.

The city continued on, moving at the same pace as ever and freezing as the cold winds howled along the alleyways and between the buildings.

The City Guard moved in squads now, backed by the Imperial Army stuck in Canhoon. There were no days of rest any longer and no times when they did not move in force, alongside the Silent Army, who moved of their own accord and spoke to no one and nothing.

Those who wanted to riot did not. They were either too afraid, or too sick.

The cause of the illness had finally been found, thanks to the poisons found on Dretta March's body. Not all of the supplies for food in the city had been tainted, but most of them had. The levels were not enough to kill, but they were certainly enough to cripple.

The food provided for the Imperial Court came from Desh Krohan himself, who did not say where it came from but managed to supply enough to keep the palace running.

Along the far southern coasts the reports kept coming in of the black ships of the Sa'ba Taalor. They were brutal and efficient, but they were not immortal. The Brellar gave as good as they got, and sank several of the larger vessels using the speed and agility of their smaller ships and boats.

They took advantage of the tactics of the Fellein, and started using arrows lit with pitch to add to the damage to the black ships. They did not have to hit the enemy. They only had to burn their ships out from under them.

It was not a victory so much as it was a standstill. The Sa'ba Taalor were not taking new ground, but they were still overtaking the Brellar a few boats at a time. Every battle won came at a heavy price and the Sa'ba Taalor had a few tricks of their own. When the Brellar came close enough to fire arrows, their enemy returned the favor, and if the Brellar came too close, the arrows were replaced with grappling hooks that tied the smaller boats down while the Sa'ba Taalor boarded. The Sa'ba Taalor were as ruthless as the Brellar.

As bad as that situation was, the black ships running up the Parmahar River toward Goltha were worse. They seemed determined to kill every person they met, without exception.

Looks were deceptive. Many of the people they encountered chose to offer themselves to a new god. Those who were willing to learn the ways of Wheklam were spared and offered new chances they would have never seen otherwise.

To the west the remains of Lored's army paused and licked their wounds. Guards were set and the remaining Sa'ba Taalor in the area took stock of their situation.

It was Blane and Praxus who built the raging fire and called for enemies of the Sa'ba Taalor. The mounts provided, having left several of their enemies alive.

Once the fire raged high enough to melt metal and the coals were a brilliant yellowish white, the bodies of the living enemies were offered to Ordna. They screamed, they burned, and in their dying they made themselves useful to the Bronze God.

There was no need for questions. Everyone already knew what was needed. The King in Bronze was dead and his replacement had to be chosen. Someone needed to lead the army of Ordna. The faithful would follow whomsoever was chosen, of course, but that decision had to be made by the god they all worshipped.

There was a glorious moment when the sparks and flames rose three times higher and flared until the nighttime sky looked almost as bright as daylight. The flames twisted around themselves and the embers and sparks from the great pyre roared and seethed until the visage of great Ordna was there for all to see. They did not prostrate themselves before their god but instead cheered and roared his name.

Great Ordna looked upon his followers and nodded. A moment later Pre'ru, the mount of Lored, let out a great roar and was transformed.

After a lifetime of service Pre'ru had been granted a second life as a mount. More time to serve and slay in the name of the gods.

Now, a third life was provided. No one asked why the mount was given the opportunity. The answer was simple: Ordna wanted it. Ordna was their god and spoke to them all with the gesture. What most already knew was that Pre'ru had often offered wisdom to Lored. That did not mean that Lored was weak or unprepared, only that Pre'ru had remained useful long past the time when most would have been dead.

Pre'ru stood and stretched her body. She was revitalized, reborn and made young again.

Under most occasions a Sa'ba Taalor crafted their own weapons and armor. That was still true, but the armor of the new king had been discarded when he moved on to a new life. Now Ordna found and replaced what had been lost, merely to expedite their journey.

Pre'ru had been born a male the first time and had served as a mount with male genitalia. Now Pre'ru was female. The king did not question this. Pre'ru was on a third life and was truly blessed by Ordna. Whatever the god's reasons they were sufficient in the king's mind.

"Gather yourselves," Pre'ru roared, even as she dressed in her clothes and gathered her weapons. "We have enemies to find, to kill, and to offer to Ordna!"

The king's followers roared their approval and one by one knelt to offer their fealty. The gesture was not necessary. No one ever defied the gods and those few who did were punished as befitted an unbeliever.

Still, King Pre'ru, Chosen of the Forge of Ordna and King in Bronze, accepted the gesture. It gave her time to plan her methods of approach. They had a long way to go and very little time to spare.

"We walk and we ride! There will be no rivers for our enemies to use against us. Keep your shields ready! Prepare your bows and spears! We shall build our war machines when we have reached our destination. Until then we are the machines of Ordna! Let our enemies tremble!"

Within the hour they were in motion, a great tide of soldiers led by a king freshly chosen by a god who had granted all of them the chance to see a godly vision.

They were renewed and they were ready.

The storm raged on. In Canhoon it was nearly a blizzard, but lower down, closer to the ground, the frozen water melted and spilled across the grounds as a heavy rain.

The storm was not really planned, but it was a blessing to the sorcerers in the City of Wonders. They had waited for a chance to strike against the Sa'ba Taalor and the storm allowed for cover and also made the task easier. Bending nature takes more energy than merely using what nature provides.

There were surprisingly few villages in the area closer to the Arkannen Mountains. The weather was often vicious and the people on the other side of the breach in the mountains sometimes forgot that the mountain range did not actually lead to another nation. There were raids constantly, and after a time only the truly desperate remained.

Those few were killed by the Sa'ba Taalor as they ran through the mountains. Tusk and Tarag Paedori alike killed or converted, and their followers did the same. Then they rode on through the breach, moving as quickly as they could to position themselves at their final destination.

The Sooth had told the sorcerers when best to strike. Unfortunately, as sometimes happened, the Sooth lied. The great rain of lightning that cut the ground beneath the City of Wonders, that boiled the river and shattered stone, did not harm the great armies of the Sa'ba Taalor, which had already passed the area days before.

Still, if the armies had been there, it would have been an incredible victory for the Fellein.

Cullen sat on her bed and read the books she had been offered by the wizard. They were tales of the sorcerers of old and they included tales of the woman who had become part of the Mother-Vine and now, apparently, was sitting inside of her.

She used to know the woman's name but it no longer seemed important.

"Her name is Moale Deneshi." Deltrea spoke with an edge of irritation.

"Why are you upset, Deltrea?"

Her dead friend moved closer, casting no shadow and still seeming more alive than Cullen felt currently. "Because you are reading books when you should be talking to me."

Cullen placed her finger in the book to mark the passage she was reading and then set it in her lap. "What are we going to discuss that we have not spoken of a thousand times before? I've heard all I ever needed to about your love life. I've relived every damned moment of the burning of Trecharch every time I close my eyes."

She sighed.

"What else is there for us to speak of, Deltrea?"

"The time when what's in you wants out."

"What would you know of that? What could you know about that?"

"I don't think it will be a good thing is all." Deltrea sat on the bed with her. There was no sense of weight at all, but the covers shifted a touch. Ghosts were peculiar things, indeed.

"Well, what should I do about it? I can't very well shit it out. I've tried."

"Get the sorcerer to help you. That's what. If he can get it removed from you, I think you'll be a great deal happier is all."

"I'll think about it."

"Think hard, Cullen! If it stays in you, it might well kill you!"

"I don't think it can." Cullen frowned as she said it. Honestly, she had no notion at all what the thing was capable of. She only knew it wasn't comfortable to carry all the time. To make that point even clearer, it shifted inside her and her guts moved to accommodate it.

"It can. I can feel it."

"Well, perhaps I'll ask Desh Krohan about it." Another twist of whatever was inside of her and she bit off a groan.

"He's been rather busy lately." Deltrea's voice cut through the discomfort.

"Yes, Deltrea, he has. He said we can go where we please

and a lot of that time I've spent with him so he can get what he needs to out of the thing inside of me, but that doesn't mean he's got time to spend on me. There's a war going on, and there's disease and famine and cold weather and a mountain range coming at us and I think he's got good reasons for being busy!" She was only aware that she'd been yelling when she came to the end of her rant, winded and red faced.

Deltrea clapped her hands, but they made no sound when they hit each other. "Look at that. You *do* have feelings left in you. I was beginning to doubt."

"Why are you here again?"

"No idea, Cullen." Deltrea crossed her legs and then rested one elbow on her thigh, and her head on her palm. "I expect it has something to do with you."

Cullen did not respond, but instead stood from the bed and walked toward the door. Her guards were outside and nodded when she stepped out. The company of anyone living sounded better than another moment alone with Deltrea. Mostly because she suspected Deltrea was right on all fronts.

Something was happening inside her and she didn't much like her chances of survival. The ghost of her associate was haunting her for a reason. The sorcerer was watching over her but seemed to be holding back a few secrets.

Cullen liked her situation less all the time. There was nothing to be done about that. But she'd have to see what she could do to possibly change that.

The snow came down heavily, obscuring everything. Even if the snow had not been a problem the clouds would have managed just fine.

Inches fell in the daylight and more as the night took over. Those stuck out in the cold huddled together and cursed their luck. Those inside thanked the gods or cursed their luck just the same.

The City Guard did their best, moving and keeping properly covered up, stopping where they could to drink something warm. The Imperials were in the same situation and did the same thing.

The Silent Army stopped moving. After a day of constantly patrolling, never resting, they simply stopped all at once, and let the snow and ice accumulate on them as if they had never been more than statues in the gardens of the city.

In most of Canhoon the night and the storm forced an unsettling sort of silence.

Not everywhere, of course. No city of any size ever truly sleeps. At best there is a quiet time, but never true rest.

The cogs continued to move in their silent machinery. The people who had to be alert were.

Deep in the depths of the palace Darsken Murdro looked at Jost and shook his head. She was never going to speak and, despite his best efforts, her mind was locked to him. To that end she remained chained to her wooden table, though he knew the places where she had been resting her flesh against the wood for days on end must surely be an agony by now, the flesh raw from constant contact, made worse with every move she made.

"If you would only speak I could give you a better place to be than this." He spoke apologetically and he meant it. Torture was not something he enjoyed. He became an Inquisitor because the truth was a powerful thing and mysteries were meant to be solved.

The girl did not acknowledge him.

Three minutes later she was alone again in the locked room. Two minutes after that, Glo'Hosht entered her cell and moved to her table. The bindings on her were simple enough: a matter of unfastening a few hooks that were impossible for even the most nimble fingers on a restrained hand to reach.

Jost did not smile when she saw her king. Instead she closed her eyes for a moment and then sighed with relief.

His hands were quick. The fastenings holding her wrists were removed in moments.

Her ankles and thighs were released shortly after that.

The King in Mercury stepped back and kept an eye on the door as Jost tried to stand and fell to the ground. No words were spoken and none were needed. She would rise on her own and she would live, or she would stay on the ground and be left to her own devices.

Life is pain. Life is struggle. If she could not manage to walk she could not be saved. It was exactly that simple. That the Daxar Taalor would send Glo'Hosht to save her was a sign of their love and devotion to her, but if she could not stand, could not walk and could not fight, she was too weak to be a member of the Sa'ba Taalor and would be remembered for what she had accomplished even as she was left to die.

Jost stood, though it took a few minutes. As she had been strapped in place for days on end, she took the time to wash herself of the waste she had been made to lie in. The stench of her alone would alert anyone passing by otherwise.

They had taken her clothes and her weapons for whatever reasons they saw fit. She did not care. Clothes and weapons could be replaced.

While Glo'Hosht waited, Jost stretched and moved her body until blood flowed once again in muscles that had been immobile save for when she could find the time to flex them. She was a follower of Paedle and staying motionless for hours or days was not unheard of; had she not been so, she would likely have been incapable of moving at all.

There were no clothes to distract her and so, when she felt she was ready, Glo'Hosht opened the door and moved out of her way.

No words were spoken nor were any needed. Glo'Hosht moved and Jost followed. She saw her king flit from shadow to shadow, barely capable of clearly seeing where he was, though she tracked him with her eyes. She did her best to follow his lead, grateful for the long corridors and the darkness of the night. There were a few torches, places where oil burned in small braziers, but mostly there was the night and the concealment it offered.

Still, there are always exceptions. Two guards moved right past the King in Mercury and stopped only when they saw her standing against the wall.

Her muscles screamed in silent agony as she stepped forward and drove her palm into the first guard's throat. He gagged but could not speak as he fell to the ground, red faced and bug eyed.

Her hands came together and met on the second one's jaw, shattering bone. He was still capable of screaming, so she broke his neck even as he inhaled.

His clothes meant nothing to her, but she took a cloak, a short sword and boots. It was cold outside. She had heard her guards complaining earlier.

The boots did not fit and were too hard for her use. The second cloak was hastily torn in two and wrapped around her feet and then they moved on again.

Muscles that had not moved for far too long continued to protest, but as blood flow returned to them she felt the relief. The areas where she had been restrained were still sore. The flesh felt bruised and thin. She did not take the time to worry about it. She would heal or she would not as the gods saw fit.

Glo'Hosht touched a wall and part of it moved. He gestured her through and they went on their way. Swech had spoken of hidden places within the palace. She must have shown them to the king. That was a fine thing.

It seemed hours, but Jost knew it was less. When the king opened the last of several hidden doors the frigid air slammed into Jost like a gust from the Blasted Lands, cold and fierce with small debris slapping against her flesh.

It did not matter.

They were free of the palace. Glo'Hosht moved along side her and whispered into her ear. "Do not go to Swech's home. She was discovered and she is dead. Go to where Freth waits. Be careful. We need him where he is for now."

The order given, Glo'Hosht moved on, disappearing into the storm.

Jost allowed herself one moment to mourn her friend and then moved on. There would be time for mourning when her enemies lay dead.

Brolley and Lanaie spent a great deal of time together, it was true, but they always did so in the company of guards, per his sister's orders. Lanaie was not the issue. Though she was a guest in the palace she was not watched as closely as he was. She was not the little brother to the Empress. It was that simple. Still, when Lanaie went anywhere, he escorted her and thus ensured she would have protection.

The princess held his hand, both securely wrapped in their heavy cloaks. Despite the fabric Lanaie's hand was as cold as ice. That was to be expected: her land was always warm and this cold was months away from where it should have been. The winter was done and the summer was coming yet here they were walking through a deep field of snow.

"You could stay at the palace, you know," Brolley reminded her. "You are a guest of the Empress."

"Yes, and I have several times and I will again, but not today. Unlike in Tyrne, my father had properties and I want to make sure they are properly looked after."

"You're just tired of me," his voice was teasing.

"That could never happen, Brolley. Not even if this winter lasted a thousand years." She looked at him with her deep brown eyes and his body reacted as it did each time he saw her. She was a beautiful woman, and despite all that she had seen she remained an innocent. He would give anything to make sure that her heart was never broken again. He'd even gone so far as to make sacrifices to Plith and Woegaia. He wasn't really sure which was a goddess of love, so he paid his tithings to both, just to be safe. Plith was a beautiful woman. He thought she was a goddess of fertility. Woegaia was half male and half female, with large breasts and an equally large penis. He thought the god was meant to represent the marriage of body and spirit. He still wasn't sure. In any event, the churches got their offerings and he kept praying for everything to turn out the right way.

"What are you thinking, my love?"

"That I look forward to us being together one day. Man and wife."

"I want that too, but now is not the time to bother your sister."

It was a simple enough equation: Brolley and Lanaie could adore each other as much as they pleased, but until Nachia gave her blessings nothing could become official. Lanaie was right, of course. It was hardly the time to bother Nachia with his desire to marry a queen who had no nation, but it was most decidedly his desire to do so.

They had discussed the matter at length. At the very least they would wait until the city settled itself somewhere. Much as he would have dearly loved to consummate their relationship, Lanaie was not inclined to part with her chastity.

They had managed a few moments of passion when the guards were not around, but only a few. She had never offered herself, but she used her hands and her clothed form to offer him release on several occasions. It was enough for now. It had to be. He would not betray her trust, though he was tempted to find a good brothel.

Some things are worth waiting for.

Too soon they were at her door and she reached out with her cold hand and touched his face, memorizing his features until she could see him again. Her face, so perfect, her eyes so wide and innocent. He leaned in and kissed her once, briefly, knowing it was against the rules. Just the same she kissed back.

Then she was slipping into her house and he waited until he heard the doors locked and secured.

The night was an endless raging snowstorm, but he did not feel the chill at all.

They would be married. It was only a matter of time.

The guards were wise enough to say nothing now and he knew they would say nothing later. Money can buy discretion. He'd learned that much from his family, if nothing else.

Inside the warmth of her home, Lanaie removed her cloak and left on the minimal clothes she could tolerate and moved into the main hall where a fire roared and the temperature was enough to make her sweat.

The fire was not normally so high, but metal cannot be

forged without heat.

Weapons cannot be shaped without heat.

King Glo'Hosht looked to her and nodded his head. She made the proper bow before her king and looked around at the others gathered with her. This was the first time that all of Paedle's followers had been in one room at the same time. It was a risk, but one the king found necessary.

"We are here to rejoice." Glo'Hosht's voice remained soft as it virtually always did. "We are here to welcome back our lost warrior."

Lanaie's eyes immediately moved to Jost, who crouched by the roaring blaze and pulled hot metal from it. The metal should have burned her, crippled her, and possibly killed her. Paedle protected the faithful as always and it was good.

Already the girl had been working on replacing her blades. She worked deftly now, her hands moving at a stunning pace, shaping the raw metal into three more blades before she tapped them against the hearthstones and used a small hammer to finish the shaping.

They would need to be sharpened, of course, but there were supplies for that very purpose.

"There is more to do this night. The mountains are approaching and we must prepare."

Lanaie nodded and spoke in the tongue of the gods. "All that was lost shall be restored, and the Great Tide will sweep the world."

"Why, exactly, are our people at war?"

Tega looked to Drask as she asked the question, and so he answered her.

"The gods demand it."

She shook her head. "No. That's not enough. Why do the

gods demand it? What purpose does the war serve them?"

Nolan March gave no indication that he cared, but Drask was not fooled. The younger man was listening at least. He could sense it. How much he understood was a different situation. Nolan had been dead when they took their fall. That he was moving at all was an indication of the power they'd all absorbed. Drask frowned. He thought Nolan had been dead. His memories were slipping away. Not all of them, just some of the recent ones. He would examine that notion soon. For now there were questions to answer.

"You must understand that the gods all tell their tales, and each tale is as different as if seen by different people."

"What do you mean?"

"What I saw when we fell into the light was not what you saw. Not what Nolan saw. I watched you climb the rope into the depths of the Mounds. You did not watch me. Each of us has our own memories and our own way of seeing. It is like that for the gods.

"I have spoken often with the Daxar Taalor. Each has given different reasons for the way we have been raised by them and for why they fight wars the way they do." He shrugged and looked up at the city, not so very distant any more. The area they rode through was burnt and blackened and stank of dead fish. The river here was littered with dead things. Mostly from the great strikes of lightning they had seen before.

Tega had explained that it was sorcery. That was enough for Drask.

"The stories all have some balances. Some things that we can guess are as true as they can be. The Daxar Taalor tell us that they were born in the Cataclysm. They were born from the bodies of the gods of Korwa.

"When Korwa lived it was the greatest city ever known, and

the greatest kingdom the world had seen. The people there had peace. Their influence spread across all of the land, but in the end that is what ruined them. They grew comfortable. They did not fight as they once had because they did not feel they needed to fight any longer. There were papers that promised peace. There were marriages that guaranteed the same. It was a time when even the weather was a slave to the rulers of Korwa.

"Until the time when others grew jealous. The Wellish had their masters. They wanted Korwa for themselves. There were several tribes of younger people who wanted Korwa and all she offered.

"It is said by all the gods that the Emperor of Korwa died, and his sister took over as the ruler of the land. And when she did, the younger kingdoms and the Wellish Overlords all demanded the same thing: that she choose a husband from among them to rule by her side and end the burning desires that had started so many difficulties in the distance.

"Even the gods do not know exactly what she said. All they know is that before a year had passed the wars had started in earnest. The smaller countries fought among themselves and soon joined forces under one king. The Wellish chose their greatest champion and with his armies leading the way they sought to take Korwa.

"The old kingdoms, the new kingdoms, none of them mattered in comparison but they all wanted the same."

Drask looked from one to the other of his companions. "They wanted the Empress. She refused. She would not be forced to serve as a puppet ruler. Her people had sworn fealty and she would not bow before others. Who could blame her? She did what she thought best. She called the armies of Korwa together to defend her."

Drask sighed. "The stories grow different here. Each of the Daxar Taalor remembers the Cataclysm differently. Some say it was the gods that ended the war. Others say that sorcerers grew too strong and killed the city and the gods with them. Still others say that the Empress of Korwa chose to kill her people and herself before accepting defeat. It doesn't matter. It is enough to know that Korwa burned and so did all of the armies that had gathered around the greatest city that ever was.

"In the end there were a few survivors and they were raised up, they were healed, so long as they promised one thing. They had to promise to serve the Daxar Taalor, who were all that remained of the old gods of Korwa. They were not the gods of the past. They were new gods, formed when the Cataclysm shattered the skies and the seas and the very land. You must understand this: everything was ruined. Everything was destroyed. All that was left of great Korwa was the Blasted Lands."

Drask shrugged.

"The rest you know. We were raised from the wounded and the dying. We were told to survive and to grow strong. Each of the gods opened their hearts to us and trained us in how to be stronger.

"Each of the gods remembered the arts of war differently and together they vowed that they would train the Sa'ba Taalor to always remember the ways of war. They made us to be stronger than Korwa, stronger than our enemies as well.

"Once, a long time ago, hundreds of years ago, the Wellish Overlords tried to claim Fellein as their own. It was the Sa'ba Taalor who struck them down. We did not claim that victory, but we crushed great portions of their armies even as they marched on Canhoon.

"Your sorcerers did the rest.

"Do you know why we let that happen?"

Tega and Andover both shook their heads.

"Because Fellein had to grow strong, and then had to grow as large as any empire that had ever been. They had to rise and spread across the whole of the land.

"They had to mirror Korwa's might before the Daxar Taalor shattered the Empire of Fellein. They had to learn a lesson.

"Your Empire is soft. Your Empire is weak. You have seen this for yourself. The Sa'ba Taalor walk across the land and crush all who come before them, just as your ancestors once stormed across Korwa and sought to destroy her.

"This time is different. The Sa'ba Taalor have been given their orders by the gods themselves. They have been forged in the hearts of the Daxar Taalor. You, Andover Lashk, have been remade in their image in a very short time."

Andover shook his head. "No. It has taken longer than you think."

"It has taken most of a lifetime, but that time has been made shorter that you might serve your purpose."

"What purpose?"

"You already know that. You are to serve as the champion of the Sa'ba Taalor, should Fellein demand singular combat."

"Why me?" Andover shook his head. In the past when he had asked that sort of question it was because he wanted to know why he had suffered. Now he asked because he could not understand why he was chosen for so great an honor.

"On this the gods agree again. It was one of the people of Korwa who offered the greatest betrayal to the Empress. It was a person she believed would be faithful simply because he was one of her own."

Drask stared into Andover's eyes. Andover looked back. "It

was a humble servant who brought the ruination of Korwa.
How, I do not know. You, Andover Iron Hands, are that
servant now. That is what the Daxar Taalor ask. That is what
you have agreed to."

"But I thought the gods chose Merros Dulver. Isn't that
why you looked for him?"

Drask held his gaze. "I do not know why the gods sought
Merros Dulver. I only know that they are not yet done
with him."

NINE

There were many wonders N'Heelis had seen in the course of his life. He had walked the Boratha-Lo'ar more times than any living being, his body painted by the colors of the crystalline bridge. He had stood in the very heart of Wrommish and been bathed in the furnace of liquid gold. He had taught a dozen kings how to fight without weapons and killed some of those very same kings in combat.

Now this. Standing at the very top of the mountain on the southern side of the river he watched on as the vast underside of enchanted Canhoon moved toward him with deceptive speed and he admired the network of stone and root as it defied all laws of nature and came closer to him, fully aware that if it suddenly stopped its flight he would be dead in an instant. That was part of the thrill.

Stastha, Tuskandru's right hand, waited calmly, her longbow notched and ready. She was not alone.

There were hundreds of archers along the ramparts built by Stastha and her group. They were secure, but they were hardly works of art. Wood, stone, whatever could be used was employed, and the followers of Ordna among them made

certain the platforms and walkways were sound. Some of
the structures were little more than added support on stone
outcroppings. Others were feats of construction that would
have been impossible for N'Heelis himself.

He readied his own bow and nodded to himself.

Stastha said, "We are ready when you are, King N'Heelis."

"Now. Make the arrows count."

She repeated the order and several others followed her
lead. Under many circumstances there would have been
horns to call the order, but not now. This was a mission of
silence. He'd have preferred it be left to Glo'Hosht, but that
was not possible. The King in Mercury was already above
them in Canhoon.

Instead of worrying about such things, N'Heelis drew
his bow, took a long, deep breath, and then released as he
exhaled. The silk streamer at the end of the arrow unwound,
dancing frantically as the arrow sought the right spot.

It was not skill. It was luck. N'Heelis knew the difference.
The arrow sank deep into a thick root, the barbs finding
purchase. Other archers fired as well and for each arrow that
stuck a dozen or more bounced back.

N'Heelis moved, grabbing the silk, pulling to test it and then
trusting to the gods to see him to his destination.

The followers of Wrommish trained first and foremost in
unarmed combat. That did not mean they could not carry
weapons, merely that they either chose not to, or that they
chose carefully.

He was finished with the bow. It stayed behind as he scaled
his way to the moving city above. Several others joined him.
More than a few of them fell as the arrows that held them
came loose from the soil and roots. Most screamed as they fell.
That was impossible to prevent. Some actually fell along the

cliffside. He imagined a few might even survive the falls, but all of his attention was on the task ahead of him.

There were secrets that had been learned by Glo'Hosht and others. They had looked carefully at the city's maps and studied the paths of the rivers that had once watered the whole of Canhoon. What they found was nothing short of a miracle, for which N'Heelis thanked the gods.

The sewers under the city were still there. They were doubtless slicked with water, sewage and ice, but there were tunnels, and those tunnels were the very best possible chance for them to gain entry to Canhoon.

Many might well not achieve their goal. They had no way of knowing where the tunnels went, or if they would hold the secret to breaching the city. They only knew the openings in the base of the city were there and that this was their best chance to gain access to the deep underbelly of Canhoon. N'Heelis had done what he could to ensure success. None wore heavy leather cloaks. There was little armor. Instead there was leather clothing and good, short weapons. More than a few of his followers made claws for their close combat, weapons that would hook an opponent's weapons and tangle them, leaving the bearers unarmed for a moment or more. Those same metal tines were well suited for finding purchase in the underside of the vast city. Some used fingers, some used claws; all counted on their years of climbing different mountains to help them through a truly terrifying climb.

Fingers grasped at stone, at mud, at clusters of broken root and frozen rock. The Sa'ba Taalor began their climb, aiming for the dark tunnels carved through the very ground, that led to the depths of the city above them. The trick was not to fall in the process.

N'Heelis caught the vine his arrow was now stuck in and

worried his fingers into the edges of the thick wood.

He looked down once and quickly looked back. The ground was so very far distant. He held even tighter when the shrill scream came: as they had feared might happen, the mountain and the city were on the same path. The only saving grace was that the edge of the mountain was just that, an edge. It would break if they were lucky. If they were not, the base of the city would break and everything they were attempting would end in death. Clouds had hidden the base of the city for days, leaving everyone on the mountain guessing if they would be capable of actually scaling to the city above.

As he had all his life, N'Heelis trusted in the gods. Just the same he clung hard to the heavy root and braced himself for impact.

Inches. Mere inches of stone collided. He heard the grinding roar of stone on stone but barely even felt the impact.

The Daxar Taalor were kind.

N'Heelis moved carefully, crawling with his entire body, hanging suspended in the heavy cloud cover and the bitterly cold mists. There was no time to think of others or their celebrations. There was only the one goal for now.

He found the edge of the tunnel and started in, not worried about what might be in there beyond ice and frozen waste.

The Empress and her closest advisors cheered their luck and drank a sweet wine that was, traditionally, saved only for victories. As far as Nachia was concerned surviving what might have ended her city and her life qualified.

"That was the hope, really." Desh smiled and spoke as if he might be discussing the migration of distant birds. "I expected the city would be just fine."

Merros snorted. "Which is why you've been dancing from

one foot to the other, like a man who needs to void his bladder."

The First Advisor tried to hold a menacing glare but failed. Like Nachia, he was simply too happy to be alive.

They came from lower on the mountain, moving in leaps and bounds, with all of the skill the gods had given them and all the strength of their second bodies. The mounts took the same chances as the Sa'ba Taalor they lived with, but in their case the challenges were different. They weighed much more, but they had claws capable of digging into the earth. They were much larger and had to find tunnels that the Sa'ba Taalor did not already occupy, but there were tunnels on the sides of the city's belly that were far away from where their companions climbed.

As the Sa'ba Taalor before them had done, the mounts tried for the underside of the mountain and the tunnels that moved above them.

Saa'thaa chose to leap high and felt his claws strike deep into soft soil before catching a good grip. His hind legs scrambled and claws once again sought purchase. All of the training of two lives was needed to avoid falling, but Saa'thaa managed. The tunnel was filthy and stank of the Fellein. The cold waste crawled over his fur and into his armor, which, as fortune had it, he could not remove without assistance.

None of that mattered. All that was important was getting through the tunnel. After that all that was important was what the gods demanded. Whatever they required he would do to receive his promised reward.

There was no sickness in the air of the tunnel, but there was death. The Sa'ba Taalor had been poisoning people and he could smell the stench of the poisons used. The shells of logga nuts, the fine, black moss that grew on Paedle's side.

These were fine things. They were also deadly if prepared the right way. A lifetime ago, Saa'thaa had known all there was to know of poisons. Now he could smell them, he knew the recipes, but he lacked the skill to prepare the potions. Paws cannot work the same way as hands. Both have their advantages, just as the powerful jaws he used now could rend the hide of a Pra-Moresh with little effort, but could not so easily form words.

Stench aside, the tunnel was easy enough to travel through and behind him he could hear the sounds of others of his kind moving through the debris and frozen filth.

In time the tunnel forked. In one direction the waste continued. In the other the tunnel rose higher and the air smelled only of fresh water. Following the latter path Saa'thaa found a vast opening, mostly dry but with a supply of fresh water several inches deep. The cave was manmade, and supported by many stone columns that ran to a high ceiling. As vast as it was, the chamber was far below the city above. High above, more tunnels led toward the surface and, all around the edges at the height of two tall men, were tunnels like the one he looked from, which dropped into the clear waters.

Saa'thaa thought hard and was rewarded with the word: cistern. Here the waters of the rivers must have run. Now, emptied of most of their treasure, the vast area was probably not even a consideration.

He did more than consider. Saa'thaa dropped into the shallow waters, sniffed carefully and then drank deep. Others would come soon. There was plenty for all, but he was first and that gave him pleasure.

Not far away King N'Heelis scaled down the wall until he could reach the water and looked at Saa'thaa to see if the waters were clear. Saa'thaa nodded his affirmation and

N'Heelis also drank deep.

A second mount came from his tunnel and then others joined them, Sa'ba Taalor and mount alike.

There was no light in the cistern, but they did not need it. The Daxar Taalor had blessed them with eyes that saw in the darkness.

N'Heelis ran his hand through Saa'thaa's matted fur and did what most would never be brave enough to do: he hugged the mount's great neck. Saa'thaa in turn rumbled his approval and leaned into the King in Gold.

"Soon, Saa'thaa. I cannot thank you enough for your patience."

The king pointed to the corners of the vast room. There were doors there, great wooden affairs that had rotted over the centuries. They looked formidable but Saa'thaa could smell their decay and see the weaknesses in them even from a distance.

"Glo'Hosht says there are stairs beyond that lead into the heart of Old Canhoon." The king looked around. "We shall wait a little longer and hope a few more have made it."

Stragglers did indeed continue to find their way. He counted over a hundred mounts and saw ten times that number in Sa'ba Taalor.

"It is almost time, old friend." N'Heelis ran his hand over Saa'thaa's muzzle, moving dexterous fingers under the war mask that covered his face and scratching all the right spots. A thousand little ecstasies rippled his fur.

"Almost time," he rumbled.

Soon enough. He could wait a little longer.

It was an hour later when N'Heelis and a chosen few climbed from the depths, and into one last tunnel. This one led to the house of Queen Lanaie, or rather to the empty stables on the small estate.

Lanaie herself bowed formally to N'Heelis, who smiled and said, "It is good to see you, Freth."

Lanaie's dark eyes grew wide as she spotted Saa'thaa. The great mount was large by any standards. The expression on the woman's face betrayed Freth's surprise.

"Saa'thaa has what we need to continue. It is time."

"The fire is hot, my king. But we must move quickly. If anyone should see him..."

Saa'thaa made a small, rude noise. "You know the way, Freth?"

"Yes, of course."

N'Heelis smiled. "Then we do not need a torch or lantern to find the path. Without those, who would look past the wall around your home?"

"I have suitors." The words were mumbled.

"Wrommish chose that form for a reason, I'm sure. Just the same, let us take care of this."

They moved quickly through the thick snowfall. In moments all signs of their tracks had been erased.

Life is pain. Every part of her screamed in agony, the heat as vast as it had ever been. The pain was gone in seconds, but the memory of it lingered.

Leg muscles that had not moved in a very long time moved now and she fell forward, out of the raging fire and onto a stone floor that was almost as hot.

The fire no longer burned. Wrommish was kind.

Swech Tothis Durwrae climbed to her feet and looked around at faces familiar and some almost forgotten in the recent months.

She looked down at her flesh and saw the scars that had been a part of her for so very long, and the gray hue that had been with her for years. Her muscles trembled only a little as she adjusted to standing on her own legs again, rather than the borrowed legs of Dretta March.

Her ash-gray locks fell around her shoulders and her hand on her stomach felt the small kick of new life that rested inside her.

The Daxar Taalor were kind beyond words.

The great mount came for her and let out a low yowl of pleasure. She heard her name called in her mind and knew that Saa'thaa was there for her.

She did not consider that he was wet, or that his fur was cold. Those things did not matter. Swech grabbed the great mane and pushed her face into his war mask, smiling and sighing his name.

"Saa'thaa. I have missed you!"

N'Heelis came close next, placing a hand on her shoulder and smiling. "You could not be left to the dead, little Swech." He grinned as she turned and hugged him. "The gods would not permit it."

"How are you here, my king?"

"It is nearly time. The Great Tide commences within days. The final hours are upon us, Swech. Where else would I be?"

As he spoke N'Heelis opened the saddlebags on Saa'thaa. Most would never dare, but a king can dare much without fear of reprisal. Swech was grateful. His kindness gave her time to stretch her body and familiarize herself with limbs that felt foreign after so long. Leather pants, a vest, a simple dark shirt. All of these things she pulled on hastily. She recognized them, of course. She had been wearing them when she returned to Wrommish and the Boratha-Lo'ar. Her boots soon followed and then her weapons. She looked more closely at the gathering of faces around her, seeing some that she knew hid the other members of the Sa'ba Taalor who had offered themselves to the gods. She did not see Kallider and she did not question that. The gods seldom considered bringing anyone back.

She silently thanked the Daxar Taalor. She had served and died in the process and thought that was all there would be.

"I have saved an honor for you, little Swech." N'Heelis gestured for her to follow, a smile on his handsome face. She followed without thought.

"I have many questions. How long have I been gone? Where is the city now? Are we truly prepared to attack?"

"Soon." N'Heelis waved her questions away. "First, Swech, I give you an honor. Wrommish gives you an honor. You have served so well and done so much and now you must be shown how much you mean to us all."

Swech frowned, puzzled. To serve was everything. It was all she had ever needed. She had a mount; despite all odds she had survived her own death; the child of Merros Dulver was still inside of her. What more could she ask?

When they reached the roof of the house N'Heelis opened a window that was just tall enough to let him climb to the roof. Swech followed with ease. Despite her time as Dretta March her body had not changed at all, had not aged. Otherwise she would have been swollen with the baby.

N'Heelis took the small javelin that had rested inside a sheath on his leg and offered it to her. The piece was handsome enough but made of pure gold. She could scratch the surface with her nail.

"I am to wear this?" She smiled uncertainly. It was hardly an adornment.

"No, Swech. You are to cast it to the north." The mountain range was still surrounding them. Though clouds hid most of the vast stone peaks, Swech could see the looming shadows through the snow and cold.

"In what direction?"

N'Heelis smiled. "If I had not asked myself, I would not know." He pointed. "There."

Swech looked around and saw that most of the people who had seen her rise from the flames were now in the courtyard below.

Swech looked to the north and took careful aim. She knew she could not possibly reach the start of the vast range, but she tried just the same.

The golden missile soared far further than should have been possible. Moving until it was well past her ability to see.

"That is a trick?" She smiled, this time with delight.

"No, child. That is an honor. Wait for a moment."

N'Heelis put a familiar arm around her shoulders. She felt the calluses on his palms and was comforted.

After almost four minutes in the biting cold her patience was rewarded. The skies to the far north grew bright red, highlighting the mostly obscured peaks of all the mountains leading in that direction. There were many jagged mountaintops.

"What is that?"

"You have chosen the place of Wrommish's new home."

Only moments after the light colored the sky, she heard the low, deep roar of the earth moaning in pain. The land gave birth to a god in the far north. The air around her vibrated with the glory of that fact.

"N'Heelis, that was yours. That was your sacred task. One mountain for every king."

"Swech, you have done so much to honor Wrommish. This is the god's way of thanking you." He paused a moment. "Upon my chest I bear the mark of Wrommish. In comparison there is no finer honor. I am glad you were chosen for this."

For a while they stood in silence as the flames grew higher and the howl of angry winds blasted toward them. So strong were the winds that they cast the snow and clouds aside.

That was just as well. The clouds had already served their purpose and hidden the army that came to the City of Wonders.

Merros Dulver stared to the north and shook his head. He'd have spat, but the rules of decorum forbade doing that in front of the Empress. In an instant, the mood of celebration that had followed the successful pass through the mountains vanished.

"I suppose I'd hoped we were done with that."

Desh Krohan nodded. "In a perfect world we would be. At least this time no cities were destroyed. There's remarkably little up that way beyond the edge of the mountains." The wizard paused and squinted in thought. "By my guess that's at the very top of the Arkannen range. Or just east of it."

Nachia was looking at the maps spread across her vast dining table. There was food on the table but all of it had been relegated to the far corner. Right now she was more interested in information than food.

"So the mountains will direct the winds toward us?"

Desh frowned and looked at her finger as it slid along the range of mountains on the map.

"Sadly, yes that's likely." The First Advisor looked at his goblet of wine and frowned some more. "I suppose you opened this too soon, my dear."

"I'll take my victories where I can find them, Old Man."

Merros appreciated their banter. It helped him stay calm

after all that had happened. He wanted to mourn Dretta March properly. He wanted to burn away every memory of her, because they were surely lies. In any event, she was heavy on his mind and he wished she were not. Thinking of her hurt.

"On the bright side, we missed the worst of the mountains." He sighed and looked first at Nachia, and then at Desh. "Do you suppose they've come to the city while it was so close?"

Desh shrugged. "I'd say they've at least tried. I'd also say the eruption was more than conveniently timed. If the clouds from that volcano come our way it's going to get harsh here. I intend to see what I can do about dispelling the worst of that. If I were you, General, I'd make sure your men were ready. If the Sa'ba Taalor have managed to get people into the city I can't imagine they'll simply sit and wait."

Nachia shook her head and then, decorum be damned, the Empress spat on the floor. "Where would they hide? How could they gain access from beneath?"

Desh shook his head. "I said before the Sisters saw openings under the city. We've had no real chance to explore where they might go."

"No chance at all?" Nachia stared hard, her voice frosty. Desh stared back, not the least bit intimidated.

She turned a hard look on Merros. "We have had one victory so far. One. We have the greatest army in the world, Merros Dulver. Prove that to me."

"Most of the army is gathering now, Majesty. They are following the orders I have sent and traveling to Goltha. If we are right, and if that is where the city will settle, then we will be prepared."

"And if we are wrong? If your damned Sooth have a laugh at our expense again?" Her gaze skewered Desh instead and

Merros was relieved.

While the sorcerer thought of an answer Merros added, "Well then, we are going to have a spectacular view of fifty thousand men chasing after a runaway city."

"Don't make me laugh, Merros. I'm trying to maintain my indignant outrage."

Desh nodded. "Picture it. Thousands and thousands of soldiers jogging to keep up with us. They'll get winded rather quickly I imagine." He raised his glass in salute to the imaginary troops.

"Fifty thousand? I thought for certain we'd have more there by now."

"We do, Majesty. They are waiting already. There is a vast army of the Sa'ba Taalor coming from our direction with plans to get there before us. There are more of them coming from the south, moving upriver along the Parmahar River. The sorcerers have done an excellent job of informing us of their motions."

"Do they outnumber our troops?"

"Not at all. There are some still coming from the west, but we killed a good number of them. The ones from the south seem to have a number of captured people with them. It's hard to say for certain, but a lot of the population of the small towns is now moving with them. I think they intend to use them as shields."

"As shields?"

"Yes, it's been done in the past but not for many years. The notion is they would put these citizens of Fellein in front of their own troops to work as a living barrier between the soldiers and themselves."

"And that works?" Nachia stared at him as if he'd grown another eye.

"Well, not often, really. That's why it isn't done much

any more. I believe the god Kanheer declared it a sin some time back and as a result no generals were willing to use it any more."

"Kanheer?"

"One of the war gods," Desh provided. "Always seemed a rather odd thing for a war god to do, forbid a method of defense."

"It is rather cowardly."

"Well, yes, but every shield has a use doesn't it, Merros?"

"You haven't answered my last question." Nachia looked from one to the other again. "Where is there under the city for the Sa'ba Taalor to hide?"

Desh responded first. "My dear, I couldn't hope to tell you. There are over a thousand years' worth of history in this city. Buildings have risen and fallen."

"Do you suppose our escaped assassin is down there too?" Nachia was not at all pleased that they had lost their one captured gray-skin.

Merros answered, "Who can say, Nachia? This weather hides any number of sins."

Desh scratched at his neck. "There were those tunnels the Sisters found. They could lead to almost anywhere and many of them are large enough for a man to climb through."

"And nothing was done?"

"To be fair, Nachia, we are over eleven thousand feet off the ground. There aren't many who have a way to gain access."

"Just anything that could have waited at the tops of the mountains."

"I could hardly send troops over the sides on ropes, Majesty. On this one we have to trust the Silent Army to keep watch."

"Which I suppose they would if the Sa'ba Taalor climbed over the Mid Wall."

"Well, yes, but I don't suppose they'd be that nice about it."

"They are not nice, Merros. They are annoying and dangerous and sneakier than a band of thieves."

Merros nodded. He had no solutions to her dilemma.

"Are there tunnels under us, Desh? Can they be filled with water?"

"Well, I suppose they could, Nachia. But where would the water come from?"

"You're the First Advisor and you have sorcerers at your disposal. Can you not manage a waterfall of some sort?"

Desh stared at her long and hard, his jaw working. "If we were still surrounded by water I could redirect it, but I can't just summon water from nowhere. Well, I can, which is why you have drinking water, but I cannot produce that sort of quantity. Magic always has a price."

He paced a moment, his jaw still working furiously as he tried to find the right words.

"It's not that I like not being able to help, Nachia. I mean that, but I can't just make an ocean. There has to be an ocean first."

Nachia stared coldly at him.

"Snow."

"I beg pardon?"

"Snow. There are mountains of the stuff here. Can you and yours not use that to flood whatever is under us?"

"I suppose so. Can't you just have your cooks brew it up in large pots?"

"You are a very rude man, Desh."

"You are a very demanding ruler, Majesty."

Far to the north of Canhoon the volcano erupted. It was violent and impossible to miss. For hundreds of miles around the air shook and the light was enough to startle sleeping animals into flight. Wrommish ripped free of the earth and shattered the closest mountain in the process.

Great gouts of flame and smoke stroked the air and spread across the sky, claiming all that had been peaceful in the name of war.

Far to the west the people of Fellein who had managed to avoid being crushed by the Sa'ba Taalor trembled. They had seen too much of volcanoes and what followed their eruptions.

To the far east the people stared in wonder at the lights and puzzled over the sounds. Those in the southern regions had already dealt with the birth of a mountain but closer to this source the people had little notion of what was happening, only that it was vast and powerful.

Along the jagged line of the mountain range the snow and ice reflected the fire until the night was nearly day, and the people in Canhoon woke to the sounds that might well have meant the end of them all. For those who had survived Tyrne and Roathes the sounds were too familiar and a cold dread seized them and would not let go easily. The world, it seemed, was ending, no matter how far they tried to go to escape that fact.

For some of the refugees it signified an end. For others it signified a time to do things differently. There had been a few who gathered their weapons and attempted to change their world by force. They had grabbed those they thought the cause of their sorrows and they had beaten or killed them, until the Silent Army handled the affair. Many once again took up weapons, but this time they approached the barracks of the Imperial Army and offered their axes and swords to the Empress.

While some were drawn to war, others did their best to find

comfort in the temples of the gods. Some were not so easily comforted; the gods had offered little that they could see – and of those little could be said, save that the miracle of the Silent Army did not seem a blessing in their eyes – but they tried just the same. The Sa'ba Taalor had faith, but for the Fellein that commodity seemed very rare.

As the heat came and melted snow into water, the Silent Army moved. Some went about their courses, looking over the city and making certain that no one chose to fight against the laws of the Empress. Others chose a different route.

There were many catacombs in the City of Wonders. Some were lost to time, unknown to any living being, but the Silent Army was not quite living in the usual sense.

Whether guided by memories from the past or by the gods themselves, three hundred of the Silent Army moved down into the catacombs beneath the city. They did not try to move quietly. They marched, and their tread filled chamber after chamber with the sounds of their feet striking the ground.

By the time they reached the spot where most of the Sa'ba Taalor were waiting, the gray-skins and their mounts were ready. The vast cistern was filled with a few inches of water, but nothing more. In the darkness of the massive chamber the warriors gathered what weapons they had and the mounts waited on the sidelines, prepared to attack when they were allowed that privilege.

The Silent Army came from all four openings into the chamber, treading steadily and wielding their short swords and their shields. They marched down the long stone stairs to reach their enemies below.

The Sa'ba Taalor did not wait for an invitation. They attacked.

Born and bred for war, the Sa'ba Taalor were nightmares of bloodshed. The Fellein had learned that the hard way, losing hundreds for every individual member of the Sa'ba Taalor that fell. Soldiers and civilians, men and women and children: all were the enemy in the eyes of the Sa'ba Taalor. Whatever weapon was needed was used. Whatever advantage could be taken was seized. A thousand years or more the Daxar Taalor had prepared their soldiers for the Great Tide.

The Silent Army did not care.

The first of the Sa'ba Taalor to strike was a man named Marro. He had served with Tuskandru and was chosen by Stastha as one of the most able among the King in Onyx's forces.

He struck the first of the stone soldiers with a hammer he had forged himself in the fires of Durhallem. The blow he delivered was powerful and sent the Silent Soldier to its knees. The skin of the stone man cracked along the shoulder.

Marro did not have time to celebrate. The soldier swung its shield in a hard arc and knocked him back four feet even as it stood up and came forward. His hammer did not dent the shield when it struck, but instead skimmed along the slightly rounded surface.

The warrior was made of stone. Marro could see that. He could not deny what he saw with his own eyes and so he reversed the hammer, using the pick-like edge normally reserved for punching through hard armor to deal his next blow. The point drove into the shield and left a break in the soldier's defenses. The soldier drove forward again, bashing at Marro with the shield, knocking him backward. Marro was a powerful figure and grunted in surprise. The first time the stone man hit him he might have been taken off guard. The second time he was braced for the assault, but it did not matter. He was hurled backward several feet. The shield came again and Marro ducked around it, moving as quickly as his opponent. He pushed himself in against the stone man and grunted again as the soldier held its place. Just the same he brought his hammer around and struck the stone soldier a solid blow that staggered the heavy form.

The short sword of his enemy came down in a hard arc and sliced through Marro's neck, his chest and his guts.

Marro looked up at his enemy as he died, knowing that even in death he had served his gods faithfully and that he would be rewarded.

By the time Marro fell dead, the nameless soldier had moved on, sweeping his arms in separate directions. His shield arm drove back a man with a sword. His sword arm knocked aside a woman attempting to grapple him.

In ancient times, when the Silent Army had first awoken, their very visage had driven half of their enemies into retreat. Statues should not move, or strike, or kill.

The Sa'ba Taalor did not care. Statue or flesh, the enemies of their gods were their enemies as well and they would destroy them by any means necessary. The woman cast aside was not foolish. Her tactics were best used against flesh. She was strong and she knew it. She had once broken the jaw and hind leg of a Pra-Moresh with her body as her only weapon. She could not shatter stone, but she could use physics to her advantage. As the stone soldier took a step forward she drove the heel of her foot into the back of the knee supporting all of the demon's weight.

Then she rolled fast to get out of the way.

The knee moved forward and the stone monster lost balance and fell back.

By the time it had landed on the ground she had gathered Marro's great hammer and prepared herself. Her fellow Sa'ba Taalor, the one with the sword, took advantage of the situation as best he could and tried gutting the stone man. His blade was well made, but the stone was unyielding and the sound of the two clashing was monstrous.

The stone man brought around his shield and drove the edge into the swordsman's midriff, pushing him back and likely breaking a rib or two.

And while he was doing that, she drove the pointy end of the hammer into the stone soldier's face. The blow was perfect and shattered a part of that face, breaking it completely away from the head.

There was no blood beneath that hard surface, merely more stone. The stone soldier stood up and what remained of the face snarled silently at her.

She retreated quickly and called to the mounts, "To us! Defend!" It is not a sign of cowardice to acknowledge a need for help. On the contrary, it is a sign of foolishness to deny that fact.

The mounts were not made of stone, but they were powerful nonetheless.

The first of the mounts lasted two minutes in combat with the stone soldier. That is longer in a fight than most will ever realize. Two minutes of constant straining, biting and clawing managed little but to knock the stone man around and leave the mount winded and shaking. Adrenaline only lasts a short time and despite the armor worn effortlessly by the mount, the stone sword and shield delivered hellish blows. Bones were broken and meat was cut and slashed and bruised. Teeth cracked against stone flesh, and claws tore free from their housings.

For two full minutes the mount roared and fought and bled before dying. For two minutes the mount felt alive again in the purest sense.

Sometimes the gods are kind.

Axes did some harm. Swords a little less. Hammers worked nicely enough. The trouble was that all of those were in short supply. Most of the Sa'ba Taalor chosen for the climb had little or no weapons worth noting save their hand-to-hand skills. Those skills were impressive in all cases, but one can only punch a stone so many times. Stones may break, but few will shatter before flesh is pulped or bones crushed to dust.

A few hundred of the Sa'ba Taalor ran. Most did not. Those who fled did so because their gods demanded it. It is possible that the Daxar Taalor spoke to many, but who can say what is in the hearts of the gods?

Those who stayed behind were killed. There were no prisoners taken this time. The Silent Army did not give second warnings.

The waters of the cistern were bloody and littered with corpses.

Nine of the Silent Army were shattered and useless by the time the fight was over. That was nine more than had ever been defeated before.

The stone soldiers were stronger than any human being. They worked fast and did what they had to do. Then they left their grisly tasks behind and headed for the surface.

There was one more challenge and they took care of that as well before once more going about their appointed tasks.

At first light a few of the people screamed. More of them cheered. War, it is said, is a harsh business, a bloody business that requires bloodthirsty souls.

What is often not said is that it is not only soldiers who can acquire a hatred of the enemy and a desire to see them suffer. Let any soul endure enough and the darkness must surely touch it.

By the time Nachia Krous left the palace with her brother and several others, the murmur of cheers and sobs alike had become nearly a roar of approval and as she stepped into the front courtyard of the palace the cacophony was nearly deafening.

Several citizens started chanting her name and more followed quickly, though she still had no idea why.

From her left Desh Krohan emerged and joined the progression, followed quickly by Merros Dulver who was still settling his cape over his shoulders.

The first sight to fill her eyes as she looked to the cobbled street was a dozen or more of the Silent Army. It took her a moment to puzzle out that the different colors on them were splashes and droplets of old and drying blood.

In the center of a circle formed by the stone warriors was a tribute the likes of which she had never expected.

At the base of a hastily formed stack of grisly trophies was a layer of heads from beasts she could barely fathom. She had seen them before, of course, but never without their war masks. The mounts were dead, obviously, but each had disfigurements she could barely fathom.

Desh Krohan spoke softly. "I don't believe what I'm seeing."

Merros Dulver nearly sighed the words, "It hardly seems possible."

Above the heads of the slaughtered mounts a towering stack of fresh heads rested. It only took a moment to recognize that they belonged to the Sa'ba Taalor.

Nachia looked at the pile of heads stacked higher than she stood and nodded as she slowly circled around it.

She raised her hands into the air and yelled, "Death to the Sa'ba Taalor!" as loudly as she could.

The response was immediate: the call was picked up by the

crowd, who carried on the chant even as Nachia made a slow, steady retreat back into her palace, imagining a thousand arrows coming at her from all directions.

Despite that dread, a smile kept trying to break on her face.

Cullen heard the noises down below, looked out into the courtyard and felt a thrill run through her. She could not decide if it was joy at the death of her enemies or joy that something, anything at all, was capable of stopping them.

The gray-skins had seemed unstoppable in Trecharch.

"You killed a few of them, you know. I don't think that I did, but your arrows struck true."

"I ran away just the same. Deltrea. I watched everything we loved die."

"Not everything I loved. That's why I'm here you know. Because I love you. You are my sister and my friend."

"And all I ever do is yell at you for talking too much."

Deltrea laughed. "You have always yelled at everyone for talking too much. I have never known anyone so happy to be alone in my entire life."

"I was never alone." Cullen shrugged her shoulders and looked away from the dead below. "I always had the trees and the wind and my thoughts."

"I always tried not to think that hard. Whenever I did I just got sad or angry."

Cullen smiled at that one.

"It's almost time, you know."

"Time for what?"

"I do not know. I only know that the time is almost here."

"Are you scared, Cullen?"

"I don't know what I am anymore." She sighed and looked out the window again, but this time at the skies, not at the ground and its dark rewards. "I only know that all I was is gone with Trecharch and all that is left wants everything to change."

"Well, I am fine with things the way they are. I like having time to do nothing."

Cullen shook her head. "Not me. I grow restless."

Deltrea had no answer to that.

TEN

To the east, the fires of Wrommish brightened an already glorious morning.

Tuskandru tore a chunk from a hard bread made of logga nut and grunted as he chewed it. The air was cold and he liked that too. Better to fight in the cold. War was hot work.

"You are calm." The King in Iron was sitting next to him and rubbing oil along the blade of his massive sword.

"What is there to be excited about, Paedori?" Tusk offered the other king a lump of bread and got a nod of thanks. The sword settled against a rock as the man ate.

"You have been angry of late."

"No. I have been impatient."

Tusk pointed with his chin to the lake in the distance. "There is our target. There is a city the size of which I did not think possible. You will come from one side. I will come from another and two more kings bring their armies to bear on this place."

Tarag Paedori nodded.

Tusk continued. "To the north Wrommish offers us new light and the blessings of a god. That is a good sign, I think.

But mostly, we are here. We are alive, and we have come to offer our gods countless sacrifices." He patted the heavy axe at his side. "I think this will be a glorious day."

The Fellein had their sorcerers who told them secrets. The Sa'ba Taalor had their gods who did the same. The deaths of so many of their brethren were not hidden from the kings. They heard of the violence and the Silent Army's brutality.

There was no mourning to be done. They had lived good lives and died for their gods. What else was there?

Tusk looked at the massive lake. It was more water than he had ever seen at one time before. He had never traveled to Wheklam's heart, had never tried to learn the ways of the water. He focused on Durhallem, instead. Very likely that was why he was a king.

The city itself was a crescent moon on the distant side of the vast lake. There were smaller cities and towns dotted here and there, but Goltha rested on the far side and waited like a treasure. The Fellein had nearly danced when gifted with gold. It was a metal, shiny enough and nice to look at, but soft and only good for hobbies. You could not make a good axe from gold, though he had been told it could kill if a fool ate enough of it. He did not know the truth of that and felt no reason to find out.

The Fellein liked their gold. The Sa'ba Taalor preferred different treasures, like a city that could be crushed.

The plans had already been discussed. Tarag Paedori was a master tactician – he followed the god of armed combat and led the armies of the Daxar Taalor, how could he be less? They had gone over the variables, chosen the paths they would take and decided when they would ride.

This was their final rest before the siege would begin. It would be a siege, too, they knew that. The armies of the Fellein had been gathering in the city called Goltha. Even from this distance the banners and flags of their soldiers could be seen.

There were no horns, no battle cries. They did not announce themselves this day. Instead they moved toward their destinations and prepared themselves for whatever the gods might demand.

Cullen stood upon his ship and stared out at the waters ahead.

He was a captain again, but somehow the title didn't mean as much this time around. The ship was given to him by the people who had killed his crew and left him to witness their deeds.

His crew was dead. The new crew was untested. To be sure they could row a boat and fish, but the Louron were hardly known for their skills as warriors and sailors. If one wanted a person tortured they were among the best, but to sail into battle was a different thing.

Still, looking at the dark-skinned people around him, he could see that they were dangerous enough.

Their demeanor gave away none of that. It was the conversations with them as they nursed him back to health and fed him that told the difference. A dozen Inquisitors had pried questions from him. They did not torture him nor were they cruel, but they were persistent. Darsken Murdro had been direct and harsh, but the others here were subtler and in some ways more cruel. The questions they asked were painful to answer, not because they used torture, but because they made him face aspects of himself that he did not like. Perhaps it was a drug in the food, or in the water, or perhaps it was simply that he needed to tell someone and they knew how to ask. They found ways to get truths from him even when he tried not to tell them anything.

Now they smiled and they joked softly among themselves, and they moved up the masts of the ship, and for over a week he watched as they painted the wood with dark inks and sang softly to themselves. The wood of the ship was no different. The shape of the vessel remained the same, but there was something menacing about the Brellar boat that had not been there before.

"What is it you have done, Daivem Murdro?"

The woman he looked at was sleek and dark and ageless. She could have been fifteen or fifty and he would not have known the difference. She had silver in her hair but her skin was smooth. Her eyes held the frank expression of an older woman but she giggled when she laughed and sounded like a child at those times. Like her brother, her hair was drawn into a dozen braids, hers all beaded and covered with wire and odds and ends. It should have looked preposterous, but it did not.

"My brother said you are a good man. He asked that we help you."

That thought puzzled him greatly. The notion that Darsken Murdro would call him a good man made as little sense as the rest of his life of late.

"Yes, and thank you. But what have you done to the ship?"

"Two crews died here. Yours and the Brellar who owned the ship, yes?"

"Yes."

Her voice carried that same lilt as all of her people and was almost a purr. "They are angry. They want justice. They want to taste the blood of their killers. If this does not happen, they will never rest properly. They will search for their killers until the end of time. Do you understand?"

"Yes. I think." He had heard of the Lourons' fixation with

the dead. He understood it well enough to know they were not to be trifled with. "And so we have offered them a map. It is carved into your boat. Their boat. They will guide you. We will sail with you."

"Why are you doing this for me?"

"For the dead. They will have a voice again, if only for a while. When they are at peace, we can be at peace."

She smiled as she spoke and then she called out to the crew around him. They called back, some loudly and some with nothing but a gesture.

Satisfied, Daivem looked to him again. "We are ready."

"Then let's get to it." He didn't give himself enough time to think and get nervous. If he did that he might well tell them to let some other fool be their captain. He owed his crew, however, and he owed the Brellar. If not for his actions they would all likely still be alive. He had led his crew, and the Brellar had been brought into negotiations with the Empire because of his suggestions and actions.

The ship lurched as the anchors were raised and the sails were spread.

Callan looked at the sky and frowned. "What is wrong with the clouds?"

They danced and shifted in a way that was not at all to his liking. They seemed oddly out of focus, even when he looked directly at them.

"The clouds are fine. We have found ways to go faster than other ships. We will meet up with our enemies in hours."

"In *hours*?" Despite his willingness to fight against the enemy, he had rather been hoping for a few weeks in which they could get more of themselves killed.

"In hours," Daivem confirmed.

"But they have had weeks."

"The dead have watched. The dead have waited. They wish to wait no longer."

He wished the woman would stop speaking of the dead as if they were alive. The thought made his skin shiver as if fevered.

Callan knew the coastline better than most. He was shocked to see that they had travelled much farther than should have been possible an hour into their voyage. The man currently steering the ship did not look his way, but instead focused on the wheel. The rest of the crew stayed busy.

Daivem was close by and he called to her. "How does he know where to go? I haven't told him."

"You do not know where to go. Why would he ask you?"

Her logic was solid.

"Just the same, where are we going and how does he know?"

"Look carefully at your helmsman and tell me what you see." The dark-skinned man was the same as before when he looked but there was something there, a smudge in the air that made no sense.

Daivem's long fingers moved up the back of his neck and into the tangle of hair on the back of his skull. "Look carefully," she whispered.

He looked and saw Vonders there, holding the wheel with the helmsman. Vonders whom he'd seen killed. Vonders whom he'd mourned.

"The dead know the way to retribution, Captain Callan. They have no secrets from us."

Callan nodded and stayed where he was, cold and dread-filled in the warm ocean breeze. The miles went quickly, very quickly indeed.

Andover woke from a doze. He was still on Gorwich's broad back. "You sleep like the dead," the mount observed.

"And you stink like the dead, oaf." The words were spoken with affection on both sides.

Andover looked around carefully. They had reached the passage between the mountains. Canhoon was above them, so high up it barely seemed possible that the shape was a city. Wrommish had moved, according to Drask. The winds from the north blew hot enough to convince Andover that the man was right, even if the gods had not told him already.

Drask rode next to him on the left, with Tega riding behind him. On the right Nolan March sat on Delil's mount, where Delil's body still rode. Nolan still offered no expression. How he rode without falling Andover could not begin to guess.

Delil did not rot. She should have been a reeking mess after the time they'd spent riding, but she was not.

"Should we not be closer?" Andover yawned as he spoke.

"We are where we need to be," Drask replied. "We are days away from the Great Tide, Andover Lashk."

"Have the gods ever raised the dead before, Drask?"

"You know the answer to this already, Andover."

"I know one answer. I know that nothing ever goes to waste. I know that the punished come back as the Broken or as the Pra-Moresh. I know that the worthiest come back as mounts. But have the Daxar Taalor ever resurrected someone as they were before they died?"

"In some of the stories of the kings, they are reborn from their broken bodies. According to some of the legends, Durhallem raised Tuskandru from the dead."

"Do you believe that?"

Drask shook his head. "No. I know that they can raise the dead, but I have never heard of it happening." He tilted his head. "They have come close. Swech died. She sacrificed herself to Wrommish to hide among the Fellein. She died there, but they have only recently given her back her old body."

"So they raised her from the dead?"

Drask shook his head. "More like they put her back in her own form. It is hard to say, I am only just learning of this."

"How are you learning?"

"Tega and Nolan and I have been changed, Andover. I think we have bathed in the blood of the gods and been transformed."

"I thought the blood of the Daxar Taalor was the metal in their hearts."

"A different type of blood, perhaps. It is hard to say. All I know is that we are changed. We are changing. You ask if gods can raise the dead. I raised Brackka. Does that make me a god?"

"You raised *Brackka*? From the *dead*?" Andover's voice was soft with surprise. He looked past Drask to Tega. She stared directly in his eyes and nodded her confirmation.

"Yes, I did."

"Could you raise Delil?"

"I think so, but I see no reason."

"What do you mean?"

"Delil lived the life she wanted, Andover. She fought for her gods, she lived well and served the Daxar Taalor. She was happy. If I bring her back that might not be the same."

Andover stared hard at the man who had been his mentor. "I don't understand. Why would you hesitate?"

"You would not hesitate, Andover. She is important in your world and you wish to be with her. But she is not important to me. She was my friend, but death is part of the world, even for gods. If I brought her back, it would not be for me or for her, it would be for you."

"Would that be such a bad thing, Drask?"

Drask looked at him, stared deeply into his eyes. "You have

already made a bargain to have her back, Andover Iron Hands. It is not my place to reach between a man and his gods."

"But if I do not keep that bargain, if I should fail..." Guilt swept through him.

"Then your desire for Delil is not strong enough for you to test your faith."

"Do you know what the gods want of me?" His voice broke momentarily.

"I have not listened to the gods since leaving the Blasted Lands." Drask looked forward again. "They have been trying to speak to me, trying to get my attention. I suspect they would like their power back." Drask looked his way again and raised his right hand. The silver there had grown, was sweeping up his arm all the way to his shoulder. "I imagine they want you to convince me to talk to them. Or they want you to kill me, Tega and Nolan." There was an edge of menace in the man's words that made it clear he would not die easily. "I will understand if you try. I have killed more than a few people I considered worthy of friendship because the gods demanded it. I will defend myself, Andover. If you attack me, I will kill you. Know that."

They rode in silence for a long while. Tega stared at Andover as if she did not know him any longer. Perhaps that was true.

When Drask spoke again, his voice was calm. "You have met all of the Daxar Taalor, as have I, Andover. That is rarer than you know. There are fewer followers of Ydramil than you might think, because to truly be Ydramil's follower, you must visit with all of the gods."

Drask studied his own hand for a moment. "I do not ignore the gods because they have offended me. That is what you must understand. I do not ignore the gods at all. I am merely doing what Ydramil has always said to do."

"And what is that, Drask?"

"Ganem is the Mirror King. Ydramil is the God of Silver, the God of Reflection." Drask looked his way. "I am considering what my options might be. I am reflecting on the changes in my life as Ydramil has always asked of me.

"It is not all of the gods that have made an offer to you. Ydramil would not. Ydramil understands my heart."

"Then why would the other gods ask me to kill you?"

"They are war gods, Andover. They will always ask for blood. It is their way."

"Then perhaps if I offered them something else?"

"You can ask. I do not expect you will like the answer."

Tega left her body, as she had done before her transformation, and dreamt herself a new form as her master had taught her to do.

The storm crow soared high, indeed, as high as the mountaintops, and then moved over the City of Wonders.

It was not hard to find Desh Krohan. He was in his chambers as she suspected he would be. It is not always easy to know a wizard, but it is far easier to know a man.

He did not need to look hard to know who she was.

Desh smiled and held out an arm. "Tega! I'd feared you dead. You have not responded in a very long time."

Rather than land on his arm as she might have in the past, Tega took her own shape and settled on the ground beside him.

He was still looking surprised by her transformation when she hugged him fiercely. She'd had no plans to cry. She'd meant to merely let him know all that had happened but instead she found herself burying her face in his robes and wrapping her arms around his lean chest.

He said nothing. Instead he merely held her and let her

grieve as she needed.

"They are all dead and it is my fault. I failed you a thousand times, Desh."

"You are alive, Tega. You have not failed me. I have failed you. I should have never sent you to that miserable place." He spoke into her hair and placed a dozen paternal kisses on her scalp.

After a time she could breathe again and pulled back from him.

Words were not enough sometimes. Instead of trying she touched her fingers to his head and showed him what had transpired. He seemed far less surprised than she would have expected. Then again he was on a floating city and an army of statues was moving about. Some events make the impossible less outrageous.

He showed her as she had shown him, and Tega burst into tears anew to learn that one of her teachers and friends, Goriah, was dead.

She was not alone. When Tega cried her grief out, Desh Krohan joined her. They held each other through the emotional storm and when it was mostly over Tega looked at him and said, "We could bring her back."

"I've thought of it. I've considered it often. I have preserved her body for the possibility, because I do not want to bury her and I do not want to burn her. I do not want to lose any of my Sisters any more than I would ever want to lose you."

"We could. The Daxar Taalor brought Swech back from the dead. That's what Drask said."

"How?"

"They are gods."

Desh shook his head. "Even gods have their limits. Or at least they should."

"There was something about her body. She was not in it and they cared for it. So bringing her back was not so hard for them."

"Resurrection is almost impossible. To heal a wound is one thing. To put a spirit into a body and bind it is another."

Tega shook her head. "You are thinking like a sorcerer, not like a god."

"What do you mean?"

"I mean a sorcerer must find the energy to do these things. Magic has a cost. You have always said this. The cost is the energy. Or the ability." She waved her arms around. "This city, the Silent Army, they exist because you could draw on the deaths of thousands to rebuild, yes?"

"Yes, of course." Desh looked at her carefully, like a parent looking for signs of a fever. "What is your point, Tega? I'm not going to kill a dozen people, even my enemies, in order to bring Goriah back. That is why those magics are forbidden. The temptation is strong, always, but it's the wrong approach."

"Desh, I have the power. It is inside me. Drask has the power inside him. Whatever we were supposed to find or not find in the Mounds, the power is in us." She paused and thought of Drask recreating the Blasted Lands and bringing Brackka back from dust and ash.

"I have the power of the gods inside me, Desh. All three of us do. It is wondrous and terrifying."

"Have you used this power?" He was calm as he asked, but he was also cautious.

"No. Of course not. I have already caused disasters without the power I have now."

Desh nodded.

"That is why I am here. I wanted to give it to you. I think I can do that."

Had she scalded him with boiling oil he could not have reacted as deeply.

He did not scream. He did not rail. Instead Desh looked at her as calmly as he could and shook his head. "I would not want it."

"Why not?"

"Because I would want to use it."

"But shouldn't you?" Tega stepped closer to him, only vaguely aware that he had stepped back. "You could bring Goriah back. You could end this war."

"No, Tega." He placed his hands lightly on her shoulders. "Once upon a time I think that was what ruined Korwa. Too many people with too much power fought against each other and destroyed that place. Do you see? The power of the gods should not be wielded lightly."

Tega frowned. "But the gods have cheated! They bring back the dead of the Sa'ba Taalor!"

Desh smiled. "How about we come to a compromise, then. We could bring back Goriah, if you truly want. But nothing else. Instead I would ask that you refrain from using any more of this power, in case, as I suspect, it could cause too much damage."

There was no hesitation on her part. Tega smiled and nodded and once again hugged her instructor and friend. He hugged her back and she felt, for the moment, happier than she had in months.

"There is someone I need you to meet first, Tega. He has spoken with Goriah. He has asked her many questions."

"I thought that forbidden, Desh."

"Not to an Inquisitor."

Within the hour they met. Tega looked at Darsken Murdro and was intrigued. She had never met a man with darker skin or eyes and no man she had ever seen wore his hair in so many braids. Even the Sa'ba Taalor she had seen, many of whom braided their locks, had never managed so many braids of varying lengths, all tied together.

When he smiled his face lit up like a child's. She liked him.

Pella and Tataya were there, along with a small, muscular woman introduced as Cullen. Cullen had a ghost. She also had something hidden within her that felt like it had all the power of a tidal wave locked in a bottle.

Desh explained enough to let Darsken know that bringing Goriah back was possible without sacrifices.

Not far away Tataya and Pella were still mildly shocked to see Tega, but happy for all that. After everything that had happened they'd feared she was dead and that they had lost another of the family.

Jeron was missing. Tega knew of his name but that was all. He was not in the city that they could see and there was no word from him. The sorcerers had lost enough for now.

"You can bring her back?" Tataya spoke softly and moved to Tega, her arms moving around Tega's shoulders and her body pressing to her from behind. She leaned into the embrace, taking comfort from the Sister. Pella looked closely at Tega and frowned in concentration.

"I cannot," Tega shook her head. "But Desh can. I can only provide a means."

Pella nodded but said nothing. Half of sorcery is understanding how the world functions. Pella looked at Tega and understood.

Desh looked at Darsken Murdro and asked only one question, "Would Goriah want to come back to us if she could?"

Darsken looked carefully at each of them. "Yes. But she knows the rules of sorcery and necromancy and would want no sacrifices to bring her back."

"Then she will have none." Desh nodded. "We will try once and only once."

Tega smiled. "I have to leave soon. I have to get back before I am missed. I think there are things that still need to be done from down below. So we should work quickly."

"What are they doing?" Deltrea looked at the gathered people and worried at a spectral fingernail. She was always curious, but now she seemed more concerned than anything else.

"They try to bring back the dead."

"Not me I hope. I don't think I'd like the shape of my body after all this time."

"No. One of the other sorcerers."

"Hmmph. Just as well. I wouldn't want to be alive again."

"Liar."

"Maybe so. Still, no one has asked me."

The short blonde woman who clung to Desh Krohan like an infant with her father looked their way for a moment and smiled timidly. Cullen smiled and nodded. Deltrea realized she could be seen by the girl and immediately waved and smiled as well.

"See? That one I like. Not nearly as rude as the wizard."

"I think they are all wizards."

Deltrea moved closer. "Is that the one they're bringing back?"

There was only one body on a table. The corpse was pretty as corpses go, but still only one more corpse as far as Cullen was concerned. She couldn't imagine wanting to be reborn into the world after all that had gone wrong. Trecharch was gone. Her home, her people, almost all of them destroyed and instead of trying to stop the enemy, the group here worried about bringing back one person. She wondered idly what made that one so special but decided not to dwell on it.

She didn't really know what to expect but it was a simple enough affair.

Desh Krohan made markings on the body of the dead girl. Some might have seen his caressing of flesh as obscene, but he obviously took no pleasure from it and he broke a sweat as he concentrated. The little blonde girl stood beside him, and he reached for her at one point and their hands clutched together.

Then the lights came. Cullen felt like she was seeing the sun for the first time. The lights were warm and bright and comforting even though their intensity scared her a bit.

The lights ran from the girl to the sorcerer to the corpse and there they danced along each and every mark that the sorcerer had made before they sank into the cold, dead flesh.

After a moment the corpse shook and took in a breath before groaning and sitting up.

She was lovely. She had cold features, but they were structured well. High cheekbones, full lips, blue eyes and hair so blonde it bordered on white.

Deltrea looked at her and spoke with a shocked voice She did not speak of the miracle they had just seen instead she said, "You fancy her."

Cullen waved the comment away. Who she fancied had never been a part of her relationship with Deltrea and wouldn't be a part of it now.

"I can feel it, Cullen. Why didn't you ever say?"

"I fancy men and women alike, Deltrea." She muttered the words, while not a dozen feet away the miracle workers held onto their resurrected friend and hugged.

"Well, yes, but you never said."

"You talked of your rutting. That doesn't mean I ever wanted to talk about mine."

"But we're friends, Cullen. I told you everything because we are friends."

"I saw how you treated a few people like me. You smiled in their faces and then said hateful things."

"I would never do that to you." Deltrea looked genuinely wounded.

"I never wanted to take that risk. In any event it is done."

It was not, however.

The recently reborn looked to the other blonde, the smaller one, and swiftly grabbed her hand.

"I need a favor from you, Tega." The way the woman spoke, it was not really a request.

"Just... Only this time, Goriah. Because you are owed that much."

Goriah kissed the other girl's cheek and then closed her eyes.

Desh Krohan said, "What are you doing?"

Goriah replied, "Revenge."

The First Advisor merely nodded his head.

They were gathered together at the estate of Lanaie, though she was not there. Once again she was walking the palace with Brolley Krous and learning what secrets could be gleaned while with him.

Swech was restless. She was back in her body and wanted combat, as is almost always the case with the Sa'ba Taalor, regardless of the body they might inhabit. It was not that she was impatient, merely that she needed to refamiliarize herself. Limbs were different widths and lengths, joints were more fluid – thank the gods – and muscles were just different enough that she felt like her whole body was wearing a new boot.

To that end, rather than pace and drive everyone mad, Swech stretched and practiced her punches and kicks as she had been taught. From time to time N'Heelis called out a compliment or a suggestion and she smiled and listened. It was good to be among her people again.

Glo'Hosht did not pace. The King in Mercury looked over a map of the city that was several layers deep.

"Here, I think, is where your people can do the most good, N'Heelis."

The King in Gold moved over to look and Swech stopped her practices long enough to look on and learn.

"Swords and blades are very nearly useless here. I think chains and staffs a better way." N'Heelis spoke casually enough. Of all the kings it was possible that they were among the closest. They had always worked well together and likely that would never change.

Swech moved closer and looked at the map. They were examining the Mid Wall.

"That is where the Silent Army is strongest."

N'Heelis nodded and pointed. "It is also where they are weakest." She smiled and crossed her arms.

Glo'Hosht stood up suddenly and backed away from the table. As he moved, his arms and then his legs twisted and popped. Bones snapped and the king fell to ruined knees.

It only took seconds. The King in Mercury screamed, a loud, harsh bellow, and then the flames erupted. Not at one sleeve or another, not at the bottom of the king's cloak or at the top of the woven hood the king always wore, but from everywhere at once. This was not the heat of the forge. It was hotter.

The fires roared along the king's body and if there was a second scream it was torn away by the fury of the flames.

N'Heelis did not have time to react. Swech did not have time to react. No one could have. The King in Mercury exploded into flames and then burned away into nothing before anyone could hope to assist. Fine soot rained down from the spot. Scorch marks painted the ceiling above where Glo'Hosht had been. The whitest ash, so fine that it shivered away in the breezes caused by motion a dozen feet away, was all that remained.

Swech sought comfort, as she always had, in the voice of her gods. The Daxar Taalor did not answer immediately.

Even the gods were caught unawares.

She took no comfort from that notion.

ELEVEN

The greatest rivers in the whole of the land all ran to the same spot, Lake Gerhaim. The lake itself was a sight that many could barely believe. Surrounded on all sides by low hills, almost any place a person stood afforded a view of the clear blue waters and the numerous villages and towns that all led to Goltha.

Goltha was a city of wonders in its own right but never had that name. The title given to the city was the Jewel of the Empire. Commerce from all portions of the country came through Goltha at one point or another, and even in winter the rivers were too wide to freeze completely. Goltha lived off the taxes claimed and the people who came to her for fortune. Not everyone succeeded, but all who came to the city knew they were in a place of magic and power. The magic was mostly for show: courtesans and street magicians, an occasional sorcerer and a thousand charlatans. The city embraced all who came so long as there was coin in the transaction. That was one of the less pleasant titles for Goltha: the Whore of Fellein.

Whore or Jewel, Goltha was very well protected indeed. Because so many wanted to seize the area, the Empire had long since made defending Goltha a priority. There were great iron gates that could be closed against ships from any or all directions. Water could pass through, but boats of any size would have to be given permission to enter once the main gates were shut. Those gates were among the greatest creation of the sorcerers of old. They had rusted, true, but not as much as they should have and never enough to weaken them in hundreds of years.

In addition to the gates there were three great walls, each higher than the last. The walls were solid in all directions save one: the waters of the lake were not blocked. That was why they had the great gates.

There were entrances in the walls, of course, but they could be barred and braced.

The sun had not yet risen when the northern and southern gates of Goltha's outermost wall were set ablaze. The fires were carefully set in the deepest part of the night and the guards who stood outside those closed gates were murdered before they could sound alarms. The eastern gate was set ablaze as well, but only after the other two. City Guard and citizens alike did what they could to stop the fires but they were massive indeed.

By the time the sun rose the gates were in ruins. Metal hinges and bars do not stop wood from burning and whoever started the fires used a great deal of oil and wood to make the blazes burn hot and fast.

Among the soldiers was Captain Leno Nethalte, in charge of the archers who had successfully slaughtered their enemies along the Inbrough River. He did not fight the fires or waste his men on that action. Instead he ordered the First Wall stationed with archers and spearmen alike. All brought shields, the better to defend their positions. All brought extra arrows and spears because one never knew how long a siege would last.

The ruined gates were quickly replaced with heavy lumber and stones to support the wood. Great wooden braces were rigged as quickly as possible.

The soldiers of Goltha were as prepared as they could be for the attacks that they knew would come their way. Alarms were sounded and the Gerhaim Gates were tended to. There seemed no issues from the north, east or west, but the Southern Gates were drawn against the black ships heading for them. Rumors of the ships had long reached the city, of course, but the reality was unsettling.

The gates were massive affairs. The walls that held the mechanical wonders were eighty feet in height and blocked off a portion of the river itself on each side. Many a brave soul had walked out along those stone barriers over the years simply for the view the gates afforded. The gates were seventy feet in height and were checked regularly by the sorcerers to make certain that everything functioned as it should. There were parts to be oiled, of course, and the metal itself, while enchanted, still required a good cleaning now and then. That was, as far as most sorcerers were concerned, why apprentices existed.

When the alarm was sounded and the gates were sealed the noise alone would have scared off the dead. Horses had to pull the latticework from below, down in tunnels along the waters. They were strong animals, and the apparatus was well kept, but still it took time to work the defense. The rumble and squeal of metal on metal as the pieces were drawn across and locked in place was a din that only a few ever heard and forgot.

That was all the alarm needed to have most of the people at the smaller towns around the river's end looking on in anticipation.

The first of the massive vessels turned and collided with the great iron gate. The ship shook, the gate shook. Nothing fell apart.

The figures that came off the ship and started scaling the sides of the gate were unexpected. The gate itself was a massive affair and while some marveled at the thing, few ever consider scaling it, at least when they were sober.

The gates were not solid. If they were, water could not pass through and the city would suffer. There were rather substantial holes in the gates but the bars used to forge the entire thing were thick and, as has been mentioned before, crafted with sorcery to back up their strength.

Once every six months the gates were closed and examined to make certain their integrity held. In all of the years of repairs and examinations it never occurred to anyone that invaders might try to climb the deterrent. The metal was harsh and uneven; holding on would be painful at the least. Handholds could be had, but not very easily and one would have to reach a great ways to grasp the next spot.

The Sa'ba Taalor scaled mountains with regularity. The gates were not a challenge.

Archers were deployed. Because the gates were important, there were always soldiers to look after them. The archers took positions atop the walls of the gates as quickly as they could and waited.

The Sa'ba Taalor had arrows too. Those atop the gates braced themselves and fired at the archers, keeping them busy. The Fellein used crossbows for the most part but here, the archers used longbows. The range was better and the speed was a blessing. Also, the king of Goltha, Kordis Neiller, preferred longbows, as he was a hunter.

More ships rammed against the wall with no noticeable damage to either side. More of the Sa'ba Taalor scaled the gates.

Further out, on both sides of the river, the armies that had previously been disgorged and now had the newly anointed with them continued on, unwavering.

The Fellein marked by the gods had made their decisions and the Sa'ba Taalor kept them to those choices. They were made to run with the People of the Forges, to eat with them and to fight with them. Those who did not fight well died. Those who fled suffered a far worse fate.

The Daxar Taalor did not brook cowardice. The first warning came in the form of crippling pain to any who tried to escape or to betray their new gods. Crippling pain meant just that, and the traitors died quickly. Those who survived did not usually try again. If they did it was time for a short lesson in what angry gods can do.

There were no dogs in the Taalor Valley. The Sa'ba Taalor encountered the creatures quickly enough and came to respect the animals for their loyalty and savagery. The freshly anointed who failed the Daxar Taalor were made into the equivalent of hounds. They were bent until their shape was that of a dog and their jaws were reformed, their teeth made long and vicious.

They suffered, as naughty children often do, and were told that the only escape was death, or to prove their loyalties once and for all.

The hounds led the way into combat, willing at last to prove themselves to their new gods.

Their feet and hands ended in long, thick claws. Their faces were warped into nightmarish lumps with too-long jaws and wide, sharp teeth. It is hard to say if the Daxar Taalor enjoyed creating the nightmares, but the Sa'ba Taalor loved setting them on the people ahead of them.

The hounds ran ahead of the armies, and they reached the gates while the soldiers from Fellein were still trying to keep the Sa'ba Taalor from the black ships at bay.

The screams of the people below made a few archers turn their attention from the approaching gate walkers.

While the fight was forming on two separate fronts, more of the Sa'ba Taalor from the ships attempted to use the gates to gain entrance to where the great locking mechanisms were housed.

Alarms were sounded and reinforcements charged to assist before the black ships could make their way inland.

In the chaos it was understandable that boats coming from the Parmahar got past without even being noticed. They had little in common save that they were all designed for fishing. They sat low in the water, a sure sign that their holds were heavy with fish, and while there was cause for panic to the south of the city, there was business to tend to in the east and on the docks.

Meggs, a dockworker with connections in all the right places, looked to Dockmaster Toast and shook his head. He spat and snorted in the cold air coming from the waters.

"You seeing this? What do they plan to do, sell fish to fishermen?"

Toast looked at the boats with no real concern at first. "Not like they've much of a choice, is it? Where else they gonna sell fish? In Canhoon?" He pointed to the small speck in the air to the west. "Way I'm hearing things, that dot up there is Canhoon. Can't sell them fish if they can't reach them."

Toast spoke with a bit of pity for the bastards. They'd come all this way and all they were going to get for their efforts was being taxed by him before they could settle in. That was the way of it. The docks were expensive to keep, and with the fuss going on to the south he doubted he'd be seeing much business from that direction, either.

"Could be refugees."

Toast shook his head and followed Meggs's example. He spat at the waters. "Emnol!"

Toast's son Emnol was a good boy, but just barely. He looked the part of a girl and more than once he'd been warned to keep his eyes alert when boats came in. He was thin, had his mother's fine face, and was too trusting at the age of ten.

"Aye, Dad!"

"Go find the City Guard. Tell 'em we might have refugees coming in."

"What's a refugee?"

"People looking for a place to stay that can't afford to ask."

The boats were still at a distance, but they came quickly. The sails were stretched and took the wind, the oars stroked hard and the vessels fairly jumped with each sweep of the long oars, and along the sides of the vessels stood the shapes of men.

And now Toast could see more clearly, the figures were the stuff of nightmares. Great shapes dressed in leathers and armor, carrying every imaginable type of weapon.

The boats came closer still, and from their decks he could hear the sounds of men calling, bellowing the same word again and again, "Durhallem," with every beat of the oars on the water.

From behind the boats tremendous wakes spread, and despite the hellish passengers aboard the boats, the water caught the dockmaster's eye and would not let it go.

"Where the hell are those City Guard?"

"If I knew I'd surely tell you," commented his friend. "What is it that stirs the water so much? Are they towing other boats?"

"No. It doesn't make sense." He shook his head. "Besides, we have other concerns. We need to get away from here before they make shore."

The boats did not slow down, but instead veered left and right, running alongside the docks and revealing the reason for the odd wake: several long ropes ran behind each of the boats, with hands holding onto those ropes from the additional Sa'ba Taalor that rode along. The people swimming toward the docks were the enemy he had been hearing about.

"This can't be real." Meggs's voice was strained. "What are they?"

"They are the enemy of our people," Toast's voice was strained. "We need to leave here. We need to alert the City Guard."

Meggs nodded his agreement and the two of them moved a few paces back, not quite daring to look away from the hell of flesh coming their way.

The ones holding onto the ropes let them go and then swam hard for the docks, grabbing at the wood or swimming alongside the edge of the docks until they could reach ropes or ladders.

The first of them that rose from the waters was not as large as some of the demons on the boats had been. Toast would easily claim this one was little more than a boy in stature, but that did not make the leather-clad creature any less frightening. It had horns running from its jaw upward and its exposed skin was deathly gray.

He was still looking it over when the thing pulled knives from sheaths at its hips and moved toward the two of them.

Toast shook his head and stepped back again.

The creature did not seem to care. If anything, it ran faster. It had taken but five long paces before Meggs was running, his body turning toward the distant hills and his legs pumping furiously.

The shape moved past Toast and he saw one scarred arm moving forward, releasing a knife that slid through the air as gracefully as any arrow had ever flown. The knife rammed to the hilt into Meggs's skull and his friend flopped to the wooden dock and did not move.

Toast looked at the creature and it, in turn, looked toward him.

He shook his head, silently begging.

The creature's eyes glowed inside his horned helmet. No, not his. The way the hips moved, the shape of the body. Not a boy at all. A woman.

She held up the bloodied knife in her hand and then pointed to his lower body. The wound was in his thigh. The blood ran in a torrent down his leg and the dockmaster felt lightheaded as a fine clear note rang in his ears.

He did not die as quickly as his friend, but Toast died just the same.

By the time the City Guard arrived, the Sa'ba Taalor had climbed to the docks, either from the waters or from the boats.

Most of the cargo holds held the mounts, and their riders went to them quickly, grabbing armor and weapons.

Tusk looked at Stastha and smiled. "As promised, first kill for seeing to the mountain raid."

"I am glad. I did not want to go to the city. I wanted to be here, for this."

Tuskandru nodded his head and hefted his axe.

"I prefer to stand on the ground myself, Stastha. I do not like falling." The king looked toward the head of the dock, where several men in armor and one young boy were looking back. "Time to kill this place."

He started walking and each step he took had the dock groaning under his heavy tread.

"Do we sound the horns, Tusk?"

"No." he shook his head and readjusted his helmet. "Lead the new followers of Durhallem for a while, Stastha. I feel a need to kill." The words were spoken cheerfully enough and she understood. Now and then leading was a task. Sometimes it was best just to find a target.

The City Guard stood and prepared themselves for the man coming their way. Tusk's tread increased in tempo and by the time he'd reached the guards he was running.

The assault was as brutal as one would expect from the head of Durhallem's army.

The boy ran. The soldiers did not. The first of them tried to meet Tuskandru full on, sword against axe. The man was skilled, and blocked the first blow Tusk aimed for him. While he was recovering from the shock of metal on metal, the king leaned in and smashed him in the face with his great helm. Fangs from a dead Pra-Moresh carved a wound in the guard's face. As he staggered back screaming, the axe finished him.

Tusk grinned and swept the axe in a wide arc, catching another guard in the hand, slicing fingers away.

The guard screamed and reached for his sword with the other hand, his face a mask of pain. Tusk's body smashed into him, sending him staggering. The sword came free at the same time that the guard fell to the ground.

The guard never had a chance to rise. By the time the slaughter was done Tuskandru had moved on, heading for the city proper and any target that might strike his fancy.

Stastha chose to follow after him. He did not need protection, but best not to divide the army this early on.

● ● ●

The hills above Goltha were littered with mansions and villas. The view they afforded of the vast lake, the city itself and the surrounding towns was spectacular.

King Kordis Neiller did not live on the hillsides above the town. He lived in a castle deep in the heart of the city as his ancestors had for quite some time.

The horns sounding to the south were not a surprise. He'd known of the black ships for some time and had made preparations should they make their way through the river gate.

It was the messengers coming with new notes of alarm that caught his attention. First, the City Guard to the east had not sent a runner. That was hardly a cause for alarm by itself, as the man in charge of the Guard was often lax in his reports. It was the culmination of other situations. The north was quiet as well. The soldiers sent that way to keep an eye on the Sa'ba Taalor who'd escaped the river assault had not reported back yet, and that was a problem.

The court sorcerer was a capable man named Theran. He was often aloof and seldom pleasant, but he was capable and that was enough. The wizard didn't much look like a wizard. He was too young and did not carry a staff, a wand or any signs that he could perform sorcerous deeds. He was also as humorless as any man Kordis had ever met. He gave daily reports about the approaching Canhoon and shared the latest information and theories as to where it would land and how much potential devastation might occur as a result of having a city the size of Canhoon dropped on the lake, or worse, dropped on the city. The results of the latter would be horrid, of course.

The results of the former would be, well, they would be slightly less horrid.

Theran said that the Sooth anticipated vast troubles in Goltha today. To that end the military was ready. The City Guard, well, he was hopeful.

The city was as prepared as it could be.

"Are you quite finished?" He looked to his cousin, who was currently working to fasten the last of the straps on the king's breastplate.

"Almost. I should rather you not die because I can't pull a leather strap, your majesty."

He took a deep breath and felt the way the armor constricted. Enough to let him know he was secure, but not enough to steal his breath. "You've done well."

The king looked out the window of his room and faced the west. He could see a disturbance near the docks. It was not small.

To the north, there was calm. To the west, there was–

"What goes on to the west, Arthun?"

"Have the soldiers returned from routing out the gray-skins?"

"No." he frowned and looked on. "I don't think so."

There was motion near the very top of the hill that hid the city from everything to the east. The people were far enough away to look like little more than ants, but whatever it was they brought with them was larger, easily seen as it came to rest.

He turned to Arthun for answers. "What are they doing up there?"

"Are they building something?"

The first of the rocks fired from the catapult missed the king's palace but shook the earth and then rolled on to smash a hole in the eastern wall.

"By the gods!" King Kordis Neiller shook his head and

moved toward the window, not believing what he was seeing. The Empress had sent messages of mountains exploding, armies of the dead and far stranger things and he could look east and see the City of Wonders with his naked eye, but this was a different affair. This was a machine that threw rocks the size of an ox and shattered walls.

"Go! Sound the alarm! We are attacked!" That last was a redundancy, of course. The city was already attacked, but this was closer than he cared to think about. Hearing about attacks on Canhoon, or retaliation from the archers under his command, that was all quite different from watching a wall destroyed only a hundred yards from his window.

Kordis's heart thundered as he moved to the stairwell leading to the main courtyard. People were screaming and he knew they would be.

"Where is Theran?" he bellowed his question even as he strode into the courtyard, feeling the thump of his sword against his side, the slap of his axe closer to his hip.

"I am here, sire." Theran's dark eyes looked at him from near the stables. The man was dressed in regular pants and a decent jacket. He didn't look the part of a sorcerer. That was part of the problem, of course. A wizard should look like he could cast a thousand different sorts of death at an enemy and the man was just there, with his dark hair and dark eyes and a face that still couldn't gather a proper beard after months of trying.

"Speak to the messengers as you can, and let them know we are attacked. Let Canhoon know that we are under siege from at least two directions. There isn't a damned thing they can do to help us but they should know what they are facing if they come this way."

"Yes, sire." Damn, but he didn't like the sorcerer. The man

was polite. He was obedient. He still made Kordis angry.

Theran's eyes grew wide. "Sire!"

He looked in the direction that the mage was staring and faced his death. From the west a vast stone came toward him. It rolled in the air and froze him to his spot. He should have run. He should have prayed to the gods, he should have done so many things, but all he could do was stare at the impossible sight. The stone was growing larger by the instant and his legs refused to move.

The sorcerer stepped to him and held out both arms. The rock came closer, faster and then bounced in the air without touching either of them.

The missile rolled across the air and then smashed into the side of the stables, scattering shattered wood and hay as it rolled on.

Kordis looked at Theran. The sorcerer trembled with strain, even now doing his best to push the stone to where it would do the least damage.

Theran spoke with a voice that trembled from effort. "My liege, I suggest you get away from here before the next stone comes. I don't know that I can do that a second time." Suddenly Kordis liked the man better than he had before.

He also took the advice given and ordered his horse brought to him. The great rock might have taken most of his attention but he was aware of other men in armor joining him. It was time to make themselves known to the enemy.

"Where is the greatest gathering of the enemy, Theran?"

"To the north, sire."

"The north?"

"Yes, Majesty. There is a very large army coming from the north. Smaller from the west, and we have heard no reports from the east, but we can make assumptions." The wizard was eyeing the hills dubiously. "I shall do what I can about that."

"I thought you were not to fight my war." It was a point of contention that the sorcerers were only to offer advice and information.

Theran gave him a dark look. "Well, yes, but I live here too, you know. I would rather not just watch on and die if I can do something to prevent that."

"Remind me to continue this conversation if we both live through the day, sorcerer."

Without another word he mounted the horse and gestured to one of his soldiers who was carrying a horn.

The alarm was sounded, and the king turned toward the north and away from his city. There was a battle on all sides and he aimed himself at the largest force.

Goltha was a large city, with broad streets and a very large military force. Though it was true that every male citizen of Fellein was required to serve in the Imperial Army, Goltha also demanded service. No one could own land in Goltha without serving. No one could marry, no one could survive the taxes levied if they did not serve. The difference here was that the rule applied to men and women alike.

When the alarm was sounded the cavalry responded. The first horn had them dressing for battle. The second had them lining up at the royal stables – what was left of them – and gathering their horses. The third horn saw them assembled, the king in the lead.

And then they rode north, charging along the main road, lancers at the front, spearmen directly behind, and archers after that.

They were not alone in the charge. The northern barracks of the infantry was ahead of them, each with a spear and a sword, some with bows as well.

The gates were closed behind them, the City Guard alerted and made ready.

By the time the king and his cavalry arrived at the northern front the infantry and archers had dug in.

The infantry had set their long shields in a vast barrier and set their pikes and spears in a thick, layered wall of sharp points. The shields did not hold themselves and the soldiers waited as patiently as they could as the massive column of the enemy came their way.

Kordis looked at the barrier of flesh, wood and steel and nodded his approval. The archers were ready. Three layers deep, the bowmen waited for the command to be given and behind them more spear men prepared for combat.

They did not wait long for the warriors of the Sa'ba Taalor. The beasts they rode were terrors. There had been reports, of course, but the stories never seemed capable of doing justice to the reality. There was no exception here.

King Kordis looked upon the warriors of the Blasted Lands with the clawed, hellish mounts, saw the odd light in the eyes of man and beast alike, and swallowed the gasp that wanted to escape him.

The first of the enemy rode forward, a behemoth of a man with heavy plate armor and a sword of impossible size braced on the saddle of the monster he rode. His face was hidden behind an iron mask with a scowling visage.

He rode two dozen yards ahead, while the army of men and monsters waited behind him, several holding banners that matched the face on the giant's armored helmet.

"Would you parley?" the man called out as if the answer didn't actually concern him.

"On what would you parley? You stand at the edge of my city and your people already attack from three other directions."

"I am Tarag Paedori, Chosen of the Forge of Truska-Pren and King in Iron. I rule over all of the armies you see coming at you from every direction. If you would hope to survive what is coming for you, now is your one chance to negotiate."

Deep within the eyes of that mask, the silvery glow showed King Kordis exactly where the eyes of his enemy were and that they looked directly at him.

"What would you ask to leave this city in peace?"

"Surrender your crown to me and I will spare the lives of every person in Goltha. No one will be killed who does not raise a weapon." He paused for a moment and tilted his head. "There is another king already here, who would not offer you any similar kindness. He and his will kill all of your people unless I command him to stop."

King Kordis considered that. He was puzzled that there was more than one king, but didn't have the time to ponder the implications.

"What of the Empire?"

"We are already at war with the Empire. We are already at war with you. But if you lay down your swords and offer me your crown, we will let all of you live."

"And if we do not agree to these terms?"

"Trecharch fell in days. You will not last any longer."

Kordis's eyes remained locked with that silver gaze as he gave his command. "Archers, at the ready!"

As one the archers obeyed, nocking arrows and preparing to draw.

Tarag Paedori looked his way, his face unreadable behind the iron mask.

"You would kill me without even a counteroffer?" The man sounded exactly the same. If he was afraid he hid it very well.

"You have asked what I cannot give to you. Your people

have already attacked my home, my people. How can I bargain with you when you attack from all fronts?"

"How can you not when you know we will win and crush you?"

Kordis smiled and shook his head. "I know no such thing."

The King in Iron climbed from his mount and held the massive sword, letting the blade's tip lightly touch the ground. From the side of his beast he pulled a shield as tall as a young man and held that as well.

"I may not survive the arrows of your archers, King Kordis. I may not survive this combat in any event. But my people will follow my orders and will seek to kill you. All of you. Every child. Every soldier. Every wife. All of you will die if you do not surrender."

"Your people cannot kill us if you are all dead, Tarag Paedori. Archers, ready!"

The archers obeyed, pulling the bows and holding steady.

Tarag Paedori called out in a language unknown and the result was immediate. The riders moved forward and spread out even as Tarag Paedori himself moved forward, raising his shield until it blocked most of his body.

Kordis screamed, "Fire!" and the archers loosed a volley of arrows across the distance. The riders were fast to draw shields and raise them into the air, forming a wide wall to the front and above the mounts and riders alike.

Arrows rained down, some sticking in shields and others sticking in flesh. Even as they did so, the King in Iron bellowed an order of his own and the whole force moved forward.

The wave of shields and bodies parted only in one spot, where the shield of the king remained, where his helmet still glared at Kordis and his people.

Most of the archers managed a second volley of arrows

before the riders were too close. The animals and riders moved fast, and charged the massive shield wall that King Kordis had prepared against assault. Spears, pikes and shields waited. The first of the mounted riders came forward and moved ahead of the wall. The archers could not fire without risking hitting their own on the closer side; the mounted rider, a woman with a spear in her hand, nodded approval of the structure.

Rider and mount strutted before the entire expanse of barrier and throughout her spear was held at a resting position. When she was finished moving in front of the barrier she nodded to herself and then rider and mount leaped. That was all there was to it. The wall itself was nearly six feet in height. No horse could clear it without being impaled. The beasts of the Sa'ba Taalor were not horses, he'd known that, but he did not expect them to jump the wall as easily as a cat might leap onto a table. But that is what happened. The great monster rose over the wall and then crashed down, and the rider hurled her spear even as the beast turned toward the soldiers making up the wall.

King Kordis had a perfect view of their faces as the great monster lashed out and ripped two soldiers away from the barrier. The wall foundered there, falling as the men were pulled away.

The spear was hurled with terrifying force and drove into the first of the archers, throwing the man sideways with the force of the impact.

By the time the spear had finished its travels, a dozen more of the hellish riders were coming over the living hedge, their beasts roaring out in battle cries that sounded as unsettling as the riders themselves. One of the mounts did not quite clear the barrier and took a spear in the shoulder that ripped a great wound all the way down its length. It fell on the barrier and knocked more shields and soldiers aside. After that, chaos. The wall did not hold, although the soldiers did their best to push forward against the rising tide of the enemy while trying to defend themselves from the great claws of the monstrous mounts. Soldiers took strides forward and then were hauled back and torn open. In the face of that fury the ranks collapsed and despite no order being given, several archers took aim and only added to the chaos. Some might have hit their targets, but not all of them.

The great wall of Sa'ba Taalor that crashed against the remaining wall of spearmen took down their enemies, bloodied and bloodying with the same zeal.

Soldiers retreated. Sa'ba Taalor charged forward. The sheer savagery of the assault left Kordis stunned and speechless.

Enough!

Kordis shook off the unexpected sight and drew his sword. Around him others did the same. Lances were no longer an option; there was simply too much chance of crushing and impaling his own. But swords were a different matter. The horses charged down toward the Sa'ba Taalor and responded to the simple pressure of knees into sides. Horse and rider worked as one, and the king swept his sword across the side of one of the mounts as it came past him, roaring. The sword smashed into heavy armor and cut but not deeply. The impact ran up King Kordis's arm and he grunted.

One of the gray-skins saw him and swept a long mace at him, but instead of striking the king, the weapon shattered his horse's face. The horse, well trained or not, was unprepared and dropped, screaming its agony into the air.

The animal fell and so did he, rolling as best he could in full armor. The impact was brutal and surely the gods favored him as his horse did not roll over him during the crash to the cobblestones.

Hooves and legs moved around him as he tried to rise and one of the great mounts landed on horse and rider alike not five feet away, taking both to the ground. He saw the thick claws hook into the flesh of the horse and peel it back with terrifying ease, revealing meat and blood and bone. The teeth focused on the man and savaged his neck, nearly tearing the poor bastard's head away.

King Kordis made his feet and gathered his sword, sweeping the blade toward the mount. The animal was faster than he'd have imagined and ripped the blade from his hand with one claw. The great, armored face roared. The rider above swept a chain over his head and brought it down on the man next to the king.

He changed targets, Kordis was certain of it. The man had planned to attack him and changed his mind.

No matter. The sword was gone but he was not without weapons. His axe came free and he swept it into the chest of the closest of the gray-skinned enemy. The man blocked his blow and shoved him backward into the side of a horse still standing despite the nightmarish mounts. Kordis stumbled and was hit again, by what he could not guess but pain crashed down his side and across his back and he stumbled but righted himself.

This was so much worse than he'd expected. The lines of combat were supposed to be formal. He'd trained for years with his sword, for years with his axe. He was a proficient archer and a skilled horseman! But in seconds it all fell apart. Where were the guards who were supposed to ride with him? One he'd seen killed but the rest could have been anywhere at all and he would have never known.

A gray savage strode forward and smashed into him, using

a heavy shield to send him backward once, twice, a third time. Kordis grunted, staggered back and fell to the ground on his ass. Each blow of the shield had hurt, but none of them broke anything.

He came up as quickly as he could and took his axe to the shield bearer; the blade sank into wood and metal but before he could pull it back the man smashed into him again, using the shield to cast him aside. The axe remained where it was, the gray bastard grinned at him and kicked him in his chest plate, sending him sprawling.

They were everywhere. Soldiers from both sides attacked, hacking with blades, swinging axes, maces, sticks, whatever they could find to attack with after a few moments of heavy struggle. People fell. Some got up while others were stomped into the ground by hooves, boots or clawed feet.

It was overwhelming! King Kordis could scarcely breathe. Hot blood from someone or something spilled across his face and into his left eye. His weapons were gone but he swung with his fist and hit someone. He wasn't even sure who, exactly, only that they'd felt the blow.

A body smashed into him from the left and another from the right and yet another was pushed into his chest as someone brought a curved blade down and cleaved the poor bastard's head open.

Kordis lunged forward, hoping to at least manage to find a shield or a blade to use. He was dealt a blow to the side of his head that dropped him again to the ground and left his ear feeling like a hot iron was pressing into it.

The hands that grabbed him were not friendly. He was lifted and spun and thrown through the air and then left to crash into the ground once more.

When he rolled over to stand, the boot that caught him in

the side felt like a mule kick to the ribs.

He could not rise. Someone was standing on his back and pressing his face into the dirt at the same time. He tried to move, but was pinned properly. Looking up as best he could he saw the gigantic form of the King in Iron over him, watched the man hack a soldier with the massive sword he wielded and felt the blood of the man wash over him.

Tarag Paedori reached down and caught him by his arm, hauling him to his feet and dragging him along through the crowd of combatants. He did not have a chance to collect himself or even take his feet properly.

"You should have surrendered, Kordis! Your life would be easier, yes?"

Tarag Paedori held him off the ground by his arm and roared, "Here is your king! Here is Kordis!" then threw him to the dirt again.

He had enough time to look up before that great sword of the King in Iron came down and cut his neck open. Kordis's life ended a few seconds later.

Tarag Paedori looked down at the king of his enemies and nodded. It was good. It was proper. They had met in the field of battle and he had won.

Now he would claim his prize. The dead man's head was mostly severed. One cut and it came free.

"Take their heads! As many as you can. We will bear them to the palace and let them know what they will face!"

A javelin was all that was required; he drove the tip of one into the bloodied stump of a neck and then raised the head up high for all to see.

"Take them! Take them all, and if your enemy is still alive, take them just the same!"

He rode forward, prize held high, "For Truska-Pren! Take them all in his name!"

His followers listened, and they obeyed.

The best of armies can be weakened by the loss of a leader. In this case the armies of Goltha did not flee, but they writhed and howled and were taken by the tide of the Sa'ba Taalor.

An army is hard to miss. A single individual is often harder to see. Theran did not stride angrily up the hill, either; he approached with extreme caution, knowing that an army waited above and that they were currently raining destruction down on the buildings behind and around him.

King Kordis amused him. The man was standoffish at the best of times and while he was a competent enough ruler, he was not a very good person. He was self-centered, a whoremonger – it did not matter how much a whore cost, he or she was still a whore and Kordis gleefully indulged in both sexes – and believed that the sorcerers should do his bidding. Some fool had told him that wizards could make the sky rain diamonds and since hearing that he'd tried several times to convince Theran to give him a ransom in the gems. The argument over that particular debacle lasted over a year, and only really came to an end a short time ago, when Desh Krohan leveled several miles of forest. After that the king looked at Theran with a great deal more apprehension and possibly even respect.

All of which meant nothing at the moment. The king was off to the north and trying to stop an enemy that was, frankly, terrifying.

And Theran himself was trying to do the same. He doubted either of them would have much success.

Are you there, Corin?

Of course, brother. I am with you. How fares your war?

I haven't seen them yet. He paused a moment as a loud groan filled the air and a moment later another boulder rolled through the air, whistling and hissing as it rose higher and higher. *I am close, however.*

How close?

I will see them in another few minutes.

What will you do?

What else? I will attempt to destroy their rock thrower and as many of them as I can.

You are worth more than a rock thrower. Be careful.

He chuckled at that. *Rest assured of that. I have no particular desire to die this day or any other.*

Corin had been his source of information and the voice he heard the most as he dealt with news of the war on Fellein. It was the other man's voice that had warned him of the ships coming their way, of the great army coming from the north. He had sources everywhere. He had not known about the eastern attack, but he had definitely warned of all others and had allowed them the chance to strike at the western wing of the attack before it came to the city proper.

Corin was his source for all the news that he needed.

Now, however, he was on his own. The Sooth were being stubborn and refused to share. Corin was easily one of the masters when it came to the Sooth and if he could not get a straight answer from them then surely they were in troubled times.

Theran did not hurry up the hill, but neither did he take his time. When he reached the crest he was wise enough to drop to the ground and look over the edge.

The closest of the enemy was close indeed. The gray man stood only four feet away and looked back at the war engine that his people had created.

The ground was mostly level, with a gentle slope, and the machine that rested on that slope had been stabilized quite well. The framework was built mostly of wood, and in the center a vast arm lay cocked back and ready, with a collection of stones and chunks of wood in a cup large enough to hold a couple of men. Two women were adding more wood to the collection, heavy branches that were burning properly. The wood inside the collection must have been treated for it caught fire easily.

It was the fire that made him move. The vast rocks had done enough damage but the fiery logs scattered among the rocks the size of melons? Theran could only imagine the destruction they would cause.

He focused on the engine itself and used what was already available to work his sorcery. Before they could do whatever it was that would send the rain of stone and fire down on Goltha, Theran forced heat and pressure through every part of the device.

Wood bulged and cracked and exploded in seconds. Several of the gray-skins were caught in the explosion that sent daggers of burning timber in all directions. One of the women lighting the fire staggered backward with a brand burning through her ruined face and fell dead – please, by all the gods, dead. That he could make anyone suffer that way was enough to cause Theran nausea. Several others cried out in pain or challenged whatever might have attacked them in their own language. Words alone did not make speech. Their need to attack and stop whatever had assaulted them was obvious.

It was enough. As far as Theran could see there was only the one machine and that was now burning and ruined.

He backed up as carefully as he could and prepared to flee.

The javelin took him in the side of his neck and drove deep. Theran did not die, but he fell flat and could not move. None of him would move. Not even his smallest finger. He could not shift his eyes, so all that he saw was the boots that came toward him, muddied and well worn.

The voice that spoke was unknown, but he heard the words and understood them.

"My king! We have a sorcerer here. One of the Fellein that can cause magic." There was a pause and he could nearly feel the eyes that scrutinized him. "I wonder what Ordna will think of him."

He had no idea who Ordna was. It did not matter. He could do nothing in any event.

In the south the black ships wallowed, stuck against the great iron wall that stopped them from going into Lake Gerhaim. The Sa'ba Taalor attacking the gates were at a disadvantage until their hounds arrived. The vile creatures roared and snapped and took arrow after arrow, distracting the guards from the attack coming from the archers off the ships and keeping them from paying much attention to the gray-skins climbing over the iron gate itself.

The iron was uneven and sawed at skin and leather alike. Many of the Sa'ba Taalor used their tools to make the transit easier, hooking metal with axe heads or wrapping their hands in leather before going further. In any event they progressed slowly across the distance and finally reached the vast openings where the gate rolled out across the waters on hidden tracks in the water.

From there it was only a matter of time. The mechanisms were mostly on a level below the ground and they climbed past the worst of it on the gates themselves, through waters deep enough to require swimming. Those who could not swim were forced to crawl higher in the hopes of finding another way, but remarkably few sailors fail to learn how to swim.

The locking mechanisms that kept the gates extended were guarded, but not by a large party. It was not long before the Sa'ba Taalor seized the areas and then started puzzling out how the devices worked.

Trial and error. Fifteen minutes after they accessed the locking mechanisms the Sa'ba Taalor managed to unlock the gates. After that all they had to figure out was how to make the gates part and recede.

Callan and his crew moved along the river at a steady yet impossible clip. He could not have traveled at the speeds he was managing, and yet he did. Miles of river roared past, though there was little breeze and no indication that he or his ship could possibly be going at such speeds.

Daivem Murdro still stood by his side, looking toward the horizon. He studied her face, the explosion of braids that ran down her back. She was dressed in a white cotton top and a skirt made from a fabric he had never seen before.

Ahead they could see the great gate had been closed. He had only seen one of the massive gates in that position once before and that had been on a different river heading for Goltha.

"That's going to be a challenge, I fear."

"We are not worried about reaching Goltha this day, Captain Callan. We are here to visit the people who killed your crew, yes?" Daivem smiled at him, mischief in her eyes. She held no weapons save her walking stick, much like her brother's but with fewer skulls carved into the hard wood, but she did not seem at all afraid of the Sa'ba Taalor.

Callan could not say the same. He was bloody terrified of

the very notion of running across the gray-skins a second time. But he would do this, because he owed it to his crew. They'd been murdered brutally and much as he wished he could forget that, he could not. He could not forgive it, either; they were a mostly honest crew who wanted little but to make a living and he'd sent them into danger and watched as the Sa'ba Taalor slaughtered them.

And the bastards had let him live. That was the worst of it, really. That was the unforgivable sin. They'd left him alive to suffer with what had happened. He wanted them dead for that.

He blinked back the sting of tears.

Daivem looked his way and nodded. "Sometimes the pain of witnessing so much death is enough to drive anyone mad."

"So let's do this. Let's give the dead their satisfaction."

Daivem nodded and then pointed toward the black ships. Shapes scaled the great iron gate and at first he thought they might try to pry the locked bars apart but instead they moved sideways over the crisscross of bars, heading across the vast river in both directions, crossing over the locked gate like ants moving over a tow line.

"What goes through their minds?" Callan spoke mostly to himself.

Daivem answered just the same, "They want to force the gates, I suppose."

"Is that even possible?"

"I have no idea. I've never seen the gates of Goltha before." She frowned a bit, smiled a bit and then bared her teeth in a wide grin. "They are glorious, are they not?"

Callan grinned back. "They are impressive, but not so much of a pleasure to see when you are waiting for them to part and lined up seven boats deep."

"What shall we do about these black ships, Captain Callan?"

Callan looked at the gathered ships. There were enough of them to be sure. Twenty or more of the vessels were pushed up along the gate that would, he suspected, be opened sooner rather than later.

There was no possible way for them to destroy the ships. Perhaps if there were a sorcerer or two on board that would be a hope, but no, there was just Callan, a few of the Louron, and a crew of dead folk who seemed to share a similar goal to his.

"You're certain none of you are proper sorcerers?" He offered Daivem his best smile, as if that might possibly make her change her mind.

"We are not, but we are willing to learn."

"I'm afraid that might take more time than we have. So let's see what we can do to cause chaos and then try to avoid dying for as long as possible."

The Brellar ship he rode on moved forward as it had before, and Daivem nodded.

Ten minutes later they had reached the first of the great black ships. From above, on the decks of the ship, a dozen or more looked down at his vessel and seemed to stare specifically at him.

Whatever it was the people on that ship said, he did not understand the words.

Rather than turn away, Callan drove the prow of his ship into the solid side of the Sa'ba Taalor vessel. Wood shattered. The two vessels became one and the newly formed shape wept water as the river rushed past broken boards on both of them.

Callan smiled and reached for his sword. If he was going to die, he was going to do his best to avenge every last sailor he'd seen killed.

Near him, not speaking, but still unsettlingly active, the

dead who'd sailed with him came forward and drew their spectral swords.

Tuskandru looked back the way he had come and smiled tightly. He was tired, but it was a good feeling, one of satisfaction after a day of hard slaughter. As far as he could see his people moved behind him, ready for more combat.

Stastha moved closer to him, her long-handled axe held over one shoulder, and nodded. "We have captured a few, those who surrendered. One says he is the lord of this city. It is his to rule. He would speak with you."

"Of course he would. He wants to surrender or to parley."

"Will you talk to him?"

He looked at her and studied her face. She had four new wounds on her chin and across the side of her head. She was smiling as much as he was. It was good to please the gods.

"Bring him to me."

He leaned back into the side of his mount and smiled. Brodem grunted and rumbled but supported his weight with ease.

The man brought to him was wounded, but not dead. He was soft, and dressed in clothes that were for show and had little to do with anything but looking as colorful as possible, near as Tusk could tell. He had armor, yes, but it covered only his chest, and the metal was soft enough that it had been dented several times and showed every sword blow as if a knife had scraped at mud.

"What is your name?"

The man looked at him and held his head high. "I am Levron of Goltha. I am tasked with ruling this city."

"You are not doing so good a job." Tusk smiled. "The city is mostly mine now. And what I do not hold belongs to other kings."

"Why have you done this thing?" Levron stared at him, lips peeled back and eyes narrowed. He wanted to kill Tusk. Tusk respected that.

"Because my gods told me to. Because the air here is sweet and I like the view when I look down at the lake. Because that city is coming here." He pointed to Canhoon, which over the course of only hours had grown much larger and loomed above the far side of the lake. "And I want that city. I want to destroy it and the people who are there."

"What has any of that to do with us? Why do you attack my people?"

Tuskandru looked down at Levron. The man was not restrained, and yet he did not attack. He wanted to. Tusk could feel how much the man wanted to attack him, to kill him.

"Why don't you do it? Why don't you attack me, Lord Levron of Goltha? I am here before you right now. You will never have a better chance to kill me in your life."

Levron blinked at the notion. "Because I am surrounded by your troops."

"Why should that stop you? What do you fear?"

"I would stand no chance."

Tusk shook his head. "And so you do not even try?"

"To what end?" The man's voice trembled with emotion.

"What are you afraid of? Failure? Death? Disappointing your gods?"

The man did not answer.

"Had you fought you might have won. I am tired and have spent hours in combat." He held up a hand to show how the fingers trembled slightly. "Braver than you have fought me and some have bled me. They died, yes, but better to die trying than to simply fail because you will not."

"You don't understand."

"You are right and I do not want to. My gods have tasked me and I obey. If I die, it is what the gods want. If I live it is to serve them." Tuskandru shook his head. "Had you tried, perhaps I would have spared you. I might have offered you a chance at surrender. But to avoid fighting because you might not win? That is cowardice."

He looked to Stastha. "Kill this dog. He is not worth my efforts."

Stastha nodded her head and turned to the man. Her first blow rattled his eyes in his skull. She hit him again and again while he tried to fend her off. She did not waste her weapons on the task. He was not worth the effort.

Far to the north the palace was untouched.

"They have stopped throwing stones now. They should come down and join in on the actual fight."

Stastha nodded her head and once again pulled her horn. She blew several sharp notes and waited. Soon enough other horns throughout the city responded.

Tusk nodded his approval. Then, "How did Tarag Paedori get across the river on the other side? I did not see a bridge."

"There was a man there who took people across the waters on a boat as long as they could pay the coin."

"I wonder if he paid."

"If he did, it must have taken many trips across the river."

Tusk shook his head. It was a question he did not want to think on any longer. The sun would be setting soon and he wanted to make camp and rest.

"Clear out the closest buildings and prepare. We will camp here."

They did not stay in the buildings, but they made use of them just the same. They were good walls, made of stone and worked to help barricade any possible ways to attack.

TWELVE

"The reports are not good." Merros looked at the others around the table and shook his head. "The city has not been completely taken, but King Kordis is dead and a lot of the area is overrun with Sa'ba Taalor."

Desh Krohan shook his head. "We have not heard from our messenger there, Theran. He has been the main source of communication with the royal house and as much as I dread the notion it's very possible that he's dead as we've heard nothing at all and cannot locate him."

The sorcerer did not outright say that was why he wanted his people left out of the war but he cast a glance in Merros's direction that made his feelings known.

There was nothing for that, Merros knew. They were beyond the point where anyone could choose not to be involved in what was happening. There were too many dead and dying and too many caught up in the growing maelstrom of conflicts.

"We are less than a day from landing, according to your calculations, Desh," the Empress said. "I know that the air is warmer, and I can see that we've been descending for the last few hours." Nachia stretched and rose from her seat, once again starting to prowl the throne room. "On the bright side at least it doesn't look like we'll just fall from the sky. That would put an end to the war, to be certain."

The Sisters stood nearby, not speaking much, but listening. All three of them. Not that Merros wasn't glad to see Goriah healthy, but there was that whole part about her being dead that made him feel less enthusiastic. Wasn't it Desh that had told him there was always a price? If so, what had the price been? Who decided who could come back from the dead if not the gods?

When it came to that last, he preferred the gods stay silent, for that matter. Dead should be dead.

Goriah looked his way, but her face was half hidden under her hood and he could not read her eyes.

"Goltha is falling," Merros said. "We have committed a great deal of our ground forces and they are not enough. We can't call any more to the city because there's no one else willing to offer their soldiers."

Nachia waved a dismissive hand. "Can't blame them. In the same position I'd act the same way."

"The city is literally attacked from all directions, and we are very likely going to be neighbor to Goltha within a day. Even with the chaos that causes, we cannot escape the fact that the Sa'ba Taalor are coming for us and so far our best defense is a gathering of statues that listens to no one but themselves."

"Well, Merros, I can think of worse defenses. They killed a few hundred of our enemies near as we can tell." Nachia paused for a moment and frowned. "Did we find the rest of the bodies?"

"Yes, Majesty," Desh answered. "They have since been pushed out of the city by the City Guard. We took the time to move them through the tunnels we think they used to enter. It made more sense than trying to throw them over the Mid Wall."

"How many were there, exactly?"

Desh shook his head. "Hard to say. Most of them were in pieces."

"So the Silent Army has kept us safe despite the best efforts of the Sa'ba Taalor. That's something."

Merros shook his head. "The lake is our best bet. That is easily the biggest body of water I have ever seen outside the ocean. Have you considered what happens when we land? The water is very deep there. We might well sink straight on down and drown."

Desh shook his head and frowned. "I have to believe otherwise, Merros. The Silent Army has lifted us into the air and taken us a very, very long way. I can't believe that it's an accident."

"You said this happened before, Desh?"

The First Advisor nodded. "I've forgotten the details. I don't mean completely. I knew that the city had moved before, but only as a sort of vague notion. It was close to six hundred years ago and no matter how much I have increased my own lifespan over the years, memories don't seem to hold as well." He shrugged. "Maybe the mind simply can't hold on to everything. I had to look through volumes of books to be certain that the city used to be in Gerhaim." Desh tapped the map in front of him. There was the image of Gerhaim and the scattered towns and cities around it. "I found an old illustration, so old that it's crumbling now, but it showed Canhoon here." He tapped the center of the lake. "Right in this spot. There were bridges. Three of them, that connected the city to different parts of the land around it. I can't remember them clearly. I know they were there and if I try hard enough I can almost see them the way a word sometimes slides around in your mind without letting you catch it.

"It's the most amazing thing. I had convinced myself that the city had always been there, back in the east. I painted over the truth and never even noticed."

Nachia shook her head. "I can barely remember what I had for lunch yesterday. I can't imagine holding as many years as you have in your head, Desh."

Merros nodded and tried to push the notion aside. "So we can assume the city will float, or find the right spot, or that the Silent Army will move it into the proper location. What we cannot assume is that the Sa'ba Taalor will just sit back and wait for us to settle in properly."

He shook his head and looked over at the Sisters. The little blonde that had latched onto Desh, Cullen, was there as well, though she was staring off at the far corner of the room and talking to herself again. Desh said she was important but he could not or would not discuss why.

Nachia shook her head and reached for a cluster of grapes. She was one of the only people he'd ever seen that just took the seeds and chewed them up as well. He wondered if it was because spitting wasn't the proper way for royalty to be perceived.

"The thing to remember is that the city itself is ready to fight. We've seen that already. We have hundreds of the Sa'ba Taalor that were killed by the Silent Army. They may not be able to reach beyond the city, but thank the gods, they are perfectly willing to handle what happens here."

"And if we should, for some reason, need to ever leave the city? If we should have thousands of those bastards come here on their black boats?"

"There are no solid promises, Merros. We know that. But it's something. They're made of stone. They killed more of our enemy than anyone else seemed to have managed, no offense to anyone in this room."

"The trouble, Majesty, is that they are not following your orders or the general's or mine, for that matter," Desh pointed out. "They are following, according to what they already said, the orders of the gods."

"Yes, but those orders include protecting the city."

"And you, Majesty." Desh nodded his acknowledgment. "What they don't guarantee is that the orders from the gods won't suddenly change."

"I have no guarantee that you won't try to take over the seat of power, Desh Krohan." She took the time to chew on a grape before continuing, her eyes never leaving the First Advisor. "You have never attempted it in the past, but that doesn't mean you won't in the future. There are no guarantees of anything in this world, Old Man." She pointed to the Sisters. "Not even death, apparently."

Desh looked down at the table. There were laws against necromancy and while Merros was not sure if what he was looking at qualified, he knew that if she wanted, Nachia could have done something about Goriah's presence.

She was not foolish enough to attempt it. Having seen what Desh Krohan could do, no sane ruler would consider attacking his loved ones.

There had been a trust once, between First Advisor and Empress. Merros didn't know if it was merely wounded or if it was shattered. Only time would tell.

"We must prepare for whatever comes. Desh, you and your sorcerers can no longer remain as isolated from this as we would all wish."

Desh stared but did not respond.

Unlike most people, the Empress continued despite his silence. "It might be required that you and your brethren live up to the standards of the past. I am counting on the Silent Army to handle the worst of what comes our way. I have faith in General Dulver and his troops, but the numbers we have already seen are…" She shook her head.

"What must happen will happen, Nachia." Desh stood up. "We have already discussed the matter. We will do what we must. We have already killed one of their kings."

Merros looked toward Goriah as those words were spoken. The Sister's mouth pulled down in a scowl, and her hands clenched.

She looked back at him and moved in his direction.

"Has the death of one of their kings altered anything?"

Nachia's question was the very one on Merros's mind.

"Not in the least." Desh shook his head and pointed to the marks on the map where they had had their one victory against the enemy. "I can't say it has made them any more or less violent. The Sooth say that we killed a king here. We know that another king is dead by sorcerous means. But we have no way of knowing if they choose new kings by election or–"

"Their gods decide," Merros interrupted.

"What's that?"

"Their gods decide. I traveled with these people. I heard their stories. According to what they told me, Tuskandru was made king because his god, Durhallem, picked him."

Desh looked at the map again for lack of anything else to look at. "Then I hope their gods make miserable choices."

Nachia sighed and shook her head. "So far they seem to be doing well enough."

Merros nodded and so did Desh.

A few moments later the meeting ended.

Merros headed for his quarters and realized that Goriah was following him. "How may I help you, Goriah?"

"You are angry with me. With my presence."

"No, milady, I am terrified by your presence."

She nodded. "I understand."

"I don't think you do, respectfully. You work with sorcery. I have done my best never to know of its existence. I saw Desh Krohan destroy miles of terrain." His voice shook and he did his best to control himself. "I saw him burn the night and the ground. Not ten minutes ago I listened to him talk about the fact that his mind can't hold all of his memories because he's hundreds of years old. He's got so many memories that they no longer fit inside him."

Merros looked at the striking beauty before him.

"He told me that all of the Sisters are unnaturally beautiful because it gives you an edge in listening to conversations and negotiation." He shook his head. "I learned an entire language in seconds because Tataya and you felt I should."

Merros was unaware of moving closer to her until he was looking into her eyes. "I've admired your beauty. I have been amazed by your grace. It hurt my guts to hear of your death, Goriah."

His hand touched her arm. "You are alive and I am happy for that, but how are you alive? How are you back when I saw your body with my own eyes? How are you back, but others are not? Why is Wollis March still dead? Why is Emperor Pathra Krous still dead? Why did I not know that a gray-skinned bitch hid inside the body of Wollis's widow? How could I fall for her? None of this makes sense to me, Goriah. None of it and I can't sleep. I can't make myself understand why nature itself bends to some people and not to others.

"I'm a soldier. It's all I've ever been. What good is a sword against what you and yours can do?"

He was trembling. His voice shook.

Goriah nodded slowly and looked into his eyes. Her hand touched his, lightly, and he managed not to flinch.

She said, "I came back because Desh missed me too much. I came back so that he could not mourn me when he should be trying to save this city." Her hand touched his face. "I am back because there was a rare opportunity. I killed one of their kings because he killed me and I wanted revenge. Without it I could not keep my mind whole. I wanted to burn that nightmare out of existence and so I did. I can do these things because while you mastered the sword I studied different weapons. I studied nature and the world so that I could learn how to bend them."

A second later her lips were close enough to kiss and moving past until she was whispering in his ear. "I came back because there was a once in a thousand years' opportunity, and Desh Krohan seized it. He considered necromancy. He thought hard of taking lives to bring me back, but in the end he could not even take the lives of our enemies."

Her arms, long and elegant, hugged against him for a moment, the kind embrace of a friend, not the embrace of a lover.

"I came back so that Desh could sleep at night. I killed the king so I could sleep." Goriah pulled back from him enough so that he could look into her eyes and she could return the favor. "What will it take to let you sleep again, Merros Dulver?"

He wished he had a good answer.

The city was descending from the sky. The sun had set behind them and the stars were out and clear, save where the city's mass blocked them. The Great Star illuminated the edges and offered hints instead of details.

Drask looked at the city of Canhoon and nodded.

"What are you smiling about, Drask?" Andover's question was innocent enough. The boy had not yet decided if he would try to kill Drask. Despite his many changes, Andover could still not easily hide his thoughts. His face was not yet a proper mask.

"This is coming to an end, whatever it is. We no longer chase the city. It lands as all birds must land."

"Are there birds in the Blasted Lands? I don't recall ever seeing one."

"There are birds. They are very, very large and feed on, well, everything. You are fortunate not to have seen one."

Andover thought about that for a while and nodded. Tega rode up ahead, and Nolan rode with her, occasionally murmuring to himself; sometimes he laughed and other times he cried. He made words now and then, but not often.

Drask rode forward, until he kept pace with Tega. She looked his way and offered a weak smile.

"You were gone for a long time, Tega." It was not a question, merely an observation. Still, she flinched just a touch as if afraid he would strike her.

When she made no answer he continued on. "You have brought back one of your own."

"She was close to me, and she was murdered without ever being a part of your war."

"It is not my war, Tega. It belongs to the gods."

"They brought back Swech." Still she cringed. She tried to hide it but she was terrified.

He nodded his head. "What they did took power. What you did took power. You both had the ability and your own reasons."

"I thought you would be angry, Drask."

"I have no place in your actions. I am merely observing."

"You are reflecting," she corrected.

A smile played at his mouth and he nodded in the way of her people. "Yes. Reflecting is a good word. It is strong and accurate."

"What do you reflect upon, Drask?"

"What we are becoming." He raised his hand again, the most obvious change in any of the three of them. In the past it had been a miracle, yes, but stylized. There had been markings made by the gods on the metallic surface. Now it was clean of those marks.

"What are we, Drask?" Her voice shook. That was the thing about the Fellein: they seemed determined to torture themselves with doubts about the universe and their place in it.

"I am Drask Silver Hand. You are Tega, apprentice to Desh Krohan. Nolan is... Nolan. The only thing that has changed is that we have been touched by the gods in a way they did not intend. I do not have a name for what we are or what we are becoming beyond that. We are changing, but the changes are physical, Tega. You are still you. I am still me."

He pointed to the City of Wonders. "In your life did you ever imagine that you would see such a thing? A city that floats in the air, and moves hundreds of miles."

"Why did you... Why did you bring back the Blasted Lands?"

"That is easy. They have been there all my life and I find comfort in them. I spent my youth hunting in the winds and storms."

"Do you think I could bring back Tyrne?"

Drask shook his head. "Durhallem rests there now. He is a god. We have power but his is greater. You could bring Tyrne back, but if you tried to place it over the mountain or to move the mountain, Durhallem would fight back."

"Do you really think we could move a mountain?"

Drask looked at her for a moment, studied the minutiae of her face. She was easy to understand. Like Andover, she had not truly learned to hide herself behind a mask.

"I raised the Blasted Lands, Tega. You raised the dead." He gestured to Nolan, who was currently drooling on his own hands and seemed fascinated by the puddle forming in his palms. "Nolan was dead. I killed him. I felt his neck break. Yet he moves, and he feels, and perhaps even thinks."

"I used sorcery. I brought Goriah back with magic, not with–"

"You used what you know. What you are comfortable with."

Tega shook her head.

"It is frightening to you. You have so much power in you and you are limited only by your own desires. That is why I reflect. I must understand what I am capable of. I must consider what is coming. There are gods at play here, Tega. Gods that move mountains and cities and have fought against each other for a very long time. So long I don't even think they know why they fight any more.

"What will you do when the city lands, Drask?"

"I will go to it. I will see what happens when gods meet." He looked at the city again. It was a magnificent sight. "What will you do, Tega?"

"I will go too. I will stand with my friends, even if that means that you and I must stand on separate sides."

Drask nodded. "I do not yet know where I stand, Tega. We shall see."

While he looked at the city above, a small shape dropped over the side. Whatever it was, it moved as it fell. A few seconds later another shape dropped. This one was definitely humanoid.

The world continued to be interesting. Drask said nothing, but reflected on that.

"What will you do when you get to Canhoon, Andover?"

Andover looked at Tega. During the few times they had spoken, he discovered that she still fascinated him. He had thought that was gone, but after speaking again, the old feelings were back. They had just changed. There was no burning desire to fuel his fascination. It was not lust. No. Not true. It was not lust alone. She was unique in the world as far as he knew.

Still, there was Delil to consider. He remained uncertain whether she would want to come back. And if she did, whether he would act on her behalf.

"I will decide when the time comes." He did his best to smile, suddenly selfconscious of the changes in his face. "I know what the Daxar Taalor want. I am to be their champion if the Empress declares a single champion for combat." He looked at his hands and then back at her. "I do not know why I was chosen. I only know that I was and that I am grateful to the gods for all they have given me."

"I should have stopped them, Andover." Her still, calm face broke and tears threatened to fall from her blue eyes.

"What do you mean?"

"Menock and Purb and the rest. I should have told them to leave you alone. I should have–"

"No." He carefully put a hand on her shoulder. The metal was stronger than flesh and sometimes among the Sa'ba Taalor he'd forgotten that fact. He would not do so with Tega.

"You are not at fault, Tega. I am not at fault. They were predators and they wanted a meal they could play with.

Nothing more." He shrugged. "I had my revenge on them. I maimed them. I made them weak forever."

"If you had never been broken by them…"

"I would have been in Tyrne when Durhallem made the city his own. I would be dead. Or I would be wandering in the city up there, hoping to find a home and food."

Tega nodded and sniffed and tried to hide the misery she felt.

"Tega, what has happened is what has happened. The past is gone. I was not the same person then. I was much weaker. I lived and breathed and hid in fear. That time is gone. I fear nothing. I have faced my fears and learned from them. The gods gave me that.

"So many fear death. I still understand that. I fear for anyone I care for, I grieve for Delil. But I do not fear pain. I do not fear injury. Those are only parts of life we cannot always control. They have no power over me."

He sighed and smiled, fully aware that his smile unsettled her. "That is a gift, Tega. I received that gift because I was wounded. I would have died from the poisons in my hands, but you changed that. Do you understand? If not for you, I would have died. If not for you, I would have never met with Desh Krohan and I would have never met the Sa'ba Taalor. Whatever else might happen in this world, Tega, I am here now because of you."

His iron hand moved from her shoulder and very carefully raised her fingers until they were close to his face. He looked over her fingers to stare into her eyes.

"All that I am, everything that I do, is because you cared enough to stop for a boy who could not help looking at you."

The look she threw his way was not one that he easily understood. She had never regarded him with that expression previously and he had no idea what to make of it.

"What will I do when I get to Canhoon, Tega? What I must. Whatever I do, know this: you helped me more than any person ever has and I am forever in your debt. Thank you."

Tega nodded and rode forward.

Andover looked up to Canhoon, where another body fell from the sky.

The snow was melting but was not yet gone. That was good. It worked to their advantage.

Swech nodded her head and then raised one hand, speaking without words to the others.

The night air was still cold, the ground still frosty enough, and the Mid Wall was dark. The time had come to try their luck.

Evenly spaced along the Mid Wall, the stairs leading from the ground to the top of the wall were unguarded. What need of a guard when the unkillable Silent Army was already performing that duty?

The Sa'ba Taalor were vastly outnumbered. There were just over a hundred of them. There were at least ten times that number of the stone men with their swords.

They would work in teams of three.

The stone soldiers stood at their posts, some looking over the wall, others looking into the city. The stairs were easy enough. At Swech's order the groups went up the access points to the top of the Mid Wall and did not wait to be engaged.

Three lengths of heavy rope and three metal weights. Swech threw her bola at the first of the Silent Army that she encountered. The soldier stood at attention. The bola wrapped around his legs at the knees and he turned toward her, his face expressionless.

He started moving his legs, trying to untangle himself, and Swech stepped closer. The mace was heavy and spiked and took a large chip out of the soldier's face. As he turned toward her and reached, Jost came in low and jammed her staff between his legs, throwing her weight into the move. One foot was off the ground already as he tried to break away from the bola. His balance off, the soldier fell backward, arms flailing. Deras, the heaviest of them, smashed his weight into the soldier from the front and sent him careening over the wall. Momentum did the rest. Swech watched exactly long enough to see the soldier grab at the small lip of ground that still existed beyond the Mid Wall. He caught it and it crumbled, and ground and statue alike soared down toward the earth several thousand feet below.

The next one in line had turned toward her by the time she reached him. He swept his sword from the scabbard and Swech smashed her mace into his wrist, which promptly broke into two pieces. Hand and sword hit the ground. Swech brought her mace around in an upward trajectory and drove the soldier back as she shattered his chin.

As he stepped back Jost was there, once again using the staff to trip up the stone man's feet. As he staggered, Deras used a heavy staff and shoved at the soldier's chest. He stumbled further, off balance, and Deras hit him again. Jost was still there, her staff catching the guard at his knees and keeping him off balance.

The stone man fell over the wall and Swech watched history repeat itself.

Further along the wall she saw N'Heelis catch a soldier's arm, shift his hips and throw one of the stone men over the wall.

Beyond him, a Sa'ba Taalor named Rander soared over the wall when he tried to use mass alone to fight the Silent Soldier. Like the stone men before him, he fell several thousand feet.

Like his predecessors, he likely shattered on impact.

The Silent Army were bracing themselves now and that made life more difficult, but not impossible.

It merely meant they had to change tactics.

The next bola was thrown by Jost and wrapped itself around the face of a stone man. The soldier reached for the weapon around his neck and face and while he did, Deras took a turn entangling the soldier's feet. The stone men weighed too much to wrestle down to the ground. Their flesh was stone. Their muscles were unmovable if they set their minds to not being moved. But creatures of all size must obey the rules of physics, which was where the training of N'Heelis and Wrommish came into play. They could not fight the Silent Army with conventional weapons and win, and so they tried a different method.

Ultimately there were too many of the soldiers and they knew it, but they did what they could.

The Soldiers were not foolish and learned a new trick. They kept their feet fused to the stone wall they'd grown from. They could not move as quickly but they could not be thrown.

That possibility had been discussed, and as soon as the Sa'ba Taalor saw that their enemy had grown wiser they dispersed, moving away from the area as quickly as they could and dodging the attempts to grab them.

Four of the Sa'ba Taalor died in the conflict. Over fifty of the Silent Army were thrown from the wall before all was said and done.

That was a victory in the eyes of the Daxar Taalor and that was enough for Swech.

They were clever moving through the city. No one gathered in groups and no one made their way back to their gathering place in the same directions.

The house of Dretta March was no longer available, but Swech had purchased several buildings and some of them were better suited than others. They gathered in a warehouse that stored raw goods and they were careful to leave a barrier between themselves and the rest of the place. The barrier was built of barrels and crates of supplies. It was heavy and solid.

They were also wise enough to have guards.

After the raid Swech took her time getting back. She moved through parts of the city that were desperately overcrowded, fully aware that Jost followed her.

As she went, Swech changed her appearance a bit, switching her scarves for lighter colors and drawing out a bright shawl to cover her shoulders and hair. She walked differently, too, moving like an elderly woman and doing her best to look like someone who was harmless, but not a victim.

That had been a problem earlier in the week when a group of men tried to separate her from her purse. Fortunately they'd been weak and easily dissuaded.

When she finally stopped, the younger woman caught up with her and they moved among the waking crowds. The sun was not risen yet but the sky was growing lighter. Many of the people in the area were already rising. They had no choice. The world they moved on was dropping slowly and whether they wanted it or not, people had to respond to the change. Mostly that meant they were gathering their supplies again and preparing to flee if everything went wrong. Town criers had been notifying people of the descent for the last two days, but the melting ice and the warming temperatures would have told anyone who wasn't brave enough to look over the Mid Wall to see what was happening.

"What happens next, Swech?"

"We wait."

"What are we waiting for?"

"The gods will tell us when they are ready, Jost. In the meantime we must wait. I know that is not what you want to hear, but we must be patient. The Silent Army is probably already looking for us."

"I just. I feel incomplete not having a king."

"You have a king. N'Heelis is with us and will guide us."

"What of Glo'Hosht? What of the King in Mercury?"

A beggar looked their way and raised a hand in supplication. Offering coin was often an invitation to get more beggars active. Swech moved on without acknowledging the hand and the beggar went back into a knot of clothes in the alleyway.

"Glo'Hosht is dead. You saw what they did."

"But who will be our new king? Why has Paedle not chosen?"

"Jost," Swech kept her voice conversational though she was tempted to roar, "never question the Daxar Taalor. It is foolish and solves nothing."

"But…"

"No. They are the parents. We are the children. They guide and love us and we accept their wisdom. If Paedle has not announced who will lead, that is Paedle's decision. In time, when we must know, we will know. Paedle must judge all of her followers and decide who among then, if any, is worthy to stand in Glo'Hosht's place."

Jost sighed. "You are right. I know this. I followed Wheklam's wishes to get here, and I had never spoken to Wheklam before." She touched the new Great Scar on her face as she spoke, moving her fingers under the scarves that hid her face away.

"We must get back. The sun is rising soon and we tend to stand out here."

Jost nodded and the two of them quickly climbed to the rooftops. Swech had learned her way around them well enough.

From one of the higher roofs the two of them could see the view beyond the western gate of the Mid Wall. They could see the vast lake that was Gerhaim in all its glory and they could see the sun reflecting off the calm surface.

"Gods." Jost's voice was very small.

"Aye. I thought we'd have hours but the city has moved faster than anticipated. We need to get to the others now."

Below, the waters looked close enough to touch. The land and the river were still under them but only for the moment. The river was marrying the lake below them and even from here they could see the massive city on the not-so-distant far shore.

An hour at most before city and lake met.

It was time. The Great Tide surely would wait no longer. The time had come.

Both moved carefully. Both smiled as they did. Some prayers are answered sooner than later.

The warehouse was as she expected it to be: secured. Swech and Jost entered from the roof, sliding through the trap door that Swech herself had worked on when she was Dretta March.

She thought of him again. What was it about Merros that haunted her? She didn't let herself worry. There were other considerations and there they came first. Still, she missed his touch. She missed his babbling conversations and the way he felt against her.

No.

No more of that. She had work to do.

Most of their people were already gathered. Some were

missing, mostly those in the flesh of the Fellein. She understood how difficult it was to escape from the other life. There were people in and among the Fellein that insisted on being with the hidden Sa'ba Taalor.

"We are much closer to the water than we expected," Swech said as she settled in. "I think we will land within hours."

Her rump had barely met the floor when the air in the room shifted. Heat bathed her body and those around her. N'Heelis looked around but did not seem worried. That was enough to make her stay calm.

The voice of Paedle moved through her, and from the responses of others around her was carried to them as well.

RISE KING SWECH. RISE AND BE SEEN BY YOUR BRETHREN. There was no question of what had been said. There was no chance of misinterpretation. Still, it took a moment for her to obey.

She did not claim that she was unworthy. False modestly is foolish to begin with, but twice so when dealing with gods. Swech stood, and the Sa'ba Taalor with her stood as well. All but one offered the same obeisance as was given King Tarag Paedori. They lowered to one knee and held out their arms, a weapon placed in their hands with grip or hilt offered in her direction. Their lives for her to take or spare as she saw fit.

The only exception was N'Heelis. He did not bow, as kings do not make the same obeisances. Instead he smiled and moved toward her. When they embraced she held him tightly. He had always been one of her closest, dearest teachers.

"I am proud of you, Swech." That was all he said.

Paedle did not speak again, not at that time. There was little they could do by way of celebration, but that was just as well. The King in Mercury had no need of celebrations.

• • •

Darsken Murdro stood at the top of the Inquisitors Tower, which was one of the largest constructs in all of Canhoon. The building was not decorative in the least and most who passed it had no idea what went on there. That was deliberate.

The Inquisitors did not want to be known. They wanted to be ignored until such time as they were needed.

Darsken did not much care at that moment what the Inquisitors wanted. He was worried about his little sister.

Somewhere out in the waters the fighting continued. The gate had been opened and the vessels of the Sa'ba Taalor moved into the waters, but they did so slowly. Most of their black ships had been wounded and a few of them were sinking. That was the result of interference that should not have happened.

When Captain Callan climbed from a watercraft that did not belong to him and told his sorrows to the Louron, one of the Inquisitors present was Daivem, Darsken's younger sibling. She did exactly as he would have wanted and when Canhoon was mentioned, she contacted Darsken himself. The message was short and to the point and asked if he knew Callan.

When she reported more of what the captain had to say, Darsken thought about the laws of Fellein and the proper actions, and told her to do what she must.

And now his sister was down below, moving on a ship that was locked in the Shimmer.

The Shimmer, for better or worse, was the gift of the Louron.

Not long before, the black ships had tried to attack Louron and learned the hard way that the people were protected. They surrendered to the inevitable only after losing several of their people and the crew of one ship. Louron was not like other places. Louron was blessed.

On rare occasions, the Shimmer could be coaxed into fixing

itself onto an object. Currently the ship of Captain Callan was one such item. The vessel was still intact. It should have been shattered by impact after impact with the black ships, but the Shimmer kept it safe.

The Shimmer was a mystery, even to the Louron. It existed. It was. It was not under their control, but they could interact with it, and sometimes it would listen to requests. Not for the first time Darsken wondered if the Shimmer was truly a god that rested or if it was something entirely different.

For those coming to Louron, it was often a threat. The Shimmer seemed to know what the intent of travelers was. Those who meant no harm seldom encountered the ripples in the air. Those who felt otherwise vanished from sight, never to return. They did not die. The Louron would have known. Instead they traveled the Shimmer and moved to other worlds, beyond the one known to the rest of Fellein.

The people riding on the small vessel and harassing the Sa'ba Taalor were safe enough. There was always the chance that they could be attacked. There was a possibility that they could be sunk, but neither was very likely. The Shimmer protected them.

The massive craft of the Sa'ba Taalor were a different thing. They were vast. Certainly the largest ships that Darsken had ever heard of, but though they were truly well constructed they were not unbreakable.

Still, there were many of them and even the ones that were damaged and foundering were not without dangers. The Sa'ba Taalor were relentless. The shore was half a mile away in several cases and still they swam across the frigid waters to reach the shoreline and continue on with their quest to conquer everything before them.

Darsken clenched his fists and did his best not to grind

his teeth.

His sister was probably perfectly safe, but she was his sister and he worried.

The shadow of Canhoon appeared on the water, a hundred times larger than the black ships, as the sun began to rise. Darsken never noticed. He was too busy looking at one very small vessel to pay attention to shadows that drifted somewhere behind him. He faced the east and the brightening light of the new day's sun. He did not care about the glare. He only cared about his sister.

The sun rose. The City of Wonders fell. The higher the sun climbed, the lower the city dropped. Well before the sun climbed to its zenith, however, the city had finished its descent.

Tuskandru, Tarag Paedori and Pre'ru stared at the falling wonder dubiously. It was really spectacularly large.

"Do you suppose the lake will flood the lower part of this city?" Pre'ru asked conversationally. Tarag studied her. When he had been a much younger man Pre'ru had been a soldier of great repute. Then he had been a mount to Lored, who was, if one was completely honest, a bit of an ass. Now he was a woman and a king. The Daxar Taalor followed their own agendas, to be sure. Pre'ru was only marginally smaller than before and just as muscular as ever. All of the scars he remembered on the great man were still there on the woman.

Tarag said, "Four rivers surround us. I expect there will be a lot of water, but it will mostly go up the rivers. The path of least resistance."

Tusk frowned. "The rivers? That is a lot of water that the lake will push against. In my experience water can be a very hard force to argue with." He paused and added, "I haven't much experience with water though. I prefer flesh and steel."

"We will know soon enough," Tarag replied.

"Aye." Pre'ru could not look away from the city falling slowly from above. Canhoon fell as a feather falls, that is to say slowly, but without the shaking and dancing. A pity that, as Tarag would have loved to see the chaos that sort of motion caused.

"Why do you suppose the Fellein brought their city here? Why not stay where they were and fight?" Pre'ru was full of questions.

"Perhaps they hope the water will stop us." Tusk looked away from the descending land mass long enough to look at the black ships. They were hard to see past the early morning mists that rose from the massive lake. "I do not think they are right."

Tarag looked at the ships, too, though they were little more than ghosts at the moment. "They're sinking."

"Yes, but that is only half the fleet and the others are on their way. Even without them, however, we can find boats as we did before."

"The Silent Army might have ways of handling boats. Or the wizards."

Tusk nodded. "Why has no one killed the wizards yet? Aside from you, I mean."

"I do not think all of them kill easily. Remember the lightning."

"I was there. I will never forget it."

"Swech is a king now." Tarag contemplated those words ever as he spoke them.

"She is a very skilled killer. I think the choice a good one."

"Of course. The gods do not make errors."

Pre'ru looked their way. "Who is Swech?"

Tusk smiled and answered. "Swech is very faithful. She has

also killed more people than anyone I have ever met, and that says a great deal."

Tarag Paedori nodded. "I am glad the Great Tide is upon us. I do not like to think about how things would end if Swech set out to kill us." Before the Daxar Taalor declared the actions against the Fellein, the seven kingdoms of the Sa'ba Taalor had fought against each other, and the individuals of the Sa'ba Taalor warred among themselves besides.

Tusk frowned and nodded slowly. "Glo'Hosht was good enough not to assassinate kings. Swech has already assassinated an emperor."

"Exactly so."

The three kings grew silent as the city continued to descend. They were only moments away from the vast, inverted mountain of stone touching the nearly still waters. Even past the mists the reflection of the gigantic city was impossible to miss.

Tarag said, "Had I not seen the gods move mountains already, I would have thought this beyond any power."

"Where will Truska-Pren move, Tarag?"

Tarag Paedori looked to his fellow king and said, "You will know in minutes."

The water surged as the lowest tip of Canhoon touched the waters of the lake. There was a sound of distant thunder to the south and Tarag smiled. "There. Just there. The southern reaches of this land are changed now and forever."

Tusk nodded and smiled and watched as the City of Wonders slowly sank into the lake, sending water in all directions, not as a wave so much as a surge. The water rose everywhere at once, and as it rose it slowly crested, moving across the lake in a circular ripple: a stone thrown in a pond.

Pre'ru said, "We will soon know if half this city is sunk in the waters."

As they were currently occupying the king's palace they were not particularly worried. They were several hundred feet above the current water level.

The waters rose and rippled outward, and as they watched, the docks and the buildings within an arrow's flight of the docks were slammed with water that shattered wood and buried the lowest buildings.

Tusk looked at the devastation and grinned.

The water continued, lifting the docks and throwing them aside, shattering the structure and sending the boats that were tied along the structure sailing through the air. The vessels rained down destruction on still more buildings as the water rose and surged and ate everything it touched.

Tusk started to chuckle, and his hands reached up, and got a companionable grip on the shoulders of both kings standing with him as the waters surged higher and the city sank lower.

By the time Canhoon had settled in the exact center of the lake and the water had risen enough to wash away all evidence that a dock had ever existed, Tuskandru was howling with laughter.

Pre'ru looked at Tusk and shook her head, an amused expression on her scarred face. "What are you laughing about?"

Tusk grunted out the words as he continued to laugh. He gestured with the hand that had been on her shoulder toward the devastation. "You see? The Great Tide is upon us, indeed!"

Pre'ru laughed and shook her head at his antics. She had not known him in the Taalor Valley where among his many reputations he was known as a jester.

Tarag Paedori smiled too, as the waters started to recede.

"Oh," he said. "I think we can do much better than that."

• • •

Desh Krohan looked from the highest of the palace windows and next to him Merros Dulver gripped his sword hilt in fingers turned white by the pressure.

Nachia stood between them, and did her best not to scream with joy. They were settled. Until that last moment she'd continued to fear that they would sink to the bottom of Gerhaim and either learn to breathe water like the fish, or die.

"Well," Merros said. "That could have gone much worse."

"Still could," Desh pointed to the black ships. They were, as one, turning toward Canhoon.

"I've enjoyed our chat, but I have to prepare for war." The way he said it, Merros sounded like it was farewell.

"Don't go." Nachia's voice was small.

"It's not an option, Majesty. I am in charge of your armies and I intend to see that you have an empire to lead."

Desh sighed. "There are more black ships coming this way. They are a day out yet, but they will get here soon enough."

"Sink them!" Nachia turned her head so sharply to glare at him that muscles pulled and twitched like fire under her skin. "You, or your Sisters or any of the sorcerers here in Canhoon! Sink the damned ships!"

"Majesty, we don't have the power–"

"If you found the power to raise the dead and lift a city, then find the power to sink those gods damned ships!"

"Nachia." Merros's voice was soft. "No. Don't. We have the Silent Army. We have the Imperial Army. If you must use sorcery, wait until the last. Don't lose that last defense."

Without another word Merros left the room, shoulders squared and cape snapping with every stride.

Nachia shook her head.

Desh moved up behind her and placed a hand on both her shoulders, and she leaned back into him as she had on a hundred occasions through her life, already regretting snapping at him earlier.

He demanded no apologies, but instead simply held her.

"We'll prevail, Nachia. I'll make sure of that."

"Don't make false promises, Old Man. It belittles us both."

Down below, horns sounded the assembly and from a dozen different quarters the soldiers came, moving from their barracks and assembling in the vast yard of the palace.

Somewhere in that crowd Merros Dulver would be speaking, talking to the forces left to him in Canhoon and preparing for the inevitable assault.

The Sa'ba Taalor were monsters. They could not be reasoned with. They wanted death and destruction. They wanted to crush the Fellein Empire and they were doing a fine job of it.

Somewhere below the very best of the Imperial Guard were gathered together to defend her. Nachia did not care. She preferred that none stay behind, none defend her. The Empire was more important than the Empress. It had to be. If not, why was she so worried?

Theran stood trembling on the shore.

His head ached. His body was cold and he could not stop his muscles from shaking even though he stood still. It was like a fever, but a thousand times worse.

He was recovering from what they had done, but it wasn't easy. Someone had pulled the javelin from his neck. He'd heard bones crunch and felt his body go numb in the places where it did not scream.

The one with the skull helmet had spoken to him, his accent thick. "You have metal where you are from?" The man grunted and sat him up. "I mean the type touched by gods. It heals wounds." Thick fingers probed the wound on his neck.

"We heal you now, so you can talk to us."

The pain had been enough to shatter him. He bucked, he kicked, he screamed and they held him still as white hot metal ran across his neck. Or at least it felt like it did until the pain vanished.

The man with the skull helmet moved his head for him and nodded. "Better."

The giants around him were terrifying. There were easily a hundred, but he could see the leaders clearly enough.

That had been half an hour earlier. After he recovered enough to stand, they did worse to him. Now, they stood around him, the largest of the people, the ones he sensed were in charge.

"I do not think he likes us very much." The one who spoke wore a vast helmet shaped like a monstrous skull, the mouth of the thing filled with teeth of varying sizes, all of them sharp and the smallest of them longer than his middle finger.

The woman next to him was large and scarred and had been the one to cause him the greatest agony in his entire life. A pain so large that five minutes later he was still trying to recover from the memory of it. He had screamed, begged and even tried to use his sorcery, all to no avail. He was too scared to concentrate on magic and his words apparently made no difference to the people around him. They were the Sa'ba Taalor, and he was ready to piss himself at the sight of them up close.

The coin she'd shown him was very large and made of gold. Her hands were smaller than the largest of the giants' but not by that much. The golden disk filled her palm.

He'd looked at her and shaken his head at first, having no idea what was about to happen. The metal was pressed into his forehead. Her palm kept it there and her fingers moved into his hair as if she meant to caress and tease him.

Then the burning started. Theran felt the heat start and jerked, trying to get away, but her fingers pulled his hair tight and even as he tried to move his head one way and then another she did not let the pain escape. He wet himself. His arms and legs twitched and kicked and he beat at her as best he could with his hands tied behind his back and one of the bastards standing on his calves while he kneeled before the bitch who tortured him. If he could have, he'd have spat in her face, but he was too busy praying for death and his eyes were screwed shut as the metal melted across his forehead.

As intense as the pain was, it only lasted a few seconds and when he looked up she was still there, looking at the palm she'd pressed into his head.

There was metal left over, hot and steaming, and she had painted it across her cheeks in two nearly white-hot streaks that had cooled down and now looked almost like the golden trails of tears. Her flesh was not burned and he could not understand that. He did not want to know what his forehead looked like. The coin she used had been quite large.

The pain was gone. Theran was grateful for that much. It was all he had. They'd let him stand when they were done and he wanted to run, wanted to hide away, but he found he was too exhausted to do more than stand and shiver.

The last of them finally lifted the faceplate on his great helm and revealed a face that glowered just as well as the iron visage that hid him away.

They spoke among themselves and he listened. Currently he was not capable of much more. The pain was gone, but the memory of it lingered and now it seemed he had a fever.

The biggest of them, the one with the iron helmet, studied him carefully. Each of the man's hands looked large enough to cover his face.

"I do not care if he likes us."

Their words were not the common tongue of Fellein or any of the other languages he knew but he understood them well enough. They had their own sorcery then.

NO. NOT YOUR SORCERY. THAT IS WHY YOU ARE HERE. THAT IS WHAT WE WILL NOW UNDERSTAND.

The words smashed through his mind and Theran fell backward, his limbs moving and dancing, his teeth clenched in a sudden fit that threatened to break his teeth in his mouth. He could not breathe, could not control his movements.

The gray-skins around him watched on, not speaking, not moving, but staring as if he were a new form of bug they had never seen.

The thunderous voice was gone, but the presence that roared at him was not. He could feel it probing him, moving under his flesh, peeling his self away layer by layer as it examined him in great detail.

It was a violation that made control of his body impossible, and he continued to seize and kick for the eternity that the assault lasted.

When it was done Theran groaned. It was the only sound he was capable of.

When he finally had recovered enough he stared out at the waters, at Canhoon where it now rested, a city that had fallen from the sky.

He and the people around him stood on the edge of the waters amid the destruction caused by the city's arrival. There was debris, of course. There were also corpses, though not as many as he might have expected. A great number of the citizens of Goltha also stood nearby, though they were not there by choice. They were injured or too scared to fight. In any event, they were there and they watched on as well.

The woman spoke to him.

"You are a sorcerer. You can make magic."

It wasn't truly a question, but he sensed that she wanted a response and so he nodded and said, "Yes."

"You have spoken to a god. You have been judged by the Daxar Taalor. They wish for you to obey us."

Theran sighed and nodded again. "Yes." He liked to think himself a good man, but he was not strong. He never had been. One of the reasons he loved Goltha was that his vices had always been easy to accommodate. Women. Otha and other narcotics. Whatever helped him feel pleasure, he could access. A good man, but weak.

So very weak.

"We want to cross the waters. As they are, we would sink. You must freeze them."

Her hand touched his hair again and he flinched. She lifted his sweaty bangs from his face and looked at the damage she had done to him with a coin and her hand. Her palm was unmarked. The gold on her face shone. Once again her fingers moved through his hair.

"You and I, we are linked. I have marked you and made you mine. The gods have willed this. You will obey me. You will do as I say. If you do not, there will be pain."

He nodded. "Yes."

Then he tried to reach out to Corin. He wanted only to warn them.

The pain was so much that he fell forward and vomited. His body felt broiled in heat, lit afire from the very inside of his bones outward. He could not move. He could not scream.

An eternity later the pain was gone. There was no lingering aftermath. It simply was not there.

"No." The woman shook her head at him. "You will never speak to them again. If you try, you will hurt."

Theran sobbed. "Yes. Yes. Yes. Yes." He nodded his head so hard he feared he might break something.

"Freeze the lake."

"I can't."

He screwed his eyes shut again, fearing the titanic wave of agony. It did not come.

"Why?"

"What?"

"Why can't you freeze the lake? Your people move cities through the air. Your kind brings lightning from the air. Why can you not do this?"

"Sorcery takes power. It has a cost. If I tried to freeze the whole lake, I would die. It would drain all of my life from me."

She nodded her head and looked to her two companions. Though they spoke, he could not understand the language. The one with the skull helmet looked to him and then pointed to the people gathered together nearby.

"Then use them."

"What?" He could not keep the shock from his voice.

"If you cannot do this thing alone. Use them. We will only kill them in any event."

"I cannot do tha–" That was all he could mutter before the pain ruined his world again.

The woman said, "Use them."

"Yes." He cried as he spoke, but none of them cared.

She crouched down next to him as he once again became aware of the universe beyond his personal agonies. For the first time he looked into her eyes and realized that they shone with their own light. He might have been fascinated were he not so utterly terrified. "If you betray me, if you attack any of us, your pain will never end. Do you believe me?"

"Yes." He nodded as hard as he could.

Her hand found his hair again and stroked through it. "Freeze the lake. Whatever it costs."

"Yes."

Theran didn't trust his legs. He crawled through the muck and the debris, barely aware of what was beneath him even as he slithered over the corpse of a dead woman and her dead child.

When he reached the waters he reached forth with his hand and the gray-skinned monster that promised him pain crouched over him. Her hand moved over his chest and belly like a person petting a dog, or restraining it. His body moved over more corpses, dead and drowned, but he didn't dare change his course.

"Not yet. Not yet, no." She looked out at the waters, and the black ships that were crawling closer to the city.

One minute passed. Then three, five, ten and finally, "Now. Do it now."

Theran did not dare disobey.

His hand touched the water and the water screamed.

Where his fingers touched, the ice started and grew quickly. The saturated mud under his body rose as ice formed, and the beach and shoreline all along the way did the same.

The surface of the water was not all that froze. He dared not take that chance. Instead he pushed with all that he had and the lake howled at the sudden change in climate.

A crust of ice ten feet deep formed in seconds and raced toward Canhoon.

Theran was aware of the screams behind him and felt his eyes sting once more with tears. They had to die. It was not a choice, still, he felt their deaths as they happened, felt the life ripped from body after body, torn from flesh that fell lifeless to the ground.

No matter their pain. He had already endured worse. He could not dare it again.

He was a good man, but he was weak. He kept telling himself that as the water froze and the air steamed with the change in temperatures.

The woman's hand moved lower, until she touched his privates. "Good. That is good." Had she been the most perfect female he had ever seen he could not have grown hard for her. She was a terror to him, a scarred, hideous beast that would haunt him for as long as he lived.

"Come now." She stood up and looked out at Canhoon in the distance. "It is time for us to run."

Around them, all along the shoreline, horns sounded a cry to war.

The Sa'ba Taalor moved, stepping onto the ice with ease, their great mounts moving with them.

Theran could not guess how many of the hellish folk there were. The fog from the frozen waters was too thick to give the faintest hint.

He could not see the corpses that he left behind, either. That was for the best. He had felt two of them freeze beneath him as he touched the water and he would never get past that sensation in a hundred lifetimes.

THIRTEEN

Captain Callan looked at the ice and shook his head, simply shocked beyond his ability to understand for a moment. One thing to hear about sorcery. One thing to even travel faster than a man should ever manage. The ice was a different beast. It was an actual impossibility made reality.

"How is that happening?" He watched as the ice overtook every one of the black ships around them. Waves froze in an instant and even the ship he stood on – a ship that had managed not to get destroyed by a dozen impacts with other vessels, that had traveled miles in minutes against all possibilities, even so incredible a boat as that – was slowed and then suspended in the ice.

Daivem looked his way and frowned. "Powerful sorcery. More powerful than any I've seen, besides that city."

They'd watched as Canhoon dropped softly from the sky and landed. They'd felt the surge of water lift all of the ships around them and theirs besides. It had been an experience not easily prepared for.

The air was warm with spring. The trees were blooming along shorelines that teemed with green, but now the whole

of Gerhaim, virtually an inland sea, was frozen in minutes.
Heavy mists rose from the ice, making even the closest of
the ships little more than a silhouette, but still he could see
the Sa'ba Taalor's shadowy forms as they climbed from their
trapped ships and started walking across the ice. Hundreds of
the bastards were heading toward the island city.

"I don't see how we can go after them at this point," he
said. "I mean, it's one thing to hit their ships and another for
a small crew to try to kill that many."

Daivem nodded and then pointed. "Still, your crew will try,
yes?"

Sure enough, the ghosts of his crew were scaling down the
sides of the ship.

"What can they possibly do?"

Daivem frowned and shook her head. "Nothing. They are
dead. They can do nothing once they leave the ship, except
remember that fact."

He wondered for only one moment what she meant. As
they left the ship and walked a short distance, they flickered
out of sight.

"Where are they going, Daivem?"

"To where the dead go. I am not dead and cannot say
beyond that." She sighed and looked his way. "I hear that they
go to a place of peace. I hope that is true."

"What do we do now?"

The Inquisitor looked at him and shook her head. "This was
never my fight. Never Louron's fight. This is your battle. We
have merely provided you with a means to get here."

He looked at the woman for a while, not sure how to
respond. "How do you mean?"

"You asked for our help and we gave it. But you have lost
your crew. What you do now is your decision, but we will

not be staying."

"Where will you go?"

"Home. The same way we got here."

"With this ship?"

"No. We will follow the Shimmer."

Callan nodded. He'd understood that something unnatural to him allowed the ship to move so quickly and he'd certainly seen the distortion around them. The Shimmer was as good a name as any for it.

"Do you come with us, Captain Callan? Or do you stay here?"

Callan looked to the city and felt the ship beneath him, and was uncertain.

Drask looked down at the ice and nodded slowly. "That makes sense."

Andover looked his way. "What do you mean?"

"Why swim when you can walk? Freezing the lake was sensible."

Whereas the Fellein were unsettled by the notion, neither Drask nor Andover was particularly shocked. Both had seen the actions of the gods.

Tega looked on and then shrugged. A moment later the mount under her moved forward.

Why it obeyed was something that Andover could not fathom. The mount had been Delil's and she was not only dead, but now she was gone as well.

The night before, with Canhoon only a short distance away, he had taken her shrouded body and laid her upon the ground. He had uncovered her face one last time. She was perfectly still, but had not decayed. The Daxar Taalor had given him that. Or perhaps it was Drask. He hadn't bothered to ask.

He touched her face one last time then covered her and set about the task of building her funeral pyre. He did not ask for help, but Tega and Drask gave assistance just the same.

There were no tears shed, but he felt the loss of Delil deeply.

In the end he could not decide if she would want to come back and so he left her death in the hands of the gods. Had they wanted her back they would have brought her back as they had Swech. Her body burned hot and the blaze was bright enough to light the area.

Eventually he slept and when he awoke all that was left of Delil was ashes.

Andover stared at the frozen lake and followed Tega and the silent fool who rode with her, Nolan.

Drask rode out onto the ice beside him. Theirs was a comfortable silence, at least for the moment. There were decisions to be made and that time was upon them.

"You should present yourself to the Empress." The words were unexpected and Andover looked to Drask and shook his head.

"You jest."

"Not at all. You were sent on a task by her cousin, the Emperor. You return now from that task and you should present yourself."

"I suspect the guards throughout the city might object."

"They might indeed, but you will be safe from them. Tega and I will see to that."

"You discussed this then?"

"Yes. It is a matter of protocol. This is not your war unless you choose to make it your war, Andover. You have been tasked with a duty by gods, yes, but your Emperor also tasked you with a duty."

"I don't see how I can go back before them. I've changed."

Drask sighed. "An honorable person is only as good as the vows they choose to make and keep. You have made vows. Would you not discharge them properly?"

"What will the Daxar Taalor say about it?"

"The Daxar Taalor were the ones who taught me about honor. There is a time and a place for conflict, Andover. If you choose to fight for the Daxar Taalor that is acceptable, and you may present yourself as their champion if they have, as you say, chosen you for that purpose."

"They have." He did not take offense from Drask's words because he understood the meaning.

"Then you have even more reason to present yourself to the Empress. Fellein has suffered greatly and will continue to suffer. That is the way of war. One side must win and one side must lose and the losers are seldom pleased with the outcome. There is death, there is destruction, there is disease and often poverty. In this case there are also the Seven Forges. Five have now been relocated. They will change the very shape of the land in all directions. That change can be gentle, or it can hammer Fellein into a new shape as it does now."

"Why do you say these things, Drask?"

"Am I not one of your instructors? Do you see any of the others here?"

Andover nodded.

"You speak for the gods on this and you must let the Empress know that she has an option aside from all-out war."

"Drask, do you not want a war?"

"What I want does not matter. The war is already happening and is the will of the Daxar Taalor. It is also their will that you are their champion and must present yourself as such. It is not me who suggests an alternative to combat, Andover Iron Hands. It is the Daxar Taalor."

Drask looked his way, his eyes glowing in the light. Andover knew the man, respected him, and still, even after all this time, found him unsettling. He was the only other member of the Sa'ba Taalor that Andover had ever seen with symmetrical Great Scars. He had the balance that Andover himself was seeking.

"As you wish, Drask."

Drask shook his head. "No. As the gods wish. In this I will act as their agent. You will reach the Empress safely."

That was all there was to say for the moment. They moved on, the mounts carrying them with ease.

The ice was thick enough to hold them and the mounts were fast. The heavy fog hid them and only hinted at the great obstacle before them. They rode hard and though he wobbled for a moment, even Nolan reacted properly. The man's hands moved to Tega's waist and held to her as she leaned forward over the shoulders and neck of the beast.

Drask leaned forward as well when the mounts moved faster and Andover followed their lead. The brutes tore across the frozen lake, claws adjusting when they started to slide, their speed whipping back the hair of every rider.

The city of Canhoon was a massive affair, indeed, easily dwarfing Tyrne. Andover had enough time to look at the vast wall ahead of them and the shapes of men that stood along it.

The wall was too high for even the mounts to hurdle and though he knew that, he kept moving forward at the same frightening pace. Tega or Drask or the gods themselves would have to either open a way or peel his broken body from the stone surface.

The shapes atop the vast wall moved, and Andover reached for his shield. They might have arrows or spears and both he and Gorwich would need the protection if it came to that. Closer still they rode and then the air flickered around him and Andover grunted, surprised to find himself in a different location.

The sun glared down, no longer hidden behind a veil of mists. The ice was gone and the ground beneath their feet was dirt and cobblestones. The yard was vast, and that was a blessing. Even the fastest mounts needed room to stop. They managed, though Andover almost fell on his ass at the sudden shift in speed.

There were easily thirty men in Imperial armor less than a hundred feet away. They were practicing with swords, and they stopped as the mounts and their four riders appeared.

For one moment he had no idea what to do and the ghost of the boy who had once been maimed by the City Guard wailed from inside his belly.

The soldiers moved quickly, forming into a proper rank and replacing swords with spears. A good sword would wound a man in close combat. A good spear would do the same but had the advantage of range. Before he had been trained by the Sa'ba Taalor and the Daxar Taalor, Andover had considered spears to be little but sticks with a pointy end. He knew better now.

Andover climbed down from his mount and patted Gorwich on the side. He looked to the men coming his way, most of them with swords drawn, and casually pulled his axe from the side of Gorwich's saddle.

"That is enough!" Andover barely recognized his own voice. "I am Andover Iron Hands, and am here to speak with Empress Nachia Krous and with Desh Krohan!"

The man in charge of the group looked at him and nodded. He seemed absolutely unimpressed. "I am Captain Alaire of the Imperial Guard, and you will stand down or you will die here and now."

Tega spoke up. "I am Tega. I am apprentice to Desh Krohan. We will wait here while you pass a message to the Empress and her First Advisor."

Drask said nothing. He merely sat tall in the saddle on Brackka's back, his hands in easy reach of enough weapons to terrify anyone who knew what he was capable of.

Nolan giggled.

It wasn't long before the four riders were escorted to see the Empress.

Nachia stared at the four who came into her throne room. They were hard not to stare at. The last time she'd seen Tega and Nolan they were on their way to examine the Mounds. The last time she'd seen Drask Silver Hand, her cousin had still been Emperor.

As for Andover Lashk, the only reason she really recognized him at all was because of his hands.

"What did they do to him?"

She whispered the words to Desh, who looked at Andover and spoke back just as softly, "I couldn't hope to tell you."

Drask Silver Hand was the first to approach and as he did he dropped into a formal bow, his arms spread to his sides and his head lowered. "Empress Nachia Krous, I return to your lands in troubling times."

"Indeed, Drask. The world has changed a great deal since last we met." She spoke formally as did he, and she sat on her throne and did her best not to fidget.

Andover came forward next. He had changed a great deal. He'd left Fellein to be an ambassador between two different civilizations and came back dressed like a member of the Sa'ba Taalor nation, with gray skin and scars too numerous to count.

"Majesty, I am Andover Lashk, called Iron Hands." He bowed formally. "I come before you as a citizen of your Empire, returned from a long journey. I come to you as a messenger of the Daxar Taalor."

That earned him an arched eyebrow. Part of her wanted to react more substantially, but there were protocols to consider.

As was often the case Desh Krohan was on one side of her. As Andover gave his speech Merros Dulver moved into the throne room and to her other side. His eyes scanned Drask, and his face spoke of a dozen sorrows. They had never become friends, exactly, but they'd shared a deep respect for each other and now stood on opposite sides of a conflict.

Desh spoke for Nachia at her signal. "You bear the hands of Andover Lashk. In most other ways you have changed a great deal."

"I have been in the presence of seven gods, Desh Krohan. I have spoken with them and been blessed by them. These are events that change a man. I remember you well. You were kind to me when my hands were ruined. You have never done me any unkindness."

Nachia nodded. "What message do you bring to me, Andover Lashk?"

"The Daxar Taalor, the gods of the Seven Forges, offer you one last chance to avoid all-out war. Even now the Sa'ba Taalor surround this city. They are prepared to attack, but they have stayed their actions long enough for you to consider the path you choose.

"I have been chosen as their champion. Should you decide that your Empire is best served by singular combat, I am the opponent your champion will fight."

Nachia leaned back in her throne.

"And how long do we have before this offer expires,

Andover Iron Hands?"

The man in front of her was larger than the lad who left her Empire. He was almost as large as Drask, who was a terrifying sight to behold up close. Andover's face was ritually scarred and he looked enough like Drask that it was unsettling. A different shade of gray, fewer scars, though still a substantial number, his hair not as black. His eyes glowed with silvery light, however, and his garb was little more than black pants and a leather vest.

And an axe made of glossy stone.

Andover tilted his head.

"The Daxar Taalor offer you one hour to decide." He stood to his full height and looked directly at Merros Dulver. "This will be the last offer of peace from the gods."

Merros looked back, one hand on his sword. He did not seem the least bit intimidated.

Nachia nodded. "There is a chamber down the hall where food can be had. Two guards will escort you there. Please do not leave that hall until I have summoned you back here."

Andover bowed again and so did Drask. Then the two of them followed the Imperial Guard out of the room.

Tega and Nolan did not leave. They were not representatives of the Sa'ba Taalor.

Merros looked at Nolan March with an expression of deep sorrow. He had the unpleasant task of telling the soldier that his mother was gone as well.

Desh nodded to Tega and she moved to him, almost immediately being folded into a protective embrace.

Merros walked toward Nolan and sighed. "I am sorry, Nolan March. I must inform you that your mother has passed."

Nolan looked at him for a moment and then looked at the far wall.

"He's addled," Tega said. "He was injured in the Mounds, and injured badly. We do not know if he is capable of thought."

"If he is not it might be a blessing." Merros looked at the young man for a moment and then moved back to Nachia's side.

He looked toward his Empress and said, "*That* was Andover Lashk?"

Nachia said, "We've less than an hour to decide if the Sa'ba Taalor will attack us or if we will choose a champion to fight for me." She gestured toward the door. "Against Andover 'Iron Hands'."

Desh nodded. "That was Andover Lashk. Now he's apparently a full member of our enemies."

Merros shook his head and sighed. "I'd dearly love to know what training regimen they used."

Nachia scowled, "Perhaps we can ask them after the war?"

Desh came straight to the point. "If you were to choose a champion, who would it be, Majesty?"

She walked over to the closest window without answering. Outside was her city. Beyond it was a frozen lake blanketed in fog, and covered for far too great a distance with the Sa'ba Taalor.

"How many do you suppose are out there?"

Merros frowned. "Fifteen thousand at the very least."

"I know the Silent Army is on our side, but that is a lot of enemies." Nachia stared at them as if by looking she could somehow make them go away. It wasn't going to work that way, of course.

"I don't know that Andover Iron Hands is all that formidable." Merros spoke, but he seemed distracted. She knew that he was simply trying to calculate all of the odds.

Tega spoke up from the comfort of her instructor's arms. "I

have spent time with him. I know that he hasn't truly been gone from here all that long, but you've seen the transformation and he told me that he literally fought thousands of enemies thrown at him by the gods in order to prepare him for this. He is likely as dangerous as he looks."

"Well then, what shall we do?" Nachia asked.

Desh looked her way. "It's one champion or a massive army. You could always try to find a really good champion."

The debates began properly at that moment.

Who can say if the Silent Army was aware of what was going on in the palace? They stood along a massive stone wall and stared out toward the vast armies of the Sa'ba Taalor which, shielded by fog, made noise as they settled themselves and prepared for the coming combat. For some time, the stone sentinels watched as the masses of invading forces came their way and they did nothing.

And then they changed their tactics.

The stone army slipped through the Mid Wall and stepped out along its edge. Their spears were held in position. Their stone faces offered nothing.

The Sa'ba Taalor, unfamiliar with much of the ways of sorcery, saw the changes and stared, shocked. How clearly they could see was a mystery, but they noted when the soldiers vanished into stone and stepped out of the wall.

The gods had spoken, had said that none should attack as yet.

They had not said that none should defend themselves.

The Silent Army looked on for a few moments, and then one of them hurled a spear. The throw was strong and fast and the point of that spear rammed through the shield of a follower of Truska-Pren and then through the heart behind that shield.

Tarag Paedori looked at his fallen follower for only a moment and then roared, "We are attacked! For Truska-Pren!" The horns sounded. The forces of the King in Iron moved forward.

It was only seconds later that the rest of the kings called for battle.

"What was that?"

Merros moved to the window and looked down. "We're attacked." His voice made the words seem inevitable, and perhaps they were. The world had already changed too much and there were too many forces involved for calm to be maintained.

"Why are we attacked?" Desh Krohan moved closer to the window and wall and studied the situation. "The Silent Army are no longer at their guard positions." He shook his head. "It might be they started this."

"Yes, well, I'll try to remember to yell at them later." Merros shook his head. "Please relay the call to arms to my battalions, Desh."

The sorcerer nodded. With a thought Desh Krohan told his followers what they needed to hear and they, in turn, passed the information on to the leaders of the Imperial Army.

Even as the massive surge of the Sa'ba Taalor charged across the ice once more, the horns of the Imperial Army called for a defense of the city.

From the barracks houses and the ready stations that had been hastily assembled, the army moved, taking up arms and grabbing shields. From the throne room they looked like ants, but they were well-organized ants as they scaled the steps to the top of the Mid Wall and prepared for battle. Shields were set to the wall, adding height and strength to the barrier.

Archers readied their weapons. Spearmen set their long spears into position between the shields, wedging hard iron tips between the flagstones so that the points thrust outward and toward the sky. Shorter spears were readied for close combat.

"Desh?"

"Yes, Merros?"

"Could you melt all of that ice?"

"Beg pardon?"

"The ice. The damned idiots we're dealing with are standing on ice. Could you melt it?"

Desh frowned, thinking.

Tega didn't hesitate. "Done."

And just like that, it was.

The ice shattered violently and as it broke apart the shards melted into water. The charging forces of the Sa'ba Taalor fell fast and hard as the effect continued to ripple outward.

Just as the gray-skins had somehow managed to freeze the lake, Tega now reversed the effect. Merros looked at her and damn near kissed her.

Drask heard the horns, of course. He knew what they meant the second they sounded.

"We are at war," he said to Andover.

Andover nodded and rose from the food he'd been picking at. Pabba fruit. He would never tire of it.

The two guards with them heard as well and reached for their swords. Under the circumstances that was to be expected. Drask stepped toward the first of them and drove his silver hand into the man's skull, cracking it like a soft-boiled egg.

Andover kicked the table where he was eating across the distance between him and the other guard. The table was small and got good clearance. The guard was fast with a sword and slow with defending himself. While he was pushing his way past the wooden obstacle, Andover cleaved him in half with the obsidian axe.

The two emissaries did not speak to each other. Instead they pushed past the door and headed for the stairwell leading down.

Then Drask said, "You may never have a better chance to kill the enemies of your gods."

Andover shook his head. "Tega is there. She would stop me, even if the sorcerer could not."

Drask nodded his head and kept moving.

"You could stop them too, Drask."

"As I have said, I am not certain where I stand. I am still reflecting."

Andover shook his head. "The time for reflection might have passed."

"No. But it soon shall."

In her chambers, Cullen sat up abruptly. The pain was no stronger than before, but there was a sense of urgency, a sense that whatever it was she had been waiting for was soon to come.

Also, there were horns sounding. Deltrea looked to her and shook her head. "You're going to do something stupid, aren't you?"

Cullen reached for her arrows and bow.

"I am going to help defend the castle. You've seen these animals in action. They'll kill everyone if they break through the walls."

"There are two walls between us and them, Cullen. Two. And they are very large walls, with many soldiers."

"Then I will simply look foolish while I wait."

She stopped speaking. That pain in her guts was now roiling. "Almost time," she said quietly.

"Almost time for what, Cullen?" Deltrea's voice sounded worried and desperate. "Gods sake, almost time for what?"

"For whatever I'm becoming. Oh, GODS!"

The pain was as vast as Trecharch. It filled her. It seethed through her. Cullen dropped her weapons and fell to her knees, crawling toward the window, looking to the north and east. Whatever was happening, it was happening now.

The Sa'ba Taalor swam. There was no other option. They had spent their lives preparing for this and so they swam.

The waters were not as deep as one might have expected, but they were deep enough. Several of the more encumbered warriors sank to the bottom of the lake, only to find that they only dropped ten feet or so. There had once been a city here and it had been locked into the land under the lake. That land was still there.

Tarag Paedori held his breath and moved, reaching for the straps that held his armor in place, pulling them as calmly as he could even when he felt like he was drowning. Truska-Pren comforted him, the god's presence keeping him calm. The chest plate fell away. It was enough as a start. He reached for his dagger and cut at the straps as he walked, concentrating on cutting his way to freedom.

When he rose from the waters the helmet came off his head. He rose in little but pants, his sword held in his hands.

He rose angry, and sought to take out his fury on an enemy.

The wisdom of Tuskandru could not be denied. The man never wore armor and he was already wading to the shoreline and roaring Durhallem's name at the stone enemy they all faced.

The first of the moving statues to reach him tried to skewer Tusk with a spear. Tusk dodged the weapon and crouched low, water spilling from him in a cascade.

The man sported a short sword, an axe with two blades and a flanged mace. He reached for the mace.

That was as long as Tarag could look toward his counterpart before he was engaged in the battle himself. A spear was hurled his way and he twisted his body roughly backward even as he swept his sword in the direction of the weapon. The sword did him no good. The movement however stopped him from being gutted by the head of the spear.

He charged, pushing out of the waters and onto the land along with dozens of his brethren.

The Silent Army was powerful, to be sure. They were also vastly outnumbered and every last one of the Sa'ba Taalor who stepped onto the land wanted them dead.

A stone sword came for him and he blocked it, sending the blade singing along the edge of his great sword. The pommel of his sword was a heavy counterweight for the blade. He used it to break the stone blade in half and then shoved himself at the stone man wielding it. For most the forward shove would have achieved nothing. But he was Tarag Paedori and he knocked the stone man back.

Even as he struggled against the defender of Canhoon, two of his people came to his aid. A sword rang off a stone arm. A hammer broke a stone knee.

A broken stone blade cut the arm from the other sword bearer and Tarag once again struck with the pommel of his sword, this time to hook the knee of the stone man and make it buckle. The silent warrior fell and Tarag pushed past him, leaving him to the mercies of the other Sa'ba Taalor.

A spear tip cut a line of fire across his chest and he felt

blood flowing. The wound was not deep and he thanked
the gods, even as he grabbed the stone spear that had been
thrown at him and dropped his massive sword. The blade was
too unwieldy and could not cut stone. The spear was a better
weapon under the circumstances.

The butt of the spear broke the nose of a stone man's face.
And the length of the pole let him knock his enemy staggering.

All around him flesh met stone, stone met steel, and
enemies clashed on the narrow strip of land around the city
of Canhoon.

Tarag Paedori roared his god's name and continued on,
reveling in the glory of a proper savage battle.

Behind him, around him the Sa'ba Taalor moved onward,
pushing themselves against an army of stone.

Swech listened and obeyed. She once again climbed to the
roofs and along with her a dozen others. They carried few
weapons and they spoke not at all. The war was on. The Great
Tide crashed along the edges of the city and Paedle told her it
was time.

There was no need for ceremony, she merely needed a
decent view.

Once high enough Swech looked to the north and east and
nodded. Morwhen. The city was famed for its barbarism and
the warriors it created. The first she heard of the people, they
were to be the probable salvation against the Sa'ba Taalor, as
they allegedly matched her people in savagery. For that reason
the gods waited until most of the soldiers from Morwhen were
on the move and heading for Canhoon before Paedle told her
it was time.

She merely looked and willed the change and it happened.

Swech was the conduit for her god's power. She was not a

sorcerer and had no desire to be one, but she was the focus of Paedle's will in this world and so she let the god's power flow through her and she felt the earth shift and the heat boil and reveled in Paedle's glory as the god was reborn on the site of Morwhen.

A war raged but still the lake and the city and the area rocked with the ferocity of the eruption. The recently unfrozen waters rippled and danced and waves slashed the relative calm.

Even before the water shifted the sky grew bright. Six gods had taken new places. The last would come soon.

Her mission accomplished, Swech sighed and prepared herself for her next task. The palace had to fall. The armies of the Sa'ba Taalor fought against the Silent Army.

All save those who were already past the Mid Wall and even the First Wall.

People like her.

They moved, silent and hardly worth noticing in the madness of the moment.

The ice was gone.

Callan stared at the waters and the black ships that faltered and foundered around him. They had no crews. The whole lot of gray-skins had run off to join the fight.

The smaller boat he'd ridden to the lake was still in fine shape, but there was no crew left.

The fogs had not dispersed when the water melted. They had thinned, but not vanished, and he looked to the shore and saw the vast army of the Sa'ba Taalor and shook his head.

"There's nothing I can do here." He looked for Daivem. "I suppose I'll go with you."

But the woman was gone, as were the others from Louron.

With no other choices that he could think of, Callan took down one of the smaller boats for reaching the shore and lowered it into the waters. He was well past the last of the foundering black ships when the rest of the Sa'ba Taalor fleet rode up the river.

There was no thought of going to Canhoon until that moment. The abandoned vessels were between him and the black ships and he was fine with that notion. He might have gone for the side of the river but more of the Sa'ba Taalor were there. Likely the ships would gather them for the next wave to attack the city.

In the meantime, he had to go somewhere and the city seemed his best bet.

Give or take the invading forces.

"I suppose we'll have to see about going around them." He said the words as if he could convince himself to avoid the fight.

He knew in his heart that wasn't going to be possible. There were too many of them and only so much land around Canhoon to step on.

He needn't have worried. Even as he considered the notion of how best to avoid being trampled under the gray-skins, they managed to breach the closest gate in the Mid Wall and started pushing inward.

Tuskandru did not break down the doors to the great gate. That was entirely Brodem's doing.

Tusk had been trying to reach that damnable door for a long while and his muscles burned and he stank of blood and sweat. It was a lovely thing to finally have a full battle against worthy opponents.

The stone men did not die easily but they did die. He had

that in common with them. Not the dying part, but the hard
to kill part. His lip was split and two teeth had been knocked
from his mouth. There were a dozen cuts across his flesh and
some of them were deep. He would worry about them later,
after the enemy had fallen.

He was still considering that fact when Brodem managed to
get over the wall.

The Silent Army was very busy trying to stop the Sa'ba
Taalor. The mounts were busy too, trying to find a place to get
out of the water. Brodem took advantage of the situation and
pounced on one of the stone soldiers. He knocked the stone
man down at the same time as he got enough momentum to
climb the wall.

There were spears in the way, and shields. He took the path
of fewer points and knocked a shield aside. Once at the top,
flesh and blood soldiers – who did the sensible thing and died
when Brodem slashed and bit at them – replaced the Silent
Army. Several spears came for him and most were knocked
aside by the heavy leather armor the mount wore. A few cut
deep and he roared his outrage at the wielders and knocked
them aside as he charged for the stairs and the level ground.

Other mounts tried to conquer the wall and most failed,
though a few scrambled to the top. More spearmen and archers
waited for them. Brodem left them to their own devices.

The great gates were closed, as one would expect. They had
been barred for a while and no one tended to them. There
was no need, as no fool in their right mind would consider
opening the doors while the city was in the air.

A lack of opposable thumbs can be a deterrent, but Brodem
managed just the same. His muzzle knocked the heavy beam
blocking the gates twice, three times and finally a fourth
before the barricade was shoved aside. After that the pressure

of bodies fighting against the wall took care of the rest. Sa'ba Taalor and Silent Army alike spilled into the city proper and flooded into the area like water.

Stone soldiers held no interest for Brodem. They did not bleed. So he went up the stairs again to kill as many of the pink skins as he could.

Tusk appreciated the assist and took advantage of the opened door. The Silent Army tried to fight on and Tusk did the same. All around him the stone warriors pressed against the Sa'ba Taalor, cutting and beating at flesh. The followers of the Daxar Taalor defended themselves and conspired to destroy the stone warriors.

Stone is stronger than flesh, it is true, but the Sa'ba Taalor carried weapons and were not afraid to take injuries even as they wore through the Silent Army's defenses.

Canhoon was breached, and the Sa'ba Taalor roared the names of their gods as they charged into the city that had escaped their fury before.

Desh ran toward the room where Cullen resided. He felt her pain, her confusion and knew he had to get there before it was too late.

Opening the door was easy enough. The young woman was kneeling on the ground, groaning and sweating in a feverish daze.

"One left. Only one. Have to stop it."

"Stop what, child?" Desh moved to her, trying to come to her aid, but she pushed him aside and shook her head.

"The gods move, Desh Krohan." The voice spoke in the old tongue, a language that had not been lost so much as it had changed. The Sa'ba Taalor still spoke it, but this form was archaic. The words were just different enough to make Desh's mind and heart ache to hear the tongue again. It was Cullen's mouth that spoke them. It was Moale Deneshi, once his lover, who uttered them.

She said, "The gods move and there is only one more location to allow them to cover this land. They will own everything unless we stop them."

"How? How do we stop them?"

"How does one ever stop a god, Desh? With sacrifices."

He didn't have to ask what that meant. She had come back from the dead but had no intention of staying. The power inside of her was that of the Mother-Vine and it existed for one reason only.

The Mother-Vine intended to live again. The question was where it would reside.

"Where does the last mountain rise? Do you know?"

Cullen shook her head. "No, but we must stop it. We must!" She writhed, her body shaking with effort, glistening with sweat.

The Sa'ba Taalor had breached the Mid Wall and would soon be trying for the First Wall of the city. The Imperial Army was gathered and would do their best to repel the enemy, but who could say with certainty if they would succeed? The Silent Army was being crushed, pushed back by sheer numbers, but he had to guess a great number of the enemy were falling in the process. It made no difference to the Sa'ba Taalor. They were fanatical in their actions. They would not stop unless their gods decreed it and their gods would not, not unless a champion was chosen to fight against the abomination that used to be Andover Lashk.

Even then, they would move the last of the mountains. The Daxar Taalor had their plans and Desh had no doubt that claiming Fellein was among them. Even if their champion lost, he knew the last mountain would go in place.

"We have to find out where. That's all there is to it. I have to visit with the Sooth."

No part of him wanted that. The last time he'd been drained and nearly crushed by the energies needed.

"Too late for that, I think. I can feel the shift in the world around us. I just can't find the spot where this will end."

Desh scowled. He was not a man who ever liked not getting his way.

Unfortunately, it seemed that gods had more pull than even the greatest sorcerers.

"Tega!" he yelled her name out loud and in his mind as well. Perhaps there was a way around the problem. Perhaps the power she had acquired would allow her greater access than others could manage.

She came to him, trailing Nolan March, who was smiling and giggling softly.

"Tega, my dear, there is one more volcano to rise in Fellein. All signs point to it. Is there any way you can discern where it might rise? I would call on the Sooth, but I've been told there's no time."

Tega shook her head. "But maybe one of the Sa'ba Taalor could tell us?"

"Well, yes, that's possible, but who?"

"I have called to Drask Silver Hand. He is coming."

"No. I am here." Drask spoke from the entrance to the chamber, where he stood with his arms at his sides and his head tilted slightly to the side, a sign of curiosity among his people. Desh looked the man over again, and was unsettled. He was really very large, but that wasn't what made Desh uncomfortable. It was that, despite his size, Drask managed to move so quietly. Too many of the enemy were like him and moved without making a sound.

Drask looked at him with silvery eyes and no discernible expression on his face. "What is it you want to know, Desh Krohan?"

"Where the last of the volcanoes will show itself."

"Truska-Pren has not shared that knowledge." He looked at Cullen on the ground, his eyes moving over her shape. "He, perhaps, is finding the place of best strategic value."

Desh nodded. "Can you guess?"

"I have not seen your maps of late, but if I could, yes."

"Then we should go to them."

"Advise your guards not to attack me again and I will keep my peace."

"And where is Andover?"

"He is nearby. He will come if I call to him."

Tega shook her head even as she reached down to help Cullen to her feet. "We need to find the maps and worry about Andover later."

"There might not be a later if we aren't quick about this." Desh moved to Cullen's other side and Drask sighed. He moved quickly, sliding past Desh on the side and lifting the girl in his arms.

"Now we can move faster."

Desh nodded and bit his tongue before he could make a foolish comment. Ego clashes over women had no place in the moment, even though a part of him wanted to protect the spirit that had once been his life mate.

He led the way and had the group of them back in the throne room in short order. The guards eyed Drask with suspicion, but the presence of the First Advisor meant they didn't do anything foolish.

Nachia was not on her throne. Instead she was looking at

the maps spread across her table and making small marks on the actual map of Canhoon. Most of the marks were made with ashes from the fireplace. They could be wiped away if need arose.

She looked up as they entered and tensed for a moment. Upon seeing Desh, the tension faded.

"Is she well?"

"No, *she* is not," Cullen answered for herself. "*She* is boiling in her own blood. The thing inside her wants out." Even as she spoke she wriggled impatiently until Drask set her down.

Her legs barely seemed to hold her weight, but she managed to get to the closest chair and settle herself.

Drask nodded to the Empress and made a formal bow before he moved to the table and the largest map of Fellein. He did not ask to examine the piece but rather moved it around until he could look at it properly.

Nachia looked to Desh with a questioning expression. He spoke clearly and concisely. "Drask is trying to calculate where the last volcano might rise. There is only the one, you see, and Cullen and the Mother-Vine are sure it will settle itself soon."

"There's another?"

Drask looked at the small cup of ashes that Nachia used to mark her map and plunged one thick finger into the mess. He looked at where marks had already been made for most of the volcanoes and smudged similar marks for the ones that had not yet been placed. Far to the south at the edge of the river, on the western side, firmly between Louron and the rest of the area. Then to the northeast, where Morwhen had been.

"The placement is not an accident. The Daxar Taalor mark the land where it will offer them the best possible strategic value." He pointed. "Each of the gods has a reason and a place they want. The Guntha Isles were claimed by Wheklam because they were the best place to change the winds along the entire western coastline of Fellein. From there the trade winds can send ashes and worse along the waters. They already have. Roathes is no more because of that placement. Louron will fall when Donaie Swarl wills it."

His finger pointed to where Tyrne had been. "Tuskandru and Durhallem chose to show a display of power here. The city was destroyed and Durhallem rose."

"Tuskandru did not place that mountain." Nachia frowned. "It was your King in Iron."

Drask's eyes locked with hers. He spoke very clearly. "No. That was a display of superiority over you. A show of power. You saw what he wanted. Tarag Paedori wanted you to see his command, but the King in Obsidian is the ruler for Durhallem and could be the only one to move the mountain."

Desh stared at Drask and nodded.

Drask continued, "Paedle has taken your Morwhen. I do not know why." He stabbed at where Elda used to stand. "Like Elda, both places were large cities and they are placed well enough to allow the surrounding of Fellein. From these places the followers of the gods, the Sa'ba Taalor, would be able to cover large areas. That might be enough."

Desh spoke up. "Morwhen was known for the formidable soldiers they trained. The same is true of Elda. A very large portion of the military to the east was trained in those areas."

Drask nodded his head. "As with Wheklam, the gods could force their hearts to spew fire and ash in these places and cover much of Fellein."

Another jab of his finger. "N'Heelis and Wrommish have claimed your north. The heart of Wrommish now beats along your mountains, and from there the volcano's fury can be unleashed along either side of the mountain range, all the way to the southern seas with little effort."

"What do you mean?" Nachia looked hard at the map.

Desh answered. "Heat from the volcano could run along the edge of the mountains and change the way storms grow, or funnel fire and Plague Winds through the whole area."

Drask nodded. "It is a good position strategically. There is no one up there, or at least few according to your map, but the coldest winters could be made milder or worse with Wrommish's desires."

Nachia crossed her arms and looked at the map. There were a lot of large Drask-finger smudges on it. "So where the will the last volcano show itself?"

"There are many possibilities." Drask leaned over the map. "The Daxar Taalor have moved their hearts. They do not follow the same pattern that existed in the valley. Now they are spread far and wide and the center of this place is empty." Drask almost reached for the ashes again and then stopped himself.

"If they wish to control all of Fellein, they must cover the northwest. That would mean placing the last heart in ruined Trecharch."

"I can't imagine them wasting their time, really." Nachia shook her head.

Drask shook his in return. "You are thinking of immediate effect. Gods have centuries. The Wellish Steppes and Trecharch are not currently held by the Daxar Taalor. They have been claimed by the Sa'ba Taalor and that is not the same thing."

"Isn't it?"

"No. The faithful are not the same as the godly. To own the land completely they would have to place a volcano in any part of that area. It might be Trecharch, it might be over the Wellish. Those areas are currently vulnerable."

"So, there?"

"A strong possibility. However, Truska-Pren is also the god of armed combat and armies. In times of war, his king rules over

all others. For that reason he might prefer a central location."
His finger tapped the map directly over Lake Gerhaim, where
the City of Wonders now rested.

"My people have been directed here. They were told to face
you at this time and this place." Drask studied the map carefully
for several seconds without speaking. No one interrupted. It
was obvious he was thinking hard. "It is possible that this
was predestined."

"What do you mean, Drask?" It was Tega who asked
this time.

"First let me finish with the previous question. Truska-
Pren, being the center of a war situation, could well decide
to claim Gerhaim. That would mean taking this spot or the
city of Goltha, or even pushing into the center of the lake.
It might mean being north or south of here, or even just
blocking off the river from the west, sealing the rest of the
mountain range."

"What? Why?" Merros Dulver came into the room as Nachia
was talking. It was obvious that he'd come in a hurry and
though Desh had not summoned him he suspected someone
had. It could have been Tega or it could have been Nachia.

"The reasons gods do anything are unknowable. Even if
they tell you, they only say what they want you to know."

Desh bit back a snort of laughter. To him the gods sounded
a lot like the Sooth.

Drask continued, "It is possible that what the Daxar Taalor
plan to do is push all of Fellein back to the east and lock them
in the Blasted Lands and the Taalor Valley. That would suit
their desires for revenge. So those are the main locations
I think could be chosen. A smaller chance is that the gods
plan to leave Truska-Pren where he currently resides, and
to encompass all of the Blasted Lands as well. I do not think
this likely."

Drask stepped back from the table and crossed his thickly muscled arms over his broad chest.

"So what were you saying about this being predestined?" Nachia looked the man over as she spoke.

Drask leaned down and tapped the map again, his finger striking where Canhoon now rested.

"This place. Even with all that my people have done to capture Goltha, they have not completed the task." His finger slid along the edge of the massive lake. "There are too many towns here, and Goltha has a large population. Taking a palace and killing a king is not the same as taking a kingdom."

Once again his arms crossed.

"Now, add in Canhoon, and you have the largest single population of the Fellein ever gathered. Am I right in that?"

Nachia nodded. "After the loss of Tyrne, Elda, Morwhen and Roathes? Most certainly."

Drask nodded again and Desh felt a cold hand slide through his guts and make a fist.

Drask, ever perceptive like most of his people, must have noticed the expression on Desh's face. "You understand, don't you, wizard?"

"Understand what?" Nachia was not a foolish person and she did not like being left in the dark.

Drask spread his arms to encompass everything. "Canhoon and Goltha together could be very easily seen as one city. The size of that city would likely rival the size of Korwa before it fell." Nachia's face crumbled. "No one knows what destroyed Korwa. For all we know, it was the gods themselves."

FOURTEEN

Plans were in action. Her followers were moving through the catacombs of the palace and were ready to strike. Swech crouched in the hidden tunnel that allowed access to the throne room. One step and she could be in the room and killing.

All they waited for was a signal from Swech. One call and the deaths would commence, but instead of calling out, she was listening to Drask Silver Hand explain that none of it would matter because they would all be dead.

"Is this all supposition, Drask?" The wizard asked the question that was likely on everyone's minds.

"Of course. I have not asked the gods. They have not told me as much. We are not currently talking."

"Why not?" The Empress this time.

"Because Tega and Nolan and I took their power."

Desh. "Beg pardon?"

"That is what was hidden in the Mounds. Under a thousand feet of rock and the remains of all the dead of Korwa there was a lake of energies. We bathed in them by accident and absorbed them."

Drask peeled away his shirt and revealed his arm for all of them to see. Swech barely suppressed a gasp. The silver she had seen on numerous occasions now spread up past his shoulder. It was growing inside him and that was impossible.

No. Nothing was impossible for gods.

"So what do we do now?" Merros spoke and her insides swam with ice. To have him so close. She did not want him dead and the gods had been kind, but for how long if he was in the same room with her targets?

"Choose your champion, or fight this war. Either way the last mountain will move and we still don't know where. But if I am right and the mountain is to settle here, then all we do is a joke and nothing more."

Merros looked around the room, nervous, tense. She knew he hated sorcery. He'd told Dretta March that a dozen or more times.

In the room with Merros and the rest she saw a younger man. His face was familiar and she once more bit back a noise. Dretta March was dead, but she'd have given her life for one glimpse at Nolan March. The boy was talking to himself, muttering small words again and again and no one in the room paid him the least bit of attention.

No. She had no time to consider the fates of dead women's children. She had no time to consider her own for that matter. Still her hand moved to her abdomen unconsciously.

Is this truth, Paedle? Will this city be taken by Truska-Pren? She spoke only with her mind. She did not need to utter words.

Paedle's voice was soft and calm. FINISH YOUR TASKS, SWECH. WE WAIT FOR THEIR DEATHS.

No answer then.

Fair enough. The gods had always kept her. They had never betrayed her trusts.

The sorcerer first. If he lived, she would not be able to finish her tasks.

• • •

Tarag Paedori ached. A hundred wounds covered his body, most of them mere scratches, but he ached from all of them. The stone men were not dead. He did not know if they could die, but most of them were broken and seemed incapable of further motion.

All it cost was a few thousand Sa'ba Taalor. Had anyone asked him if it were possible to lose so many of the Daxar Taalor's chosen he would have laughed at the notion. But these were not the normal enemies. They were stone and stone does not bleed.

Pre'ru's people bashed at the great gate into the city and above them the Fellein fired down arrows. The orders were given and most of the Sa'ba Taalor raised shields over their heads to avoid the deadly fire.

Tarag had no arrows or he'd have killed them all. Instead he satisfied himself with finding spears and javelins and doing what he could.

The lancers came from the left. The spearmen came from the right. Fellein soldiers, fresh and ready for combat. Soldiers who had not just spent hours in hard effort against stone soldiers.

Tarag nodded his admiration. He would likely have done the same thing were he in a position to.

Of course, there were a few who could offer surprises on his side, as well. The arrows did not come to a complete stop but they slowed and then faltered even more.

"Form two walls!" He bellowed the order and heard it repeated and the Sa'ba Taalor did as they were told. Shields were raised to the left and to the right, and the worn, shaking soldiers set shields in a barrier against the approaching enemies.

The lancers came without their mounts. Their horses were dead. They came just the same, bearing spears and short swords instead of their usual weapons. Still they had the advantage. They were rested and fed.

Tarag Paedori did not care if they were rested. They would die. As the Fellein approached he waited and then, "PUSH!" The walls of shields pushed into the enemies approaching as the Sa'ba Taalor held their wall and charged forward.

A few arrows came down and hit flesh. A few more of the chosen fell, but others walked over the dead and dying to take their places in the walls.

While above the combat N'Heelis and Swech's forces cut away the archers, quickly eliminating their targets and moving on to the next. As often as not the archers dropped from the wall and landed on the bloodied ground at its base. Any that lived were quickly eliminated.

Pre'ru roared her approval as the doors finally splintered under the assault from the rams. Several houses had given up their wood in order to make the battering posts but it was worth the effort. The great posts were dropped to the sides and the Sa'ba Taalor surged past the final wall of defense for Canhoon.

There were more soldiers. There were also civilians, who had held too much faith in a wooden gate. The latter ran back, fleeing the scene. The Fellein solders came forward, marching in unison and forming proper barriers.

Pre'ru gave a sharp whistle and the mounts came in. There were fewer of them than there had been, but the remaining war animals did their part. They came in hard and fast and charged at the Fellein. The soldiers facing them were brave enough, but they were shaking already, the ranks falling apart.

No, Pre'ru realized. The Fellein were not moving in fear, they were letting something past.

The dogs were everything she had heard them to be. They were fast and savage and fearless. There were also a lot of them.

They came in low and worried at the mounts. The mounts stepped back and tried to understand what had just happened because, as Pre'ru knew from experience, few were the creatures that would willingly take on a mount. Still the fighting continued. The enemy had spears and they used them. Several attacked the mounts who were distracted by the dogs, but most threw harder and aimed for the masses of the Sa'ba Taalor.

Her people knew how to respond and so they did. Arrows flew, spears were thrown and some even took on the hounds, hacking at the animals as they fought against the mounts.

Pre'ru caught motion from the corner of her eye and turned to look at the wall she had just breached. There was movement; she was not wrong. The stone shifted and as she watched on a man walked from the stone, pulled from it, was birthed from it.

The Silent Army came forward again.

Pre'ru did not have time to question it. She instead called to arms, alerting all around her of the new attack. She had not seen the shattered remains of the Silent Army drawn into the stone of the Mid Wall like ice melting into a puddle of water.

She saw instead the end result of that action on the far end. The Silent Army lived again, unmarred, born of a different color stone, and ready to repel the enemies of Fellein.

Had she known more of sorcery she might have been prepared. She chose not to waste time thinking on the matter. The enemy was upon them and she would kill them all if she had her way.

"Ordna!" She called her god's name and charged the closest of the stone men. She would live or she would die but in all cases she would serve her gods and do them proud.

• • •

Merros read the message quickly and reported.

"The last wall is broken. The Sa'ba Taalor have reached the inner city and are on their way here."

Drask nodded. "As I said. Your best chance is to choose a champion. Andover Lashk is a very skilled warrior, but he has doubts inside of him and those can be exploited."

"What sort of doubts?"

"He fights for the Daxar Taalor out of a sense of gratitude and honor. He does not fight with the love and devotion that most of the Sa'ba Taalor fight with. He does not believe he will be doing the right thing if he dies in his efforts."

"How do you know that?"

"We walked a long ways before reaching your city. We had time enough to talk."

"You think I should choose a champion?" Nachia paced. She was nervous. She had to be.

"Yes." Drask looked at her and nodded his head slowly.

"Who should I choose?"

"Someone who can win."

Merros sighed and stepped forward. "I will gladly be your champion, Nachia."

Nachia smiled and him and nodded. "I know, and I love you for that."

Then she pointed to Desh. "Go get ready for combat."

Desh looked as if his pants had suddenly fallen away and left him with his privates flapping in the cold wind.

"Beg pardon?"

"You are my First Advisor. You are my champion. Prepare yourself for battle against Andover Lashk."

"I don't see how you expect me to–"

"Go! Prepare yourself! You will be fighting for your life and the life of Fellein!"

Desh looked at her for a long time, not speaking, his eyes

studying her face. Finally he nodded.

When he'd left the room she sank back on her throne and shook her head. "I've lost my mind."

Merros crossed his arms, a small smile playing on his face. "No. I think it's brilliant."

Tega shook her head, "What have you done? One way or the other you've condemned one of those men to death."

"There's no choice in this, Tega." The Empress suppressed a desire to argue. Merros could see her working to maintain her calm. "Andover is an unknown quantity. He could very well be as dangerous as Drask. We do not know. So I chose someone that could hold his own against any soldier. I chose someone who has power and skill and a long history of thinking his way out of problems."

Tega shook her head. "This is madness."

Drask looked her way. "No. This is war."

Tega bristled and walked closer to the man. He was almost twice her size and she did not seem to care. "And have you changed sides, Drask Silver Hand?" She looked up at him and he looked down, their eyes locked in a staring contest.

"I remain uncertain as to where I stand on this conflict."

"Why?"

He shook his head. "Because I have not made up my mind."

"No, I mean why now, after an entire lifetime of devotion, do you question your gods?" Tega jabbed her fingers at his stomach like a dagger. He did not seem to notice. "Your entire life you've answered without question. You followed the orders of your gods until you reached the Mounds. So why change now?"

Drask nodded his head. "I see. You want to understand my reasoning. That is simple. For the first time in my life I am aware that my gods have lied to me."

"Shouldn't you be punished for thinking that way?"

Drask nodded his head. "Yes."

"But they have not punished you. So again I ask, why?"

Drask crossed his arms and refused to answer. Or, perhaps, he was considering the best way to answer. His facial expression was not querulous so much as it was baffled.

The dogs did their work. Many of the mounts were wounded, and badly. They bled freely from gashes along their sides and bellies and across their flanks.

The mounts did their work, too. The dogs were dead. Tuskandru's body warred with itself. On the one side he was tired and bloodied. On the other he was exhilarated and happy. He lived for this and this alone. He warred. He served his god. He had offered up a hundred sacrifices to Durhallem today and that did not include the stone monsters that came back from the dead and fought again.

The obsidian stick hissed and melted and burned with the fires of Durhallem as it sealed his torn flesh. He would have howled out his pain, but he was a king and had to set an example. The spear had cut him from neck to groin and now that ruptured flesh pulled itself back together and seared itself shut.

Tusk closed his eyes and smelled his own flesh burning. The scent mingled with the blood, the mud, the death all around him. It was a heady aroma.

When he opened his eyes the fighting had slowed. And then, surprisingly, it stopped.

The pain had been too much to let him listen but he heard now. There would be a fight between champions. One battle to choose who would win.

Tusk shook off the last of the pain and moved toward Tarag Paedori. The King in Iron was currently the King in Torn Pants. Most of the rest of his clothes were gone, discarded in the water or shredded by combat.

As he walked he grew angrier.

"Who is this champion?"

He nearly barked the words at Tarag, who looked at him and shook his head. "Andover Iron Hands."

Tusk's rage at that moment was nearly white hot. He clenched his fists until knuckles popped and tendons pulled.

"Say again?"

"It will be the same words. Andover Iron Hands is the chosen of the Daxar Taalor for this combat."

"And what are the terms?"

"You already know this, Tuskandru." Tarag Paedori's words were surprisingly gentle. "If Andover Iron Hands wins, then we win. If he loses then we go back to the Seven Forges."

"You and I know this cannot be. Six of the seven have moved."

The King in Iron nodded, then lowered his head. "Yes, and regardless the seventh moves soon. We do not go back to the Taalor Valley. We go to where the Forges now rest. We are victorious in that, but we might not keep this city."

Tusk's mouths opened and closed.

Tarag leaned in closer and put hands on both of Tusk's shoulders. It was a calming gesture and because it came from his friend and a fellow king, Tusk allowed it. "The Daxar Taalor have spoken, Tusk. We have no further claim in this."

"Aye." His voice was hoarse. "Then I will retreat with my people."

"What?"

"Why stay here?" Tusk frowned. "We have either already won or already lost. In any event, there is nothing for us to do here. I will retreat with my people and we will rest."

"What if the Fellein do not listen? What if their champion loses and they decide to fight on?"

"Tarag, King Swech and her assassins are already in place. You know this and so do I. Regardless of betrayal, the Empress will fall today. One way or another." Tusk sighed. "I will fight for my gods. I will serve my gods. If they tell me right now to wait here, I will wait. But otherwise, the fighting is done and I am tired. I would rest before being called back to war."

"Where will you go?"

"Only to the wall for now. I am tired, not foolish. Call if you need me."

Without another word to his fellow king, Tusk walked away. Moments later the horns of Tuskandru's people called a note that none had ever heard from them before. Moments after that the Obsidian Army retreated. Those that still could. Those that were still alive.

FIFTEEN

Andover Iron Hands paced the courtyard that had been designated for the final battle. The ground was level, the dirt soft but not so soft that one could sink into it.

The wall at the edge of the courtyard carried several different sorts of weapons, but Andover did not bother looking. He carried his weapon of choice: the axe created by the gods themselves to help him win this combat.

He had not expected Desh Krohan as his enemy. The thought made him want to piss himself.

Desh Krohan was known for his powers of sorcery. He had killed men from half way around the world with a word. He had helped raise the Silent Army, which even now was guarding the access points to the courtyard. The Sa'ba Taalor stood on one side of the area, the Fellein on the other and, in the middle, in the courtyard, Andover looked at both sides.

Desh Krohan had not yet shown himself. Still there was plenty to see. The Sisters stood on the side of the Fellein, and next to them Tega watched on. General Merros Dulver stood there as well, next to the Empress, who stared hard at Andover and made him feel uncomfortable, if only a little. She was the enemy here, today. She and her Empire had crushed down the Sa'ba Taalor for far too long. They were weak, and they were soft and they were fatted like calves and ready to be sacrificed to the gods.

And yet....

Brolley Krous, who had almost started this war on his own, looked on from the other side of his sister, his face unreadable. Next to him Queen Lanaie stood, her arm wrapped around Brolley's bicep.

On the other side Andover could see Drask Silver Hand standing near Tarag Paedori and several others he did not recognize. Drask did not stand still. He talked with the King in Iron and then moved on.

He knew there were more of them within the city. He could not see them, but they were there.

The Fellein parted and the striking shape of Desh Krohan came forward, dressed in his robes and nearly gliding across the ground. Was he as massive as Tarag Paedori? No, still he struck an impressive figure. His hood was up and his face lost in shadows and he seemed, at all times, to be staring directly at Andover, even when he was obviously looking elsewhere.

Tega stared at him, and Andover felt his stomach freezing over again. He had loved her once, or thought he did. And now she was looking his way and he couldn't quite make our what was going through her head. Was she angry with him for his choice to be the champion of the Daxar Taalor? Or was that pity, she with the knowledge of what her master could do and how very easily he would kill Andover?

Back in Tyrne there had been a man to announce the combats. Andover remembered him. No such man was here.

Desh Krohan entered the courtyard. One second it seemed he was near the Empress and the next he was only paces from Andover.

Tarag Paedori moved onto the field. He carried no weapons

and still he intimidated.

"We all know why we are here." It was not a question, still Andover and Desh alike nodded their heads.

"Step back and choose your weapons."

Both stepped back and Andover considered the javelins and spears. Finally he grabbed one of the spears and hefted it.

Desh Krohan took a spear as well, which rather surprised Andover.

Tarag Paedori stood at the edge of the wall and bellowed, "Begin!"

Andover sighted and threw his spear. Desh Krohan did the same. Andover's spear cut the air and struck the sorcerer in the chest, falling to the ground.

The wizard's spear tore through Andover's shoulder, easily slicing meat.

Andover moved in, ignoring his bloodied arm and gripping his axe. The sorcerer moved, not foolish enough to wait for an attack. He stepped to the side and Andover swept the axe toward his chest.

The blade hit the wizard's robes and cut through them where the spear had failed.

Desh Krohan let out a yell and backed away, looking at the axe. Andover did not wait. He came in hard and fast and used his body mass to knock the man sideways. Before Desh could recover, the axe was whistling down at his head.

Desh reached out with his hand and caught the edge of the blade. The obsidian blade sliced into meat and through bone, taking Desh Krohan's fingers.

The wizard fell back, bleeding freely from his wounds. Tega let out a yelp of dismay and Desh Krohan stepped back again and this time he nodded.

The obsidian axe exploded. Had Andover not had the weapon behind him it would have surely killed him, but instead it only tore muscles away from his right leg.

The pain hammered at Andover. Chunks of the obsidian blade now shivered in the muscles of his thigh and brought about exquisite agonies.

Desh Krohan held his wounded hand and stared at Andover. Andover in turn pulled the largest pieces of the axe from his leg. Had he had hands of flesh he would surely have lost the one holding his weapon. Even now his fingers screamed and his palm ached and his wrist felt like it was broken. It was not. He tested that theory before he moved forward.

The sorcerer waited for him and Andover reached out, planning to throw the man to the ground.

Instead it was he who was thrown. Whatever the man did, it knocked Andover back a dozen feet and left his body twitching.

He looked at the sorcerer with an effort. Desh Krohan stood in the same spot and slowly raised his good hand, letting the other bleed. The flow of blood was weakened, but not gone. Andover didn't think it was blood loss alone. The man was healing himself somehow.

Iron fingers clutched at the dirt and he made a fist.

As Andover rose he sighted and as he stood he aimed. A moment later he was hopping toward the sorcerer and the man was preparing. He had cost Desh Krohan fingers; he suspected he would not be long for this world if he did not win quickly.

The dirt hit the sorcerer. It slipped under the cowl covering his features. Desh Krohan stepped back and shook his head, momentarily blinded with any luck, and Andover charged. His leg was weak but holding him. His fist went into the cowl, and struck flesh and bone.

At the exact same moment, the wizard slapped him in the chest. Andover flew backward, his eyes blinded, his ears ringing with a deafening peal, and he did his best to roll as he smashed into the ground and bounced all the way to the distant wall.

His muscles did not want to respond, but he still managed to reach his hands and knees.

Andover blinked furiously as a great blue veil of afterimage covered his vision. There was sight, but it was blurred.

He managed to stand, but only with a great deal of effort.

"Easy, Iron Hands. Easy. You've won."

Andover recognized the voice of Tarag Paedori and slumped a bit.

He was doing his best, but the pain was overwhelming.

His eyes finally focused enough to let him see Desh Krohan lying on the ground. The man was breathing, but he was not moving much beyond his chest.

Tega and the Sisters moved to him, surrounding him.

"Get me metal! Iron Hands needs aid."

"Is this a victory? Or is this a draw?" Tarag cried. "Neither of our champions can fight any longer." He looked toward Nachia Krous as she called from her side of the courtyard.

Andover spat blood that tasted wrong in his mouth. He worked hard to form the words as he forced himself to stand. "I am not dead and I can stand." He was shaking as he reached for another spear. "If needs be, I can still kill your sorcerer. Do you want that, Empress Krous?"

To make his point clear he walked toward the downed sorcerer. All around him the Fellein looked on, genuinely horrified. The Sa'ba Taalor remained calm, waiting to see the outcome of Andover's words.

His skin was black in places. He was burned and very badly, he knew that. It was not the fire of the Forges. That would have caused him no injury. It was the fire of the storms. The light striking his chest had been lightning. The roar had been thunder. He looked at the iron hand that held his spear. It was smoking. The metal was scorched but seemed unharmed.

Tega looked up at him and pulled Desh Krohan's broken face into her lap, using her body to protect him. Andover did not look her way.

"I do not want to do this, Empress! I have a great fondness for Desh Krohan, but you have made him your champion. Do you accept defeat or do I kill him?"

He walked on, ignoring the parts of him that howled for his attention. It was only pain and life was pain.

No one spoke. Not from either side, but Tega sobbed softly and broke Andover's heart again.

"Please, Empress. Do not make me kill this man."

He raised the spear, prepared to bring down a deathblow.

Tega looked at him with wet eyes and shook her head.

Nachia Krous, Empress of Fellein, looked at the sorcerer on the ground and then looked at Andover Lashk.

"Fellein yields."

Andover nodded and dropped his spear. The war was over.

Tarag Paedori nodded and three of the Sa'ba Taalor moved to Andover's side. The clothes were carefully peeled from the vast, blistered marks on his body.

Had he not seen it himself, the King in Iron would have denied the possibility. The man had been struck by lightning and thrown across the field of battle. His skin was blistered in a hundred places and a blackened handprint adorned his chest where the sorcerer had touched him and cast electricity through his body.

Tarag had watched, had seen the lightning arc through him. He had seen the boy fall and expected him to be dead. And then Andover Iron Hands had worked his way to his feet.

Burnt, bleeding, injured inside and out, the champion of the Daxar Taalor had managed the impossible and taken down the Fellein's sorcerer.

He watched as metal was used to heal a dozen life-threatening wounds.

He watched and felt the gods reach down and touch Andover Iron Hands, healing his vast injuries.

Then Truska-Pren spoke into him. The god said, IT IS TIME. I WOULD BE REBORN.

Tarag Paedori nodded and looked toward the city of Goltha.

The city would burn. The world would understand the power of the Sa'ba Taalor.

He felt the power roaring up inside him as he stared at the ground just above the city.

Truska-Pren would rise. The great towers and walls of Prydiria, the Iron Fortress, would be his once more.

"So let it be done."

Tarag Paedori looked across the lake.

Drask Silver Hand looked at Tarag Paedori.

Not far away, lost in the crowd of the Fellein, Cullen let out a whimper and fell to her knees on the stones of the courtyard.

Desh Krohan did not miss much. He did not miss the fist that moved under his cowl and broke his nose, his jaw, his left cheekbone and eye socket and seven teeth. Iron Hands. Iron fist, more like. He may as well have been struck in the face with a mace. A few seconds after that he missed completely, as he was knocked into a stupor by Andover Iron Hands.

He should have still been in that state. His face had been shattered, his fingers cut off and he was suffering from massive blood loss. He'd also just used lightning on another person and that was draining beyond most people's comprehension.

His head rested in Tega's lap. He felt the power she was using to mend him even as she cried over him and half-shielded him from Andover's view.

Andover, the poor bastard, looked as bad as he felt.

And then he was healed and Nachia was conceding her Empire to spare him his life.

Then the power in the area shifted. When Tarag Paedori had made his move before and driven his sword into the ground there had been no perception of power. That was because, as Desh had recently learned, the power had not come from the King in Iron but from Tuskandru.

This time the sensation was entirely different. Every one of the Sisters, Tega and likely every sorcerer in the city felt the power that moved through the King in Iron.

The Sooth had power. No two ways about that. Even contacting the Sooth took a great deal of power and preparation. Dealing with the Sooth was like trying to stand in a fastmoving river while juggling a dozen rocks and singing drunken songs at the loudest tavern ever built. It was noisy, draining, and required incredible self-control. The smallest mishap could cause injuries and true mistakes sometimes led to death.

The force that moved past all of them made the power of the Sooth seem like a candle next to the sun.

All of them were moved by it. The Sa'ba Taalor looked to their King in Iron and roared Truska-Pren's name. The Fellein stood their ground but blinked and paused as if a great wind had cut across their path unexpectedly. The Sisters and Desh shuddered as the power moved past.

Tega did not shudder. She looked toward Drask Silver Hand.

Drask looked to Cullen and nodded. Desh was aware of all of that simply because he had trained himself to be aware.

He heard Drask Silver Hand's words. "Now. It is now or not at all."

Tega closed her eyes and something vast jumped like a bolt of lightning from her to Cullen.

Cullen jerked and seized and fell jittering to the ground. Desh sat up immediately and felt the world tilt madly as he looked at the young guardian of the Mother-Vine.

Drask Silver Hand stepped past him and reached for the cloaked shape of Nolan March. He did not ask. He took.

Desh could feel the power rise from the boy and get drawn into Drask Silver Hand.

He dared look at the man and wished that he had not. Most of the people around him were looking to the east, where the ground shook and started to break above the city of Goltha.

Desh did not. He looked to the man with the silver arm who wrested a power greater than any Desh had ever seen from a simpleton who fell screaming to his knees.

Whatever that power was, it seethed and whipped around that metallic arm. And then Drask Silver Hand released it. The energies he had stolen bullwhipped around him and then ripped across the air toward where the last wave of energy had left Tarag Paedori.

The King in Iron roared and charged for Drask.

The ground settled and stilled near the city of Goltha.

Cullen screamed again and fell motionless.

Desh fell back, his senses nearly blinded by everything happening around him.

There was nothing to see. Callan was sure of that, but still he looked. His senses were drawn to the far side of the lake and to Goltha. He could not have said why in a thousand years, but he was compelled to look.

There was nothing else to do, really. He had stopped trying to fight the Sa'ba Taalor when they stabbed him in his side.

He'd patched himself fairly well and then settled back against the Mid Wall to either live or die as the gods might decide. He was never a soldier, not like the Fellein or the gray-skins. He was a captain who liked to make money by moving people and things from one place to another. He was a man who liked an occasional woman. What he was not was a fighter. He would rather couple than kill and that was all there was to it.

Se he decided to sit this one out and he was staring at Goltha when the first Thing happened.

Never much of a man for words, that was his phrase when the disasters hit. They were Things.

The storm that sank his father's fishing boat? It was a Thing. The Sa'ba Taalor taking Tyrne? Another Thing.

He felt the power tear across the lake. He even saw it. The waters slashed apart from each other in a vast wave, as if a ship of truly impossible size were cutting the lake in half to reach a new destination. There was no impact when that trail hit the land, but only seconds later the land above Goltha began to bulge and become a Thing. He did not know what would occur next but he could guess. There would be fire soon and it would burn the lungs right out of him even from across the lake.

Then it happened again. The lake shivered and whatever it was that moved across the water skittered and danced like a snake just under the surface. The waters ripped and rippled, danced and twisted, and any poor fool who was out on a boat would surely have been sunk as easily as the black ships of the Sa'ba Taalor. The water and the Thing hit them at the same time and they shattered. That was the only word to describe it. Wood bulged and popped and flew apart.

That one actually moved his hair and Callan winced at the feeling that ran through his body. It wasn't uncomfortable so much as it was damned BIG.

A moment later the ground beyond Goltha stopped bulging.

And then the air above Goltha screamed.

The city itself did not escape. Whatever was up there, whatever it might be that fought, it shattered several of the taller buildings as easily as the ships. The stone blew outward and some of it even melted. He was looking right at the stuff and though it was very far away he saw light flaring on stone and then stone spilling out in a cascade that looked like burning water.

Callan stayed exactly where he was and wished he had a bottle of wine.

Whatever it was that moved over the city, he could see it if he squinted. There were two Things and they warred and he suspected they planned for death.

Cullen wept.

The pain was gone. Whatever had been inside her was gone and the lack of pain alone was enough to make her feel empty and cored out.

There was nothing left of her. Her muscles felt as if they'd been flattened in her body and she could barely breathe.

Deltrea squatted next to her.

"Come on, Cullen! It's time!"

"Time for what?"

"For whatever is going to happen. You aren't supposed to stay here. You're supposed to join with that thing."

"How the hell would you know that?" She sounded petulant even to herself. She was not speaking out loud this time. She couldn't. Her jaw refused to work. There were people around her now, looking down and stepping back, horrified by whatever they saw.

Deltrea reached out for her and hauled on her arm. Cullen moaned as she was lifted into a sitting position.

"Come on, Cullen!"

"How are you holding me?" Even through her pain she

knew that should have been impossible.

"Shut up, and come with me you fool or it's all for nothing!" Deltrea was smiling, which made as little sense as everything else.

Cullen looked to the east and heard the sounds of battle. Something roared and something else screamed and when she looked there were shapes up there, vast as the heavens, and fighting. Most of the fools around her were looking at her and ignoring the spectacle across the skies and over the lake and moving north at a frightening pace and–

"MOVE!"

Deltrea pulled at her and something tore and the next thing Cullen knew the world was spinning.

"The Mother-Vine needs you. You're a part of her now. She's got to win this and she can't do it without you."

The pain was gone and Deltrea's words sank into her. As she moved, she recognized the shape of the Mother-Vine for what it was: an endless expanse of tendrils offering life and protection. It was not real. There was no mass, but that was the shape just the same as it writhed across the skies and slashed at the hard lines and angles of the nightmare trying to crush the Mother-Vine once and for all.

Madness, of course, except that there was another presence with her, distant and dying, an ember that had once been the mate of the First Advisor.

That ember glowed brightly one last time and urged Cullen on without words.

The Mother-Vine was not dead, not even dying, but she would be soon without Cullen. There was no question of this in her mind, no doubt about the validity of the notion, and no time to consider in any event.

"Now, Cullen! Now!" Deltrea's voice rang in her mind and she nodded, annoyed and grateful to her friend at the same time.

Cullen reached out and touched the Mother-Vine, uncertain how she could move so far, so fast, or how she'd learned to fly.

Far below, the crowd looked on as a few people tried to revive the body of a girl who'd fled Trecharch when the dead walked and the Sa'ba Taalor killed all on their path.

Their efforts were wasted. There was nothing left but flesh and meat.

"Do they honor the pact?"

Jost stood next to Swech and looked on as the Fellein stood around.

"I cannot say."

Swech tried to speak to Paedle. The instructions were simple. If the Empress did not yield, the Empress died.

Jost looked on, trying to comprehend what was happening. Andover Iron Hands had won, they knew that.

He had taken down the sorcerer and let him live. Then he had fallen, and then Truska-Pren moved through Tarag Paedori.

All made perfect sense until that moment.

It was easy to discern what was supposed to happen. The great mountain would rise and the glory of the Seven Forges would be seen by everyone.

And then the King in Iron charged at Drask Silver Hand.

Drask turned toward the King in Iron and defended himself, stepping past the boy on the ground before him. Tarag grabbed and Drask moved and Swech could have easily predicted what happened next.

Tarag Paedori smashed into the ground and came to a rolling stop. He was not injured but his pride likely hurt.

"You betray us!" Tarag stormed toward Drask again.

Drask shook his head. "Your god would see us all burned for winning the day, Tarag Paedori. I merely defended myself and everyone here."

Swech shook her head. She could understand nothing that Drask had done.

"You betray the gods, Drask Silver Hand! Face me!"

"I have not moved, Tarag." The man's voice was filled with regret. "You have won your victory today. The Empire is yours and belongs to your gods. Let this be enough."

The larger man shook his head and moved closer again and the gathering of Fellein around them wisely moved out of the way.

Swech called to Paedle, seeking guidance. But there was no sound, no voice to guide her and she felt afraid for the first time in her life.

She reached further, called to the other gods and once again received only silence as an answer.

"Where are they?" Swech was unaware that she was even speaking aloud.

"Where are who?" Jost frowned and looked her way.

"Where are the gods? Why don't they answer?"

The look on Jost's face a second later told her all she needed to know. Her young friend was hearing nothing but silence as well.

The battle ended. The raging energies of Truska-Pren and the Mother-Vine crashed to the earth, and the ground where they struck shattered.

The burned ruins of Trecharch bulged, and seconds later Truska-Pren rose from the ground, the vast black mountain reborn in only seconds. The explosion blew down the ruined trees and shook the air for a hundred miles. The heat blasting down from the mountain would have burned away anything in its path, and the cloud of smoke that rose into the skies was as black as the space between the stars.

Where normally the Sa'ba Taalor would have been howling their approval to the gods, instead they stared around, stunned by a silence they had never heard in their lives before.

The Daxar Taalor were silent.

Beyond the reach of Truska-Pren the Blasted Lands grew quiet as the storms there faded again. From the depths of the mounds the ground shook and split, and what remained of the vast stone monoliths collapsed.

Tarag Paedori stood facing Drask Silver Hand and shook his head. "What madness is this?"

Drask's eyes narrowed. "I do not know what you mean?"

"Where are the Daxar Taalor? Where are the gods?" Tarag Paedori's voice shook with suppressed rage and he took a long, menacing step toward Drask.

"Where they have always been. I hear them calling for you. Why do you not answer?"

"Liar!" Tarag came toward him another step and Drask stood his ground, rolling his shoulders and preparing for the fight he knew would happen.

"I have never lied to you, Tarag. You know this. You have only to open your mind to the gods and you will hear them as I do."

"It is not just me!" Tarag's voice was filled with grief like a blade that cut his soul in half. "Who among you can hear the gods?" He looked to his own people and heard no one say anything positive. Most were only just now trying to find the gods and failing to hear a response.

Drask shook his head. "Truska-Pren wants to speak with you. He calls your name, King in Iron."

Tarag looked around with desperation in his gaze. This was an impossibility.

Andover Iron Hands, only recently healed, nodded his

head. "I can hear him, Tarag Paedori. I hear his call. He wants you to come to him."

"I'll kill you for this!" The challenge was offered to Drask.

It was not merely a threat. His honor was on the line, his faith in the gods was on the line. He heard the gods, heard them calling and refused to accept the madness of a foolish man who had suddenly gone deaf. "You have challenged me, Tarag Paedori and I accept your challenge! Face me!"

Drask moved, sliding effortlessly to the wall of the courtyard and entering it.

The King in Iron came his way, hurdling the wall with ease. He grabbed a sword as he moved.

Drask chose instead to use the bullwhip he carried coiled around his waist. The king charged and Drask moved aside, backing away hastily. He could have killed Tarag with a glance. The power he'd absorbed was still there. That was why he took the well of energies from Nolan.

A second charge and Drask ducked under the swing, stepping in fast and driving his elbow into the King in Iron's ribs. He felt bones snap. The king paid them no heed and drove himself against Drask before he could catch his balance. The sword came down again and Drask caught it with his silver hand, gripping the blade tight and pushing.

The blade shattered in his grip.

Tarag drove his forehead into Drask's face and knocked him sprawling.

A moment later the broken sword was coming for him and Drask rolled, hissing as the jagged metal cut a line of blood across his side and back.

"What have you done to me?" Tarag's voice broke with raw emotion and Drask, on the ground below him, swept the king's leg and knocked him down. The fingers of his silver hand caught in the king's hair and he yanked the man closer, even as he wrapped his legs into the king's own legs and bent his body and crushed.

The sound of Tarag Paedori's thigh breaking was a sound he would never forget. It hurt him deeply to cause a man he considered a friend pain, and yet as always he did what he felt he had to do.

"Yield, King in Iron. Accept defeat and go home to your god." He leaned in closer and pressed his elbow against the king's neck and jaw. They both knew that he could shatter the man's skull if he applied enough pressure. They also both knew he was capable of it.

"There is no dishonor here. The gods cannot reach you and I have not been fighting for endless hours. Go home. Go to Truska-Pren and find out why he has been silenced. Let him heal you, Tarag Paedori. I will make certain no one brings you harm."

The king trembled. It could have been rage, or fear or simple exhaustion. "I yield. This day, I yield. The battle is over, if not the war."

"No. This war is finished. You have yielded to me."

Drask rolled off the other man and made himself stand. "The King in Iron yields! Go home to your gods and find your way back into their graces!"

There was anger on the faces of the Sa'ba Taalor. There was also fear. An army that had true faith in their gods might be unstoppable, but that faith had been ruined, at least for the moment.

It took hours, but the Sa'ba Taalor left. Most of them at any rate. There were several of the children of the Daxar Taalor who were still hidden in the flesh of the Fellein. None of them left. Through one means or another the rest made their way across Gerhaim heading in several different directions.

They abandoned Canhoon, heading for the homes of the Daxar Taalor.

Drask and the Silent Army watched them leave.

SIXTEEN

In the far distant remains of the Blasted Lands the ground shivered in a thousand places. At the heart of the place once called the Mounds the great vine pushed itself from the ground and began spreading far and wide. It rose into the air and spread itself like a dozen arms reaching for the horizon. As it spread, the ground beneath it offered up trees and shrubs and deep, green grasses.

Deep within the center of that great vine, Cullen moved and sighed and stretched herself. The Mother-Vine was renewed. That was all she could hope for.

Deltrea's voice spoke to her softly. "That wasn't so horrid, was it?"

"By all the gods, Deltrea? Why are you still here?" She spoke with no mouth and was not the least concerned by that fact.

"I have no idea. But here I am and here I'm staying."

The notion of eternity was not particularly pleasant at that moment.

Nachia Krous stared out from her window and shook her head. "What exactly happened?"

Desh Krohan rubbed at his jaw and mirrored her headshake. "No bloody idea." He raised his hands in mock surrender when she looked his way. "I could not hope to be more serious."

Drask Silver Hand moved into the room. He did not knock.

Nachia frowned. "I'm not sure how this works. Their champion rose and beat my champion. I accepted defeat and offered up my Empire and then you came along and defeated them."

"If I had any desire to rule an empire, I would have the right to yours."

Desh looked his way. "Would you?"

"Nachia's Empire was technically in the hands of Tarag Paedori as the head of the Daxar Taalor's armies. When she conceded, the Empire was his to claim in the name of the gods. I defeated him in honorable combat. I could claim your Empire as my reward."

"Why not claim his kingdom?" Nachia looked at the gray-skinned man dubiously.

"The gods choose who is king. I am not currently in their favor."

"So what would you do with this Empire if you had it?"

Drask shook his head. "Leave you as my regent and leave. I have many things to consider." He looked them both over. "You are either the Empress or the regent to the Emperor. Either way, you will likely see me again."

Drask left the room that easily and the two of them looked after him.

"I don't suppose you could just turn him into ashes."

"No, Nachia. Don't even jest." He worked his jaw and heard several light crackles.

"How do you feel?"

"Humiliated. I was punished by a boy."

"And you were cheating."

"I was not!"

"He dropped you without benefit of sorcery."

"He has iron hands!"

"You wear robes that can stop a dozen arrows. You were beaten by a boy who was smart enough to figure out your weaknesses."

"What happens now?" Desh liked a good jest but there wasn't time. There was never time. After centuries he was beginning to understand that notion.

The war was over. Nachia was Empress. They had to do better when the next challenge came around.

"We need to rebuild our armies. We need to find a way to speak properly with the Silent Army. They have not yet gone to rest and they might know something we do not."

"They were ruined. You understand that don't you? They were broken and defeated and I still don't understand how."

"The Daxar Taalor and their chosen." Nachia shook her head. "I have never seen more brutal soldiers. They are relentless. You saw Andover! You ruined his leg with your sorcery. You burned him alive, and he kept coming."

"I truly hope he doesn't hold a grudge." Desh was looking down at the courtyard where the fight had taken place. Andover Lashk was down there. He knew it. He didn't have to guess. Merros Dulver had told him as much.

Nachia nodded her head and moved closer to him, resting her head on his shoulder for a moment. "I have never been this tired, Desh."

"So sleep for a while. I will be here waiting."

The Empress of Fellein, or regent, depending, nodded her head and moved to the antechamber where she had a small bed concealed. Now and then, rest was a beautiful thing.

• • •

Merros Dulver looked at Andover Lashk and headed his way, carrying two Pabba fruit and a knife.

The young man looked him over, read his posture and assessed the contents of his hand with a glance.

One quick stroke of the knife opened the hard rind of the fruit. A second slice and the other was opened. Merros offered both to Andover and let the lad pick. As soon as he had made his choice Merros peeled the rind back and took a bite of his prize. The best way to make the lad comfortable was to show that he meant no harm.

"I'm surprised you don't have me in leg irons."

"Personally, I don't feel like losing that many soldiers today. We've had enough injuries of late."

Andover meticulously pulled away the rind and then tore segments from the sweet Pabba. Watching him eat was unsettling and fascinating at once.

"You are staring."

"I'm sure you did the same when you got those... things on your jaw."

"They are marks from the gods."

"Do you still hear them? Your gods?"

"Yes," Andover nodded. "They still speak to me."

"What do they say?"

"I can come home to them or stay here as their... ambassador."

"Do they wish to sue for peace?"

Andover shook his head. "They are gods of war. They will never sue for peace. They will simply bide their time."

"And do you think we should accept you as their ambassador?"

"Honestly? I still don't really know what an ambassador does."

Merros chuckled. "From what I've seen they mostly sit on

well-padded seats, eat food and flirt with the Empress."

"That is hardly the life I was planning to live."

"You could work a forge. I've seen your work."

Andover shook his head.

"Then how about this? How about you work with me to train the Fellein Army?"

"How's that?"

"By all the gods, lad, you took down Desh Krohan. You knocked the greatest wizard of the lands down a few pegs."

"He did not want to kill me any more than I wanted to kill him." That said, more of the fruit went into his mouths and Merros forced himself not to stare.

"Maybe. But he would have."

"He very nearly did."

"Help me train the troops. They will follow your commands."

Andover nodded. "Until one tries to kill me."

Merros grinned and pulled a slice of his own fruit free. "Then you get to keep your senses sharp. Stay more alert than I did when I went into the Blasted Lands."

Andover closed his eyes for a moment and nodded. "For now I will stay. It is what the gods want and what you want."

"Excellent. I expect honesty from you, Andover. A vow not to kill anyone here without a fair and proper warning, regardless of what the gods will say."

Andover looked at him for a long moment and sighed. "You have been talking to Drask Silver Hand."

"Drask and I respect each other. I would have the same sort of respect with you, Andover."

"Done." He shrugged. "I will not betray the kings or the Daxar Taalor. But I will offer you this. If I am ever told to kill anyone, I will leave the city for two days first."

"What good will that do?"

"Do not insult me, General Dulver. You have had people

watching me since the Sa'ba Taalor left."

True enough and he couldn't argue the point.

Merros nodded. "We will work out the details soon. In the meantime you may stay in my chambers until we work out the final details."

"Where will you be?"

Merros tried to smile and looked away. "I lost someone to the war. I will go to her home and find a way to say goodbye to her."

Andover looked at him and nodded. "I have lost someone as well. I wish you the best at finding peace."

Merros moved away and left his last thoughts unuttered. There is no time for peace, even after war. There is only time to prepare again. His people had forgotten that for a very long time and it had cost them almost everything.

It wasn't a lesson he intended to forget a second time.

Tataya was the one who found Captain Callan's body. First she called the Sisters to her and then she called on Darsken Murdro.

"How do you suppose he died, Darsken?"

The Inquisitor looked at the dead man and shook his head. "He died at sea, fighting the Sa'ba Taalor. He died as he was meant to die, as a hero."

"How do you know these things, Inquisitor?" Pella's voice was soft and low and lovely. Her eyes looked into his and he smiled, content to know that he could drown in her eyes as easily as any of the Sisters. They could enchant a soul with ease and chose to leave his alone.

"When he died he drove his ship to Louron." He shrugged. "Sometimes the spirits find their way to us and we do what we can."

"Did he know he was dead?"

"He did not. He had a small seed of talent. His anger was

so great that he dragged the spirits of the dead with him. So, of course, we did what we had to, to help him. In another life he might have been a sorcerer. Instead he took to the seas and had his fun and games dodging the military and the City Guard."

Callan's skin was cold, but surprisingly well preserved all things considered.

Tataya almost asked, but before she could Darsken answered her. "It's the waters. They are very cold and hold off decay. Now that he is here, on the land, the rotting begins." He looked down at the man and shook his head. "A pity. I liked him."

"I remember you yelling at him very clearly."

"I had hoped to convince him to try a different career."

"Apparently soldier was not the right choice, either." Tataya's voice was touched by sorrow and she touched the captain's face.

Goriah's voice was soft and cold, "Was it you, Darsken?"

"Was what me?"

"Did you silence the gods?"

"Who am I to silence gods?"

"There are many tales of what the Louron can do."

"Do any of those tales speak of silencing gods?"

"Well, no, but it was not us."

"Had I that ability I would have used it long ago. The Louron do not believe in gods, after all, and having them silenced would work to our benefit." Darsken rolled his shoulders. "We can call this one a war hero and give him a proper ceremony. He and his crew killed several of the enemy and foundered their ships. Besides which, he was a good man. I will send the City Guard to claim him before the birds can feast."

The Sisters nodded as one and moved with him. Darsken did not mind the company.

Not far away a member of the Silent Army looked out at the waters, guarding against whatever might come.

They were all disheartened. They were all, to the last, broken. They could not speak to their gods and that was as great a sin as if they'd had their ears ruined and their eyes cut out.

Still, the Sa'ba Taalor were fighters. They moved across Fellein using whatever methods were available to them. Many walked, others ran. Some cut down trees and took to the waters, building small vessels to let them find their way to Wheklam. There were a lot of small boats and more stolen along the way.

Tuskandru found his way home easily enough. He killed any of the Fellein who crossed his path on the trip and he took the time, now that the war was at least halted, to get to know Stastha better. They lost themselves in their lust and it eased the pain of their broken contact with the gods. At least for a while they could connect with each other. Also, his second seemed determined to break some kind of personal record. Who was he to argue?

Every king made it back home. The first of them was Swech, who rode Saa'thaa to the mountain where Morwhen no longer stood as if her very life depended on her being first. In some ways it did.

She followed the rules, of course, and made her way to the heart of the mountain, crawling and climbing as was needed Through the Thousand Veils of Paedle she worked her way until, finally, she stood at the heart of the mountain, naked and afraid.

"Where are you, Paedle? Why can I not hear you any longer?" The stone beneath her bare feet surged with warmth and she heard the voice of her god.

I AM HERE, SWECH, I HAVE NEVER LEFT YOU.

She wept and dropped to the ground, pressing her face to

the warmth of the volcanic heat below her. "I have been so alone, so very alone." She wept. They were tears of joy at finding her world was not destroyed irreparably.

THE DAXAR TAALOR LOVE YOU AS THEY HAVE SELDOM LOVED ANY OF THEIR CHILDREN. THAT IS WHY WE HAVE GIFTED YOU SO MANY TIMES.

She nodded, feeling the love of the gods and returning it.

"I thought you would make me kill him. I would do it, you know. If you asked, but I am grateful that you did not."

HE IS AS SPECIAL TO US AS HE IS TO YOU. MERROS DULVER HAS NOT YET COMPLETED HIS TASKS FOR THE DAXAR TAALOR. Swech felt the warmth move over her and concentrate on her belly, where the life within her continued to grow, a sign that she and Merros were meant for different things.

IT IS NOT MERROS DULVER'S TIME AND IT IS NOT YOUR TIME. YOU HAVE MANY THINGS TO ACCOMPLISH IN OUR NAMES.

Swech rolled over and looked up at the stone ceiling above her. At a distance she could see the opening to the heavens and the Great Star above her. For the moment she was content in the love of her gods and in the knowledge that they loved her still, despite her flaws.

Her hand rested where the baby stirred inside her, growing slowly.

It was enough. For now, it was enough.

The Pilgrim listened to the words of Empress Nachia Krous and ignored them. Rebuilding themselves from the ground was easy enough. The giggling man, Nolan March, had found him and asked a simple question of him. He had asked if the Pilgrim could make the Sa'ba Taalor suffer.

After consulting with the gods, he had said yes.

The idiot godling fed power into the Pilgrim and the Pilgrim shared that power, bringing back the defeated Silent Army and then striking in a way the Sa'ba Taalor could never have expected.

The Silent Army could not silence gods, but they came close. They deafened the followers of the gods. In time the effect would wear off. Eventually the Sa'ba Taalor would reach their gods and the connections would be reestablished. Until then the enemy fled, uncertain how to react when they could no longer hear their gods.

It was a simple trick, really, but one with heart-wrenching implications. The Pilgrim and his faithful devotees would have been just as lost if their gods stopped speaking to them.

Drask took little with him. He had little to take. His weapons stayed with Brackka and so they came along. Just to his side Tega rode in comfortable silence and Nolan March held onto her as he always did.

He did not know how Nolan had silenced the gods. He did not care. The lad had ended the war and that was enough.

"Why do you suppose he silenced the gods?" Tega was looking at Nolan as she asked.

"Perhaps they offended him when they killed his mother."

"Did they kill her, truly?"

"Swech did as she was told. She is no more responsible than a sword blade."

"Are you a sword in the hands of your gods?"

"I am not Swech. Her faith has always been greater than mine." He paused a moment. "Are you certain you want to come along?"

"I cannot stay here, Drask. Desh will ask too many questions and I must have my time away from him before he learns what I did."

Drask nodded. Tega climbed atop the saddle and looked around as her mount purred.

"Where are we going, Drask?"

"Wherever you would like."

"You have no destinations in mind?"

"I have not read a thousand books telling me of the past. I have only lived in the now. The past is as good a place to look as any, but you are the one who knows where wonders might be hidden."

"Perhaps across the sea."

Drask nodded. "Wherever you like. For now we can see the world and later we can consider what the world is trying to tell us."

"Can you still hear your gods?"

Drask nodded. "They are angry with me." He tilted his head a bit. "They are also weak at the moment. Now is a good time to leave, before they grow strong again."

Nolan chuckled to himself as they started off. Sometimes Drask suspected that the boy knew more than he showed. On other occasions, he was certain of it.

ABOUT THE AUTHOR

James A Moore is the author of over twenty novels, including the critically acclaimed *Fireworks*, *Under the Overtree*, *Blood Red*, *Deeper*, the Serenity Falls trilogy (featuring his recurring anti-hero, Jonathan Crowley) and his most recent novels *Blind Shadows* and *City of Wonders*. He has twice been nominated for the Bram Stoker Award, and spent three years as an officer in the Horror Writers Association, first as Secretary and later as Vice President. He lives in Massachusetts, USA, where he is working on the first of a new saga, The Tides of War.

genrefied.blogspot.com • *twitter.com/jamesamoore*